GENEVA PUBLIC LIBRARY DISTRICT

W9-BTA-837

12/12

WITHDRAW

Geneva Public Library District
127 James St.
Geneva, Illinois 60134

ALSO BY HEATHER MCELHATTON

Jennifer Johnson Is Sick of Being Single
Million Little Mistakes
Pretty Little Mistakes

Jennifer Johnson is sick of being married

HEATHER McELHATTON

wm
WILLIAM MORROW
An Imprint of HarperCollins*Publishers*

GENEVA PUBLIC LIBRARY DISTRICT

This book is a work of fiction. The characters, incidents, and dialogue are drawn from the author's imagination and are not to be construed as real. Any resemblance to actual events or persons, living or dead, is entirely coincidental.

JENNIFER JOHNSON IS SICK OF BEING MARRIED. Copyright © 2012 by Heather McElhatton. All rights reserved. Printed in the United States of America. No part of this book may be used or reproduced in any manner whatsoever without written permission except in the case of brief quotations embodied in critical articles and reviews. For information address HarperCollins Publishers, 10 East 53rd Street, New York, NY 10022.

HarperCollins books may be purchased for educational, business, or sales promotional use. For information please write: Special Markets Department, HarperCollins Publishers, 10 East 53rd Street, New York, NY 10022.

FIRST EDITION

Designed by Diahann Sturge

Library of Congress Cataloging-in-Publication Data has been applied for.

ISBN 978-0-06-206439-4

12 13 14 15 16 OV/RRD 10 9 8 7 6 5 4 3 2 1

For
J. C. Smith
and all who sailed with him.

First mate of the schooner *Appledore*
June 6, 1986–January 17, 2012

Contents

Jennifer
Johnson is
sick of being
married

On Your Marks

1
Paradise Lost

Not all honeymoons are erotic carnivals. They're not all bliss. Champagne, roses, and sex may or may not be a part of your honeymoon experience.

There are no guarantees in this world.

I went on my honeymoon with a few expectations. Kill me. After decades of consuming popular honeymoon images featuring white-sand beaches, tranquil breezes, and newlyweds barely able to contain their matrimonial lust for each other, I pretty much thought that was what happened. I'd hung on to the possibility that a few moments in life *might be* perfect, really *should be* perfect if God loved us even the smallest, tiniest, teensiest bit. He doesn't. He's a bored trickster with a penchant for ironic calamity, just dreaming up new ways to ruin us.

Our honeymoon *did not* include any of the aforementioned fun qualities, but *did* include illness, injury, and the unrelenting soundtrack of severe gastric distress and loud calypso music being performed live in the lobby at all hours of the day and night. Sharp, tinny, percussive beats that tapped like a wasp inside your skull. An inescapable rhythm audible anywhere you went, including the hotel room and the marble floor of our bathroom with several towels wrapped around your head. They say you attract the things that happen to you. Maybe it's true, and if it is, I must search out the specific mistakes that allowed my honeymoon from hell to happen. Perhaps uncovering the choices that led our prepaid, nonrefundable little piece of heaven to transmogrify into a baffling personal hell will prevent it from happening again.

So here we go.

Mistake #1: Letting Brad's parents plan the honeymoon. Brad's parents are generous, rich, religious, and controlling. They paid for our wedding, which is why we had "Mary and Joseph" (the most popular couple in the Bible) as the theme at our reception and little hay mangers for table centerpieces, each one with a clothespin Baby Jesus.

They also paid for our honeymoon, which is why it was at a Caribbean Christian resort called In His Palms on Saint John island. Brad was happy about it. He'd just gotten his dive certificate . . . well, he'd almost gotten it. He hadn't finished all the classes, but his stupid dive-instructor buddy gave it to him as a wedding present, just handed it over even though Brad hadn't learned all the hand signals. I was livid. What if something went wrong down there and Brad *died* because he didn't know the hand signal for some *critical* message, like:

"APOLOGIES, FELLOW DIVERS. I JUST SHAT MYSELF."

"HAS ANYONE SEEN THAT BALD GUY WE WERE DIVING WITH? WE GOT A LITTLE TANGLED UP EARLIER AND I JUST REALIZED I'M STILL HOLDING HIS MASK. "

"DOES ANYONE KNOW WHERE A SAND DOLLAR'S ANUS IS? THIS ONE EITHER SPAT AT ME OR POOPED STRAIGHT UP AT MY FACE AND I WANT TO KNOW WHICH."

"HELLO, NEW FRIENDS! I NEED ASSISTANCE. I LOST MY ORIGINAL DIVE GROUP AFTER BECOMING FASCINATED BY A WEIRD-LOOKING TURTLE WHO LED ME, ALMOST KNOW-INGLY, INTO A STRONG UNDERWATER CURRENT WHICH WHISKED ME AWAY AND SHOT ME OUT INTO A VAST KELP BED. THERE I BECAME LOST AND WAS FORCED TO OUT-SMART A MEAN DOLPHIN AND A PARTICULARLY INTELLI-

GENT GROUP OF STARFISH, WHO MAY OR MAY NOT HAVE POOPED AT ME REPEATEDLY. MIGHT I JOIN YOUR GROUP? IF NOT, I WILL DEFINITELY DIE, NOT THAT IT'S DEFINITELY YOUR PROBLEM. THE LAWS AT SEA ARE TRICKY. MAY WE PLEASE HURRY, THOUGH? THE STARFISH WILL BE BACK. "

Mistake #2: Going to the Caribbean in the summer. We got married on June 10 and were in Saint John the next day. We stepped off the plane and into a solid wall of humid steamy air. It felt like walking around Africa with damp wool blankets wrapped around your body and heaped on your head. It was like being inside someone's mouth.

Mistake #3: Checking our luggage. Bad weather on the first leg of our flight left us circling over Miami for two hours. Once we'd landed, we were forced to sit on the runway for another hour with babies crying and toilets overflowing. It was the kind of situation *20/20* does investigative stories about. By the time we got to a gate, we'd missed our connecting flight, as had most everybody else. I thought we should spend the night in Miami and fly out the next day. Brad, however, was determined to get us to Saint John *that night*, so as passengers lined up en masse at a ticket counter in the terminal, Brad used some new travel app he had on his phone and found us two seats on the last flight leaving Miami.

"Got it!" he said. "I got it!"

He booked two seats on a flight leaving for the neighboring island of Saint Thomas . . . which was leaving from a different terminal, of course, located somewhere on the other side of the globe, and was departing . . . in about forty-two microseconds.

I told him I didn't *want* to run. He said running would be good for me. Then he snatched up his bag and just took off without me. Suddenly I was standing there in the Miami International

Airport by myself, watching Brad's quickly receding figure. In an instant, he was gone.

I blinked. Then I shouted, *"Brad! Wait!"* and fumbled to grab my stuff and bolt down the corridor after him. By the time I caught up with him at the connecting gate, I was furious. Teary-eyed, I refused to speak. Did Brad notice the distraught condition of his new bride? *He did not.* He was too busy congratulating himself on his victory of finding a new flight.

I managed to hold my fury down for about half the flight. Brad finally nudged my arm and said, "Hon, you okay?" I maintained my pensive stare and refused to look at him, while studying his every expression closely in his reflection in the dark window. Finally I lifted my chin defiantly and said, "I'm fine." He of course assumed that meant I was actually fine . . . and he went to sleep.

WIFE-TO-ENGLISH TRANSLATIONS

WHEN A WIFE SAYS	WHAT SHE REALLY MEANS IS
(Nothing . . . is silent)	She is gathering evidence and ammunition before issuing punishment.
"It's fine."	"You will pay."
"Am I pretty?"	"I opened an online dating account."
"It's no big deal."	"You ruin everything."
"I'm going out with the girls."	"I'm going out with the girls to tell them about your weird testicles."

HUSBAND-TO-ENGLISH TRANSLATIONS

WHEN A HUSBAND SAYS	WHAT HE REALLY MEANS IS
"I'm good."	"When will you stop talking?"
"No, he's the kicker."	"For the love of Christ . . . leave."
"Your mother is coming?"	"Prostitutes make sense."
"I guess we could go."	"This'll cost you a blow job."
"You guys go on ahead. I've got work to do."	"You guys go on ahead. I'll watch porn with the dog."

Brad slept for the rest of the flight while I ground my molars into a fine powder. When we landed in Saint Thomas and learned that our luggage *had* in fact been left behind in Miami, I already had my reaction planned. I stared stoically off into space and said nothing. Brad proceeded to tell me everything was fine. They'd deliver our bags in a few days. He wasn't surprised they had lost our bags; they never could've gotten them on board our new flight. It took off in forty-two microseconds, after all. Remember?

I smiled at him and felt rage.

We took a ferry from Saint Thomas to the smaller island of Saint John. As we crossed over the water in a jolly wooden boat painted aquamarine and yellow, I silently and furiously inventoried all the contents of my luggage: carefully selected resort wear, tropical-hued makeup, complicated lingerie, industrial-strength foundation garments—items all selected to make our honeymoon perfect. Items that were irreplaceable, absolutely essential, and officially no longer in play. Of course Brad thought it was no big deal. But I *needed* my luggage. He could stagger around wearing dirty boxers all week, but I couldn't. Men can stop shaving and wear rumpled clothes and people think they look rugged. Women do that and the only people who acknowledge them are stray dogs and lesbian folksingers.

When Brad asked why I was being so quiet for the third time, I uttered a small teeny-tiny concern that our honeymoon was now *ruined*. Brad thought I was being high-maintenance. He said they'd probably deliver our luggage in the morning, which they did not. In fact, they did not deliver it all week. In fact, we never saw our luggage again.

Mistake #4: Staying at an all-inclusive resort. "All-inclusive resort" is another way of saying "friendly prison." We arrived quite late at the In His Palms resort and found the harried concierge barely had time to give us our ID key cards and a hefty list of rules. You had to carry ID on you at all times. You were discouraged from leaving the resort grounds at any time. The Olympic-size pool, which was in the shape of a giant cross, closed every night at nine. The hot tub was for "married couples only," not that anyone would take a Jacuzzi in that heat. There were also an ominous number of signs indicating forced jocularity and management-controlled merriment.

SMILE, YOU'RE IN PARADISE!
AND ON 24-HOUR SURVEILLANCE CAMERA!

TRY OUR NEW LIME TAFFY NO-BIG-BANG DAIQUIRI!
YUMMY AND ALCOHOL-FREE!

BIBLE BINGO and CHRISTIAN SCRABBLE NIGHT!
PRIZES INCLUDE:
- "IN HIS PALMS" TOWEL VEST
- 36-OZ. TUB OF OUR PATENTED
"NOW I LAY ME DOWN TO TAN" SUNSCREEN
- RAPE WHISTLE
- GROOVY "WALKIN' WITH THE J-DOG" FLIP-FLOPS

TRY JOY-GA
NON-SATANIC YOGA!
YOU'VE STRETCHED WITH THE DEVIL . . . NOW REACH FOR THE
LIGHT!
DAILY/10 A.M./JOY-GA STUDIO (BEHIND DUMPSTERS)

FOOTPRINTS IN THE SAND SUNRISE BEACH WALK!
IF HE CAN GET UP EARLY, YOU CAN TOO!

VISIT THE HOLY WATER PARK . . .
WHERE FUN IS CONTAGIOUS!
SO ARE GERMS! DON'T FORGET TO APPLY BLEACH SOLUTION
BEFORE YOUR SWIM!

Worse than all this, however, worse than the heat, the enforced fun, and the number of judging Christians all around me, was that to my complete dismay the resort was 100 percent alcohol-free. There was not a drop of liquor anywhere on the premises. Nor was a drop allowed to be brought on. An hour after we arrived, I looked at my new husband and said, "Darling, get me a drink or I won't be held responsible for my actions."

Brad paid the guy at the front desk ten dollars and he told us there was a bar just down the road that stayed open until about two A.M. We found the bar, which had no name, and it was a small plywood hut with teal-blue walls, metal road sign tables, and a rotating fan nailed to the ceiling. Nobody was there but the bartender. He made us cocktails, a rich touristy drink for me, with Appleton rum, canned pineapple juice, and room-temperature cream, and a virgin Bloody Mary for Brad, who doesn't drink anymore. He poured our drinks into two beat-up-looking coconut shells. I loved them. Brad did too. We clunked our coconuts together and kissed. This was the moment I'd been waiting for. We were newlyweds in paradise. We were happy. Our romantic honeymoon had finally begun.

Mistake #5: *Accidentally going to a sex club*. On the way back to the resort, we passed a sign on the road that said CHICKEN. The sign had an arrow pointing up toward a white stucco building with dark windows and a muscle-bound bouncer at the front door. "Are you hungry?" Brad asked, and I said, "Famished!" So we went into what we *thought* was a restaurant that served chicken. Inside, the music was low and thumping. Figures moved around on the dance floor. We found an open booth on the far side of the room, and I peripherally caught the strange shapes and jerking motions occurring at the tables and booths we were walking past.

"Did you see that guy wearing a mask?" Brad whispered when we sat down.

"What guy?" I looked around as our waitress arrived and asked what we wanted. Having no menu, I shrugged and asked if they had chicken. She nodded and said it was ten dollars for ten minutes. I didn't understand her. She repeated herself. "Ten minutes of . . . *chicken*?" I looked over at Brad, whose eyes were suddenly wide, wide open. "Hon," he said. "We're in a sex club." I scanned the room and forced my eyes to focus. It was true. People were screwing all over the room. On the tables, in the booths, against the walls. My horrified eyes accidentally locked on the pear-shaped ass of a big chubby white guy wearing nothing except a fanny pack. His fat rolls jiggled as he banged a corpulent black girl, whose ass was lodged in the salad bar's lettuce bin. It was like watching giant lumping albino walruses slapping squid-bits together. I will never get the images out of my head.

Mistake #6: Forgetting our ID cards. Our walk back to the resort took forever. Traffic whizzed by, kicking up gravel and dust and skittering beer cans across the road. Then the resort's front gates were locked. We hollered until the front desk guy came out and said we needed our ID key cards to get in. We'd left them in the room. After twenty minutes Brad wadded up a hundred-dollar bill and chucked it at the guard's little hut. Moments later, the gates swung open and Brad started to argue with the guard, threatening to tell management.

I calmed Brad down and steered him toward the restaurant, promising we'd both feel better after we finally ate. Unfortunately the restaurant was closed and the kitchen staff had all gone home. Room service stopped at eleven P.M. I told the front desk guy we were really sorry to inconvenience him, but we were really hungry and could he heat us up some soup? He agreed, after I gave him twenty bucks, and asked what kind of soup we wanted. Spicy black bean or creamy crayfish bisque? Well, anyone who orders beans before their first night on their honeymoon is insane. We ordered two bowls of the crayfish bisque and the desk clerk smiled and bowed his head. "The bisque," he said. "Excellent choice."

Mistake #7: Ordering the crayfish bisque. The cramps didn't set in until we were asleep. After wolfing down two large bowls of crayfish bisque and then adjourning to our honeymoon bed, we passed out. I woke around two A.M. feeling hot. There were frogs outside our window, croaking through the slats, sometimes in unison, sometimes in a baffling cacophony of independent sounds. They dominated the world, it seemed, controlled the airspace in our heads. (Brad said he liked the sound, it was soothing. It made me feel insane.) I lay there and listened to them while I stared at the ceiling fan and wished it was on. Suddenly my stomach gurgled. A stabbing sensation tore through my bowels and felt like a saltwater-taffy-pulling machine had hold of my intestinal tract and was now twisting it into loops. I doubled over in pain. The frogs outside croaked louder.

When the first wave hit, I managed to make it to the bathroom . . . but barely. I rivaled any Olympic gymnast as I bounded across the room and planted my posterior on the bowl just in time. Brad, however, was not so lucky. Twenty minutes into one of the most violent bathroom episodes I've ever experienced, Brad started pounding on the door. He was shouting something desperately at me; I couldn't say what, because for once in my life I'd had enough sense to lock the door. He begged me to let him in, but there was *no way*. Unable to stand, I was only able to shout through the door in short telegram-like sentences. "*Can't . . . move,*" I shouted. "*Can't stand . . . up. The crayfish did . . . it. Oh . . . Jesus.*" I doubled over in pain. Eventually, the pounding ceased. Brad bolted for the nearest toilet, which was downstairs in the lobby.

That night, we hardly slept. We just lay there groaning and gurgling and cramping up and wanting to die and listening to the death frogs, all the while intermittently lunging for the bathroom. I took carefully worded guesses at what had caused our gastric distress. There were the turbulent flights, the mismatched alcohol, the *warm* dairy products. Upon hearing those words, "warm dairy products," Brad groaned loudly and gripped the bed.

"No crayfish bisque ever again," he said. "No crayfish *anything*."

We lay there and panted as we speculated and sweated and

tried to keep still. Moving was tricky; roll too fast or far and the crayfish insurgency was right there to rise up and meet you. Fail to shift the voluminous gas building up inside you and it stabbed like a knife. This is how we spent the first night of our honeymoon. The smell alone made it something we'd want to forget. Around dawn we fell asleep in twisted-up, foul-smelling, and sweaty sheets.

The next day we staggered downstairs pale and weak, our bones like sharp glass. We went to the resort's mirth-free brunch, with virgin Bloody Marys and the "no-touch conga line." I ordered weak tea and dry toast in the dazzlingly bright dining room, which, judging by the sudden sharp warning gurgles in my stomach, was already pushing it. Then my brother-in-law, Lenny, and my sister, Hailey, came bounding toward our table. I'd almost forgotten they were there. My mother-in-law had sent them along with us. They had more energy than golden retrievers and were so tanned and smiley I wanted to vomit. They'd caught their flight and gotten in early. They'd already been snorkeling and had seen dolphins and a huge sea turtle.

Rage.

I listened to them as long as I could, but when the sadistic calypso band started up in the lobby, I said I needed to go back upstairs, before a gastronomic event happened. We passed a smattering of joyless Bible Scrabble players sitting on the sun-dappled patio. A man nearby let out a sigh. "Goll darn it," he said. "Almost had the bonus word. Look at my board. I had 'pro-lice.'"

We stopped at the front desk and discovered our luggage was still missing. The manager was apologetic but wholly unsympathetic, especially when we told him we might've gotten food poisoning from the soup we ate last night. He found that unlikely. None of the other guests had complained. In fact the kitchen was serving it again that night, and he directed our gaze to the nearby menu board. At the mere sight of the words "crayfish bisque," Brad fled up the stairs. I smiled politely and asked where the nearest bathroom was.

There, I pondered my clothing situation, which was dire. The outfit I'd worn on the plane could be washed in the bathroom only so many times and I didn't dare send it to the cleaners. I didn't want it out of my sight. Hailey offered to lend me clothing, but she was two agonizing sizes smaller, and so I declined. But I had to do something, so I decided to brave the resort's gift shop, Onward, Christian Shoppers, a tacky crap emporium filled with cheap plastic and neon colors. You could buy a lime-green bucket of bleached starfish for twenty-eight dollars or a king-size Snickers bar for six. I wound up buying two muumuus at eighty bucks each. One was neon safety-orange; the other one was bright Day-Glo pink. I donned my new tent-size attire in the room and Brad said, "What . . . what are you wearing?"

He looked horrified.

"This is a muumuu, darling," I told him, and climbed into bed. "It's the official attire of women who've given up. Get used to it."

He laughed. Sort of.

I also laughed sort of and we lay there, assuring each other that the worst of the food poisoning had surely passed and we'd feel better soon. An hour later there was a horrible gurgling in my stomach. Gurgling with intent. "It's *happening*!" I shouted, and flew from the bed to the bathroom. The bisque was back. The next wave hit Brad a few hours later. This wasn't some shitstorm that would pass over with a handful of Tums. No. We named it the Crayfish Jihad. The concierge gave us the number for a doctor, who agreed it was either food poisoning, a virus, or a bacterial infection. So basically, he didn't know what we had. He called in a prescription at the local pharmacy and said for insurance reasons the hotel would be unable to pick up the prescription for us; we had to get it ourselves. An eighty-dollar cab ride and several sudden stops for the bathroom later, we found the pharmacy, which informed us they only had enough antidiarrheal medication in stock for one prescription.

We were quiet on the ride home and decided to split the medication, ensuring that neither of us got better. Not completely. You'd think the trouble was gone and then *pow,* you were sprinting for the bathroom. Our recurring episodes of gastric distress continued to alternate throughout the remainder of the trip and were obviously present to one degree or another in every photo we took. In all our honeymoon photos one of us looks worried. Either Brad has a deep crease in his forehead and is poised at the edge of the photo to sprint for the bathroom, or I have a panicked smile on my face, saying, *"Hurry. Take the damn picture."*

Meanwhile Hailey and Lenny were having the time of their lives, surfing, swimming with dolphins, dancing to that damned calypso music. (They bought two CDs of it to bring home.) We, on the other hand, were still terrified to venture too far from indoor plumbing. Our honeymoon was almost over and we hadn't had sex once, which didn't upset Brad nearly as much as the fact that he hadn't been scuba diving once. Stubbornly, he donned a snorkeling mask and went for a short paddle around the reef, while I sat on the beach with Hailey and Lenny reading magazines. I seethed with rage at my copy of *Cosmo,* which was brimming with gorgeous supermodels who aggravated and vexed me. *We're perfect and you are not. Whatever you have, it's not enough. Whoever you are, you're not who you should be. Whatever you want, it's just out of reach and always will be. You will never be finished, fixed, or free.* They should just call the magazine *You Will Never Be Happy.*

Suddenly Brad came roaring out of the water like a wet moose, bellowing and stumbling toward the beach. I was afraid it was a level-six crayfish insurgency. He charged toward us, his howling louder and louder. Lenny put down his copy of *Crappie Fisherman* and told us that if a man hollered like that on the Iron Range, he'd find his snowmobile spray-painted pink by morning. *"Pee on it!"* Brad shouted, hopping on one foot.

I tried to comprehend his gestures. (I *knew* hand gestures were important.)

"I stepped on a freaking sea urchin!" Brad howled. *"Jesus freaking Christ, somebody pee on my foot!"*

"Pee on your what?" Hailey squinted at him.

"Pee on my freaking foot!"

Lenny finally stood up, muttering, and unzipped his pants. "Shit," he said. "I'll pee on your damn foot, all right? Why dontcha quit hollering? You're scaring the damn seagulls. *Shit.* Peeing on a grown man's foot. I don't know what to think anymore."

Mistake #8: Getting lost and winding up on the kitchen loading dock. I got lost while trying to get back to the room and wound up wandering down some employee-only service hall and turning down another service hall, and then I was in the kitchen. Through the steamy racks of stainless steel kitchenware I saw a loading dock and sunlight pouring in through a partially open garage door. I headed for the light, thinking I'd get my bearings more easily outside. Ducking under the door and stepping into the blinding sunlight, I found myself standing outside on the loading dock with three young men, presumably members of the kitchen staff, judging by their dirty white aprons.

They were sitting on folding chairs and smoking. One kid with dark greasy hair and a pimple-pocked face tore off a hunk of bread and hurled it at a bunch of dogs standing on the cement slab below. There were a dozen dogs or so standing there, all rough looking and full of mange. They snapped and snarled over the thrown morsel and I asked the boys why all these dogs were there. The kid with greasy hair told me they were stray dogs. The island is full of them. They roam around in packs and knock over garbage cans. "It's a problem," the kid said. "That's why we poison 'em." Then he whipped another hunk of bread at them.

"Poison?" I croaked. "What do you mean, *poison?*" Apparently it's common practice to feed stray dogs food laced with rat poison. It cuts down on the population. I watched the boys throw three more chunks of bread to the dogs before it dawned on me and I asked them, "Is there *rat poison* in that bread?"

Yes. There was. Didn't they just tell me that?

"But . . . but . . ." My brain raced stupidly around my head for an answer. "But that one is *a puppy*!" I finally said, pointing to the little pudgy mutt pawing the gravel below us. He was all white except for a black dot near his tail. Somehow *this* was the only argument I came up with, as if people who poisoned dogs for fun would care that one of them was a puppy.

"Yeah, get him," the greasy-haired kid said lazily, as though I'd just alerted him to which dog I'd like them to poison next. A boy chucked a bread ball at the little dog and without thinking I shouted, *"No no no!"* while leaping over the edge of the loading dock, landing painfully on my ankle. On the ground I started clapping my hands and stamping my feet, separating the dogs and driving them away from me. The dogs all stared at me, not sure what I expected.

That's when it occurred to me that there was nothing I could do if they decided to attack, and wouldn't that be perfect? UN-LUCKY WOMAN ON VERGE OF WONDERFUL LIFE WITH NEW HUS-

BAND TORN TO DEATH BY WILD DOGS ON HER HONEYMOON. "Shame on you!" I shouted. I was looking at the dogs but shouting at the boys. I didn't know if either group was aware of this. "That's *no way* to treat a *living* animal!" I yelled. "You should be *ashamed* of yourselves!"

Using disgust as a shield, I pushed my way toward the little dog and scooped him up. The puppy let me do this without so much as a whimper and I held him up with both hands. That was when I realized the poor little guy only had three legs. "Shame on you!" I repeated angrily at the boys. I cradled the pup, sniffing his neck, which smelled like garbage left out in the sun. I left, indignantly brushing past surly canine faces around me. "You should know, I'll be informing the hotel manager about this," I told the boys on the loading dock. They hadn't moved from their chairs. "I'm going to tell him that you're out here poisoning these dogs!"

Mistake #9: Complaining to the hotel manager. My ardent appeal to the mean little hotel manager was met with irritation. It turned out he paid the kitchen crew extra to "assist with maintaining the hotel's ongoing high standards." He paid them to poison dogs, five bucks a body. The hotel manager scolded me for entering restricted employee-only areas and then he started asking me where the dog was. "What dog?" I asked.

"The one they said *you took*? The puppy?"

"Huh. Never heard of him."

The manager said *any guest found with an animal in their hotel room will be kicked out immediately, and all refunds will be forfeited.* I told him he was one heck of a *Christian*, letting his staff kill God's creatures left and right. I defied them all. I hid the three-legged puppy in our bathroom for three days, refusing to let housecleaning in. I put newspaper down on the floor and sneaked him bacon. Brad, recovering in bed, said I was crazy;

there were dogs running around loose all over the island. "What difference does saving one dog make?" he asked me.

"It makes a big difference to one person I know. To Ace."

I named the puppy Ace, because he's a lucky little guy.

I was lucky too. Ace was great company. He accompanied me all over the island as Brad slept in the room. I hid him in my bag with loose muumuu over him and sneaked him past the front desk. We went out for lunch together, we went to the beach, we went sightseeing, we even went on a paddleboard ride together. Then Brad got better and started accompanying me on short trips downstairs and the maids found Ace snoozing on his bed of towels in the bathroom. They reported me to the manager, who threatened to kick us out.

Brad calmed him down with a large cash bribe and he promised we'd get rid of the dog immediately. Luckily I was able to find Ace a new home, with an elderly woman living nearby. She sold baskets by the roadside and kissed him on the forehead. "I can be a good mama for him," she said, and agreed to take Ace home. I gave her enough money for a year's dog food supply. My ever-indulgent husband let me. He just shook his head and said I was crazy.

Mistake #10: *Booking a romantic moonlit dinner.* We only had one night left, so I booked what was to be the *highlight* of our trip, a romantic moonlit dinner for two on our own private island at sunset. We decided after much debate to go for it. We let a festive wooden boat drop us off on a tiny island three miles offshore, and they told us they would return in two hours. The captain said we'd find our gourmet candlelight dinner waiting off the end of the dock and bathroom facilities just beyond it. We nearly ran down the dock to the beach, where we found a small raised platform and a lovely table with plates covered with silver domes. It looked just like the brochure.

Under our plates were round battery-operated plate warmers, which kept Brad's filet mignon warm and my chicken Kiev toasty. A chilled bottle of champagne rested in its battery-operated cooling bucket. As a spectacular sunset unfolded before us, we sighed, smiled at each other, and clinked glasses. Finally, a small piece of sanity. We ate dinner, then we ate dessert, which was chocolate cake with fresh strawberries. After dinner we took a leisurely stroll around the circumference of the tiny teardrop-shaped island and found a sand dollar, a pretty feather, then another feather, and then a desiccated dead seabird. We kissed, hugged, and reviewed the many events of the past week. Finally we made our way back to the dock and waited for the boat. We waited . . . *and waited* . . . *and waited*.

No boat. Once we thought a boat was headed for us, but then it turned and veered away. We hadn't even thought to bring cell phones. It was getting cold. And windy. I thought briefly of sitting on a plate warmer. As the sky darkened we discussed our options. We talked about the currents, the tides, and every castaway/maritime disaster and shark movie we'd ever seen. We could see the lights twinkling on the shore and even tried to light a signal fire, but without matches and only dying plate warmers, it was useless. We huddled together under the table, now strewn with empty glasses and debris. The only other structure on the island was the Porta-Potty, and I just couldn't. We were rescued the next day by a passing pontoon boat of teenagers. We staggered into the resort sunburned, dehydrated, and covered with bug bites. Nobody at the hotel had noticed we were gone, not even my sister.

The only not-mistake? The only decision that wasn't a mistake was one I made the morning we left. It was raining and we packed in silence, despair setting down on my shoulders like a heavy, damp blanket. I kept trying to think of something funny to say that might lighten the mood, but everything I thought of sounded stupid. Finally we piled into a pink taxicab and headed for the airport. A few yards away from the hotel, however, I shouted *"Stop!"* and the cab screeched to a halt. I jumped out and Brad stuck his head out the window. "Jen? What's going on?" I marched toward a row of aluminum garbage cans by the side of the road. There he was, poor little guy. Ace. He was eating garbage by the side of the road. That devious old woman took my money and tossed my dog out the minute I wasn't looking. Ace started hop-walking toward me, tail wagging. I scooped him up and we got back into the taxi.

Brad said, "Honey, you can't bring a dog home. They'll stop you."

"Well, darling"—I put on my sunglasses—"they can certainly try."

2
Home Is Where the Hell Is

Airport security is not what it could be.

Ace sails through the TSA inspection, riding through the X-ray machine while sound asleep in a bundle of muumuu fabric inside my canvas bag.

"But what're we going to do with a *dog*?" Brad asks when we're in the air. "My mother won't like a dog in the guesthouse." I remind him we're not going to live in his parents' guesthouse for very long. He promised we'd move out as soon we came back from our honeymoon.

"Remember?" I say, smiling.

Brad just groans.

"You said we'd find a house of our own, Brad. You know, our own house with its own address and its own cable connection? So your mother never lectures me on Satan's grip on the Independent Film Channel again?" I say this as sweetly as my shattered nerves will allow. The truth is, we've been fighting about it for eons. "Besides," I tell him, "your mom will love Ace. He's like her first grandchild."

"Right." He snorts. "What about Trevor?"

"Trevor's not a grandchild. He's like a grand-oddity."

We land on schedule and Brad's parents pick us up at the Minneapolis airport. Mother Keller wears a pea-soup-colored linen pantsuit. She's surprisingly pleased with Ace. "My goodness, it looks like you've started your family after all!" she says. Mr. Keller, who says I should call him Ed, gives me a big squeeze and winks at me. "Bring us back any other souvenirs, Jen-Jen?"

"Um . . . like what, Ed?"

"We were hoping for a bun in that oven!" He grins.

Ick.

No surprise though. Are they ever hoping for anything else?

Hailey and Lenny take a cab home while Brad and I bundle our ragtag luggage into the car. It's warm out but not humid and tropical like Saint John. The Kellers drive us home in their big white Lexus SUV, which smells of new leather and continually broadcasts Christian talk radio. Ace sleeps on my lap. Mrs. Keller peppers me with awkward questions, questions I don't want to answer, like, *How was the trip? Did you guys have fun? Did you get to go scuba diving?* Finally, when we're almost home and salvation is almost delivered . . . Brad's father turns down the wrong driveway.

"What's up, Pop?" Brad says. "Why're we going to the Morganthalers' house?"

"A-*ha!*" Mr. Keller says, his eyes twinkling. "It *was* their house, dear boy. *Was!*"

I sit up; my heart skips a beat. *"What's going on?"* I nearly whine. I'm so exhausted. I just want to get home and take a bath, where I'll begin concocting the elaborate lie that will take the place of my actual honeymoon.

"Don't worry." Mother Keller pats my knee. "You'll see."

Right. It's when she says "don't worry" that I worry the most.

The car rolls up to the front door of the Morganthalers' house, a huge behemoth of a house, a monstrosity of confused design best described as a New American McMansion with Swiss turrets, Victorian elements, and Mediterranean accents.

Ed stops the car.

"So," he says. "We have a little surprise for you kids!"

I moan quietly and Ace starts to get squirrelly in my lap, licking my face.

"Welcome home, son!" Ed Keller beams.

"What?" Brad says.

"*What?*" I echo.

"We bought you a new house!" Mother Keller says. "Isn't it wonderful?"

"You bought us a house?" I chirp, looking out the window.

"Right next door!" she says evil-gleefully.

"No . . ." I shake my head.

"Oh yes, we did," she says. "Come and see!"

They all pile out of the car and I sit there in stunned silence. "But . . . this is the Morganthalers' house," I say meekly. "*They* live here."

"It *was* their house, Jennifer. They moved. Now it's *your* house. *You* live here!"

"*No . . .*" I groan.

Brad tugs me out of the car and I lose my grip on Ace, who wakes up and springs happily out of my arms, tumbling after Ed Keller through the front door. I'm lost in a daze. Speechless. It's like a slowly unfolding nightmare. You want to wake up, a voice in your head keeps repeating, *It's not true, it's not true* . . . yet it is true, and waking up is not an option. I find it's all freakishly, inexplicably true. We have a nasty dose of reality here; it's undoubtedly a good thing that I'm too jet-lagged and exhausted to voice my opinion too clearly. It's enough just to wrap my gerbil-size brain around the situation. The Kellers bought us a house . . .

The house right next door.

Kill me.

You could lob a ham sandwich from our front door to theirs, if you wanted to. Or a bomb. We tour the airplane-hangar-size monstrosity and find all our belongings have already been moved in. All our books, clothes, pots and pans—even our toothbrushes are there, sitting in engraved silver toothbrush cups in the master bathroom. Mother Keller did it all while we were on our honeymoon.

"Mom, this is incredible!" Brad says. "Hon, isn't this incredible?"

"Incredible . . ." I smile weakly.

Mother Keller went ahead and decorated the whole house herself. She picked out all the pastel furniture, the flocked wallpaper, even the porcelain figurines and dried flower arrangements. After all, we didn't own nearly enough furniture to fill up this place. Trying to fill this behemoth of a house with our scrappy belongings would be like trying to fill the *Titanic* with the contents of a rowboat. Unfortunately the furnishings Mother Keller chose are more to her taste than mine. The place is all sweet and pastel-y and frilly. It looks like a gynecologist's office mixed with a Christian Science Reading Room, slammed inside a Céline Dion video. I hate it.

The front hall has white marble floors polished to a high liquid shine and a sweeping spiral staircase that twists up around a large, low-hanging chandelier of queer citrine yellowy-green crystal. The living room is douche-commercial peachy pink and dominated by huge peach upholstered couches and brass accent lamps. In the kitchen I find a copy of *Cooking for Dummies* and a plaque on the wall that says LORD BLESS THIS MESS! Upstairs in our walk-in closets, I find all of our clothing hanging up or neatly put away in drawers. I burn with shame and the distinct memory of leaving a pair of dirty underwear on the floor in the cottage. Dear God, I hope Mother Keller didn't see them. The tour's almost over, and I'm contemplating suicide by way of skewering a brass fireplace poker into my eye socket, when Mother Keller flips on the lights in the dining room and my whole family leaps out shouting, *"Surprise!"*

I nearly have a heart attack. My first thought is, *What's* wrong *with you people?* which isn't fair, because they're only trying to congratulate us on our amazing new house. They've been silently waiting there in the dark, even Hailey and Lenny, who took a taxi from the airport. Dad hugs me, Mom kisses me. They take turns holding Ace, who's nearly hysterical with joy. He bounds up and down the staircase on three legs faster than most dogs can go on four.

Everybody congratulates us on our new home and they all start asking questions about the honeymoon. I don't even get to lie about it, because idiot Hailey is already there blabbering away. "They had a honeymoon from hell!" she hoots. "They had diarrhea all week!"

"It's always *something*," Mother Keller says.

"I *told* you to pack Imodium," Mom says with a sigh.

"That's a doozy of a honeymoon!" Ed laughs out loud.

"Oh!" Mother Keller yelps suddenly. "Jennifer! The dog is peeing all over the house!"

"Ace?" I look around, bewildered.

"Oh my, what a mess!" she says, blotting the carpet. "Quick, grab that napkin. Oh, Jennifer, really. You're not here *two minutes* and you've already turned your house into a mess."

My house. What a joke. I feel like I might faint.

Brad's older sister, Sarah, arrives and she starts in immediately. She tosses back her shiny auburn curls and says, "Diarrhea on your honeymoon? What a *loser* my brother is! It's always a disaster when he travels with women. Always. Like the time he went on spring break with what's-her-name. The Asian one. Anyway they both got gonorrhea."

She gives me a big saccharine-sweet smile.

That's Sarah for you. A Prada-wearing piranha.

"All right then!" Ed says. "I'm getting everybody some apple cider! Hey, Bill here?"

Sarah says her husband is outside. She made him repark the car. Poor Bill.

Being married to Sarah must be like marrying a black widow spider. The question isn't whether she'll kill you, it's when, and how much of your dry husk will remain. Mother Keller offers to show my parents the new snow blower in the garage and I'm alone with Sarah momentarily. She turns and whispers conspiratorially. "Did you know Dad's retiring?"

"I heard he was thinking about that."

"Oh, I'll *bet* you did." She winks. "Bet you want to know who's the new president too! Don't assume Brad's becoming president."

"No, he hasn't even mentioned—"

"Oh, of course," she snorts. "My brother never tells you anything, does he. Poor thing. Always in the dark. Don't you just wonder what *secrets* he's keeping from you?"

"Not really . . ."

"He probably has a harem of Asian hookers somewhere. He's always had Egg Roll Fever, you know."

I choke-chortle awkwardly, wanting to punch her in the face.

Her eyes dart around the room quickly. "I'll tell you something, Jennifer. I've worked for years and years at the company.

My brother just got here. While he was off *fucking up his life* and drinking himself into whatever stupor my parents found him in, I was *right here* the whole time. You know? Working and waiting for my turn. Now Brad thinks he's in line for the throne?"

"No, I don't think he——"

"You know what? I'll tell you what. *No way* am I handing over the helm to my idiot-dipshit little brother. Not without one motherfucking *hell* of a fight. Got it?"

I nod, afraid she might sprout fangs and eat me right there on the spot.

We hear a child shriek in the front hall and my eyes go wide with fear.

Trevor?

Demon Trevor speeds around the corner full-tilt, arms open, and slams painfully into me, grabbing my legs and hanging on like a koala bear, his hands sticky with something.

"Auntie Jen! Auntie Jen! *Guess how old I am.*"

"Forty-seven?" I say. "Forty-six?"

"Seven and *three-quarters*!" he shouts at me.

"Trevor!" Sarah grabs his arm. "You have candy. Why do you have candy? I said no candy! Give me that candy."

"No!" He sticks his hands behind his back. "Daddy gave it to me."

"Oh, I'll *bet* he did," she says. "Give me that candy this minute, Trevor, or I'll tell Santa Claus that you get no presents *ever again.*"

He looks at her.

"I mean it," she growls.

Trevor lets go of my legs and stares up, his lips trembling. "*Santa?*" he says, and I want to call child services.

"Did you hear me?" Sarah shouts at him. "Give them to me . . . *now!*"

Trevor thrusts two peppermint candies out and starts crying.

"Go wash your hands," she says. "They're filthy!"

Weeping, he trudges toward the kitchen, head hung low. I swear, there is not enough therapy in the world to fix that kid. "You know," I say carefully, "a little candy isn't *that* bad . . ."

"*Bill?*" she shouts as her husband walks in. He still has his coat on.

"What?" he says. "I was parking the car. Oh, hey, Jen! Welcome back."

"Bill!" Sarah snaps. "Did you give Trevor candy?"

"Oh. Yeah. It's . . . that sugar-free stuff your mom got. For him."

Sarah rolls her eyes in disgust. "He doesn't *know* it's sugar-free, Bill. He's got to learn about healthy eating habits or he'll end up with *weight issues* like his father!"

Bill sighs. "All right then." He nods. "Better go wash up." He disappears to the kitchen.

Poor Bill.

"God." Sarah shakes her head in disgust. "Men! Can you believe that?"

"Nope." I sigh. "I really can't."

Ed returns with our burning peppery handmade apple cider, which I gulp down, or try to, and Mother Keller returns with my parents, who are mightily impressed with our snow blower.

"That's some snow blower you got out there, honey," my dad says. "You should make sure that snow blower's on your home insurance."

Mother Keller announces dinner is served, directing us to the stack of plates on "my" sideboard, where a banquet of her most vile dishes awaits us. "Eat your clam blankets before they cool," she warns us. Somehow all her dishes always sound vaguely and specifically sexual at the same time. Clam blankets are baked clams and bacon. There are also codfish balls, which are diced cod, potatoes, and egg pressed into balls and baked. Mulled fish-wives are sardines soaked in sherry. Meat jelly is exactly what it sounds like. For dessert there's prune whip: Take unsuspecting prunes, soak, and chuck in blender with heavy cream. Puree until they sing and the rest of us weep. I mournfully survey the buffet table.

Hailey winks at me. "We stopped at McDonald's on the way over," she whispers.

"Not fair!" I whine. "Then why is Lenny eating?" I nod at my brother-in-law, who is heaping up a big plate of grub. Hailey shrugs.

"I don't know," she says. "He'll eat anything."

"Damn this looks good!" Lenny grins. "Shit, I'm hungry enough to eat the balls off a low-flying duck."

We sit at the table and Brad raises his glass for a toast. "To Mom and Dad," he says. "You're *the best*."

Mother Keller basks in her son's glow. "It's our pleasure, dear," she says. "Your father and I realized you couldn't stay in the guesthouse and raise a family." My cheeks turn pink. I hate it when she starts in about Brad and me having a family. She's always insinuating that I don't *want* a baby, or worse, that I can't have one, and I do want one and I can have one. She never gives me a chance to tell her *how much* I want to have a baby, she just starts harping on how we better hurry up and start trying before my ovaries are like dried-up beef jerky. I have half a mind to tell her that I deliberately stopped taking birth control even before Brad proposed to me. That might shut her up. Then maybe she'd finally believe that I want to have her son's baby.

Ed leans over. "Have I ever told you how much you look like my cousin Ada?"

I nod at him. Ed's told me many, *many* times that I remind

him of his cousin Ada. Almost every time he sees me. Ed has this weird relationship with his cousin Ada, and every time he mentions her, Mother Keller gets very quiet and looks like she does right now. Like she swallowed a bee. "Ada's a real beauty," Ed says. "And a wonderful cook."

Mother Keller stares down the table at him. "A wonderful cook?" she snaps. "She once set fire to the stove on Christmas morning."

Ed ignores her. "Ada can sing too," he says. "Did I ever tell you about Ada's voice?"

"You did, Ed." I smile politely. "You definitely did."

Suddenly the swinging door opens and an ancient-looking woman shuffles in. She has dark yellow skin that's deeply creased and wrinkled. Her face looks like dried apple. She's wearing a black burlap sack; the waist is tied with a piece of yellow cord. We all look at her and the table falls silent. "Heavens, I nearly forgot about little Bi'ch," Mother Keller says.

"*Who?*" I sit up. It sounded like she said "little bitch."

"Bi'ch!" Mother Keller repeats. "Since poor Jennifer here has *no* experience running a house properly, I wanted to make sure she had enough help."

"Help?" I repeat.

"Your maid," Mother Keller says. "Everyone, please meet Mrs. Bi'ch Fang."

The woman's last name is "Fang," as in wolf fang. Her first name is "Bi'ch" and rhymes, unfortunately, with "ditch." She's Hmong; she came from the Bridge Program at church, which Mother Keller says relocates displaced immigrants looking for a new home. Bi'ch will be our maid. "Oh, I don't need a maid!" I say. "Thank you, but . . . it's not necessary!"

"Oh my, yes it is." Mother Keller smirks. "Bi'ch is going to help you keep your house in order. *For once*. I had to get you a maid, Jennifer. We all know how you keep a house!"

The whole table chuckles together happily as I glower.

"But where will she . . . live?" I ask gloomily.

"Right here," Mother Keller says. "In the little guesthouse out back."

"She's going to live *here*?"

"Of course. It's all been arranged."

So there it is. The super-awesome cherry on top of my super-surprise sundae. Not only has my mother-in-law decided *where* I'll live and *how* I'll live, she's even selected *who* I'll live with. A woman who looks like her last position was cleaning up the prehistoric cave of some Neanderthal man. Fine. At least she won't be afraid of Brad's laundry. Some of his socks stand up for themselves. Literally. Especially the ones he masturbates in.

Nine million years later, everyone's leaving. I'm so tired, I feel like I might pass out. "It'll be so wonderful having you all right next door," Mother Keller says, air-kissing me good night. "We'll get to see you *all* the time."

After everybody leaves and we're finally alone . . . we're not alone. The strangely shaped Bi'ch clanks and shuffles around in the kitchen. As Brad and I lie in bed, I fight back tears. I don't want to ruin my first night back, especially since we're both worn out and exhausted.

I finally break down though, and my shoulders heave as I start weeping. Brad asks me what's the matter and I tell him everything. How I'm distraught about the honeymoon and feel like a complete failure. Now we come home and his parents have picked out our house? It feels claustrophobic, manipulative, and overbearing. I wanted to get away from his parents. I wanted to start our own life. Now we're trapped here . . . for how long?

Forever? Brad works his jaw and says this is a fine way to thank his parents, who shelled out $3.2 million for a house.

"Our house," he says, looking around the room. "You see them here? No. Because this is *our* house. Not theirs. There's a lock on the door, Jen. Use it."

"That's not enough, Brad. You shouldn't have said we'd take the house. You always let your mother run your life. You never ask me what I want to do."

"We always do what you want to do!"

I look at him, aghast, and have my ammunition ready. My eyes well up with tears. "You . . . *left* me!" I cry.

He looks around, confused. "I left you where?"

"At the airport! You took off running without me!"

"I didn't leave you," he snorts. "Jen, I told you to run."

"You *told* me to run? Am I a child? Am I a German shepherd?"

"Jen, what are you talking about?"

"What are *you* talking about, Brad? One minute you're swearing to honor and protect me, the next minute you've abandoned me at Miami International Airport! I find that concerning. I really do."

"Come on, the Miami airport? It's perfect for you! It's got stores and massage chairs, and I saw at least two Cinnabon joints. You'd be set!"

I stare at him and grab my cell phone off the nightstand. "I actually *timed* you, Brad. I timed you to see how long it took before you looked for me."

"You timed me?"

"Yes I did." I frown grimly at the imaginary numbers on my phone's screen. "It was *not* good, Brad. Not good at all."

"How long did it take?" He leans over, trying to see my phone, but I turn it off and shake my head. "Let's just say that in the amount of time it took you to look for me, I could've been kidnapped by Norwegian sex traffickers."

"Aw, Jesus." He shakes his head. "What is it with you and the Norwegian sex traffickers?"

I start to cry in earnest.

He comes and sits by me on the bed. "Babe, please. Don't. I'm sorry I made you run at the airport. I am, but you gotta understand there was never, ever a single chance in *hell* we were sleeping in Miami that night."

"I know." I wipe my eyes. "Because you *have* to win. You have to get your way. You were determined to get the last seats out of Miami. God forbid anyone else did, screw any old people or orphans who needed them. Well, congratulations. You won and I got to spend my entire honeymoon with no luggage."

"But . . ." He shrugs. "I had to get you on a plane that night. Don't you get it?"

"No, Brad, I really don't."

"It was our *honeymoon*. Babe, did you really think I'd let you down on our honeymoon? Just scrap our plans and find some hotel in Miami? I would've chartered a private jet if I'd had to. I would've built a bamboo raft and rowed you to Saint John *myself* if there was no other way. Jen, nothing could've stopped me from getting you to Saint John that night . . . you know why?"

I smile and shake my head no.

"Because we just got *married*, babe, and that was our honeymoon . . . and you? Honey, you are my *wife*!"

"Oh, Brad . . ." I whisper.

He kisses me on the forehead as tears spill down my cheeks. "Screw the orphans and the old people," he says. "Only the best for you."

We make love. Sort of. We're both exhausted and still a little queasy from the food poisoning. I lie there in his arms afterward, recounting everything that's happened. "I'm sorry I got mad about the house," I tell him. "Just promise me you'll fix it, okay?"

When he doesn't answer, I look over and he lets out a huge snore.

He's unconscious. Deeply asleep and blissfully gone . . .

Once again without me.

3
Queen of Keller's

The next morning I take Ace to the vet, Doc Hodge. An excellent vet with a personality akin to irritated oatmeal. He's boring, but he gets cranky if you don't do things right. Mother Keller took her beloved Pomeranian to him and Doc Hodge kept that awful little creature alive much, much, *much* longer than it ever should have lived. A large woman in a bubblegum-pink smock leads us down to an examination room.

Ace is not happy. He's been highly suspicious of this situation from the get-go and now he whimpers pitifully, locking his legs up so I have to carry him. "Sorry about all this darn mess," the woman says. "Got a buncha construction going on this week. Expanding the physiotherapy room." She leaves us alone in the room and a construction worker wearing a safety-orange jumpsuit pops his head in.

"Oh," he says. "You in here?"

I look around and sigh. "Apparently."

"Mind if I do some work real quick?"

"Where?"

"Ceiling."

"Why?"

"Pipes."

"Oh."

He comes in clattering a long aluminum ladder behind him and nearly takes my head off swinging it around. Ace squirms as the guy sets up the ladder. I realize he's actually kind of cute, in a rough Steve McQueen way. His stitched name tag says NICK. He climbs up the ladder and starts monkeying with the ceiling tiles while we sit there for ten hours or so. I get bored. "So you're in construction?" I ask him. His head is stuck up in the ceiling tiles.

"Nope."

"An electrician?"

"Nope."

"Well, you're not a plumber."

"Why am I not a plumber?"

"No plumber would wear moccasins."

"Maybe I'm a *poor* plumber."

"No such thing, unless you're a plumbing social worker. Out there helping PVC pipes get into low-income housing, finding jobs for unemployed faucets. Trying to keep caulk guns off the streets."

"Funny lady," he says flatly.

"Oh, I can go on."

"I have no doubt."

Ace whines and Nick looks over his shoulder. "Doesn't like the vet much, huh."

"He's never been before. I smuggled him here from the Caribbean."

"Wasn't having a good time down there?"

"Neither of us was."

"Yep." He sighs. "Paradise can be hell."

"Where're you from?"

"You know, I always hated that question."

"Why, are you from Wisconsin?"

"Wow. She's mean too."

"I'm not really that mean."

"Too bad. You just got interesting."

"Really? Well, you're lucky. I'm still waiting."

He snorts and shakes his head, grabbing a wrench from his belt. "Wisconsin's not all bad. Wisconsin's like Minnesota's storage shed. It's where we put all our messy, dirty, and dangerous crap. Like firework factories and cheese plants. The Wisconsin Dells too. Plus all our serial killers."

"I know." I shake my head. "What's with Wisconsin and serial killers?"

"No idea. But if I lived in a storage shed, I might make buttskin lamps too."

"What?"

The door suddenly swings open and Doc Hodge walks in. Ace starts growling at him and pretty much keeps on growling the entire time we're there. The doctor asks if I bought Ace from a breeder or a pet store and I say, "Yep! They were having a half-off sale."

Doc Hodge stares at me. He gives Ace a full examination and about an hour later, after multiple blood tests, fecal smears, and X-rays, he frowns at me. "So *where* did Ace come from?"

"Where?" I look over quickly at Ace and Nick clears his throat.

"I ask, Mrs. Keller, because Ace has some intestinal parasites normally found only in the subtropics."

"He isn't sick, is he?"

"Nothing too serious, it should respond to antibiotics, but if Ace came from a subtropical climate, he'll need to be quarantined."

"Quarantined? No, no . . . he's from here. He's a rescue dog."

"A rescue dog from where?"

My mind goes blank and the ladder guy clears his throat again. "Wisconsin! I rescued him from Wisconsin."

"Where in Wisconsin? We'll need to get his paperwork."

"Oh. I just found him . . . down by the old . . . cheese mill."

The doctor looks at me. "The old cheese mill?"

"Yep. Ace was just walking along, eating some cheese. He loves cheese."

"Cheese is very bad for dogs, Mrs. Keller."

"Nope. I don't ever let him eat cheese."

"All right, well, we'll have to do some more tests and I'd like to fit him for a prosthetic at some point, but for now I'm giving him an antibiotic for the parasites and antifungal drops for his ears. I'd like him back in two weeks." Doc Hodge leaves and Nick, still up on his ladder, shakes his head and chuckles. "Lady," he says, "you are the worst liar in the *world*."

"I know. Damn it! It was the cheese mill. Why did I say 'cheese mill'?"

The cheese mill fucked me up.

Ace and I drive home, where he runs around the yard like a lunatic. He's so happy to be away from pokey-proddy-pinchy Doc Hodge. He gallops down the dock, where Bi'ch is fishing with a chubby little Hmong boy, who says he's her grandson.

It turns out Bi'ch Fang lives in our guesthouse with her entire family, including her glittery sixteen-year-old granddaughter, Star Fan; her chubby fourteen-year-old grandson, Pho; and Pho's eleven-month-old son, a little dumpling of a baby named Pac Man. Pac Man was conceived by Pho and his girlfriend at the Kenwood Rec Center in the handicapped bathroom stall. Anyone who thought they were too biologically young to conceive children . . . was corrected. Now the whole Fang Gang lives with us: Bi'ch, Star Fan, Pho, and Pac Man. Leave it to Mother Keller to find me a maid who's ancient, can't cook or clean, and comes with her own village. I decide to *not* freak out and instead focus on the afternoon, which is important.

There's a big board meeting this afternoon about Ed Keller's retirement plans and who might succeed him as the new president. It could even be Brad. Imagine that! If you went back in time and told me I'd be married to the president of Keller's someday . . . I'd think that was about as likely as my marrying the president of the United States. After the board meeting there's a pep rally in the lobby. Ed wants me to be there because all Keller's royalty should be. That's what he said, a statement I found both bizarre and heartwarming. Imagine me as a queen.

The Queen of Keller's.

I get ready quickly, throwing on my trusty black dress and my "no problem" black pumps, which I can walk a mile in and not get a blister. I know because I walked a mile in them once, when Christopher and I went to a club downtown and his car broke down on the way home. Christopher's my best friend, my little gay bee who goes *buzz-buzz-buzz* all around me. He works at Keller's Department Store, in visual display.

He dresses the mannequins and does the store windows, and I'll never understand why a bigger store hasn't whisked him away yet. We've known each other since high school. Without him they would've found me hanging from the aluminum bleachers on the football field. The secret to surviving a religious high school or any war zone is to find your people. Even if it's only one people.

One is enough.

I meet Christopher for lunch before the pep rally. He hasn't seen me in weeks, not since the wedding, and the first thing he says to me isn't "Hello" or "Welcome home" or "Gee, you look terrific!" It's "Seriously, Jennifer? I thought we decided you weren't wearing black anymore."

He hates it when I wear black, but I look good in black. Half my wardrobe is black. It's the gold standard for girls with body issues. He says I'm just addicted to being boring.

"So I don't understand," he says. "Brad's parents just *gave* you a house?"

"Yep! The house right next door. Hideous. Like a Ramada Inn crossed with a ski chalet."

"Still, it's right on the water. Must've cost—"

"Three point two million." I nod.

"Huh. A bargain! Still, how delightfully manipulative. So Disney evil queen. I love Mother Keller, she's like a . . . Christian Cruella de Vil."

"It's true." I shrug. "You've always loved evil queens. Ever since your first boyfriend."

"Come on," he says. "You have to admit, it's the perfect trap. It's a gift you can't refuse, it makes them look ultra-generous, and Mother Keller gets to keep her baby Brad tied nice and tight to her apron strings."

"Christopher, please stop calling him a baby."

"Sorry! I calls 'em as I sees 'em."

I glumly sip my water.

"So how was the honeymoon?" he asks me, taking a bite of scampi. "Was it filled with condoms and horses galloping down the beach?"

"No. It was sponsored by a three-legged dog and Imodium A-D. I'm exhausted. The wedding was brutal, but the honeymoon was from hell."

"I'm not allowed to have a wedding."

"Consider yourself lucky."

"I consider myself discriminated against."

"Well, that too."

"Still, a girl can dream. The senate's voting on the Family Equity Act soon."

"I forgot about that."

He sips his water. "I have our whole wedding completely planned out, just in case the bill passes. I want to be the first married gay bee in Minnesota."

"Does Jeremy?"

Christopher shrugs. "Jeremy doesn't care what party he goes to, as long as there's dancing."

"It's not a party . . . it's a binding legal union."

"With a party at the end. Besides, marriage was meant for gays. The pageantry! The drama! The dresses! Why do you straighties even care about who gets to have one?"

"It's not that *we* want it, we just don't want anyone *else* to have it. Are you registered?"

"At Williams-Sonoma, Ralph Lauren, and Discount Sex Barn."

"Didn't you register at Keller's?"

"Why? Do I want crappy wedding gifts?"

"Don't talk to me about crappy wedding gifts. We got some of the crappiest wedding presents ever given. Brad's aunt gave us a basket of ceramic walnuts. What is someone thinking when they decide that of all the things in all the world . . . what you need is a basket of ceramic walnuts? Brad thought they were real. Nearly cracked a tooth. Then he set them out on the deck, hoping to piss off the squirrels."

"And the ceramic walnuts are officially . . . awesome."

"We got four fruit hammocks too. Heard of those? It's a miniature hammock . . . for fruit."

"It's also an uncomfortable sex act involving dental floss."

"Well, we own *four* fruit hammocks now, which require *four* handwritten thank-you notes. What am I supposed to say to these bastards who completely ignored my bridal registry and gave me something so stupid it shouldn't even exist? I'm supposed to write them a thank-you note? When they've essentially slapped their dicks in my face . . . on my wedding day?"

"Lovely image."

"What am I supposed to say? 'Thanks for ignoring our gift registry and getting us something so stupid it makes me want to kill myself'? 'We love weird fruit-containment systems, how did you know?'"

After we finish lunch Christopher asks if this is what I'm wearing to the pep rally and I say, "Yes, Christopher, it is. I'm not Cher, I wasn't planning a costume change." He sighs and says all I do is hurt him.

Then he leaves me to go buy hair-care products, which he has to do on the sly and then sneak them back home, where he transfers them into different bottles. His boyfriend, Jeremy, has his own product line, which he sells at his chic salon in Edina. Christopher hates the stuff, though, and only pretends to use it. That's how I know they really love each other. Christopher transfers his shampoo so he won't hurt Jeremy's feelings . . . and Jeremy never lets on that he knows about it, just so he won't hurt Christopher's. They are definitely together forever.

I walk through the skyway alone.

I pass Frontier Travel, the wide glass windows filled with exotic travel posters and sleek white cruise ships on aquamarine water. I see my old pal Susan sitting behind her desk and I wave. "Hey, lady!" I say, popping my head in.

"Hey, Jen! Come to accept one of my humble writing assignments? I need an article on Spam Jam in Austin."

"Really? Nobody's snapped that up yet? A weeklong canned-meat festival?"

"Come on, Jennifer. You have to start somewhere."

"Yes, but does it have to be covering Spam?"

"No! I need loads of stories for the guidebooks. There's the Bean Hole Festival in Pequot Lakes or the Eelpout Festival in Walker . . ."

I arch an eyebrow at her. "What's a . . . bean hole, exactly?"

"You could even do something more edgy, like Gnosticon or Polka Fest!"

"Tempting."

I politely decline her kind offer and promise to let her know if I change my mind. All the while I'm wildly *thanking God* that I was spared from a life as a writer. I can't believe that once upon a time, I actually wanted to *be* a writer. A real one. I wanted to pen the next great American novel and break hearts with my searing insights and razor-sharp wit, but then there were bills to pay and rent to make and thousands of meaningless items to buy with high-penalty-interest-rate credit cards. No matter how much money I made, I needed more. I could hardly cover my expenses, let alone luxury items like unprocessed food or basic health insurance. So I took a job as a copywriter at Keller's Department Store and there I honed my craft, weaving together the perfect ad campaigns for preteen bra sales and men's incontinence underwear.

The rest is . . . history.

I pass the Cinnabon counter quickly, ignoring the sweet, cinnamon-scented air swirling around me. If I had a nickel for every calorie I consumed at that godforsaken counter, I could buy Keller's Department Store myself.

I nod at the girl behind the counter, who wears a red hat. She's the seat of evil itself.

The Cinnabon girl.

"Hey, Satan," I say.

"Hey, haven't seen you around for a while."

"I've been . . . away."

"Well, looks like you're back."

A colorful poster catches my eye.

JOIN THE
CINNERS CLUB
FOR CINNERS . . . JUST LIKE YOU

"What's that?" I ask.

She says it's an all-you-can-eat-Cinnabon club. You just pay one low annual fee and you can have as many Cinnabons as you want. They also deliver. My jaw drops.

All-you-can-eat Cinnabons?

I shudder at what I might look like if I had a membership. I'd become some blobby glutinous mass that oozed out everywhere. I'd look just like a Cinnabon. She tries to hand me a glossy pamphlet, but I don't take it. "I'm doing a gluten-free thing these days," I tell her. "And no sugar. I feel like a new person basically. I'm running marathons . . ."

She just looks at me and holds up a key chain. "Every membership comes with a free scratch-n-sniff Cinnabon keychain. It smells like a real Cinnabon. It's warm too. There's a watch battery inside."

"That's . . . that's . . ." I'm too overwhelmed to speak. I pivot on my foot and march away.

She's the devil.

I take a deep breath as I walk through the heavy glass doors of Keller's Department Store. How strange to be back, to walk through the doors as a Keller family member and not just a lowly copy girl in the marketing department. I try to maintain a semblance of dignity as I walk through the store. I walk in a stately manner, like Cleopatra balancing a book on her head.

It's still too early to go up to Brad's office, so I sneak up to the marketing department, where I used to work. Where I spent untold hours writing mediocre crap, reworking old sale copy, recutting used radio scripts, refreshing stale slogans . . . or trying to, constantly resurrecting the same dead marketing ideas that were dead for a reason. God, I hated myself while I was doing that. I would've been better off selling makeup. At least I wouldn't have had to watch my own hands butcher the English language so much.

Walking back into my old office is icky, weird, and hot. Nothing's changed. The ceilings are still too low, the carpet is still worn out, the heat's still on too high, and the same torn motivational poster is still Scotch-taped to the break room door. Two little acorns rest on a bed of moss and it says: THINGS THAT ARE SMALL NOW CAN BECOME GREAT SOMEDAY. It might be more inspiring if the acorns didn't look like small brown baby testicles.

It's the perfect time to look around; the whole department is at the weekly roundup meeting. I peek at them through the conference room's glass window. I do not miss that meeting, which is run by Carl, who's still wearing the same upsetting crotch-bulging khakis. I used to terrorize myself in meetings just to stay awake by imagining that for some post-apocalyptic reason, I had to have sex with Carl, because the fate of the planet depended on it.

I see my soul-crushing cubicle, Old Ironsides, where I worked every day, underneath flickering fluorescent lights that eventually would induce seizures. I have no idea who sits in my cubicle now. Ted's still at his old desk; his *Star Wars* action figures are positioned in some sort of group orgy. Ted was my fellow inmate, my friend, and my Bookmark Guy. The guy I always held a place for in my mind if nothing else worked out. He's so nice . . . but he's a redhead, and not in a good way. We both toiled together underneath the thumb of my old boss, Ashley. Ashley was shocked when I started dating Brad, more like horrified actually. She just couldn't believe Brad Keller picked *me*. She certainly didn't think it would last and told me so often. Now, here I am, Ashley, so suck it.

Finally it's time to go. I take the elevators up to Brad's office, where Brad introduces me to the store's new head of finance, Todd Brockman. Todd's a big broad-shouldered guy with a blocky head and blindingly white teeth. He wears a shiny blue suit and has a short frosted crew cut. He looks like your average TV anchor or high-end car salesman. He says I should call him what all his friends do: *The Brock*. I smile and tell him to call me Mrs. Keller.

Brad leaves us to take a call and Todd shows me his new office, which has a bookcase loaded with football trophies. "So, kiddo!" Todd grins. "Welcome back! Hey, I got a question for ya. Big bad Brad and I are working on this spiffy new deal with a foreign investment group, buncha nice guys. Great suits. Anyway, we're trying to raise a little capital-cashola and they're looking to invest in a retail chain. We're hoping to get them on board here at Keller's and the *upshot-a-rino* is . . . we'd like you to throw a little dinner for them."

"You want *me* to throw a dinner?"

"Heck yeah, you don't want us fellas microwaving frozen fish sticks for 'em! We need a real nice home-cooked meal. They love that crap. Take me to a steak house, but these fellas want a '*mi casa es su casa*' scenario. Fine by me, as long as I don't have to cook!"

"But you want *me* to cook."

"No way! We want a caterer to cook and you to be your super-charming self!"

"Oh. Okay . . . I guess that's—"

"Great! Emily has the deets. *Hey, Em! Grab that Jap-dinner file for Jen!* All righty then, the Brock has to bolt. Emily'll shoot you some intel on that dinner and you call me if you need anything, got it? *Hey, Em!* Grab those files for Jen to sign too! Em's got some papers for you to sign. Just employee file stuff. All righty then, we good?"

"Um . . . we're good."

"Super-great to meet you, Jen!"

Todd leaves and Emily the executive secretary hurries in, dropping files all over the floor.

"Oh no!" she gasps, kneeling down to retrieve them. "I'm so stupid!" she mutters. "I'm such a klutz!" Then she looks up with tears in her eyes. "Oh! I didn't know you were in here, Mrs. Keller! I'm so sorry . . ." She's all flustered and continues to spill files even as she picks them up. I adore her. She reminds me of when I started working at Keller's. Uncertain of anything except that everything's her fault. Actually, that still sounds like me.

I kneel down and help her.

"I'm so sorry, Mrs. Keller, Mr. Brockman's always telling me to *think* before I do something stupid."

"Well, that's not very nice."

"Oh, he's just trying to help me improve."

"I'll bet." I ask her if she'd tell *me* to think first if I dropped papers all over the floor, if she thought that would that help *me* carry files better, and her eyes go wide. "No," she says. "I'd tell you it's no big deal and . . . not to worry about it!"

"Exactly, and that's what this is. No big deal. Right?"

"Right." She nods, blushing. We get the files picked up and Cute Emily says, "Thank you so much, Mrs. Keller! I'm so glad I met you. Everybody said you were nice!"

"Please." I smile at her. "Call me Jennifer."

Emily gives me a pile of papers to sign. Health insurance, employee benefits, tax crap, just basic information, but I'm useless of course; I can't remember our new address or our new telephone number. She pulls out a tax ID form and I write down both my social security numbers. "This is the one I use, but this one pops up from time to time and it's a total pain."

Emily looks impressed. "How'd you get two?"

"When I was a baby my mom took me to Denmark and left her purse in a cab. Lost all my ID. Then when we got home, the government issued me a new card with a new number. No idea why, maybe because I was a baby, but that stupid first number still pops up from time to time, so just keep an eye out for it. Otherwise things can get confusing."

"Oh!" Her eyes fly open. "I almost forgot the investor dinner packet! I'm sorry, wait here, I'll be right back. Mr. Brockton will *kill* me if you leave without it." She brings me a manila envelope and says everything I need should be inside. As I'm leaving she apologizes for dropping the files again. She says she hasn't been sleeping well lately because she's getting married in the spring. "There's so much to do, everything is just spinning!"

"Oh, honey." I smile gently. "It'll be . . . what it is. The most important thing is you're marrying someone you love, right?"

"Right!" She grins and I think to myself, *Christ, is that the most important thing?*

"And, Mrs. Keller," she says. "I wonder if . . . I might ask you to lunch sometime? For, um . . . wedding advice and that kind of thing?"

"Wedding advice?"

"Oh . . ." She blushes awkwardly. "It's just that my mother died when I was kind of young. I don't have anyone to help me with . . . I don't even know what I need help with! Stuff you already know. Advice for brides, I guess." Her sweet heart-shaped face has gone pink and I pat her on the shoulder.

"Lunch we shall have, my dear. It would be my pleasure."

Brad appears in the doorway. It's time for the pep rally and we leave the office together, riding down in the elevator to the first floor. "We first met on an elevator," I remind him.

"How could I forget?" he snorts. "You threatened to pepper-spray me."

"Yep. Say what you will, babe, we've always had chemistry."

The elevator doors open onto the wide white marble lobby, and the smell of roses and gardenia perfume washes over us. I start to feel nervous as we cross the crowded lobby and head for the stage. People make way for us and start smiling. I feel like a contestant on *The Price Is Right*. It's worse when we get up onstage and have to stand there like idiots smiling, waiting for Mr. and Mrs. Keller to arrive. Sarah and Bill are already there, along with a very hyper Trevor, who hops back and forth from one foot to the other while his mother tells him to stop. "Auntie Jen!" Trevor whispers. "I got tap shoes today!"

"Really? Sweet."

"And where did Mommy say you could use your tap shoes?" Sarah whispers tightly.

"The basement!" Trevor grins.

"That's right. *Only* the basement."

Suddenly the crowd starts to clap as the Kellers come in. Ed's wearing a dark gray suit with a red tie and Mother Keller's in a complementary slate-gray shantung silk dress with a large gemstone-and-pearl brooch. They join us onstage *smiling, smiling, smiling*. Mother Keller practically beams at me, and I actually look over my shoulder thinking her affectionate face must be for someone behind me.

Ed begins his speech. I stand beside Brad like a wax statue riveted in position, a smile frozen on my face and staring off at an unfixed point in the crowd. I feel like an idiot up here. It hurts to smile this much. And speaking of pain, my no-problem pumps start to feel like bear traps biting into my feet. I feel progressively more awkward with every second that ticks by. Horrible thoughts cloud me. *What if I have spinach in my teeth? What if I pass out suddenly? What if I get a nosebleed? What if I develop Tourette syndrome right here and now, uncontrollably blurting out foul language?* I burst out into a cold sweat. Great. Now I'll have pit stains. *Shit!* Suddenly I hear my name and Mother Keller's hugging me, kissing me on both cheeks. The audience is clapping and someone's handing me a huge bouquet of roses.

What the hell is happening?

"Isn't she great, folks?" Ed beams. "We really hit the jackpot! Welcome to the Keller family, Jennifer! We wouldn't want anyone else for a daughter-in-law! Now . . . we just need to start making some junior Kellers, all right?" The audience laughs and my head starts swimming. Trevor gives me a big drawing he made of the whole family and Sarah kisses my cheek. I can hardly see anything now, because I'm holding a bouquet of red roses so big, it's more like a shrub. Ed thanks everyone for coming and suddenly . . . we're all leaving. It's only as we're leaving the stage that I notice the banner that's been unfurled for who knows how long behind me that says WELCOME, JENNIFER, TO THE KELLER FAMILY!

I'm thunderstruck.

I can't believe it. This pep rally was to welcome me . . . and I managed to miss almost the whole thing by nonstop speed-worrying. I feel completely ashamed. They were trying to do something nice for me. I get teary as Brad kisses me good-bye and say, "It was just so nice of them to do this for me." He says they should've thrown me a big dinner. They did that for Bill when he married Sarah. I kiss Brad and tell him I don't want a big dinner. All I want is him.

He has more meetings, so he stays behind at the store while I drive home alone. I promise to pick him up something delicious for dinner. Later that night I take a big bubble bath and pour myself a glass of wine. I put music on so no one can hear me and I let myself have one hell of a cry. Am I happy? Am I sad? Am I worried that I can't pull this whole marriage thing off?

Absolutely. All of it.

I stay in the bathtub for another hour, adding hot water as needed. I dry my eyes and open the manila envelope I got from Cute Emily. Inside the envelope I find a schedule, a contact list, a guest list, and a Xeroxed article titled "How to Throw a Party for Japanese People!"

I call Emily.

"Um . . . Is this really all I need to know for the foreign-investor dinner?" I ask her. "I mean, I don't see any phone numbers for a caterer or a florist or—"

"Oh, that's all been taken care of for you, Mrs. Keller. Did you see the caterer's schedule? She was supposed to list all the setup times."

"I have it. It says the rental place delivers dinnerware and linens at nine in the morning, then the catering staff sets up at ten thirty and the florist delivers orchids at noon. Guests come for cocktails at six and dinner is served at seven."

"Sounds perfect," she says.

"Yes, because it won't be *me* in the kitchen. I seriously can't cook anything."

"Oh, of course you can, Mrs. Keller!"

"Call me Jennifer, sweetie, and no, I literally once set fire to tap water."

I stay up and read the article on entertaining Japanese people. I make copious notes and commit to memorizing everything. I want this to dinner to go perfectly.

I climb into bed around ten and take my journal with me. There, tucked into the covers, I take out a pen and make my very first list for Emily, starting with the basics.

Top Five Things Virgins Should Remember

1. Nine out of ten penises are ugly.
2. The art of foreplay was lost with the Incas.
3. Sex feels like being hit by a shopping cart.
4. You might be shaved and waxed, but he'll still be hairy. Be prepared when he takes his sweater off; it might look like he's still wearing a sweater.
5. You'll never appreciate the word "deflowering" again.

It's just for fun. Obviously I would never show this to her, even if it is accurate and potentially helpful. Sex is no ballet. The faster you accept that, the better.

When Brad finally comes home, it's late. I'm already in bed, having fallen asleep with all the lights on. Brad gently shakes my shoulder. "Babe? You up? I have something to tell you!" He's terribly excited. I manage to put on my bathrobe and reheat his dinner—takeout from D'Amico—as he explains the situation.

Apparently, Ed Keller is putting both Brad and Sarah on

"probation" until next spring, and at the end of that time whoever proves to be the better candidate will get the job. He says it's the way to get everything he wants. To run the company without his sister. Brad says our entire future depends on what we do in the next several months. How we act. Who we are. How we seem. "We have to become the obvious candidates for the position," Brad says. "Dad wants to see which of us handles the pressure and the responsibility better. He's going to watch us and test us, and whoever does better gets everything."

I can't believe Ed's pitting his *own children* against each other. What am I saying? Of course he is. When Great-Grandpa Keller built the company, he designed the bylaws so that no individual family member could own the company outright. He made it impossible for any one family member to own more shares than the others. He knew what a pack of jackals they could be. The rule was to prevent hostile takeovers among loved ones.

Smart guy.

"Right now, I can't own more shares of the company than Sarah does," Brad explains, "and vice versa, but if I become the president, I'll have veto power. I can petition for and even force a board member's removal."

"You'd get rid of your sister?"

"Jen, I'm not trying to sound dramatic . . . but she's evil. She buried me alive once. *Literally*. She buried me in a cave up at the cabin. Then she told my parents I ran away. It took them three days to find me."

"You know she tells that story differently. In her version you're evil."

"Todd says once I replace her—and enough of the board members—I can petition to change the bylaws themselves, which means I can own the whole thing!"

"Todd?"

"I like the Brock," he says. "The Brock is on our side."

I want to say *the Brock* is on my hit list . . . but I don't want to dampen the mood.

We put together the perfect plan for becoming the perfect couple right then and there. It's a concept I've been working on all along, but it's nice to have my husband on board. Brad is determined to show his parents that *we* are worthy of running Keller's and I'm so glad/honored/relieved to be in on one of Brad's schemes for once, I pour cup after cup of coffee and eagerly agree to all his ideas. I promise to be the most perfect wife around. Ed Keller will see our amazing, awesome life and he'll have no choice but to hand Brad the store. Like all strong military campaigns, ours has a name. We call our plan Operation Hotdish.

I'm to become a trophy wife, a beautiful, poised, and gracious goddess of all domestic skills. We'll go to the Kellers' house for supper; we'll attend church and show up at the country club for all the right social occasions. Brad will work strict hours at the office; he'll have dinners, drinks, and regular tee times with investors, importers, clients, and key customers, not to mention with the dusty old white-haired board members. We'll both attend any and all company functions, parties, picnics, and employee pep rallies. And since Horrible Todd Brockman holds the keys to Keller's financial kingdom, we'll befriend him as well.

Joy.

We'll be disciplined and learn to live the way his parents want us to. We'll have to work hard because Sarah has the upper hand right now. She's older, she's been working at the company longer, and she's not a recovering alcoholic, like Brad is. "Also she has a kid, which is massive points for the grandparents." Brad looks over at me and says, "Babe, we need a kid."

I melt. I smile at him and say, "I thought you'd never ask."

Then we head back upstairs and have sex for the rest of the night. Brad's so excited and happy right now, I don't have the heart to tell him that the whole plan to act like people we aren't in order to dupe his parents into trusting us sounds a little evil. Every time I think I might mention it he gives me a long deep kiss and I see fiery stars. I've never been so happy.

This must be how Eva Braun felt.

4

Operation Hotdish

The perfect woman is actually three women rolled into one: Mrs. Howell, Mary Ann, and Ginger from *Gilligan's Island*. Three women who when combined become the whole package. The refined lady, the demure sweetheart, and the sultry sex kitten, all in one. A woman who can bake coconut pies, charm cannibals, and cavort on white-sand beaches in six-inch stilettos.

Simply put, the perfect woman is a sweet rich slut.

Being a trophy wife is something I know nothing about. Yes, I have a wealthy husband, a beautiful house, three dozen matching wineglasses, and a legal cable connection . . . but how any of this happened is a mystery. I come from more of a Spam-and-spray-cheese set. My people polka. They drink Bud Light and spend more money on their snowmobiles than their life insurance, because as Lenny says, if you got one, you really don't need the other.

I turn to Christopher for help, because let's face it, he knows more about being a woman than I do. I tell him about Operation Hotdish and Brad's plan to become the perfect couple, and he's 100 percent behind it. "This is the dream challenge of a gay bee's lifetime!" he says. "To transform a plain lump-of-coal midwestern girl into a sparkling grande-dame diamond."

"I don't know. I hate hair spray."

"Fear not," he says. "We will tame you, my little shrew."

"Easy on the shrew metaphors, Petruchio."

"We'll turn you into the bitchiest of bitchy divas. You'll be magnificent! And just think, you already have the bitchy part down perfectly!"

Top Ten Traits of a Trophy Wife

1. Gorgeous/sexy/big boobs/small waist
2. Is seen and not heard
3. Without too many opinions of her own
4. Skinny/loves working out
5. Always elegantly dressed and immaculately groomed, even when sick, sleeping, or giving birth
6. Elicits high-five signs from other men
7. Elicits true hatred from other women
8. Skilled in the domestic arts, or at least in delegating to maids
9. Appreciates fine wine, fast cars, and her husband's Viagra prescription
10. Sexually advanced: expert at oral/open to anal

We begin researching other attributes of the perfect trophy wife, skimming almost a dozen online articles, glancing over at least two advice columns, and mostly watching tens of hours of television, including such classic trophy-wife-centric shows as *Desperate Housewives, Dallas, The Real Housewives of Beverly Hills,* and *Falcon Crest.* What we learn is: Every group has a different set of rules. One man's trophy wife is another man's white trash. For example:

Top Ten Traits of a Hells Angels Trophy Wife

1. Big tits, tiny waist, and leather lingerie collection
2. Likes loud bikes and long roads
3. Hangs on, sits still, and shuts up
4. Wears buttless black leather chaps to bed
5. Wins lube-wrestling contests
6. Packs a G-string Derringer .38
7. Has pierced at least three lobes of skin
8. Tattoos her man's name somewhere sexy, like crotch
9. Serves Jägermeister shots in her navel
10. Will give cops a blow job to spring her man out of jail

Top Ten Traits of a Fundamentalist Mormon Trophy Wife

1. Intact virginity
2. Doesn't have a driver's license or a social security number
3. Unaware of the outside world or of government programs like social services
4. Sews her own burlap menstrual pads
5. Doesn't sass
6. Obeys her sister wives—all twelve of them
7. Can feed a family of forty people on forty cents a week

8. Can simultaneously churn butter and slaughter a chicken
9. Her children are Good & Plenty, her uterus is Good & Fertile
10. Patiently reads Bible while husband is in adjoining shack, banging another wife

Trophies look different to everyone, so we must build the perfect trophy for this particular group, and since we're trying to impress Brad's parents, I need to become *their* idea of a trophy wife. They're white upper-class Minnesotans with heavy corporate overtones, ingrained Lutheran values, and Norwegian-themed clothing. When I make a list of what attributes they prize most, however . . . I realize that my recently reformed bad boy of a husband hates all the things they revere. He may want to impress them, but my goal is to impress *him* . . . He's a ne'er-do-well, black-sheep bad boy who likes fast cars and strong drinks and has none of his parents' core values whatsoever. I need to run two races at the same time, his and theirs. Two completely different races, two opposite trophy wives . . . one me.

No problem.

Where there's a determined woman . . . there's always a way.

BRAD'S PARENTS' IDEA OF A TROPHY WIFE	BRAD'S IDEA OF A TROPHY WIFE
A girl who loves America and Jesus	A girl who loves porn and bacon
A sweetheart who bakes cookies like Grandma	A temptress who grills steak in a thong
A timid soul who doesn't like to touch or talk about money	A confident woman who pays her own bills
A predictable woman who embraces routine like an autistic child	A spontaneous firecracker who's wild and unpredictable, unless he wants to stay in
An avid baker who can win any pie contest at the state fair	A chesty bombshell who can win any wet T-shirt contest in Florida
A properly dressed lady who orders pantsuits from Talbots	A real stunner who wears sleek power suits with stilettos
A kind soul who's also a trained nurse	A trained nurse who's also a trained stripper
A pious lady who's fertile and regards sex as a grim necessity	A sexpert who's like a porn star in bed and also on the pill
A cranky virgin who wears a floor-length plaid flannel nightgown to bed	A free spirit who wears nothing but baby oil to bed
A good wife who's as clever as she is clingy and able to track down their son like a Saint Bernard	A cool wife who's as easygoing and nonjudgmental as a golden retriever and never asks where he was or who he was with, just wags her tail whenever she sees him

Examining the statistical data of these two different trophy wives, we find that despite the many differences, there are also a few crossover areas that both groups value, and we tackle those areas first. The most obvious area is how I look. Everybody wants me to look damn good, all the damn time. It makes me wonder if there are any living creatures anywhere in the world that *don't* care about looks. I mean, even penguins are pretty picky about only hooking up with other penguins . . . so they're making a few judgment calls out there on the tundra . . . and penguins seem like the nicest group around, so it's down to only one possibility. The Mole People.

God bless you, Mole People.

Dig on.

Up here aboveground, people are dicks. I hate that I have to "look good," especially since "good" means an elastic-waistband pantsuit to the Kellers and buttless chaps to Brad. I'm not really okay with either one, but that's clearly beside the point. Using a rather sophisticated virtual-makeover program, Christopher starts putting together some looks for me incorporating elements that might appeal to both groups. Basically, I have to find a way to look like a sexy conservative.

The idea makes me nervous, and not in a good way. We're now wandering into the scary and sometimes insane territory of Michele Bachmann Land and Sarah Palin City. Say what you will . . . those women have balls. I do not.

I'm screwed.

Christopher compiles "look books" showcasing the various styles of conservative women. I'm supposed to pick one I like, or even pick more than one and he'll blend them together. I consider Ann Coulter's "Severe Sweetheart" look, Michelle Malkin's "Perky Assassin" style, Pamela Geller's "Aristo-Slut" ensembles, and little Meghan McCain's "Cupcake with a Knife" look. Of course there's always Sarah Palin's ever-popular visage, which Christopher calls "Fresh as a Daisy, Kill-Kill-Kill." I have no idea who to choose . . . so I make Christopher do it.

"Just pick one for me," I beg him.

He happily agrees to, certain his choice will be far superior to any of mine, but he takes his time, which makes me really nervous. "You're not picking something crazy, are you? Like Laura Bush or Tammy Faye Bakker?"

"Huh. Well, now that you mention it . . ."

"Christopher, this is serious."

"I know!" he says. "Don't worry. I got this."

He surveys my wardrobe to see if I have any pieces that would work for his new look. "You have way too much black in here," he says, frowning at my closet. "I thought we decided you weren't going to wear any more black."

I remind him that *he* decided that. I wear black when I feel fat . . . which is always.

"Jennifer, come on," he says. "I don't care if you're the size of a water buffalo . . . you can't wear all black to Hillcrest Country Club, or the only friend you'll make is the headwaiter."

"Don't be silly. Black is elegant. It's the color of midnight and tuxedos . . ."

"That's Manhattan, sweetheart. In *Minnesota,* the only people who wear black are cops, poets, drug users, Democrats, and depressed teens wearing capes, and none of them are welcome at Hillcrest Country Club. There are no colors in here. Where are your muted jewel tones? Your sparkling champagnes? Where are your Cuban reds and canary yellows?"

"I don't know, but I'm guessing Cuban red is somewhere near Miami."

Christopher makes me try on every single piece of clothing in my closet and hates almost everything, mostly because of the colors. He says black makes me look tired, olive makes me look old, oxblood is communist, eggplant should exist only on actual eggplants, and all shades of gray are shady—"Like black's suspicious cousins." Finally I give up. I tell him I'll figure out my wardrobe on my own. I'm not throwing everything dark away.

I'm comfortable in black. I like black. He ignores me and unhappily sorts through my clothing, lecturing me all the while.

"This is your new life, Jen. You worked hard for it. You sacrificed things you wanted. You overcame your fear of sleeping with men who wear Dockers . . . you even learned how to use *a coaster*, for God's sake. *A coaster!* I never thought I'd live to see the day. Now you've arrived. It's a new world, so why not try new things out? Sure, you could wear your old army fatigues and eat cold cereal out of the box like you used to, but why? Why not look around and see what the natives do? And I'll tell you what they do. They wear things that are happy. You need clothes like that, that are happy and cheerful and unaware of the recession."

"How about this skirt?" I ask him. "It looks mildly amused."

"No. You want clothes that look expensive, fragile, like you couldn't wear it in a coal mine. We need to get you more soft colors. Think tranquil and soothing. Think hospital gowns for the criminally insane."

I can't handle it anymore.

I hand over my gold card and tell him to go shopping without me, which might sound like he's doing me a huge favor, but in Christopher's case it's more like telling a two-year-old he now owns a candy store. Besides, I'm way too busy with a million other Operation Hotdish projects, like befriending Sarah. Brad wants her to like us more . . . which results in my offering to babysit Trevor. Before I know it, her silver Mercedes is pulling into our driveway every other day and Trevor bursts through our door like a tornado looking for a trailer park.

So added to my list of duties are "Try to keep Trevor from killing himself" and "Try to keep yourself from killing Trevor."

Neither comes naturally.

Here's a typical morning. Brad's already gone to work and

I see a flash of light cross the window and hear a car honk. I go outside and single-handedly carry in whatever sundry activity bags, art supplies, dance equipment, or ant farms Trevor's chosen to bring over that day. As I struggle toward the house, Sarah gabs on her cell phone and backs down the driveway while Trevor races back and forth up and down the driveway beside her . . . getting closer and closer to the road until I yell at him to *please* come inside. He'll refuse until I promise to make him a milkshake. Then *bam*! He slams through the kitchen door, usually knocking a framed photo onto the floor, which shatters into tiny splinters of sharp glass. He's already kicked off his shoes by now and I scream, "Don't move! Don't move!" I promise him *two* milkshakes if he just holds still. Then I scramble to jam my feet into Brad's oversize boots and shuffle across the shattered kitchen floor to pick him up and deposit him somewhere safe, like the kitchen island or the downstairs bathtub. There he'll start crying, demanding his treat, *now, now, now!*

If I'm not quick enough to answer him, he'll shout, "Feed my worm!" and throw a slimy pink earthworm that he named Mr. Wormy at me. It's not always a worm. He's thrown spiders ("Feed my spidey!"), beetles ("Feed my buggy!"), and even eggs ("Feed my baby chicken!"). These performances usually result in my screaming, shrieking, and doing a get-it-off-of-me Riverdance thing, which more often than not results in more property damage.

Plus I'm trying to renovate the house, which is almost impossible since every contractor in Minnesota gets booked up six summers in advance. We get a new cool space-age refrigerator, a wedding present from Brad's investment group. It's an Ice Empress 3000 and takes a forklift to get into the house. Pho walks into the kitchen and stares at the massive chrome beast and says, "Is that . . . an Ice Empress 3000?"

"Yep. Heard of it before?"

Pho scowls at me. "Have I *heard* of it before? Have I heard about the hottest nanotechnology appliance to come out this decade, designed by space-station architects at NASA?"

"I'm guessing . . . you've heard of it."

"The Ice Empress showcased at the Tokyo Design Fair last year and caused a *stampede*. Do you know how hard it is to make the Japanese *stampede*?"

"No . . . do *you*?"

Pho points to the dark green computer screen set into the door. "You haven't gotten the computer turned on yet?"

"Not yet. I'm trying to."

Pho takes the manual from me and gives me a tour of the appliance's features: the micro-ecosystem temperature controls, the automatic vegetable-misting nozzles that *sense* when produce is thirsty, the smoked-meat cubby, and the solid teak cheese-aging drawer. It even has a hydrothermal champagne chilling station. "The second-coolest thing about the Ice Empress 3000 is its *zero-tolerance* pest policy. The Ice Empress has a satellite monitoring system inside that detects harmful pests and bacteria; it signals a purification program and built-in infrared lights murder any bugs inside. This cool steam gun sterilizes the kill zone."

I look at him and blink. "My refrigerator has a kill zone?"

"Afterward, the aromatherapy jets mist the air with a scent of your choice . . . Japanese cherry blossom, huckleberry pie, or roasted Tahitian vanilla bean."

"So, you said something about the purification system being the second-coolest thing? What's the coolest?"

Pho walks over to the Ice Empress. "You know about the on-board geisha, right?"

"The what?"

He pushes some buttons on the inside panel and shuts the door. The dark green computer screen lights up and Pho steps back beside me. Together we watch the chrome doors.

"Here she comes!" Pho whispers.

Suddenly a disembodied geisha head floats on the dark green computer screen. "What the hell's that?" I point at her. She has a flawless oval face and bright pink lips like a strawberry.

"That's the Ice Empress," Pho says.

"Naniga hoshiino?" the geisha says suddenly. Ace starts barking at her and I look over at Pho.

He shrugs at me. "Do I look like I speak Japanese?"

"Well . . . yeah. You do."

He rolls his eyes at me.

The Ice Empress bows deeply at us. *"Moshi moshi!"* she says.

"Hello." I bow back.

"You are *American?*" she asks, smiling. How the hell did she know that? Pho says it's her voice-recognition software. She can detect accents. I tell her we're Canadians.

"Why'd you tell her that?" Pho asks.

"Because nothing good comes from being an American. Trust me. You all want your green cards so badly, but I'm telling you, it's the pits."

"I *am* an American," Pho says flatly. "I was born in Milwaukee."

The Ice Empress giggles. "My name is Ice Empress!" she says. I roll my eyes. "We have an empress in the house." I sigh. "Great. How high-maintenance is that? It's like *Real Housewives of the Upscale Appliances.*"

"You're funny!" She giggles. "You are a funny little American!"

"Pardon?"

"I'll name you Aho-Onna!" she says. "That means 'funny lady with pretty face'!"

"Right. She can learn names?" I ask Pho.

He nods. "She has a wicked proximity linguistics program. She learns new words and uses them."

"Actually, my name's Jennifer," I tell her. "You can call me Jen. I guess."

The Ice Empress bows deeply and says, "*Moshi moshi,* Jen Aho-Onna."

"Um, Ice Empress?" Pho whispers. "You can call me Pimp-Ninja Pho."

The Ice Empress bows at Pho. "You are handsome!" she says. "I will name you Inpo Pho. That means 'handsome one.'"

"Why is she naming *us?*" I ask him.

He shrugs.

"And what exactly is a *pimp-ninja?* Should I keep you away from geishas?"

He says he's a ninja with computers and a pimp with . . . cars.

"Okay, whew." I nod. "Cars. Cars is fine."

I hear something behind me. It's Trevor standing in the doorway.

"Who is she?" he asks, transfixed by the geisha.

"Trevor, this is the Ice Empress."

He walks up to the glowing screen and the Ice Empress smiles at him.

"You're so pretty," he whispers.

She bows deeply. "You are very wise," she says. "I will call you Akiko."

Trevor nods solemnly and bows deeply back.

"What else does she do besides name people?" I ask Pho.

Pho shrugs and asks the Ice Empress for a Yoo-hoo.

"*Hai!*" she says, and the dispenser lid flips open, revealing a cold chocolate Yoo-hoo sitting in the frosty little nook. Pho takes it and I ask Trevor if he wants anything. He says no. It's the first time ever he doesn't want something, and when I ask him why, he says, "I don't want to bother her." I don't mind bothering her. I ask the Ice Empress for a Coke and she tilts her petal-white face at me. "You mean a *Diet* Coke?" she says.

I say no, a *regular* Coke.

"A *Diet* Coke?" she repeats.

"No!" I shout. "A regular Coke!"

She giggles and tells me I'm funny. Then the lid opens and a chilled Coke sits there in the frosty nook. I take it, keeping my eye on her.

"So long!" She waves good-bye. *"Kutabare!"*

"Why did she ask me if I wanted a Diet Coke?" I ask Pho, and he shrugs. I can't help but think she's insinuating something. Great. That's just what I need.

Another critic in the house.

Finally the big day for my trophy wife transformation arrives. Christopher's finished all the shopping and assembled all the products and services and other gay bees I'll need. He's bought all my new clothes, shoes, makeup, and jewelry. I haven't seen any of it but I know he's spent a bloody fortune. The credit card company has called twice. He says not to worry, we can return anything that I don't like, but I don't have the stamina to go through all this again. It will be whatever it will be. I welcome and accept his decision . . .

Just like I welcome and accept death.

Christopher books an entire day for me at Jeremy's salon and has no fewer than *seven* other gay bees of various industries and artistries meet us there to help do my hair, nails, teeth, skin, and makeup and of course . . . clothes. I have no idea what look they're trying to achieve; I clamp my eyes shut and tell them, "Just do it."

Six hours later I emerge from a cloud of perfume with sleek platinum-blond hair, smooth, tan skin, and blindingly bright white teeth. I'm wearing a tailored coral suit with cream cuffs and a simple strand of pearls. On top of my glossed blond head is a small coral pillbox hat, pinned neatly into place. "So," Christopher says. "Did we get it right, honey?"

I stand there, staring in the mirror. The room gets very quiet.

"I look like a Fortune 500 powerbroker . . . crossed with a Stepford wife . . . and with a little Dallas cheerleader sprinkled on top."

Christopher looks worried. "Is that *good*?"

I touch my face to make sure it's me in the mirror.

"It's . . . amazing. I look like I belong on *Housewives of the GOP*."

A huge cheer erupts in the room and everyone starts laughing and clapping. Christopher comes over and smiles at me. "I think we tamed you, little shrew."

I nod and tears start to well.

"Oh no, honey!" Christopher says. "Blink it back now . . . blink it back! You *cannot* cry until those lash extensions are set. Understand me? *Jeremy!*" he shouts. "Jeremy, we need tissues ASAP! It's an emergency!" I hold perfectly still until emergency tissues are flown in from the sidelines and he carefully dabs my tears away.

"There," he says. "All better."

"How did you do it, Christopher? What look did you pick?"

"Looks," he says. "This is three rolled into one. Callista Gingrich, Betty Ford, and Flight Attendant Barbie."

"I love it . . . I really do."

"Well, if you like this, then you have an entire new wardrobe waiting for you . . . a style I created and named just for you."

"What's the name?"

"You, darling, are 'Elegantly Invincible.'"

5
Grace Under Fire

Brad and I start going to church. His parents' church, Grace-Trinity Lutheran. I've been dreading it and putting it off as long as possible, but I knew it was coming. We couldn't put it off forever. Plus, I want to support my husband in his never-ending quest to convince his parents that we're exemplary citizens and pillars of the community.

Sitting in the pews, we certainly look the part. Brad has on a blue Brooks Brothers suit and I'm wearing a tailored plum peplum dress with pearls. So what if my pantyhose have duct tape on the crotch? I tried to dry them in the toaster oven this morning, when they were still damp from the dryer. Bad idea. It doesn't matter though, because here it's not what's on the inside that matters, it's what's on the outside . . . because that's the part people see, judge, and gossip about.

Randomly Handy Church Rules

- Look nice, but not too nice, or you look braggy.
- Skinny women are suspicious. Chubby is cheerful.

- Direct eye contact is an act of aggression.
- Candles are wicked unless they're apple-cinnamon scented.
- Bring a hotdish or stay home.
- Supper is served at five. Sinners eat at six.
- Catholics are going to hell, but it's impolite to mention it to them.
- Unmarried women are discouraged.
- Everyone over twenty-one should have children. No exceptions.
- God likes: Minnesota, Canada, and Disneyland.
- Satan loves: New York, New Jersey, and Florida.

I make it *clear* to Brad that while I might attend church physically, I will never set foot in the door mentally. I have no intention of listening, learning, reading, understanding, engaging, growing, or participating in one single red-hot thing. Not an idea, event, or action. Not even a sesame-seed-size one. I'll sit beside him in the sanctuary with a vapid expression on my face and think of nothing. I will consider it my meditative downtime.

That's the attitude I go in with anyway. I quickly discover, however, that I've underestimated the strength, fortitude, and sheer stubborn willpower those church ladies have. Mother Keller is cochair of the Trinity Committee, otherwise known as the God Squad, a highly organized group of frighteningly unfunny women who plan the church's social functions. Nothing happens at Grace-Trinity Lutheran without the God Squad's say-so. Not a bake sale or a charity drive or a bingo game goes down without their express consent. Nobody goes up against the God Squad. Peril awaits those who do. They're like a terrorist cell with casseroles.

The last lady who defied the squad was Edith Stanley, a strident woman who threw an unsanctioned bingo party in her basement rumpus room and lived to see the consequences. The God Squad discovered her insubo8rdination, and at the next church bake sale, a church elder found a pubic hair in one of Edith's butterscotch brownies. Her humiliation was complete. Nobody ever saw Edith Stanley or her freewheeling, godless deli meats ever again.

Who would voluntarily spend time with these people? Personally I'd rather get a root canal in a butcher shop outside Kazakhstan. The group is populated by orthodox Lutherans, descendants of hardscrabble Scandinavian pioneers and founders of the Finnish Temperance Society, the prim wives of church deacons, and an impressive roster of unkillable blue-haired widows, wealthy dowagers who've inherited fortunes from their dead husbands, all captains of various industries. Mother Keller is vice president of the committee. The *president* is the preposterously shaped Martha Woodcock, a woman whose oddly shaped body resembles a pile of sea lions that have been unjustly trapped inside a large bolt of floral-print fabric. She is Mother Keller's best friend and ongoing nemesis. I don't think Mother Keller has any other kinds of friends.

On our first visit, after "Big Church," we go to the Newcomers Welcome Party, where someone asks if Brad's my "hubs," as in "husband." I learn most Christian wives refer to their husbands as "Hubs," "Hubby," or "Dr. Hubstable." Pastor Mike greets us; he's your average, run-of-the-mill Lutheran pastor: in his late sixties, friendly, smiles a lot, and believes women are good for making hotdish casseroles and babies. Pastor Mike is a widower, which ups the sexual ante quite a bit for the God Squad, especially for Martha Woodcock, who's had her eye on him for years. She'd make a great pastor's wife; she runs a tight ship.

When she asks if I've picked my volunteer committee yet, I say I'd like to wait before signing up for anything. She smiles tightly at me and her eyebrow flinches ever so slightly and I hear a *beep beep beep!* Then she presses a little button on her wristwatch, which she says is actually a rage counter. "My doctor gave it to me for high blood pressure. Every time I get angry, I just push this little button down and the rage counter measures my skin temperature, my heart rate, and my blood pressure, and it keeps track of how many rageful events I have every day, week, and month. Then it tallies up my overall rage scores, so I can keep track of my progress . . . if there is any! See?" She beeps the little button again. "There it is . . . one hundred and fourteen rage events so far today."

I nod, wondering why she just hit the rage button again. Did she have some supersonic flash of invisible rage just while standing here, smiling at me? Good Lord, if there's ever a sniper in the church bell tower, all my money will be on sweet, smiling little Martha Woodcock. "That sounds like a lot of rageful moments," I tell her.

"Mercy no," she says. "You should've seen where I started. Back when I was writing the church newsletter with a typewriter . . . typos left and right. Once when our youth basketball team was playing I wrote, 'Come out and watch us kill Christ the King!' Mercy no, I have improved. I would've had three hundred rage events by now, just six months ago. My goal is to get the total number of rageful moments to under a hundred a day."

"Well . . . good luck with that," I say.

After we all have coffee cake, we enter the sweltering back garden, where we're presented with a white Bible, a welcome packet, and a little clip-on air freshener "Travel Angel" for the dashboard of our car. The angel holds a banner that says SWEET

FOR JESUS. She smells like peach. "She's actually a real-life guardian angel," one woman tells me.

"Really?"

"Absolutely. My angel's saved me many times."

"From unwanted odors!" I joke.

"And sin," the woman says flatly.

I should let it go but I can't. "So, you're telling me this little piece of plastic, which is made in . . . the People's Republic of China, is a real-life guardian angel? I just clip her on the dashboard and God won't kill us?"

"Jen . . ." Brad smiles at me warningly.

"She absolutely *is*," the woman says. "She's heavenly and helpful!"

"Not to mention heavily scented!" I add quickly, before Brad has a chance to pinch me.

After church we have brunch at Hillcrest Country Club. The club is like the Keller family's other home; Ed plays racquetball there almost every afternoon and Mother Keller attends at least two social functions there a week. Brad works out at the gym, Sarah plays tennis on the club team, and Trevor takes karate lessons.

I go to Mother Keller's bridge game, which she plays with a brittle coterie of octogenarian cronies every Thursday in the solarium. The powdered ladies sit on wicker chairs, sipping iced tea and nibbling sugar cookies as slow bamboo fan blades turn overhead. They volley back and forth across the table, tirelessly working together on vicious, iridescent threads, weaving gossip more masterfully than black orb spiders spin webs.

I witness all this firsthand, sitting up straight in my prim apricot dress as I try to keep up with the mind-bogglingly complicated game. The ladies aren't mean to me exactly; they don't seem to even see me. I think I fall into a category of importance similar to that of a waitress or a sleeping infant or a potted fern. On balance I'd say the experience fits somewhere between Dante's second and third levels of hell, but they do serve cake.

I try to fit in with Brad's club buddies. I join them a few times for a scotch in the clubhouse bar, a dark wood-paneled room with brass railings and deep upholstered wingback chairs. "Unpleasant" sums it up. Not only do I think scotch tastes like cat piss, I am bored beyond belief, caught between a mind-numbing conversation about football at the table and a soporific golf game up on the super-jumbo TV. The only thing worse than watching golf on TV is watching golf on a huge TV, and worse still, in *high definition*. I white-knuckle my way through the keen urge to stand up and scream, *"For the love of God, why?"* But I don't, partly because I have no backup. I am in fact the only woman there. I know the clubhouse is sort of the guys' hangout, and the women usually gather in the solarium.

These aren't rules, however—at least I didn't think they were, but judging by the *malocchio* dagger eyes I get from several women on my way to the bathroom, maybe they are rules and nobody likes my breaking them. Nobody says anything to me . . . they just give me looks and without one word uttered, the message is conveyed loud and clear.

Back off, BITCH.

It's like I've broken some sacred tribal law concerning gender roles or womanhood or menstruation or something and now my clitoris will need to be mutilated into the limp shape of a dick. Plus it never fails to amaze me how good women are at conveying information without speaking, using just their body language and/or facial expressions. We must learn it from each other, because it doesn't work on men. I can shoot Hailey a look and she'll pick up my transmission word for word. Like when she took the last bagel on our family camping trip and I made her cry after facially projecting to her this message:

YOU TOOK MY FREAKING BAGEL? SERIOUSLY? STUNNING. I'M NOT TRYING TO BE DRAMATIC, BUT YOU'RE MORE SELFISH THAN HITLER. THERE ARE FIVE PEOPLE AND FIVE BAGELS. I HAVE HAD *ZERO* BAGELS. CAN YOU DO THIS MATH? JESUS. THIS IS *JUST* LIKE THE TIME YOU PROMISED TO WALK MR. BARKY AFTER SCHOOL AND THEN WENT TO MARY-ANN LEWINSKY'S HOUSE INSTEAD AND MR. BARKY PEED ALL OVER THE BRAIDED RUG IN THE KITCHEN AND THEN POOPED IN MOM'S KNITTING BASKET AND SHE YELLED AT *ME* AND WENT LIKE *LEVEL-NINE NUTS* BECAUSE THE CHORE CHART SAID IT WAS *MY TURN* TO WALK THE DOG, EVEN THOUGH I EXPLAINED WE SWITCHED, SO I CLEANED THE GUNKY DRAIN AND *YOU* WERE SUPPOSED TO WALK THE DOG, BUT MOM DIDN'T CARE BECAUSE HER CRAFT CLUB WAS COMING IN AN HOUR AND SHE BURNED HER PECAN BARS RIGHT AFTER FINDING POOP IN HER KNITTING BASKET. SHE WANTED TO KNOW *HOW EXACTLY* A DOG POOPS *INSIDE* A KNIT-TING BASKET *WITHOUT HELP*, LIKE I WAS IN ON THE DEAL OR SOMETHING AND NOT ONLY HAD I FORGOTTEN TO WALK MR. BARKY, I HAD SOMEHOW HELPED HIM POOP IN A BASKET. I HAD TO CLEAN UP EVERYTHING BY *MYSELF*, EVEN THOUGH I WAS GAGGING THE *WHOLE TIME*, BECAUSE YOU WERE GONE AND SHE HAD TO QUICKLY MAKE MORE PECAN BARS. THEN YOU CAME HOME, EATING A POPSICLE AND WEARING MARYANN'S BALLERINA

TUTU, AND MOM ASKED IF IT WAS *YOUR TURN* OR *MY TURN* TO WALK THE DOG AND I THOUGHT, *HALLELUJAH. HERE WE GO, THE TRUTH AT LAST.* BUT YOU STOOD THERE AND LIED THROUGH YOUR TEETH AND TOLD MOM *IT WAS MY TURN* TO WALK MR. BARKY AND MOM DIDN'T KNOW WHO TO BE-LIEVE, SO SHE JUST SENT US TO BED AND THAT WAS THE END OF THE "INVESTIGATION." I KNEW RIGHT THEN JUST *HOW* EVIL YOU REALLY WERE. WE WERE LIVING WITH A POPSICLE-EATING, TUTU-WEARING *MONSTER* WHO WOULD STOP AT NOTH-ING TO GET WHATEVER SHE WANTED AND STILL DOES TO THIS DAY, AS EVIDENCED BY YOUR NAZI *BAGEL THEFT.* THERE WAS NO JUSTICE THEN AND THERE'S NONE NOW. YOU LIE AND GET POPSICLES, I TELL THE TRUTH AND GET DOG POOP. THE END. (P.S. YOU WOULD MAKE A TERRIBLE MOTHER.)

Yep. Hailey got the whole message. I could've given Lenny the same look and he probably would've just thought about bacon and farted. After some back-and-forth Hailey finally ad-mitted she *had* promised to walk Mr. Barky and I scramble-ran to get Mom so she could hear Hailey's full confession, but she just made a face and said, "We had a dog called *Mr. Barky?*"

I feel awkward at the club and uneasy. Often mildly nauseous. I have zero friends there, because in order to *make* friends, you have to *have* friends, and nobody wants to be friends with some-body with no friends. At the club's social epicenter are the Rath-bone sisters.

Addison and Eloise Rathbone, "Addi" and "Ellie" to close friends. They're two of the wealthiest, most popular women in the whole club and they're so cliquish, they only hang out with each other. If I could just get them to like me, everyone would like me. If they decide to include you in their machinations, you are also at the epicenter. If they don't, then like me you basically don't exist. It's like high school all over again, but now everyone drives luxury cars and gets routine Botox injections.

In an effort to win popularity points, I try to join the Hillcrest women's golf team. I don't really fit in with these stocky Republicans, who all have zero tolerance for arts and culture, or any other colossal waste of time, but who spend countless hours on the golf course, chasing around a little white ball. Still, when in Rome . . . I attend the club's semiannual Ladies' Golf Brunch wearing a brand-new pair of expensive all-white ladies' golf shoes and an expensive perky canary-yellow ladies' golf outfit, which consists of a piqué cotton canary-yellow golf shirt, a matching cotton canary-yellow-and-baby-blue plaid pleated miniskirt, and a thick canary-yellow headband. The headband pinches, the shirt feels too tight, and I think the skirt is definitely too short. I look like a preppy prostitute. It's perfect.

I even buy a new set of clubs, with Brad's blessing. He knows there are only two types of golfers on the course: players who own their own clubs . . . and posers, who don't. I want to be a player, not a poser, so I buy a set of expensive golf clubs after reading an article online called "What to Ask Yourself Before Buying Your First Set of Golf Clubs." It asked what my golfing goal is, which is to bamboozle other golf players into becoming my friends. Then it asked if I'm *in it for the long haul*. What's my level of interest? This, of course, is *zero*, but my level of dedication is high. That's why I bought a titanium super-pro extra-deluxe set of golf clubs that cost five thousand dollars. The golf bag is made of white leather and has a built-in cooler for my ice water.

Ice water turns out to be a real necessity for the Ladies' Golf

Brunch, which is held on a swelteringly sticky late August afternoon. I pour half a bottle of baby powder down the backside of my underpants and wear a pair of disgusting disposable sticky-backed armpit guards so I don't sweat through my perky yellow shirt. Sweat stains on the golf course are a no-no—for women, that is. Men can sweat like pigs skewered over a fire pit, but ladies must remain cool and dry.

I wish I could say that I did.

My first mistake is eating biscuits and sausage gravy at the bruncheon. Why they'd serve us biscuits and sausage gravy before a long hot day playing golf is a good question, but an even better question is why I'd eat them. My stomach begins to gurgle on the way out to the first hole, while I'm riding in a golf cart commandeered by two league captains, who both go on and on about how painful it is to play with amateurs and how everyone bets on which newcomer will be named worst player. This year they're betting on the octogenarian woman with asthma or the clumsy brunette who knocked over the pancake trolley during the bruncheon's welcome speech.

I quickly realize my many other mistakes, like that I bought a nine-thousand-pound golf bag that has no legs. Everyone else's golf bag has nifty little tripod legs that let the bag stand up on its own and be rolled merrily along without any effort. I have to haul my bag on my back. We only get to ride golf carts from the clubhouse to the first hole; for the rest of the time we have to walk. It's like the Bataan Death March. When we finally get to the next hole, I have to lay the heavy bag down on the grass, then pick it back up again, which feels like repeatedly picking up and laying down a hot human corpse.

I also forgot to wear sunscreen, and while everyone else is wearing a sun visor or a hat, I only have my canary-yellow headband on. Soon sweat starts dripping off my forehead and stinging my eyes so I can't see anything but a smeary saltwater sun. I also forgot to buy gloves, which results in a massive blister forming on the web of my index finger and thumb; this happens about four holes into the game, forcing me to swing like a paraplegic, not that anyone's watching me by then. They've already marked me as a phony.

It happened somewhere between the first hole, when my nine-iron went whipping out of my hands on the very first swing, nearly bludgeoning the octogenarian woman with asthma, and the third hole, when I sent my golf ball whistling into the dense tree line along the fairway. To make matters worse, I try chipping the ball out of the woods and my wedge catches on something, causing me to stumble and kick the ball backward, shooting it right out of the trees and onto the fairway's seventh hole, going in the opposite direction.

According to all the sticklers around me, I must play the ball from where it lies, even in this preposterous situation, and so I traverse the golf course backward, thwacking my way through irritated and amused groups of women who shake their heads and stare at me. This humiliation is compounded by the fact that I desperately need a bathroom. The rumbling in my tummy is worsening and gets to the point where I deliberately rewhack my ball into the bushes so I can take an emergency poo at the edge of a large half-hidden sand trap.

By the time I reach the eighteenth hole, it's dark. Everyone else has finished and is up at the clubhouse, which I correctly choose to avoid, instead retrieving my car while towing my nine-thousand-pound golf bag along. "Here, just pop the legs out," the valet says, clicking some mystery button, which causes a neat set of tripod legs to eject. The next day I discover I won the "Worst Player" award and they now all call me "Fern," because I so often went flying into the trees.

It wouldn't be so bad if Brad wasn't watching me fail. I'm depressed by my ongoing failure to be popular at the club, but Brad seems devastated. Between my pooping in a sand trap and not getting invited to any cocktail parties or soirees, Brad's utterly stumped.

"Why don't they like you?" he asks me forlornly. "You're doing everything right! The dress, the hair, the nails . . ."

"Thanks, sweetie," I tell him. "I guess it's just—"

"What's wrong with you that I'm not seeing?" he asks me darkly.

I look at him, stomach sinking.

"There must be something wrong with you that I'm not seeing," he says, and I feign indignation, anger, and outrage at the idea. Inside, however, I'm thinking, *God help me*. If Brad ever figures out all the things that are wrong with me, especially the things he's not seeing, he'll stumble across quite a long list of flaws, and unlike golfing, my flaws are definitely here to stay for the long haul. There's nothing I can do about them. Because like all players on the golf course of life, you have to play it . . . as it lays.

6
Selling It Like It Is

September is a big month for Keller's. It's the time of year kids buy back-to-school clothes and people are getting ready for winter, buying various arctic gear. I was hoping to see the trees turn colors, but instead of a long lovely fall filled with rich red and deep golden leaves, we get a cold snap and all the just-yellowing leaves drop off the trees overnight. Then we're smacked with a snowstorm. It's fall, then *whoomph!*, it's winter.

Which sucks.

Today I'm taking Trevor down to the store for a photo shoot. He's going to be featured in the Valentine's Day catalog as chief cupid. I shower, shave my legs, wrestle myself into my cruel foundation garments, take an hour to apply my makeup, and then put on a tailored wool suit topped by my thick navy blue peacoat and black-watch plaid scarf. Trevor shows up in a sweatsuit. God, I wish I was seven again.

We go downtown, where I drive around the block after spotting a protest outside the store. It's a small picket line on the sidewalk with twenty people shouting and holding up signs that say BOYCOTT KELLER'S! KELLER'S IS ANTIGAY! KELLER'S HATES GAYS!

"What're all those people doing?" Trevor asks. "They look angry."

"I'm not sure . . ." I tell him. "I can't read the signs . . . Can you?"

"Um . . . no."

"Good! Here we go." I pull into the underground VIP parking lot. A picket line always forms outside the store when gay rights are concerned, because Keller's is widely known for being antigay . . . mostly because they are. Also there happens to be a gay lounge across the street from Keller's called the Fairy Tail, a little joint that does drag shows and throws gay bingo night every Tuesday. Christopher stops in at the Fairy Tail after work sometimes, but he uses the back-door entrance, which everyone inside understands. That's why the back-door entrance is there. Today the protesters are responding to the news that the senate is postponing the vote on the Family Equity Act. As usual it's mostly employees and patrons of the Fairy Tail picketing; the drag queens stop over in between gigs, which is why so many of them are wearing pink wigs and glittering high heels. I drive around the building and down into the underground lot, so we can take the elevators up to the lobby. The last thing I want is Trevor telling his mom he crossed a gay picket line. She'd probably be afraid her son would join them.

The Keller's photo studio is in the basement. I lead young Trevor down there, lying to him the whole way. "This'll be super fun, Trevor! It'll go by really fast. Isn't it cool Grandpa Keller wants you to be in the store catalog? You'll love having your picture taken. You're a star. You're the most handsome boy in the world." I know it's bad to lie to kids, but the truth seems worse. *This is seriously going to suck, Trevor. It'll take an excru-*

ciating amount of time and the pictures will haunt you as an adult because your family is exploiting you. Plus you may not know it now, but you are one weird-looking kid.

We take the elevator up to Cute Emily's desk, because I have to sign some papers before the shoot. "Well, don't you look nice!" she says. "Great suit."

"This?" I say. "I just threw this on."

She has me sign a raft of miscellaneous papers that Todd left for me while Trevor tugs on my arm, hugs my legs, bounces off the walls, and shouts, "I wanna go now!"

"Trevor," I say. "Enough! I have to sign these papers first."

"Mommy said I could get a new lunch box today!"

"I told you we're not getting a lunch box."

"*Lunch box!*" he shouts. "*Lunch box! Lunch box! Lunch box!*"

"Stop it!"

Of course he *won't* stop it until I promise to buy him a lunch box. I could argue with him and make threats and swear at him at the top of my lungs, but by the time I've bullied him into going, I'll be worn out, red faced, and wanting to commit nephew-cide as well as suicide. It's much easier to just buy him the damn lunch box. When I'm finally done signing everything and Emily is done double-checking each signature, my right eyeball is ready to rupture. Trevor and I dash over to the Kidz Korner! department for a new lunch box.

"Pick one," I tell him. "And hurry."

"Should I get one with Batman?" he asks.

"Sure. Grab it."

"What about Spider-Man?" he asks.

"Fine. Same guy, different leotard."

"But Mom says all the cool kids get Incredible Hulk lunch boxes."

"Then get the Incredible Hulk."

"But I don't like the Incredible Hulk."

"Then don't get him, Trevor. I don't care which one you get. Just pick one!"

"What about a silly one? Like Barbie?"

"Sure. Great. Can we hurry, please? Alan is waiting."

"But Barbie is silly, right?"

"I don't know, Trevor. They all seem pretty silly to me, but it doesn't matter what I think. It's your lunch box, it'll carry your lunch, not anybody else's, so pick Spider-Man or Batman or Barbie. I don't care, just pick one."

He picks Barbie.

The saleslady charges it to our account. Then we run for the basement, almost twenty minutes late. When I tug open the studio's heavy door, all the familiar smells greet me. The hot lights, the burned coffee, Awful Alan's aftershave. He's our catalog director and he's barking at Nell, the lovable but hopeless wardrobe assistant. "What do you mean, they're not here yet?" he shouts. "I don't give a flying freak!"

I wave at Nell.

"Hi, Jen!" She smiles. "You look awesome!"

"This? I've had it for a thousand years."

Alan glares at me. "Well!" he says. "Glad you could join us! Need anything else before we get started? Coffee? Smoothie? Twenty grand to pay for another shoot if we can't get this one done in time?"

"Hi, Alan. Glad to see you're doing well."

"Hey, Trevor," he says. "Remember me? You ready for your big photo shoot?"

"*No,*" Trevor says. "No, no, no!"

"But you're the star, buddy."

"You're stupid."

"Well, it's gonna be pretty cool," Alan says. "Look at this cool camera we got. Wanna look through the lens?"

"No!" Trevor shouts. "Cameras are dumb."

"Well, that's just *great,*" Alan says, taking off his glasses. "Perfect! I think it's dumb too. Unbelievable. They can't spring for a real model, so they send us this kid every year, who gets nuttier each shoot and takes more and more time . . ."

"Alan?" I look at him. "Take it easy." I kneel down and whisper in Trevor's ear. His face lights up and he nods at me. "Okay. Trevor's ready."

"Is that right?" Alan says.

"Yep."

I pull Nell aside and tell her what I told Trevor, that he could keep his angel wings after the shoot if he did everything Alan said. "But, Nell . . . don't tell anyone, okay?"

She nods.

"The kid's . . . a little different, that's all. He'd rather wear angel wings than play football, you know, it's no big deal . . . but I don't want people to tease him."

"I got it," she says. "I'll make sure they go home with him."

Trevor is already at the makeup table, getting his wings attached. Next to him are two perfectly perfect little blond girls wearing pancake makeup and white sequined shorty-shorts with matching white wings. They look like midget Victoria's Secret models. I fight the impulse to throw blankets over them and whisk them away to some far-off land where parents wouldn't allow things like this to happen. I wait for a few minutes and when they take Trevor off to wardrobe, I make a break for it and crash right into . . . who else?

"Ted!"

"Jennifer! Wow. Nice suit. Are you delivering a speech at the UN?"

"Thank God it's you." I sigh. "Where've you *been*?"

"You know, more women should thank God when they see me," he says. "Well done."

"Coffee?" I ask.

"Love to," he says.

We head upstairs, stopping at Christopher's basement design lab first. This is where he designs and builds all his fabulous store displays and fancy window dressings. He's the queen bee of a ferociously talented hive, a small army of fashionable youths who wear alligator shoes and jaunty scarves while constructing his elaborate displays.

Christopher calls them the Gay Bee Brigade.

I think it's completely unfair that they're all working today, considering they had to cross a picket line claiming their employer is antigay, but that's the Gay Bee Brigade for you.

Forever loyal to the queen.

The design lab is in full production for Valentine's Day. Half-naked mannequins are posed around the room in various states of undress. Disembodied arms lie strewn about like it's a war scene and an entire chorus line of fishnet-stockinged legs erupts from a large cardboard box in the corner. Sewing machines whir and whiz in the next room; a radio hooked to a rack of clothes rushes by. Bolts of fabric spill gently down a wall of metal shelving and cascade colors to the floor, where a spilled tub of pink sequins glitters.

Christopher works at a tall wooden drafting board at the center of the room. It looks like an island or a blocky ship moored at sea. "Jennifer!" he says when he sees me. "Ted! Come in, come in and see what magic we're making! First let me see the suit, Jennifer. Give me a spin. Okay . . . okay . . . very good, but, honey, my God, why stockings with a seam? Are you a hooker at the wharf?"

"No. Why? I thought they were sexy."

"They're slutty. Take them off."

"They're fine, they just need—"

"*Off*," he says. "Now."

"Fine. God." I kick off my shoes and peel off my stockings. Christopher shouts for Tim to bring him a pair of nude nylons. Tim's his assistant and my other favorite gay bee; he's so cute, like a tiny little pocket gay, and has a high voice like Truman Capote's. Christopher gets horribly jealous of my affections for him. "Timothy!" he shouts. "Please hurr— Oh."

Tiny Tim walks in wearing a herringbone jacket with the cuffs rolled up and a jaunty scarf. "You rang, Your Highness?" He's so cute. I wonder if he has to buy suits in the children's section.

"Yes, Timothy." Christopher sighs. "I need a pair of—"

"Nude nylons." Tim hands him the nylons. "I'm not deaf, you know."

"Or mute," Christopher says. "Thank you. You may go."

Tiny Tim rolls his eyes at me and clicks his heels together. Then he leaves, whistling. It's always like this between them if I'm nearby.

"Hey, have you got any Angel Bears in?" Ted asks.

"Yes I have." Christopher sighs. "Unfortunately."

"Can I grab one? I need it for the shoot."

"Be my guest. Take all of them. Horrid creatures. Look, look at this sketch for the window display. It's a travesty unfolding." He shows us the big sloppy sketch on his drafting table. "I can't make beauty with nasty, cheaply made things. Look at this stitching!" He grabs a little white teddy bear from the shelf, which has cheap shiny silver wings sewn on its back crookedly. The bears have a satin heart on their bellies that says ALWAYS BE AN ANGEL!

I tell them Trevor's doing the Angel Bear shoot today and Christopher says, "Bet he loves wearing those silver wings!"

"Yeah." I sigh. "I was trying to hide that fact from Alan."

"It's nice you watch out for him. I had an aunt, Ariel, like that. She lived with us after my uncle Dale died, and she knew what I was before I did and protected me from my parents, who . . . well, you know. She even convinced my mother that I had asthma and couldn't play during recess, so I stayed inside every day, while all the other kids beat up Clyde Owens outside because he didn't have an Aunt Ariel."

"Can I give this bear to him?" I ask.

"You could . . ." Christopher says, "but I don't think you should. They came in boxes with these creepy hazardous-material labels on them."

"Hazardous-material labels?" I look at him. "Seriously?"

"Seriously."

"That's not right. Show me."

Christopher shouts for Tim. "Tim! Bring me another box of awful bears!"

There's a rattle in the next room and Tiny Tim comes in rolling a huge cart stacked high with boxes. He's barely visible behind them.

"Thank you, Timothy," Christopher says curtly. "You may go."

"Oh, may I?" Tim says, and steps out from behind the boxes.

"Yes," Christopher says. "You may."

"Hmph!" Tim stalks out, insouciantly flipping his scarf over one shoulder.

I look at the boxes and don't see any hazmat signs until

Christopher carefully peels back the shipping label, revealing a nasty-looking black diamond with a big yellow skull and crossbones at the center. "Whoa," Ted says. "That can't be good."

"Well . . . maybe they're just reusing old boxes," I say.

Christopher snorts. "Yeah, and maybe they're hiding the fact that these bears are toxic."

"You could check the ship's manifest," Ted tells us. "They're required by law to put anything hazardous on the ship's manifest, to prevent explosions at sea."

"Where are we going to find the ship's manifest?" Christopher asks.

"We could ask the guys on the loading dock," Ted says.

"You can ask them," Christopher says. "Last time I went there they put me on a shelf."

"Now, wait a minute," I say. "Nobody's going to the loading dock. Let's not get carried away."

"I work constantly with these things!" Christopher says indignantly. "If they cause cancer, I'll be the first to get it!"

"More like the second!" Tim snaps from the other room.

"C'mon," I say. "I'm sure everything's legal."

"Really?" Christopher throws a bear at me. "Why's that? Because you know it for a fact or because you're scared to cause any trouble?"

"You know"—Ted clears his throat—"we better get going."

"Oh sure, ride in to her rescue," Christopher says. "Like always."

"Well, why not?" Ted smiles. "She knit me a scarf once."

Christopher snorts. "That thing that looked like a bath towel connected to a washcloth? That was a scarf?"

"Drop it, Christopher," I tell him.

"Oh. I see! You say drop it . . . so we're all expected to drop it? Just stop worrying about our health so your husband can make more money by importing crap products? That's fabulous, Jen. You seem more like a Keller every day."

"Ow! Stop throwing bears, Christopher! That's not fair!"

"Especially to any children who get one for Valentine's Day! 'Hi, Jimmy, the Keller's Angel Bear of Death loves you!'" Christopher starts pelting us with bears until we scramble out and run into Tiny Tim, who flips his scarf and says, "Sorry about that. He's really in a mood today. Come back later, I'll put some Benadryl in his coffee."

Ted and I sit in the cafeteria with two Styrofoam cups of coffee and a half-eaten blueberry muffin. I ask him what's been happening at the office and he tells me the most shocking piece of gossip. I can't believe it. "Ashley seriously got a *divorce?*"

Ted nods. "An ugly one. He had an affair with a ShopNBC girl."

"No! Really? Which one?"

"The new brunette."

"The new brunette? I love her! I'm vacation-gay for the ShopNBC girls. Like if one of them was into me, I'd totally take a vacation with her somewhere and be someone totally else for a day. Or a week . . ." A shadow falls across our table.

I look up and nearly let out a yelp.

It's Ashley.

"Heaven have mercy," she says. "It's *Jennifer Keller* in the flesh."

"Hi . . . Ashley."

"Oh my . . . did you *lose* weight on your honeymoon?"

"I did . . ."

"Okay, that's not even heard of, pumpkin!" Her face twitches ever so slightly. "I just can't believe it! Look at you . . . all important and married, for the time being . . . Gosh! Miracles really do happen, don't they? Crazy miracles . . . that make no sense!"

"Hi, Ashley," Ted says, and she looks almost startled, like she hadn't noticed him.

"Ted," she says flatly. "You're here too? Wow. Sorry, I was just so excited to see . . . our Jennifer here in her . . . splendor. Um, so you obviously know, Jen . . . I'm getting a divorce."

"I . . . I did not know that." I lie for Ted's sake. "I thought you two . . . were for keeps."

Ashley turns bright pink. "Okay then, Jen! Hafta get back to . . . work. Imagine! Having to work . . . not you, though. Not anymore! Well, not everybody went and slept with the president's son, so . . . Some of us have to do it the hard way I guess! Okay, bye-bye!"

I wave at her as she leaves, and just as I think my head might explode, she's gone.

"Oh my God." I stare at Ted. "I'm so sorry, I didn't know what to do. I always say the wrong thing when I panic!"

"I know." Ted sighs. "If it weren't so entertaining, it might get really annoying."

7

Fishwife

I wake up at six A.M. after a tortured night of sleep.

I kicked and thrashed around so much Brad went down to sleep in the guest room. I hate it when he does that, but I knew the odds were against my sleeping. Today is the big Japanese investor dinner. My Day of Judgment has finally arrived. Who knew it would be unseasonably cold? One of those late-September days that feels like deep November. Arctic wind from the lake whips up the steps and hammers on all the windows of the house, rattling the doors and trying ceaselessly to find a way in.

I can't worry about the weather. The house looks perfect anyway. I cleaned the whole mausoleum myself. Actually I gave Star Fan and Pho twenty bucks each to dust. I was told Bi'ch was a qualified maid, but I have no empirical evidence of this. She makes huge messes, speaks intermittent English, and is terrified of all electric appliances. The espresso maker in particular causes her to flee. Animal husbandry seems to be the one area she thrives in. She fishes constantly, and I discovered a chicken coop she built behind our house, and a fledgling chicken pen beside it housing six fat squirrels, which she dotes on and feeds. Are they pets? Meals? To be used in rituals? I'm too traumatized by the situation to inquire further.

Just like with the chicken coop, I choose not to panic about today.

Relax. Breathe. I can do this.

After all, everything is already arranged. The party-rental delivery is at nine, the catering staff sets up around ten, and the florist delivers the orchids at noon. Guests arrive at six and dinner starts at seven. God, that seems early. I just have to pick up a few things for tonight and go to the spa and get my hair done. No need to fret. No need to catastrophize and picture in my head every conceivable scenario in which the dinner could be a disaster. Before I leave, I double-check the kitchen; I want everything to be ready for the caterer when she arrives. Star Fan lumbers into the room and I frown at her. "Were you smoking?" I ask her.

"No." She scowls through smudgy kohl eyes. I know that look. I know why her hair is all kinked up in the back too. I clear my throat. "Star Fan," I say, "are you on birth control?"

"You can't ask me that."

"Well, I just did. I'm sorry, but I'm concerned. I think one preteen parent in this—"

"Naniga hoshiino?" the Ice Empress shouts, causing me to curse and swear.

No matter how many times I approach the stupid refrigerator, I can't get used to seeing a disembodied geisha head appear. "Is she changing outfits now?" I squint at the chrome door. "Star Fan, is she wearing a different . . . Star Fan?" I look up. She's gone. I tug on the door but it won't open. I sigh and say, "Ice Empress, open the door please."

She giggles at me. *"Moshi moshi,* Jen Aho-Onna!"

"Yes, hello," I yawn. "Sayonara, Fuji Film, et cetera . . . Can you please open the door?"

"Oooops!" She giggles. *"Damatte-yo! Kono ama!"*

"Why isn't the door opening?" I tug on the handle. "Speak *English,* Ice Empress!"

"Oooops! Sorry, Jen Aho-Onna! Time for express steam-clean! *Wheeeeeeee!"*

"No, I want coffee right now. No steam-clean!"

The Ice Empress giggles and bows. *"Kutabare!"* she says, and the door stays locked.

Bitch.

I groan, banging my head lightly on the door, and shout up to Trevor that it's time to go. I have him for the whole weekend because Sarah's at some leadership conference. As Trevor and I leave, the overhead light in the front hall flickers.

"Auntie Jen, why does the light keep doing that?"

"Because the house is cursed, honey. We're all damned. It's nothing to worry about."

We get into the car and head for the Mall of America. The Mall of America is evil. Also, it's fun! It has everything you could ever possibly need and everything nobody should ever own. Karaoke golf carts with neon light shows, giant robot dinosaurs that fight, a collection of magnets in the shapes of every known animal's poo. A huge amusement park sits at the center of the mall with a roller coaster and a Paul Bunyan flume ride. The amusement park is ringed like a stack of doughnuts by five floors of movie theaters, restaurants, department stores, food courts, and hundreds of specialty stores that allow you to shop for two weeks straight without ever going into the same store twice.

I drop Christopher off at Kidzilla, the Mall of America's baby-sitting emporium. I read about it in the paper; it's like the Las Vegas of day-care centers. Trevor's heard about it too, and he's nearly hysterical with glee when I slap down my gold credit card and sign him up for a Godzilla Pass, which includes unlimited access to all the Kidzilla attractions and activities, like the Zero-Gravity Chamber, the Tsunami Soak Pool, the Mega-Paintball Canyon, the Big Lizard Exotic Animal and Petting Zoo, and Planet Snacker-Snacks, just to name a few.

Trevor busies himself at the Welcome Wagon while I sign legal waivers and medical consent forms. "Great," a Kidzilla counselor named Joe says. "Does he have a bathing suit?"

"Why does he need a bathing suit?"

"Tsunami Soak Pool? He'll get wet. You can rent him a suit too."

"That's fine. Rent away."

"Cool. Most moms get all weird about their kids wearing used bathing suits. I tell 'em they got nothing to worry about. There's more industrial-strength bleach in that pool than there is water." He gives Trevor a pair of neon-green swim trunks, which Trevor rejects in lieu of a neon-pink pair. He also gives Trevor a waterproof name tag lanyard and a neon-green electronic GPS tracker, which he clamps around his ankle.

"Is that really necessary?" I ask.

Joe sighs and shakes his head. "Lady, you have no idea."

I sign a few more release forms and conspiratorially whisper to Joe. "Look," I say. "I don't care *what* Trevor does today, as long as he comes back to me exhausted. Got it?" I slip a fifty-dollar bill across the counter and Joe smiles at me.

"Lady," he says, "don't worry. That kid won't know what hit him." I turn to say good-bye to Trevor, but he's already shooting down the Adventure Launch Tube. *Lucky kid.* I wish there was an Adultzilla for women. It would have well-oiled men doing laundry and lush fountains of sangria. Adultzillas for men would have roasted meat platters and naked waitresses and be one big fart-contest room.

Wait, that's Hooters.

I make my way to the spa called Mallspa, the mall's spa, where I have a ninety-minute massage done by a very small girl who still beats the living tar out of me . . . in a good way. I'm all kneaded and unknotted when I get my hair colored and my nails done. Then I buy new earrings, stockings, lipstick, and over-the-counter weight-loss pills. I pick up a specialty bottle of Shimizu-no-mai sake, which I ordered at a specialty store called Hot Socky by the mini-putt place. They sell expensive Japanese sake there and also expensive socks to wear. Many people come in for both products at the same time and say warm feet really complement good sake and vice versa. I take advantage of the complimentary spring water and swallow three of my over-the-counter weight-loss pills. I want to look slim and alluring in my dress tonight.

On my way to retrieve Trevor, I'm feeling quite confident and relaxed as I walk down the colorful chaotic halls, passing loud roller coasters, fragrant fudge factories, and clusters of small kiosks selling odds and ends. Cell phone cases, glass paperweights, whirligig kites, clip-on ponytail hair extensions . . . I take the escalators up to Kidzilla, where Joe tracks Trevor's GPS anklet down to a heating duct near Planet Snacker-Snacks.

"What's he doing in a heating duct?" I ask.

"Happens all the time," Joe says. "Don't worry, it's all mostly escape-proof."

A special captivity task force catches my nephew and loads him in the Adventure Termination Tube and *whoomph!* Trevor gets spit out from an air vacuum tube, wide-eyed and grinning. "Auntie . . . it was *so cool*!" he shouts. "This was the best day of my *life*!"

I beam at my adorable nephew. Maybe I'm not a failure as an aunt after all. Maybe I could even be his Aunt Ariel one day. Trevor yawns and trudges behind me all the way to the car, where he falls deeply asleep in the backseat. Thank you, Joe at Kidzilla.

I love you.

Fifteen minutes later, however, Trevor wakes up and projectile-vomits all over the car. He keeps going and brings up about three times his body weight in puke. He starts groaning so badly I call the emergency room on my cell phone. The nurse asks me what he ate, and in between moans, Trevor tells me he ate: two triple-meat cheeseburgers, a basket of cheesy chili-pepper French fries, six grape juice boxes, a supersize Kidzilla sundae, a jumbo banana milkshake, a bowl of maraschino cherries, a box of blue Popsicles, and a cupcake shaped like a robot head. "How could you eat that much food?" I hiss.

He looks up at me and says, like John Wayne gasping his last line in a dramatic spaghetti Western, *"Unlimited . . . candy. I had to . . . get . . . the . . . candy . . ."*

"Um . . ." I say to the nurse. "He had a little *candy*."

She says to keep him hydrated and to bring him into the emergency room if he keeps vomiting. I get off the phone and say, "Trevor, buddy, I have a big event tonight, so please stop vomiting. Okay? I will buy you *any toy* you want. Okay?"

"Okay," he says.

Then he vomits.

He proceeds to keep projectile-vomiting until my car is merely a vomit-transportation system with a nearly weeping woman at the wheel. We're a mile from home when I can't take it anymore. He looks deathly ill. I turn the car around, heading for the emergency room. *Goddamned kid.* He better be terminal. As I sit in the ER waiting room I get my first painful cramp. Gas from the diet pills. I go into the bathroom, where I burn with shame in my stall after accidentally letting out a loud fart. To think Lenny and his buddies have farting contests . . . but to me it is the epitome of all shame.

Four eternities, six encyclopedias of hospital intake forms, an illegal signature claiming to be Trevor's legal guardian, and a two-hundred-dollar pair of sunglasses lost in the emergency room later, the doctors determine Trevor has an upset stomach. Probably from eating candy. *Gee, ya think?* They give him some Imodium and tell him to drink clear fluids. *Imodium*. I have Imodium tablets in my purse and a bottle of liquid Imodium in the glove box of my car.

"That's a far cry from being terminal, Trevor."

We race home.

When we get there, the house is empty. No party planners, no glasses or linens, no caterer. I check the upstairs. The upstairs furniture is there. Bizarre. I run around double-checking every room. Ace runs around barking at me. In the kitchen I run into Pho, who's drinking a bottle of Yoo-hoo. "What happened?" I ask him. "Where is everyone? Where's the *furniture* downstairs?"

Pho shrugs and says, "They came and put it in a van."

"*Who* came and put it in a van?"

He shrugs. "How should I know?"

"Pho, didn't you think it was *strange* that people were putting our furniture in a *van*?"

"No." He takes a gulp of Yoo-hoo. "I don't know how white people throw parties."

Unbelievable.

Not only is the house empty of furniture, it's empty of food. The caterer is completely missing in action. She was supposed to be here this morning, but at ten to five, there's not a chef or a chafing dish to be seen. My head is swimming. "Okay, let's not panic," I say to myself. *"Yes, let's!"* I shout back. "We have no furniture and no food, and the guests are coming in an hour? What else is there to *do* but panic?" I look around. *"We can do this.* We have half an hour. All we need is a meal for a dozen people and a table and chairs. We don't even need chairs. They're Japanese, we'll sit on the floor . . . *Pho!"*

"What?"

"Jesus, you scared me!" He's standing right behind me like a chubby ninja. "Go get your sister and your grandmother. Check and see if the Ping-Pong table is still in the boathouse. Hurry!"

He sighs and shuffles off. I race to the refrigerator and the Ice Empress bows at me.

She says *"Moshi moshi,* Jen Aho-Onna!"

"Ice Empress, tell me in *English,* do we have enough food for twelve to fifteen people?"

She giggles. "Sorry! We are still steam-cleaning! Steam-clean . . . wheeeeeeeee!"

"What?" I tug on the chrome handle and it still won't open. I can't believe this.

"Pho!" I shout. "Pho, come and fix this damned thing! Make it stop steam-cleaning!"

"So, what do you want me to do first?" he says. "Find my sister or my grandma or a Ping-Pong table in the boathouse . . . or fix that?"

"Yes!" I nod, then take a dramatic gulp of air. "Oh my God, we're all going to die." *Okay, think.* I look at the clock on the wall. How fast can I get to the store? Panic rises in me like a balloon. When Star Fan and Bi'ch come into the room I say, "Okay, D'Amico can't deliver any food in time so listen up. We need to brainstorm here . . ."

"Grandma B fishes wicked good," Star Fan says.

I look at her. "Fishes?"

"Yeah . . . you know, like fishes for fish? That swim in the lake?"

I stare out the bay window at the wide expanse of water in our backyard and parrot back blankly, "The lake?"

Star Fan nods.

That's when it hits me. *My God! We can serve fish from the lake!*

I ask Star Fan if Bi'ch can fish fast and she says, "Faster than you, that's for sure."

"Okay . . . let's do this. Let's *do* this!"

Star Fan goes to get the fishing poles and I shout for Pho just as he walks through the door. "Did you find the Ping-Pong table?"

"Yeah," he says. "It's down there."

"Well we need it up *here*! We need it *here*! Go get it . . . Go!" He rolls his eyes and trudges back down to the boathouse. "And then come get this Goddamned geisha to open up!" I shout after him. Five minutes later I'm down on the dock with Bi'ch as she puts something sticky and tarlike on my hook and points to the water. *"Tod,"* she says, pointing. *"Tod, tod!"*

"Put it in there?" I say. *"Tod?* Okay, I'll put it in *tod*. Ew . . . here we go."

Two minutes later we have both our poles in the water. Ten minutes later heaven has taken mercy on us. We're reeling in fish. My line jerks and Bi'ch shouts, *"Zoo tod!"* which apparently means "Reel it in!" We slap fish after fish into the bucket. Then Bi'ch quickly builds a crackling fire by the shoreline while I haul our impressive catch up to the kitchen. Star Fan cleans the fish over the sink. Pho has monkeyed with the refrigerator and gotten it to open up. "Great!" I shout. "Now look for anything in there that makes fish sauce!" He looks around inside and shrugs. As I sprint back outside, he thunks a bottle of mayonnaise on the counter.

I go to the garage to get the saw, which I use to shorten the legs of the Ping-Pong table. Pho helps me haul it into the dining room. I tell him to go find a clean sheet and throw it on the table. Outside Bi'ch is roasting fish, five at a time, wedged inside a handmade reed box. She grins her big toothless grin at me and says, "I cook!"

"Roasted over an open flame. I can't believe you know how to do all this! I mean, this is amazing! We caught all of this—right here in Lake Minnetonka!"

Even Star Fan smiles.

"Did Bi'ch make that reed thing she's roasting the fish in?" I ask her.

Star Fan nods. "She made it in like five minutes, from shit she got from the shore. Bi'ch can do anything. She's badass. She led a resistance group through Laos."

"She did?"

"Hell yes. She was their survival guide. She was the reason they ate."

Amazing. I'd always thought of Bi'ch as some helpless little old woman, when she's actually like a MacGyver who can't sing. Bi'ch stands up, dusts off her skirt, and points to a basket of greens, which she also apparently collected while I was inside. "Oh yeah," Star Fan says. "Grandma B found salad." Bi'ch gives me a big toothless grin. I pause for a moment and then seize her by her tiny waist and twirl her once around. "Aiyeeeee!" she shrieks, and I kiss both her dried little apple cheeks, laughing before setting her down.

"Thank you!" I say. "Unbelievable. Unprecedented. Bi'ch saves the freaking day!"

"You have ten minutes before they get here," Star Fan says.

I race upstairs. Ace and Trevor are on my bed watching TV. "You feel okay, buddy?"

"No."

"You need anything?"

"Yes. A Coke."

"No Coke ever again, mister!" I get him a glass of water and then hurry to get ready, wrestling into my most severe foundation garment to date, then pulling on my white sweater dress with the green alligator accent belt and matching green alligator pumps.

I review the article on Japanese etiquette that Emily gave me while putting on my makeup. Japanese people like frequent hugging, touching, and eye contact with strangers. Signs of respect are finger pointing, snapping, and whistling. Lots of touching, kissing, finger pointing, and something. Got it. I take tea candles from the bathroom, carry them downstairs, and put them on the sawed-off Ping-Pong table. It looks far more elegant than I could've hoped.

The sake!

I forgot the sake out in the car. I run to get it and have to wash the bottle off in the sink. It's covered with vomit. Looking over my shoulder, I quickly open it and take a generous swig. Not bad. I take another one. "Careful," Pho says, cruising by. "That stuff's strong."

"Let's hope!" I say, and take another one. "Hey," I shout at him. "How would you know?"

I use my last remaining seconds to tidy up the front hall and prepare the sake tray. The chandelier overhead flickers. I toggle the switch back and forth but it's still flickering. *Why can't they just fix the damn thing?* Finally I stamp my foot on the floor and the flickering stops.

In the same breath of air, the front door opens.

There's Brad. I watch his face as he comes through the front door and sees no furniture. He manages to smile as if everything is just fine. "Hello, sweetheart!" he says, and introduces me to twelve Japanese businessmen, their translator, and two unexpected, unwanted, and unhelpful guests, Mr. Cartwright from the Minnesota Department of Public Health and his radish-shaped wife, Laura. I call her Hateful Laura because . . . well, because she's here.

I graciously greet each guest with a big bear hug and a light butterfly kiss on the right eyelid, which is called the Emperor's Greeting, the highest form of respect one can give. I can tell they're impressed. They quickly bow and back away, saying nothing. I don't know what the translator is translating but he's whispering a mile a minute in their ears. Brad waits for an opportune moment and whispers hotly, *"What is going on?* Why is there no furniture in the dining room?"

"I have no idea, darling!" I whisper back. "Let's just get through it!" I hurry to fetch two more pillows, muttering under my breath but smiling all the while. Then I snap my fingers at each guest, asking if they'd like some sake. Everyone's a taker. Except for Cartwright and his hateful radish-shaped wife. They're no fun at all.

The group tries to mingle, but it's awkward, as there's no furniture or artwork and nothing to show them room-wise. I quickly lead them to the dining room, figuring we might as well start dinner. When I finally sit down, Brad shoots me a look and nods at the table. That's when I realize Pho put his own bedsheets on the table. They're Superman sheets. Every other inch of space is stamped with a blue and red letter S.

Nobody mentions it.

We sit silently, cross-legged on the floor. I have gas pains again and use every ounce of effort not to break wind as Bi'ch serves roasted char-blackened fish. *"Why are the fishes' heads still on?"* Brad whispers. I look down at my plate. The tallest businessman sits to my left. He seems to be their leader, probably because he's the tallest. He nods slightly and says, "Mrs. Keller. May I ask what kind of fish this is?"

"I was wondering that myself," says Mr. Cartwright.

I smile painfully at them. "Roasted walleye, I think."

Bi'ch moves at a glacial pace and spoons gloppy pink sauce over our fish heads. I think it might be mayonnaise and Tabasco sauce. Next she goes around like a steady snail and—*thwap!*—slaps a greasy spatula of sautéed greens on each plate. One of our Japanese guests asks to use the bathroom and I gratefully get up, which is no small task when seated at a sawed-off Ping-Pong table, and lead him to the guest bathroom by the hand. I myself dash upstairs and vault over Ace, who's parked on the top step. He growls at me as I sail past. "What's *your* problem?" I ask him, running into the bedroom, past Trevor watching TV on the bed, and I slam into the bathroom, where I sit on a stack of towels, hoping to mask the sound, and fart.

Ace starts barking. Damn dog. All this and I still beat our guest back to the table. He takes a long time to come back and we sit there silently, the food getting cold, waiting for him to return before we start eating. Ace starts barking again upstairs. I'm going to kill that dog. I'm about to go get him when our bathroom-bound guest returns and we start eating. Oh, how I yearn for that wonderful time a minute ago, when we weren't. The fish is bitter and gritty, riddled with sandy bits we must discreetly spit out. Each bite of fish is followed by . . . would I call it a burning sensation? Yes. I might.

I smile at the Japanese man seated next to me and he bows his head slightly. I bow my head slightly back, hitting it on my water glass. "Do your people eat this kind of fish?" I ask. "Do you mind that your fish has a fish head?"

"What's wrong with you?" Brad whispers.

"I was just asking!" I whisper back.

Mr. Cartwright sets his fork down. "What *is* this kind of fish? You said walleye?"

I nod and smile at him. "We caught it right here, off the end of our dock!"

One of Mr. Cartwright's bushy eyebrows crawls like a caterpillar up his head. *"What?"* he says.

I repeat myself. "We caught it right here in the lake, off the end of the dock."

"The fish we're eating . . . came from *Lake Minnetonka?*"

"Yes, sir!" I grin. "Now that's eating locally!"

Mr. Cartwright puts his napkin on the table. "So, I take it, Mr. Keller, that you're not aware of the public health warning for Lake Minnetonka . . . banning all fish consumption?"

I freeze and say, "Pardon?"

Mr. Cartwright stands up. "Laura, get your coat."

I look over helplessly at Brad. *"What's happening?"*

"Blue-green algae!" Mr. Cartwright says. "That's what's happening! The heat wave caused blue-green algae to bloom all over the place!"

"Well, we just scraped that off . . ." I tell him.

"Really! Did you scrape off the neurotoxins too?"

"Probably . . ." I say blankly.

"Mrs. Keller, fish caught in a blue-green algae bloom causes bacterial infections, tissue damage, paralysis, respiratory failure, even tumors."

The Japanese start looking at each other and whispering. I distinctly hear one say, *"Law and order."* I'm hoping he means the TV show. I throw myself on Mr. Cartwright's mercy. "Oh,

Mr. Cartwright, I beg you, please don't go! You don't think one little piece of fish could cause—"

"Liver cancer!" he says. "Chromosome loss! DNA damage!"

The translator goes apoplectic.

"Now, Mr. Cartwright," Brad says. "I can assure you that my wife didn't know there was any fish advisory in effect—"

"Well, I can assure *you*," Mr. Cartwright barks, "that there *is*. Now, pardon us, but this is nothing to mess around with."

"Where . . . are you going?" I ask.

"The hospital, to get an antibiotic shot, and I suggest you all do the same." The translator rattles off what must be the Japanese equivalent of "Your hostess has tried to kill you; please follow the fat white man if you'd like to possibly survive." All the Japanese businessmen get up quickly and head for their coats in the front hall.

Overhead the chandelier flickers.

"Please accept our apologies," Brad says, his voice soaked with defeat. The tall Japanese man bows slightly. He begins to say something, but his sentiment is cut short by a strange sound above us, a queer clinking of glass crystals that makes everyone look up.

There's a creaking sound in the ceiling.

"*Oh no . . .*" I whisper.

The chandelier suddenly gives way.

Thwissss-*ba-boom*! The massive chandelier plummets down, crashing with an explosion on the marble floor. We stand motionless, in a rising plume of dust. Nobody was hurt, which is too bad. A little blood and we might've all known what to do next. Instead the Japanese stand there staring at me in a V formation.

Then I fart loudly.

Get Ready/Get Set

8
Rule of Thumb

Brad is furious with me.

He won't even look at me the next morning. I try to make him talk to me, which is a mistake. I'm following him into the bathroom, begging him to listen to me, when he steps right in a pile of fresh dog poop with his bare foot. "What the fuck!" Brad shouts. "Why's that fucking dog always shitting in here?" Ace has a thing about pooping in the bathroom. I think it's because we use it for that function and he assumes he should too, but Brad says it's because I potty-trained him in a bathroom on our honeymoon and he's too stupid to unlearn it.

He pushes away the towel that I try to hand him and sticks his whole foot in the sink, blasting the faucet. "Tell me this," he says. "Why does everything always go to shit when you're around?"

"What?" I stand there staring at him and holding the towel.

He snorts and shakes his head. "You know, we gave you *one thing* to do. One thing. We even got a fucking caterer to do the cooking, since everyone knows you can't be bothered!"

"I would've cooked!"

"You *did* cook, unfortunately! Jesus, I give you one damn thing to do and it's a total disaster! You nearly killed everyone!"

"I don't think the fish I served was that poisonous."

"Do you hear yourself? Is that honestly a sentence that anyone should have to say in their lifetime? And what am I supposed to say to the next batch of investors we want to entertain? 'Hey, guys, come on over to our house, my wife might kill you, but she might not! She's wacky that way!' No, what do you care? Serve the fish and see who keels over later. *Jesus,* I wish I had your problems. You sit around here all day worrying about what shoes to wear while I'm out there every Goddamned day, everyone watching me, my Goddamned sister breathing down my neck, just *waiting* for me to fuck up so she can run and snitch to Daddy. Do you know what she'll do with this? She'll have a fucking field day. That's what. She's been telling Dad all this shit about me, saying how she'd do a better job, how she has more experience, how she isn't a drunk, blah, blah, blah . . . She has him halfway convinced to cut me out!"

"Brad, your father would never cut you out—"

"Oh really? He told Mom he wasn't sure about my negotiating skills. That's why he had us throw the dinner without him here. He wanted to see if I could close the deal without him. Well, ha-ha! I closed the deal, all right! Slammed the door right in their faces! They're all on a flight back to Tokyo! Won't be seeing them any time soon."

"But they still might—"

"Nope! They're out. Todd just called."

"No. Really?"

"Yep. Really."

"I'm so sorry."

"Me too. Sorry I ever thought you could pull this fucking

thing off. I should've known you'd screw it up. Mom said you would."

I stand there, my face burning with shame. Tears start to well.

He turns off the faucet and blots his foot on a dirty towel on the floor. "And would you get rid of that fucking maid?" he says. "Jesus! She's freaky as hell and she can't clean for shit."

"But . . . your mother hired her!"

"I don't give a fuck! Get rid of her."

"But it's not their fault the dinner went wrong! It's my fault, it's all my fault! They were only trying to help, you can't fire them because of something I did!" Hot tears start rolling down my cheeks. "Please, Brad!"

"Oh Christ, now you're crying? Terrific. Why are *you* crying? I'm the one who has to fucking tell my dad the Tokyo deal is dead! Fine, don't fire them! Do whatever the fuck you want to. I don't even care anymore. God, I have to get out of here, I can't stand being here." He pushes past me and storms out of the bedroom. A few minutes later I hear the front door slam shut. Then he's gone.

I run and go get my phone. I have to find out what happened. I have to prove last night wasn't my fault! Okay, the fish might have been my fault, but I should get an "A" for effort and I still don't think the fish I served was that poisonous.

I call Emily at work and then I remember it's Sunday. I hunt down her home number, but there's no answer there either. I call three more times and leave two messages asking her to *please* call me back. Then I call the caterer. No answer there either. I am getting pissed beyond pissed. I want answers, dammit! I grab my purse and drive all the way out to Burnsville, where I storm into the caterer's shop, march right past the girl at the front desk, and burst into the steamy kitchen demanding an explanation. The caterer, who has a smudged apron on and a spatula in one hand, looks at me, confused. "But . . . we're loading up for your party right now," she says.

"What?"

"Your office called and rescheduled it."

"*Who* rescheduled it?"

"Someone named Emily? She called last week. Said you had to move dinner to tonight. I had to scramble just to find wait-staff. We already had two other events scheduled."

I thank her for her time and storm back out to the car. I sit in the parking lot and speed-dial Emily forty-two times in a row until she gets out of the shower and answers. She's confused too. "But . . . M-Mrs. Keller *told* me to change the date," she stammers. "She called last week to reschedule it."

"My mother-in-law?"

"She said you had to change the date because of a personal emergency."

"What?"

"Oh no, I should've double-checked the date with you! This is all my fault! I'm so so so sorry . . . I'm so stupid!" She breaks down crying and ten minutes later I still can't get her to stop.

I finally hang up on her and call Mother Keller, who, oddly, picks up on the first ring. She pulls a stunningly impressive award-winning denial act and says she has *no idea* what I'm talking about. She never changed the date of the dinner. That's preposterous. "Really, Jennifer," she says indignantly. "It's bad enough you tried to poison your guests, but blaming it on me? Pitiful. I would've thought you'd be better at taking responsibility for your mistakes by now, there've been so many."

My heart is racing. I want to reach through the phone and strangle her. I tell her, "I did not do this! Emily says *you* called her and *you* changed the date!"

"Oh, I see! Is that what Emily said? And does Emily have any proof of that? A voice mail, perhaps? An e-mail? Something written down on paper?"

"Well . . . no . . ." *Oh shit.*

"Then it's her word against mine, isn't it, Jennifer? Now, think back and tell me exactly what happened. Naturally I'll believe you. If you say she said I changed the date, then I'll know she's been lying to you and I'll have to terminate her immediately."

"You can't do that!"

"Ah, but I can. She has no proof to back up her statement and neither do you."

My eye twitches slightly. I think I might be having a stroke. "So," I whisper. "It's just that easy?"

"And it always will be."

A palpable tension races between us. I have no idea what will happen next.

"Of course, if this was just a miscommunication," she says, "then I'd understand. I know how hard it can be to work with you. Oh, and doesn't young Emily have a wedding coming up? How terrible to lose her job now. Of course it *was* just a miscommunication between the two of you; she must feel awful. Maybe we should give her a little raise to cheer her up? They always get so excited when you toss a few pennies at them, don't they?"

I can't seem to breathe.

My head is like a tiny balloon floating miles above earth.

"Now, I'll believe whatever you tell me, Jennifer. So just tell me the truth. Is Emily lying and claiming that I changed the date? Or was there just a miscommunication between you two?"

It is an act of fierce will to reach through the flames of anger in my head and try to form words. "I . . . think it was," I whisper.

"Was what?"

"A small . . . miscommunication."

"Ah, I thought so. Pity. But these things do happen. Best thing is to learn from your mistakes and move on. You know, young brides deserve nice presents. Why don't you pick out something nice for Emily and tell her it's from all of us?"

"Sure."

"Oh, and do tell Brad I need to speak to him. All right?"

"Okay."

I drive home, sailing along empty ribbons of road. Overhead, deep V's of geese bisect the sky, all flying south for the winter, and it takes all my strength not to turn south and fly right along with them. When I get home, there's a Lemon Fresh Furniture Cleaners van parked in my driveway and two guys are carrying furniture back into the house. "Hey, got a big party tonight, huh?" one says. "Bet you throw big parties all the time!"

"Yep." I smile at him. "Big party tonight. Big big parties . . . all the time."

I take a long hot bath and stare at the water. I check my messages. Nothing. I have no idea when Brad is coming home . . . or if he's coming home ever again. The thought of him leaving ignites cold panic in me. I call him sixteen times in a row, but he never calls back.

On Monday I take Emily to lunch at Pastamania! She orders the Minnesota linguini (linguini and Swedish meatballs) and I order the pasta carbonara. "Here," I say when we're seated. "I wanted to get you something." I hand her a small silver envelope. Inside is three thousand dollars. Her face falls when she sees it and she says, "Are you firing me?"

She thinks it's a severance package. I explain it's quite the contrary. "I messed up, Emily. My mother-in-law left me a message about changing the dinner, but dingbat me . . . I didn't listen to the whole message. So, I just wanted to tell you how sorry I am and . . . Mrs. Keller knows it wasn't your fault. It was mine. Just a . . . miscommunication."

Emily's so happy she cries into her linguini.

Over the next few weeks, I see very little of my husband. He leaves the house early and comes home late. Often after I'm already asleep. He doesn't talk to me, gives me only monosyllabic answers to any questions I ask. It's like we're roommates who aren't even friends. Like some awkward twist of circumstance has thrown us together here temporarily, and we just have to make the best of it until we both go our separate ways. Only I'm still here, right where he left me. I watch him when he sleeps, so sweet curled on his side, one hand tucked under his chin. I study his face. So gentle when he's asleep, so stern and unforgiving when he's awake.

On long, lonely nights, I try to occupy my hours with healthier pursuits. Yoga, meditation, journaling, reading self-help books like *The Complete Idiot's Guide to Self-Esteem.* My shelves used to be filled with self-help books for single girls, but now they're filled with self-help books for married women. The advice is actually quite similar. I purchased a wagonload of them at Barnes & Noble. I asked a smiling bookseller named Kelley for popular titles concerning marriage. She was the one who helped me buy all my self-help books about being single. She pointed me down a self-help aisle. I wound up with a bookshelf filled with books like:

Keep That Man!
Get Him Back NOW!
How to Seduce Anyone in Five Dates or Less!
What Men Want

Why Men Leave
What Women Do Wrong
Marriage Isn't Supposed to Be Easy
Save Your Marriage, Save Yourself
Ten Ways You're Driving Your Husband to Drink

I write down the upshot of all my studies for myself, and possibly for Emily. I admit my current sour mood forces me to put a somewhat negative spin on things . . .

Top Five Traits of Good Wives

1. They cook, clean, and shop. (*Translation: Become a gourmet chef and economical wizard and keep a ready-for-surgery-clean home.*)
2. They're not high-maintenance, and they're proficient at organizing and making budgets for the home. (*Translation: Shop like a frugal Depression-era war widow for yourself, but gleefully purchase any item your husband requests, like Brad's new electric shoe buffer.*)
3. They speak positively about their husbands in public. Always. (*Translation: Glow about hubby. When he's accused of scandal, weep and deny.*)
4. They keep their minds and bodies in shape. (*Translation: Go easy on the gravy boat, lady! And the independent thinking.*)
5. They enjoy having a healthy, monogamous sex life. (*Translation: Enjoy whatever sexual positions/acts/routines your husband does. Whatever he likes is to be considered "normal."*)

Top Five Traits of Bad Wives

1. They neglect household duties. (*Translation: Don't leave scum rings in bathtubs or forget to buy toilet paper.*)
2. They're unwise with money and make secret purchases. (*Translation: Don't buy anything you don't have permission to and don't hide your expensive purchases in the garage.*)
3. They tease and speak negatively about their husbands in public. (*Translation: Don't say anything bad about your husband ever. Even if he throws you down a flight of stairs, smile and say he's wonderful!*)
4. They dress in a slovenly manner and are careless about their appearance. (*Translation: He can wear sweatpants to bed but you can't.*)
5. They trick their husbands and pretend to enjoy sexual relations. (*Translation: Don't agree to oral sex and then use a sock slimed with hand lotion to do the job.*)

I can never show these lists to Emily. She'll think I'm insane. There's so much that's hard to talk about. Like loneliness and how that seems to be a large part of being together. Sometimes I walk through the empty house and I turn on every light, until each room glows and the house is ablaze. From bay windows I watch warm light from our windows dappling the dark water. People ask how I'm doing and I say great. I can't bring myself to tell them the truth. I have no close friends I see anymore, no close family. My husband ignores me and his family dislikes me. I don't fit in at all and yet I can go anywhere I like, buy anything I want. I've never had so much, and somehow I've never felt like I had so little. I never had much at my little apartment, but everything I had was mine. My retro toy collection, my squidgy bath mat . . . and Mrs. Biggles, my beloved cat. Here . . . what do I have? *What can I say is mine?* Other people chose everything. I've never been this safe and this close to starving at the same time.

When Brad finally comes home there are strange calls late at night. He runs vaguely worded errands that sometimes last for hours. I'm starting to really believe he's having an affair. How would I know? It's not like I can ask him. Instead, I ask the online community, read articles on how to tell if your husband's cheating. The culmination of reading hundreds of such articles is:

Top Ten Signs Your Husband Is Cheating

1. You get recurring yeast infections.
2. Your husband's laptop and cell phone have a password.
3. You find strange receipts in his coat pockets for bars and nightclubs that have names like Liaisons, the Beaver Club, and Paroxysm.
4. Arguments ensue when you ask your husband where the *fuck* he goes at night.
5. He gets repeated late-night phone calls from secretaries, paralegal assistants, dental hygienists, pregnant porn stars, or any other female strangers.
6. You smell perfume on your husband's trousers that isn't yours.
7. Missing cash.
8. Missing jewelry.
9. Blondes named Candi, Melodi, or any name ending with an "i" keep stopping by your house and sitting on the doorstep crying.

10. Oozing sores of any kind on your husband's body, especially on the tip of his penis, which he says are just an allergy to something, like linen.

I obsessively take online quizzes like "The Cheater Test," "Big Cheater Quiz," "Find Out If He's Cheating on You," and "Did He Ever Even Love You? Find Out in Five Questions or Less." They all ask questions like:

Has your husband seemed distant lately?
Not at all. Brad maintains the distance of most rogue cosmonauts drifting through deep space and orbiting far-off planets like Oh Baby Yes Baby and the exotic Escort Service 9. He's fearlessly explored countless moons and I know he frequents his favorite galaxies: the Big Fat Liar's Way and Jesus, That's My Wife Again.

Does your husband check in with you regularly?
Brad checks in very regularly. He sticks to a strict schedule and calls me every single never. He started to never call me back when we first met and he's so cute about it, he's kept it up even to this day. He *still* never calls me. Never. Didn't call yesterday, won't call tomorrow, and any minute now . . . he won't call today.

Have you and your husband stopped having fun together?
Stopped having fun? Of course not. That implies we even started. Brad and I have always made it a priority to bicker, argue, and sulk whenever possible. We try to put petty things aside. We never let a sunny day or our anniversary get in the way of what's *important* to us, which is finding out who's

right, crucifying the one who's wrong, and of course, assigning blame.

Does your husband check out other girls?
Brad only checks out one kind of woman: *women with eyeballs.* He's so specific, it's weird. He will *not* ogle a woman if she's missing even *a single eyeball,* no matter how gorgeous she is. It's his thing. Once we saw a woman at the mall wearing a patch over her eye, like a lady pirate. I thought she looked mysterious but Brad was almost grossed out. Luckily we ran into some teenage girls trying on bikinis and *whew.* They had eyeballs and my sweetie was right back in the old leering saddle, mentally doing each underage girl there. *Relief.* I feel silly getting upset about it. How can I deny him something as small as an eyeball?

Does your husband get phone calls or text messages late at night?
Does he ever. That's like peak texting time. I'm not sure about phone calls; he usually jumps in the car and takes off when the phone rings. I asked him where he was going one time, and he said to the corner of Nacho and Beeswax.

As the weeks drag by and the weather gets colder I read self-help books and watch helpful YouTube videos about the signs of an unfaithful spouse. Also about developing a reasonable action plan to make sure the son of a bitch stops getting his icky sticky. It's all information written primarily by women for women, and horror stories abound. Each one is more awful than the next. There's the woman who caught her husband having sex with both her best friends, the woman who walked in on her husband four-to-the-floor going at it piston-style with *her gay brother,* the woman who watched her husband ker-floomping a Swedish exchange student live in their hot tub while his buddies watched, and of course the woman who caught her husband playing Pink Lipstick with their beloved Great Dane, Alphonso. She sued him for divorce on the grounds he had an extramarital affair.

I try everything I can think of to get Brad's attention. I go to Jeremy's spa and rebleach my hair, and I buy more expensive clothing, better makeup, sexier lingerie, but he takes no notice of all my improvements. He's always working, and when he's home, he seems busy and annoyed. Nothing is quite good enough.

Not even when Mother Keller nominates us for this year's annual Heck of a Home Designer Home Showcase. We're selected as a featured house, which means thousands of people will troop through our home and admire our lifestyle. A woman from the showcase calls and says she's putting together the official catalog. Can she schedule time for a photograph? I tell Brad the exciting news and he says, "Well, you better make sure you get the house cleaned up. You don't want them to see it this way."

Everything seems hard. My life seems like a low-budget community play. All the scenes are awkward, every line is inauthentic, and every movement is skeptically scrutinized by a surly audience and deemed inferior. A trip to the grocery store, a quick run to the club, a quiet dinner for two at home, and I'm so nervous, unsteady, and panicked I'm ready for a double hit of Benadryl and a glass of wine as big as my head . . . even if it's noon.

I wake up sweating, in panic. Maybe our marriage was doomed before it ever began. I'm working on this awful theory that some people are just not designed for happiness. They lack certain wiring or are unable to make enough of the right chemical compounds to feel happy. If our eye color and hair texture and taste buds are so specific as to be completely unique in the universe for all time in all directions . . . then why wouldn't our brains be that unusual too?

I thought things would get easier in time, but they've only become more complicated than I ever could have imagined. My low-grade anxiety's become outright ugly panic. I don't know, I'm looking around this place and I have everything I ever wanted. Maybe I just didn't want them in the first place . . . but— and the thought makes me queasy—what if I'm programmed to be unhappy no matter what I have or where I am or who I'm with?

Maybe some of us are just broken.

Maybe this sadness is an inseparable element of my bones and blood.

9

Onward, Christian Shoppers

Snow.

Lots of it. The whole lawn looks like one enormous Sara Lee pound cake. I fight the urge to run through it zigzagging like we used to do when we were kids. There's something so refreshing about tromping on un-tromped-upon banks of freshly fallen snow. Brad's out of town, and I don't know that we already have a snow removal service, so I shovel the whole front walkway by hand, panting and feeling near death when I'm done . . . which is about twenty-two seconds before the guy in the little Bobcat shows up and plows the whole driveway in under five minutes.

Tonight is Supper Club. Supper Club is a dinner that Hailey and Lenny throw at their house every month or so; it's like a potluck dinner party for friends and family and people who keep showing up. They've been throwing these strangely themed dinner parties for years, even though by now they're fairly tame. They used to be somewhat dangerous.

The infamous Hotdish 'n' Heavy Metal Supper Club had many poorly aimed and very illegal fireworks, which were set off to deafeningly loud heavy metal music. The night ended with a citation from the police, many crying children, and two dead pigeons that had unfortunately been flying overhead.

Twisty Chili Supper Club got messy quick when guests had to play Twister in high winds while eating piping-hot bowls of chili. We stopped after Lenny accidentally dumped a Crock-Pot of molten-hot cheeseburger chili on somebody. Lenny kicked it up a notch for his final activity-themed Supper Club, Gumbo 'n' Guns, which basically ended before it began, when Lenny accidentally shot Chucker in the leg with a BB gun. Chucker still has the BB in his leg.

Tonight's Supper Club theme is Fucked-up Pancake Night. There are rum pancake shakes, a deep-dish steak pancake bake, pancake chowder, pancake bacon, sugared pancake balls, pancake Jell-O, and pancake pudding cups. Mom has left already by the time I get there—I guess Dad's not feeling well—but she left me a note that says she's cleaning out the attic and I should stop by to sort through some of my old junk. Lenny comes up and hands me a beer.

"Lookin' pretty fancy-pantsy there, Jen."

"Am I?" I'm wearing chocolate jeans, a buttery-soft nutmeg-colored cashmere turtleneck, and a long green leather Marc Jacobs jacket. Accent pieces are tall leather riding boots and yellow topaz chandelier earrings. I thought I was dressing down. The truth is, I'm starting to have the opposite problem of the one I used to have, which was being constantly underdressed. I wore sweatshirts outside, something I'd never do now, unless it was a designer sweatshirt. Now I'm overdressed for things.

"Where's Pee Boy?" Lenny asks. I tell him Brad's been really busy. He had to work.

"Oh, I'll *bet* he's busy," Lenny says, swigging his beer. Lenny's the foreman of the Keller's loading dock. They gave him a job after Lenny lost his job at Hormel, though we still sometimes call him the Ham Man. "Got an awful lot of *cheap crap* showing up at our *American* warehouse," Lenny says. "I'll tell you something else, my union guys ain't too happy about them Chinesey products comin' through the store."

"Shut up, Lenny," Hailey snaps. "Don't say *'Chinesey.'*"

"*Ow!* Quit it, woman! What's wrong with 'Chinesey'?"

"I told you at our wedding, you don't say 'Chinesey'! You're supposed to say 'Oriental.'"

"No, no you're not!" I shake my head. "I told you guys that at your wedding, remember?"

"Why? What was Chinesey at the wedding?" Lenny asks her.

"God, Lenny! Only everything. All the lanterns and the kimonos my bridesmaids wore. Well"—her eyes dart over at me—"that *some* of them wore."

"Don't start," I warn her. "Don't give me that look."

I've told her a million times that the bottle of Drano *fell* out of the cabinet on top of me and bleached my dress before I could even stand up. That's my story and I'm sticking to it. I grab another beer. I ask Hailey if she wants one and she shakes her head no. Lenny's still confused. "Man, I thought our wedding had a Mexican theme," he says. "Or like, chili peppers."

All of a sudden loud music blares over the speaker and I moan.

"No, not 'The Pancake Song'! No no no . . ."

"The Pancake Song" is this weird children's song Lenny found about a pancake named Flapjack who runs away from home and some sort of Butter Pat people help him escape the Bacon Man and he becomes unlikely friends with Pokey Fork. The plot's a little hard to follow. Anyway, on the chorus, "*Watch him rumble, see him tumble, run-runaway pancake you're in trouble!*" the whole room stops what they're doing and starts doing the pancake dance, which involves wheeling your arms around like a windmill while twirling. There's always a lot of spilled beverages afterward. I wind up whirling right into Lenny, and I shout, "Lenny! Just out of curiosity, how hard is it to find a ship's manifest?"

"*A what now?*" he shouts back.

"A ship's manifest! How do you find the actual cargo ship a product was shipped in?"

"The ship?" he says, knocking the drink out of my hand. "Dunno, we mostly got trucks at the dock!" When "The Pancake Song" is over, I go get a new beer. I hear someone say, "Hey, chief," and I turn around. There's Nick, the guy from the vet's office, wearing an orange hoodie, grinning at me.

"Hey, Nick!" I smile. "Stalk me much?"

"Much as I can!" He nods. "Meet my new pal, here. Pastor Joe."

"Hi, Pastor Joe." I shake his hand. "Pleased to meet you."

Pastor Joe is creep city. He has dark eyes and a fucked-up crooked haircut and he's wearing a JCPenney beige turtleneck sweater with patches on the elbows and a white collar sewn on the turtleneck. He says he's living next door, in the creepy rental house that's been empty for six months. He got locked out and came over and peered through the windows. Naturally when Lenny saw a freaky-looking peeping-tom "man of the cloth" leering into their windows, he invited him over. "The Lord works in mysterious ways, children," Pastor Joe says, and wanders away.

"*What a weirdo!*" I whisper to Nick.

"Weird as hell," he says. "That's why I came over here. I was sure he was gonna start shooting people. Thought you might provide protection."

"You can count on me, Nick. Call me Jennifer."

"Well, Miss Jennifer, the only thing I think that anyone can count on in this crazy old world . . . is that Pastor Joe *will* kill all of us. Probably one day very soon." He smirks. "Saw you do the Pancake Dance."

"Oh, too good for the Pancake Dance?" I ask him.

"I'm better than the Pancake Dance. You should see my Waffle Trot."

I snort, despite trying not to. "Sounds very sexy," I tell him.

"Too sexy." He sighs. "Got caught up in it. Wound up in a seedy Tijuana bar, showing my puff pastry for bread crumbs. I'll never let anyone near my waffle again. At least I saved my doughnut hole." Hailey walks by holding a bottle of lemon spring water and I tell her to start drinking like a man. She ignores me and heads for kitchen. I excuse myself and follow her.

"Why aren't you drinking?" I ask her.

"I am!" she says. "I had a couple beers earlier."

"No, you didn't. I haven't seen you drink a beer all night."

"Oh, okay, Matlock. Good to know you're on the case."

"Oh my God!" My eyes widen. "You're wearing . . . yoga pants."

"So? You look like a contestant on *Star Search*."

"You're . . . you're pregnant!"

"What?" She makes a face. "No I'm not."

"You *are*!"

"Shut up already, I'm *not*."

"Liar. You totally, totally *are*."

"Just keep your voice down, would you? I gained a little weight. That's all. Plus I got my period yesterday, so I'm bloated. Okay? That's why I'm wearing my yoga pants."

I stare at her, speechless.

"Jen, I'd tell you if I was pregnant, wouldn't I?"

"No," I snort. "You'd totally lie about it."

"Well I'm not." She sighs. "Absolutely positively *not*. Okay? Trust me. I'm just *fat*."

I gasp and nearly drop my beer bottle. "You *are*!" I hiss at her. "*You're freaking pregnant!* The only reason you'd say you were *fat* is so no one would think you were *pregnant*!"

"*Jennifer, please!*"

"Oh my *God*! You look so . . . like you're about to burst or something. What's in there? *Quadruplets?* Are you like an Octomom? Shit, I can *see* it. Everything on you looks *pregnant*. Big. Ripe! Like you're gearing up to . . . *hatch*! Your face has this weird shine and your eyes are bright . . . like a vampire's!"

"*Shit*." Hailey sits down. "How could you tell?"

"Wait. Seriously? You really are?"

She rolls her eyes at me. "Yes. I am. It happened on your honeymoon."

Then it's like the room tips and all the sound drains out. I can suddenly hear my heart beating. Slow, steady. "My honeymoon?" My sister got pregnant . . . on my honeymoon? Of course she did. That's so typical. "Right, I should've known you'd get pregnant on my honeymoon."

"*See?*" Hailey says. "That's why I didn't tell you. I knew you'd be all weird about it. I'm having . . . twins."

"Twins?" I stare at her. I can't believe this is happening. I walk out of the kitchen and into the backyard for some fresh air. This is the worst night of my—*whooomph!* A snowball beans me right in the side of the head. I hate everything right now.

I go home to take a hot bath.

Then I drink my weight in red wine and watch the Lifetime channel because it makes me cry, every time. Tonight it's a movie called *When Love Fails, Sometimes Only Sick Children and Lost Dogs Can Bring People Back Together*. I grab hold of Ace and cry my eyes out until he starts to howl. I fall asleep with the TV on, amidst wadded-up tissue and empty wine bottles.

The phone wakes me up.

It's Sarah. She's calling in a cold rage.

"Did you buy Trevor a Barbie lunch box?" she says.

I don't have any idea what she's talking about.

"Oh, at the store? Yeah, Trev wanted to get a new lunch box, so I let him pick one out."

"You *let* him *pick* one?" she snaps. "Seriously?"

"Is that a problem?"

"A problem? I can't believe how unbelievably *irresponsible* you are!"

I can't believe her. "Am I missing something, Sarah? Trevor wanted a new lunch box, so I let him pick one . . . at Keller's Department Store. What's the problem?"

"The *problem* is that he picked out a *Barbie* lunch box!"

"Oh. Is that . . . bad?"

"Is that *bad*?" she says.

"Based on your tone of voice, I'm guessing it's . . . bad."

"Of course it's bad! You're unbelievable! Truly! Did you even *know* Trevor picked out a Barbie lunch box?"

"Well, if memory serves me, I believe Barbie's name *did* come up in the lunch box discussion . . . but so did Spider-Man's and the Incredible Hulk's and a few others. I just thought it was best to let Trevor work it out."

"You did? You thought you'd let Trevor *work it out*? Fantastic, Jennifer. Do you know how hard we work to get him to pick gender-appropriate toys and clothing? It's constant with that Goddamned kid! Barbie is banned in this house. *Banned!*"

"Well, I didn't know that. We were running late and it was a . . . confusing moment."

"A confusing moment? I'll give you a confusing moment! How's this? Imagine Trevor bringing a bright pink Barbie lunch box to school with him! A prestigious *Christian* school with *strict rules* and *firm values*! They suspended him!"

"Why?"

"Because a little boy does not bring a pink lunch box to school! Especially if it has a perky blonde on it, wearing a rhinestone bikini and rhinestones in her ponytail!"

Then she curses and hangs up on me.

Classy.

As the weeks drag on, I start occupying myself with anything I can find to distract me.

I finally submit myself to the God Squad and am immediately voted in almost unanimously. One person says nay, but the vote is anonymous, so I'm left with my own imagination. My best guess is it was Mother Keller trying to make me look bad, or I did something to set off Martha Woodcock's rage counter.

I volunteer on the Youth Program committee, figuring it has to be more fun than organizing charity jumbles or scheduling confirmation classes or choosing industrial tampon receptacles for the girls' bathroom toilet stalls. My committee organizes youth group events for our high school students, like the Boundary Waters Camping for Christ and Salvation Canoe Trek and the annual Back to Basic Morals and School Prayer Picnic.

They launched the new "Episco-Pals" program, an international Christian-based pen-pals program that became controversial after several girls fell in love with their overseas opposite-sex correspondents. Parents demanded the program be pulled before any daughters ran off or lobbed their maidenheads at the feet of whatever swarthy foreigners starting showing up at the door. The subcommittee is also planning the youth group's Valentine's Day Abstinence Dance and has already booked Urge Alert, a Christian sex-ed dance troupe, who'll perform their hit abstinence dance routine: "Don't Scratch the Itch."

The big event that everyone's excited about is this spring.

On Fire for Jesus is an action-packed teen worship rally up at Camp Wapi-Wapawee in Minnetrista. There'll be food, games, arts and crafts, nature walks, a Maypole, and a huge maze made of hay bales. The rally is aimed at underprivileged inner-city youth, who'll be bused in from all over the city and treated to Jesus-approved fun. As a welcome present, I'm given the honored task of overseeing the big bonfire and wrap-up sermon given by Pastor Mike. Luckily I'm given two other women to help me, both named Louise.

Louise and Louise look alike, talk alike, and both have watery blue eyes. I have a heck of a time telling them apart and decide to call the Louise that's slightly bigger Big Louise. The other one has a slight peach fuzz on her lip. I call her Dirty Louise. The Louises are tasked with helping me plan activities for the kids as they sit around the big bonfire. The fun and games will lead up to Pastor Mike's campfire sermon and his invitation to the unsaved to accept Christ. It's like the big sell right at the end and we're the warm-up act.

My first thoughts for fun activities teens can do around a bonfire are of the ones I enjoyed, which were primarily illegal, unadvisable, and/or dangerous: drinking, smoking, whipping batteries into the fire, and having a whole lot of unsafe sex. My subcommittee members have more sanitized ideas. Dirty Louise wants campfire tales with a moral ending and Big Louise votes for skits. She *loves, loves, loves* skits.

I hate Big Louise.

I also volunteer for the Senior Fit! program. It's a low-impact exercise program for the over-seventy gang. It's the day I'm supposed to help the dance teacher teach the senior citizens basic dance steps but then the dance teacher calls in sick at the last minute. I'm stuck there alone, and then of all things, I see someone who looks like Brad walking down the hall with a tall mysterious female. My stomach gets queasy. I feel cold. Brad's supposed to be out of town.

I quickly excuse myself from the classroom and follow them to the parking lot, where they get into a car I don't recognize. I call Christopher on his cell and say he has to get down here and teach this class for me—it's an emergency. He sighs and says, "Oh, Lucy. You so crazy."

I tell the restless seniors that their dance instructor will be here in five minutes. Then I take off in search of Brad. True to his word, Christopher arrives and saves the day. He teaches the senior citizens of Grace-Trinity some basic dance moves, which he picked up in San Francisco while working in a bar called the Manhole.

They're stripper dances.

The first move is called Pickin' the Cherries, where you stand in place, reaching up to pluck imaginary cherries from the air. The second move is called Driving the Bus, where you hold your hands straight out, as if you're grasping an invisible steering wheel, and you turn the wheel back and forth while swaying your hips. The third move is called Flossing the Teeth, and you smile wide while holding a fist on either side of your cheeks, then you pump your fists from side to side, like you're flossing your teeth with a three-foot-long piece of invisible string.

It was all in vain, however; when I got back to the parking lot, Brad and the woman were gone. Pulse racing, heart beating, I still got in my car and started off in the direction I thought they probably went and wound up circling around aimlessly for hours.

Why does everything feel dark and wrong? What am I supposed to do in that big empty house all alone? What is everyone else doing? Are there other unhappy housewives drinking wine alone? When I get home I pour myself a glass of wine and I actually take Brad's binoculars and peer through the trees at our neighbors, scanning across the tangled spans of dark branches for lit windows. I'm not trying to spy, I just want to see what they're doing.

All I can see is dark trees.

Then Brad calls from the airport. I can hear the loudspeakers announcing flight departures in the background. He's on his way home, he says. Do I have anything at home for dinner? That wasn't him with another woman. Still, that doesn't mean he hasn't been with one while he was traveling. It doesn't mean anything. Brad comes home and we sit through a sullen dinner at the dining room table. "You missed Supper Club again," I say sulkily.

"I was working."

"You're always working."

"Hey, we can switch places any time you like, Imelda."

"What's that supposed to mean?"

"It means I don't like how much I work either, but someone has to pay for your world's-most-expensive-shoe collection, so lay off."

"Oh right. You're doing all this for me. I forgot. I just thought husbands spent time with their wives. I guess I was wrong.'"

"You know *why* I'm gone all the time, Jennifer? Because I'm out there trying to scare up new investors, since the Japanese investors strangely *pulled out* after you tried to poison them. I mean, do you think Donald Trump has to deal with this kind of shit? Do you think Ivana accidentally burns dinner up or loses track of where the dining room table went?"

"He divorced her."

"Can I count on you for help? No, I can't. All I can count on you for is being negative and bitching at me. I actually have another dinner tomorrow night with an investor group from church. Did you know that? Did Todd call you up, or Emily, or my mother? Did anyone ask you to help out with it?"

"No."

"Know why? Because they're all scared to death you're going to ruin it! That's why. These people might actually be able to bail us out of the mess we're in . . . if nothing goes insanely wrong during dinner! But you know, you still managed to make it awkward, because they're all bringing their wives and they asked me to bring you, but I can't, can I? Because you're not normal. Because nobody knows what completely fucked-up thing you're gonna do next, right?"

Hot tears well up in my eyes. "I'm sorry," I whisper.

He pauses and pinches the bridge of his nose, as if stanching a headache. "I'm going to bed," he says. "Good night."

"Okay," I say in a small voice. "I'm sorry."

"Yeah . . . me too. For a lot of things."

"I know you're tired of me."

"Jen . . ."

"I know! I mess everything up, so I try harder, and then I just mess up worse."

"Jen, I gotta get some sleep for the meeting."

"Okay. I understand. I do."

He shakes his head. "Look. If you want . . . If you want to go to dinner tomorrow night, they'd like to meet you and I'd like to do anything that makes them . . . happy. So, if you think you can handle it, just be ready by six thirty. Okay?"

I look up at him and nod. "Okay," I say. He leaves. I stifle a sob. I have to win him back.

The next day I'm ready right on time for the new investor meeting. At six o'clock sharp I'm standing with my coat on in the front hall, wearing dark chaste colors and a chastised expression. I stare at my shoes as the clock ticks five, ten, fifteen minutes past six . . . I figure my husband has bailed on me. Can't say I'm too stunned. Then the front door flies open and Brad is there, looking dashing in his suit.

"Oh good!" he says. "I was hoping you'd be ready!"

I smile with relief and we hurry to the car.

He tells me more about who we're meeting on the way over.

"You can't laugh, though," he says.

"Never."

"You can't."

"Brad, I won't. I promise."

He says the dinner meeting is with a missionary group that's started a global import/export business and they're represented by some of the largest churches in America. The Baptists, the Methodists, the Nondenominational Free Church . . . These guys travel all around the world, to some of the poorest places on earth, and build missions for some of the poorest people on earth. They got the idea to start making villages self-sustaining and invested in little start-up operations in far-flung places, importing products in bulk from their partner-affiliates.

"What about this is funny?" I ask him. "It sounds pretty serious and amazing."

"The group's called . . . Christian Lambs of God, or CLOG, Industries."

I say nothing. I stare straight ahead. Then we hit a bump, and I snicker.

"You said you wouldn't laugh!"

I clam up immediately, but then Brad can't stop himself from laughing either.

"Who would have initials like that?" he says. "CLOG?"

We pull into the parking lot of Applebee's. "What are we doing here?" I ask, confused. "Aren't we going to the club?"

"Nope. We got some down-to-earth pastors here. The leader of the group is a millionaire, but . . . he likes Applebee's."

I look at him and nod. "See this?" I point to my face. "This is me *not* laughing."

"That's my girl," he says, and leans over to kiss me.

Inside Applebee's plump people munch happily on deep-fried everything. God, I miss this place, but I pretend to be morally offended. "It's all just deep-fried trans fat on a plate!" I whisper, watching a plate of delectable deep-fried steak waft by.

We sit in a large booth with Todd Brockman and his vapid fiancée, Cyndi. He introduces us to the import/export missionary group, led by the Reverend Coy Jones from Atlanta First Baptist and his permanently startled-looking wife, Jolene. Then we're introduced to Deacon Bill Davis, from the United Free Church of Houston. His wife, Arnelle, took sick tonight, poor illness-riddled thing. She's suffered endless maladies ever since they came back from the mines of Bembezi, Zimbabwe.

Finally we meet Pastor Joe Goodrich from Chicago's Christ Church Evangelical and his "wife" Lee, who I'm 99 percent sure is an Asian boy. "Well, God be praised!" Pastor Joe says when he sees me. "I met this wonderful woman at my neighbor's barbecue! Wonderful people! The Lord surely works in mysterious ways, brothers. Here we were, praying for a sign, asking God to lead us in our decision to invest with the Keller's company or not . . ."

Todd gives Brad a sly smile.

"Pastor Joe, are you saying what I think you are?" Reverend Coy asks.

"I am, Reverend Coy. The Spirit is speaking to me even now."

"Praise be!" booms Deacon Davis, whose giant fist bangs on the table and makes everyone near us look.

"Let's pray on it together," Reverend Coy says, and the

whole table has to hold hands while Reverend Coy prays out loud, emphasis on "loud," which makes it sort of awkward for the waitress when she tries to deliver three Sea Lover's Snack Platters, which sizzle as they rest on her meaty forearm. She waits patiently as a saint for the pastor to say, "Amen!" before she serves them . . . then she runs off, to apply first aid lotion to her burns, I'm certain.

We celebrate that night.

Brad, Todd, Cyndi, and I go to Nye's Polonaise Room and Brad pulls me onto his lap. He keeps tickling me and saying, "It was you, babe! They loved you! You're my lucky charm!" We go home and Brad falls asleep before I even come out of the bathroom, but I don't care. I turn off the light feeling happy. We spent the night at Applebee's with a bunch of weird preachers . . . but it was still wonderful.

The most romantic night I can remember in recent history.

I'm achy and hungover when I hear Sarah honk her horn. She drops Trevor off, despite her grave trepidations about my moral character, with a note pinned to his jacket.

"It's the new rules." Trevor sighs. "There's a-lots of them."

I read the note with growing disdain. I can't believe the amount of control Sarah assumes she can assert over not only her son but his free day-care provider . . . *me*.

New Rules for TREVOR *(Which Are Assumed to Be Obvious but Apparently Are Not)*

Trevor CANNOT
- ✔ *Eat sugar*
- ✔ *Eat processed foods*
- ✔ *Watch television or movies*
- ✔ *Buy clothing, toys, or books*

- ✔ Make playdates with unapproved parties
- ✔ Take part in dangerous roughhousing activities

<u>Trevor CAN</u>
- ✔ Read preapproved books
- ✔ Watch preapproved videos
- ✔ Play with preapproved toys sent with him

"Trevor!" I immediately shout.

"What?"

"Wanna go eat some sugar and processed food and then go buy banned books and videos and make playdates with . . . I don't know, homeless circus performers living in burned-out vans down by the river? If we're lucky they'll teach us dangerous roughhousing activities."

"Yay!" Trevor shouts.

"We'll start at Kidzilla and you can see if there's a heating duct you can break. I'll sign you up for the Godzilla Pass again. I heard they just got a go-kart track put in."

"Yay!"

"There's only one condition. You can't eat so much junk food, okay?"

"Okay!"

What inspires this direct insubordination? What makes me think I can do this? Because clearly I am this kid's Aunt Ariel. Or I should be. Someone's got to keep his spirit alive, with all these mud people slapping mud all over his fun heart. Damn. I think it was getting approval from the pastors last night too. I feel like doing something nice for myself for once.

And for Trevor.

We pile into the car and head for the Mall of America. I'm dropping him off at Kidzilla before I run for my massage when who do I bump into but Ellie Rathbone, the country club queen herself? She's dropping off her son, Cody, who, it turns out, happens to be on the same soccer team as Trevor. "Well, hi there, Trev!" Ellie says. "Didn't think your mom let you come here!"

"His mom doesn't," I tell her. "If she finds out she'll kill me. I'm his . . . aunt."

"My husband thinks Cody is at an afterschool science class."

"Well, have you seen Planet Snacker-Snacks? That's a science lab."

"I'm Ellie," she says, reaching out her perfectly manicured hand. She's wearing an absolutely adorable tennis outfit underneath her coat, which accentuates her itty-bitty waistline and toned arms. She's impossibly stupidly unfairly skinny. Like she keeps her organs at home in a jar. "We haven't officially met," she says.

"Jennifer Keller," I say warmly.

"My son Cody's in the same class as Trevor. He's eight too."

"Hi, Cody." Trevor hops around and waves at the boy, who silently stares at him.

"You look familiar," Ellie says.

"Oh, do you go to Hillcrest?" I ask casually.

"Oh yeah . . . wait a minute, now I got it—" Her phone rings. "Hang on a sec," she says. "Sorry." She takes the phone call and I hear her voice drop; she speaks in hushed tones and annoyed inflections. Without straining to hear her conversation, I can tell she's arguing about who will pick Cody up. "You know, *we* could drive Cody home," I tell her when she's off the phone.

"Yay!" Trevor shouts.

Ellie looks at me and blinks. "No," she says. "That's . . . sweet. But, I, um . . . we can figure something out."

"It's really no trouble," I tell her. "My day is wide open."

She looks at me, calculating something in her mind.

for me, if Trevor needed a ride. It's really no trouble, Ellie." I think it's this last touch of using her name that seals the deal. She rolls her eyes and smiles, relief flooding her pretty, perfectly toned face, and she gushes with thanks, writing down her phone number, address . . . all of it solid gold. "Hey, let's grab lunch at the club," she says as she's dashing away. "I'll grab your number from the Hillcrest directory. Bye for now, guys. Bye, Trevor. Have fun!"

And just like that, I have a lunch date with Ellie Rathbone.

Unbelievable.

I chalk it up to my extreme exhaustion, my ever-changing weight-loss pills, and my constant low-grade anxiety. Christopher has always said this is the secret to popularity. If you want to make new friends, then be a new you. The absolute last thing you should do is be yourself. You should be the opposite of yourself, or rather you should be the epitome of those you desire to know. If you were so great you'd already have friends. Anyone who tells you to be yourself is probably plotting against you. So that's what I did when I met Ellie Rathbone.

I seemed cool, detached, and easygoing.

Everything I am not.

10
The Cuntry Club

I'm as happy as Wedding Day Barbie. Sick to my stomach with joy. I'm about to have lunch at the club with Ellie *and* her infamous sister, Addi. I go all-out getting ready. I get my hair and nails done and Christopher finds me fourteen different Elegantly Invincible outfits that are all "perfect" for a fall club luncheon. I try each of them on seven different times and finally pick one of the more conservative looks, which I call "Sexy Librarian on a Fox Hunt": an ivory silk blouse with a ruffled front, a rich nut-brown Burberry cardigan, and a tailored tweed pencil skirt that I top with a thin black patent leather belt. I wear tall leather Ralph Lauren calfskin riding boots and small teardrop pearl earrings. If there's a fox hunt at Hillcrest today, or if Hemingway wants to have a scotch, I'm ready. I'm actually just spritzing perfume on my wrist when Ellie's car honks outside.

She's here!

Tummy butterflies get all fluttery. I'm nervous! It feels like a date. I hurry downstairs, putting on my cashmere camel trench coat and almond-colored pashmina. Now if I only had a pith helmet and a martini, I might qualify for a vintage safari too.

Outside I nearly slip on a patch of ice, and in an attempt to summit the passenger seat of Ellie's tall white Land Cruiser, I slip and painfully bang my knee.

"Oh! You okay?" Ellie asks me.

"Yep!" I whisper, tears welling in my eyes. I take my seat and buckle in. Then I wait for . . . ten minutes? fifteen? as Ellie fastidiously prepares to leave my driveway. She puts her sunglasses away, checks her cell phone, texts somebody, flips down her visor and looks at her teeth in the mirror, pops a Tic Tac in her mouth, dabs lip gloss on her bottom lip, digs in her purse for the better lip gloss, sips her bottle of water, turns on the stereo, clicks through the satellite channels and settles on the classical music station, then monkeys with the rearview mirror and asks me if I want an Evian.

"Ah . . . sure," I say.

She pushes a button and a rectangular lid slides open on the armrest next to me, releasing a vaporous cloud from the refrigerated compartment below. Inside is a neat assortment of chilled beverages. "Help yourself," she says. "But don't take Cody's juice box. If he doesn't get his juice box after school, it's not . . . pretty."

I grab an Evian and the lid rolls shut.

Ellie rechecks her mirrors. By the time she eases the mammoth white Land Cruiser carefully out onto the street it feels like an eternity has passed. Like lunch should be over. I'm worn out already and realize my face hurts because I haven't stopped smiling and nodding the whole time. We take off and roar onto the highway; Ellie talks all the way to the club. About what, I have no idea. I'm too distracted to track it. I'm much more aware of my pencil skirt digging into my sides; it now feels like it must be two sizes too small.

I do this all the time. I try things on and concentrate on how they look, completely oblivious to how they feel. I could stand in front of a full-length mirror with my feet jammed into bowls of broken glass and not even notice the blood spurting out because I'm trying to decide if they make my feet look too "chunky."

By the time we arrive at Hillcrest, I'm ready for my nap and we haven't even eaten yet. We're having tea in the solarium, a pretty room overlooking the garden with tall French windows and a domed glass ceiling. It's like we're all canaries in a giant birdcage. We're led across the room, past a dozen tables with pink skirting and pink hand-painted japan. On each table is a silver tea service. Our table has a wine decanter on it and no teapot. There's a little sign on the tablecloth saying RATHBONE PARTY. No one else is there. The room and our table are empty.

"Big surprise." Ellie sighs. "Addi's late."

A Hispanic waitress appears in a peacock-blue uniform.

"Mara!" Ellie says. "Martini, please. Also a Pellegrino with sliced lemon on the side, and a decaf skim latte with *one* shake of cinnamon and *one* shake of nutmeg. I have to drink caffeine when I drink alcohol or I collapse. Just *one* shake of cinnamon and nutmeg, okay? Last time he went a little nutmeg-crazy and my coffee tasted like, well, liquid nutmeg. Ick."

Mara nods. I'm worried she's not writing this down. I panic-order a martini too. I never drink them. I can't usually even get down a sip of one; the alcohol burns my retinas so bad that my eyes start to water.

Suddenly the solarium doors burst open and in sails a coiffed blonde, smiling and tanned, draped in silks and satins, cuffed with sparkle-chunk diamonds. Addi Rathbone flashes her blinding, trillion-kilowatt smile. She's known for her excessive augmentations, her luxury obsessions, and her astronomical divorce settlement, as well as for never being on time.

She sits next to me and holds out a perfectly manicured hand.

"Call me Addi," she says. "And I know who you are. Ellie told me all about you. Dumping your nephew off at Kidzilla every afternoon? For shame!"

"Oh." I look over at Ellie and blush. "I . . . um . . ."

"The real shame is you can't dump his ass there every night too! God. If I didn't have a full-time nanny I'd have sent Fiona to a nunnery in Milan by now. He's your nephew, right? The weird kid."

"Trevor."

"That's right. Fiona had him in her tumbling class. Please. If you can hand him back in anything but a body bag you get full marks from me."

"Trevor's all right."

"Oh, they're all wonderful in doses. Doses, darling, like acid!"

Mara serves us drinks and Addi orders a glass of Burgundy. When Ellie sips her latte she makes a face at me. "Nutmeggy," she says. "I knew it."

"Hey, are we ordering any food?" I ask hopefully.

"Ugh. Not me." Addi frowns at her cell phone. "The Tin Man upped my Trimexa, thank God. I may never actually eat again. Hooray!"

"What's Trimexa?" I ask her.

"Do you take it too?"

"No, I . . . just asked you what it was."

"You should be on it! We all should be! It works, Goddammit. You can eat three stuffed-crust pepperoni pizzas and four pints of ice cream and then give Godzilla himself a blow job and you won't gain an ounce." I have no clue what she means about Godzilla, unless she means swallowing his . . . oh God. I down the rest of my martini and order another one. Now I see why these women drink so much. So they can stand each other.

"You shouldn't take that stuff," Ellie says. "It'll kill you."

"Well, *of course* it'll kill me," Addi says, rolling her eyes. "Say something more obvious. That's why it works, dummy. Anything that *works* kills you. But look on the bright side, think about how pretty my corpse will be." Both Addi and Ellie burst into identical fits of loud honking laughter. Ellie dabs the corner of her eye with a napkin.

"How do you even get a prescription? It's illegal in all fifty states."

"Ah, but it's *not* illegal in the U.S. commonwealth of Saipan."

"Where's Saipan?" I ask.

"Who knows? Who the fuck cares?" Addi shrugs. "You've seen one nuclear experiment on a coral atoll, you've seen them all. Trust me. My doctor, the Tin Man, can prescribe trial drugs, many of which, I might add, actually *work*."

"And many of which sometimes kill you," Ellie adds cheerfully.

"Well, there's always *side effects*," Addi says. "Jennifer, you should go see the Tin Man and get some Trimexa. I can get you an appointment if you want one."

"Don't do it," Ellie says. "That guy gave her stepkids dog tranquilizers."

"Um . . . because I asked him to," Addi tells me. "And dog tranquilizers were too good for those *little beasts*. Hell on earth is three boys under twelve. Literally. You go to hell, and Lucifer hands you three disgusting smelly hormone-crazed perverts who like to order spy cameras online and then hide them in your bidet. I packed those monsters off to boarding school the minute I got pregnant. I was sure they'd kill the baby. You know what they did their first week there? Lit the dean's couch on fire and locked a classmate inside a chicken coop. Left him there all night. To this day that kid will only talk to chickens. Seriously. Stockholm chicken syndrome or something. Anyway, if I hadn't shipped those animals off they would've probably lit my baby on fire and stuffed her in a chicken coop too."

"Fiona," Ellie says.

"*Fiona.*" Addi rolls her eyes. "My little drama queen. Where does she get it? Hollywood will never know what hit them. Anyway I saved my daughter from years of persecution, didn't I, and I also saved my couch from being burned to the ground, which is more than I can say for Dean Weber."

"Where are the boys now?" I ask her.

"God knows! Probably in jail somewhere or sailing the seven seas with my ex-husband."

"Kenneth," Ellie says.

"*Kenneth.*" Addi rolls her eyes. "King of the idiots."

"Addi's quite proud of her divorce," Ellie says.

"I'm quite proud of my divorce *settlement,*" Addi says, correcting her. "You'd be proud too, if you ever divorced that walking sodball of a husband you have."

"Rick's not bad."

"No, he's awful. You should just put my divorce lawyers on retainer."

"Who, Henckles, Luststerben and Grump?"

"Henckles, Luststerben and Grump!" Addi cheers. "Ferocious German divorce lawyers. All women, who specialize in high-impact divorces."

"High-impact divorces?" I ask.

"King Idiot never knew what hit him." Addi grins. "You should've seen my lawyer in court. Ursula Henckles is the biggest, baddest, meanest supercunt in any divorce court from here to Düsseldorf. She was spectacular."

"Addi, *please* don't use that word," Ellie says. "Really!"

"What word?"

"The C-word?"

"'Cunt'? What's wrong with 'cunt'? I love 'cunt'! It's such a pretty word, like 'cut' and 'hunt.' Plus it sounds like a German tank rolling over and popping a ball sack."

"I'm sorry, Jennifer." Ellie sighs. "She gets this way sometimes."

"Don't apologize to *Jennifer*," Addi snaps. "She's a cunt too, like I am! Aren't you, Jen?"

I mutely sip my martini. At this point I'm just hoping to get out of the dining room alive.

"Well, I find the word offensive," Ellie says.

"That's because you *aren't* one. You're a bitch; it's quite different. Bitches do just that. They bitch and moan and complain. Cunts take action. Right, Jen? We don't let anyone hold us down. Joke. Seriously though, we kick and fight and scream if we have to, right, Jen?"

I nod politely, dreaming of faraway places.

"Come on, Jen," Addi says. "Say it, I know you're a cunt. I have very good cunt radar. Come on! Say it! Say you're a cunt!" I look around the room, wondering if there's a hidden camera. Maybe I'm part of some guerrilla documentary about sociopathic adult bullies. "Come on," Addi says. "Just say it *once* and I'll be happy."

"She'll keep asking," Ellie says. "She won't stop. That's what she does."

Addi prods me again. This time literally. "Fine!" I smile ferociously. "I'm a cunt! Okay? I'm a big fat hairy cunt! There you are, happy?"

"I knew it!" Addi smacks the table. I hear whispers on the other side of the room and look up to see a group of older women come in. I think they're friends of Mother Keller's. They heard me say, "I'm a big fat hairy cunt." Oh my God . . . My cheeks burn bright red.

Then the maître d' appears and I feel like we're teenagers caught by the school monitor swearing in the lunchroom. The maître d', a short, mean-faced little man wearing a burgundy bolero vest, looks down at me and smiles disapprovingly. "Is there a *problem* here, ladies?" he asks.

Addi yawns. "Yes, Louie, I need another fucking martini."

"Yes, madam. Some of the other members ask that your guest might refrain from—"

"My *guest?*" Addi looks around like someone just slapped her. "What guest? Louie! This is Mrs. Jennifer Keller! A VIP club member and daughter-in-law of Mr. Ed Keller, the club's third admiral viceroy? Perhaps you've heard of him?"

"Yes, madam."

"Well. I'm quite surprised you don't know a VIP member when you see one." Addi looks at him like he just dumped a pile of dog shit on the table.

"Yes, madam. It won't happen again, madam. My apologies to you, Mrs. Keller."

"Oh, please." I smile broadly. "Please just call me—"

Addi shoots me a look. "Mrs. Keller is a very old and *dear* friend of mine," she says to Louie. "Understand?"

Louie smiles at me and bows deeply. "Of course," he says, and either this balding man deserves an Academy Award for acting or I see true remorse in his eyes, as well as something resembling true respect. He went from disdaining me to liking me, solely on Addi's request. I'm angry at Addi for humiliating him and I'm also weirdly grateful to her for sticking up for me like that, even lying and calling me her dear old friend. It's odd. When someone lies for you, a connection forms. A bond. You've silently entered into a pact. At least for the moment, you're on the same team.

Louie reluctantly leans over and whispers to Addi. "Madam, the other table complained . . ."

"Oh!" Addi looks over at the table across the room. "Are we bothering those ladies?"

"Only *slightly*, madam."

"I see, well, I'm so sorry, Louie! We'll keep it down. Could you please send the offended party a bottle of Veuve Clicquot along with my sincere wishes?"

"Yes, madam!"

"My sincere wishes that they suck my cock in hell?"

"Madam?"

"Only teasing. Just give them the bottle and tell Mrs. Starling she won't be needed on the museum's Jubilee Committee after all."

"Very good, madam."

"Oh, Addi, don't." Ellie clucks.

"Louie, where's my martini? Quickly, before I ship you back to whatever banana republic you escaped from!"

"Addi!" Ellie frowns. "Louie's from *Costa Rica*. Aren't you, Louie?"

"Yes, madam."

"Oh, please." Addi sighs. "Like anybody knows the difference. You've seen one monkey fucking a banana in the jungle, you've seen them all. *Trust me*. Louie, *where's* my martini?"

"Right away, madam." Louie bows and hurries off.

Louie doesn't return to our table.

Mara brings a round of martinis and several three-tiered silver trays filled with little tea sandwiches—watercress-cucumber, chicken curry, and egg salad—with their crusts cut off. There are also miniature pastries, tiny éclairs, finger-size Napoléons, and apricots dipped in chocolate. Before we can eat, a flustered

woman hurries over from the table across the room. "Addison?"
She smiles.

"Mrs. Starling?" Addi says without smiling. She keeps her eyes on the three-tiered tray, carefully selecting pastries from the plates.

"Um . . . thank you!" Mrs. Starling says. "For the champagne!"

Addi says nothing. She just studies an apricot.

"Um . . . Louie said something about the Jubilee Committee?" Mrs. Starling says. "I'm still on it . . . right?" Her cheeks are flushed.

Addi sighs. "No," she finally says. "I'm afraid not."

Mrs. Starling catches her breath. "But, I've already been—"

"There's simply no room anymore," Addi says. "There was, but now . . . there's not."

"There's not? But how? Who—"

"Jennifer here got the last slot," Addi says, and smiles at me. "Have you two met?"

Mrs. Starling looks at me, terrified.

"Actually, if you'll excuse us, Mrs. Starling, we must catch Jennifer up on all the Jubilee details. It's such a big party! Oh. I do hope we weren't being too loud?"

Mrs. Starling shakes her head. "No . . . I—"

"We weren't bothering you?"

"No, not at all . . . we just heard . . . *shouting* and wanted to make sure you were *all right*."

"How sweet!" Addi says. "Actually, *your* party seems quite loud."

"My party?" Mrs. Starling looks back at her table. "We've just been playing bridge."

"Don't you think you'd be more comfortable in the lobby?" Addi asks.

"The . . . lobby?"

"Yes."

"Oh."

"If you'll excuse us, Mrs. Starling. Jennifer hasn't made all her final decisions, so . . ."

"Of course." Mrs. Starling crosses the solarium and sits down at her table. A moment later, all the women gather up their cards and purses and various belongings . . . and leave.

"*Bitch*," Addi says.

Ellie rolls her eyes. "Oh, please."

"No, you see, that woman is *a bitch*. All she and her cronies do is complain. Now, if she'd come over here and been *a cunt* . . . I would've handed over the Jubilee crown."

"Oh really?" Ellie says.

"Absolutely."

"Sorry." I raise my hand. "What is the Jubilee?"

"The museum's big annual donor party and art auction," Ellie says.

"Oh. Okay . . . am I really on the committee?"

"*On it?* Honey, you're *the head* of it."

"What?"

"Mrs. Starling was the committee chairperson."

Finally, Addi sighs and says, "Well. It's time to get Tallulah from her therapist."

"Who's Tallulah?" I ask.

"That's Fiona's current name," Ellie says.

"*Fiona*." Addi rolls her eyes. "She's seven years old and just told me she wants to switch therapists. This one doesn't seem *emotionally reliable enough*. That's what she said."

"Fiona sees a therapist?"

"And her own acupuncturist, her own nutritionist, and an on-call dream interpreter for night terrors. Every single hyperactive nutbag in her class has their own team of specialists. It's unbelievable. When we were little, our mother didn't reach for some specialist every time we got a hangnail."

"No," Ellie says flatly. "She reached for a bottle of white wine instead."

Mara brings the check and Addi quickly signs it.

"Did you want me to . . . I mean, should we split it?" I ask, and Addi looks at me so strangely I don't even recognize her expression at first.

"Absolutely not!" she says, her face changing from whatever expression it was to a look of haughty amusement. "Splitting the bill." She sighs. "Maybe you *are* a guest."

We stagger out the front doors. There's a round of air-kissing, cheerful name-calling, and friendly insult-hurling. Many cunts were had by all.

Then Ellie drives me home. I lay my head back on the seat's headrest, alcohol thrumming through my blood. "I'm not used to drinking this much," I tell her.

She says I'll get used to it. I might, but my liver never will. Ellie apologizes for her sister's behavior, but not overly. She says Addi's a complicated woman.

I'll say. I was charmed by her, then repulsed, intrigued, angered, and finally . . . I felt deeply grateful that she stood up for me. Ellie says Addi's got a heart of gold. She might come across as crass, foul-mouthed, and bullying sometimes . . .

"*Sometimes?*" I croak. "Sorry, I was only supposed to think that. Not say it."

Ellie smirks. "It's true she has a hard exterior. Inside, though, she's uncommonly kind and protective. She paid for all of Mara's dental work, and Louie, that maître d'? She stopped the INS when they tried to deport his family. Then she used God knows what channels to buy them all green cards."

"That sounds difficult and . . . expensive."

"Well, Addi has more money than the Pope," Ellie says. "She can afford it. She won *thirty-two million dollars* in her divorce settlement."

I open my eyes. "How much?"

"Exactly. So like I said, the dumb bitch can afford it."

"No, Ellie, no! *You're* the dumb bitch," I tell her, giggling. "She's the stupid cunt. Remember? Me too. I've been crowned a stupid cunt too . . . so back off, bitch!"

We both titter with laughter. Ellie sighs. "*I'm* not quite so lucky. It doesn't even matter if I want to leave . . . Rick and I have a prenup; if either of us leaves, we both lose everything. Enough to drop down several income-tax brackets. The stocks, the house, not to mention the kids . . . it's all tangled up."

"Like badly cast fishing lines . . ." I say softly.

She looks over. "Like what?"

"It's a line from a Katherine Anne Porter story. *'How I have loved this house in the morning . . . before we are all awake . . . and tangled together, like badly cast fishing lines.'* "

"Beautiful." Ellie sighs. "And true. You know a lot about literature?"

"No. I wanted to be a writer once, but not anymore."

"No?"

"Not really."

"Do you and Brad have one?" she asks.

"One what?"

"A prenup."

"Oh. We do. But—"

"Let me guess." Ellie pulls into my driveway. "You'll never actually *use* it."

"We won't." I smile and start laughing at myself. "God, I sound like an idiot, don't I."

"No more than any of us did in the beginning."

"I know, I sound drunk and like an idiot but I'm seriously serious, Ellie. Seriously. Brad and I are good. We are. We only signed that prenup for his parents, who are . . . Jesus, they're awful." I sit up wide-eyed and stare at her. "Shit! Tell me I didn't just say that out loud!"

"I think they're awful too," Ellie says. "But you know what? Addi and I like you. We're going to help."

"Really? How? Can you crucify Brad's mother? Shit! Sorry."

"Go in and sleep it off."

"Thanks for the ride, Ellie . . . and the tea and everything."

"Bye, hon. Be careful."

I'm almost to the stairs when I lurch back to her car window. "Seriously, though," I tell her. "I will *never* get a divorce. *Ever.* I promise, just you and me . . . just one stupid cunt to a dumb bitch. Okay?"

"I know you won't." She sighs. "That's what we all said, isn't it."

I wave as her white Land Cruiser ambles off down the street like a friendly elephant. Then I go into the house and up to the bedroom, where I fall facedown in the mountain of piled-up clothes in my closet. I sleep there with Ace curled up beside me.

My first lunch at the Cuntry Club is over.

It was so fabulous, it nearly killed me.

11
Army Wives

My brain is the captain; my body is the war zone.

I size up what can stay and what must go, carefully delineating enemy territories, like my ass, my thighs, my bingo-lady arm fat. Everything must be invaded, conquered, nipped, tucked, cut off, sanded down, or plumped with injectable filler.

Addi sets up my first appointment with the Tin Man and I drive over to her sprawling Excelsior megalomaniac mansion, where we're supposed to have lunch and then drive together to the clinic. I'm going for assessment and she's going for a quick eyelid scruffing. I'm already twenty minutes late when I ring her doorbell, having struggled more than usual with my outfit, which I'm not happy with. It's a pale plum Ann Taylor suit and makes me look dumpy.

Addi answers the door wearing a short red kimono and drinking white wine.

"Sorry I'm so late," I tell her. "There was a huge accident on the freeway."

"Don't talk to me about accidents!" she snaps. "Talk to my maid."

I take off my jacket and pull off my boots.

Addi starts to say something and stops short. "Jesus, what're you wearing?"

"This?" My cheeks pink. "I just wore something old."

"How old? That thing looks like it lost a Republican caucus in 1983."

"Well, it's just a—"

"Can you please just . . . I can't even concentrate because of what my maid just did. I'm so angry I want to scream. Come look at this."

She leads me through the foyer and an elegant living room with vaulted ceilings, duck-egg-blue walls, long yellow satin couches, and other assorted Chippendale furniture. She marches me into her gourmet Mediterranean kitchen, which is three times the size of mine, and opens a silverware drawer. "Here's your accident," she says. "Look!"

I peer into the drawer.

"Can you believe it?" she says.

"No. I . . . can't." I have no idea what she's talking about.

"See! Jennifer can't believe it *either*, Juanita! Everything is just tossed in here!"

A young Filipina maid cowers in the corner, carefully slicing ingredients for salad.

Addi's nostrils flare at her. "Did you finish slicing the figs?"

Juanita looks down at the cutting board.

"Juanita!" Addi snaps. "This is your last chance! Do you understand me? Toss my good silver in with the day silver one more time and you'll be back in Manila within the week! I couldn't possibly recommend you to anyone, understand me?"

The maid nods quickly.

I clear my throat. "You know, my maid's afraid of our coffeemaker. Can you imagine? She's terrified of it!"

"*What?*" Addi looks over at me.

"My maid can't make coffee. Can you imagine?"

"No. I can't." She looks back at Juanita.

"So where's this closet everyone's talking about?" I ask her. "I bet mine's . . . bigger!"

Her head snaps back toward me. "Bigger?" She smiles. "Not likely, you stupid cunt. Want some wine? I'm drinking Bordeaux."

"*Really?*"

"Jesus, why do people get all *judgy* about wine!"

I frown at her glass and shake my head. "Oh, no, it's just—"

"Okay, fine. I'll open a bottle of red. You are *such* a snob. Ellie was right about you."

"What?"

"Would the Château Lafite Rothschild meet your high standards, m'lady?"

"Sure." I shrug. "Sounds good." It does *not* sound good. I don't like to drink at eleven in the morning; it knocks me out. I'll get tired. Still, I'm already learning it's easier to go along with what Addi wants . . . or at least to pretend to. I wander out into the dining room, looking at all the large oil paintings on the walls, hoping Addi will follow me and we'll avoid another Juanita tirade.

"Jesus, Jen," she says. "Wait up!" She sweeps into the room in her red kimono and hands me a glass of wine. "Here's your wine, Queen Cunt."

We sit down in the dining room at a long polished cherry-wood table and Juanita brings us cold duck salad with goat cheese and figs. We're sitting there eating our salads and talking and I'm looking right at a large antique cabinet on the other side of the room when suddenly the cabinet door opens. I shriek when a little Asian man steps out holding a pair of shoes. He quickly looks at us and then darts into the kitchen. I look over at her. "What *was* that?"

"He's just my silver polisher."

"Your silver polisher?"

"He comes once a week and works in the cupboard so I don't notice him."

"Why was he holding a pair of shoes?"

"Because I told him to take his shoes off before he got into the cabinet. I don't want footprints tracking all over the place. God, it's already getting late. Drink up, QC, and I'll go throw on some clothes."

"What's 'QC'?"

"Queen Cunt!" She smiles. "Congratulations. You know they needed a queen."

I sit at the table and sip my wine as she goes upstairs and changes.

I can't imagine living in this huge house alone. *Wait, she has a daughter . . . where's little Fiona?* I wonder. She probably lives in a closet under the staircase.

Juanita comes to clear our plates and with a lowered voice I tell her I'm sorry that Addi yelled at her. Juanita just stares at me. Suddenly we hear Addi coming back and Juanita drops a fork, which skitters under the sideboard. Panic floods her eyes and she freezes momentarily before dashing back into the kitchen, just as Addi saunters in wearing an all-white velour tracksuit with a bright red scarf knotted at her neck.

"What was that?" She stares suspiciously at the table. "Was Juanita in here?"

"Nope. Haven't seen her."

"She's not supposed to come in here unless you call her. Did you call her?"

"Nope. Addi, this wine is delicious. Have some!"

"Well, it should be delicious, dummy. It cost two thousand dollars a bottle."

I nearly choke. My face goes red as I desperately reach for the water.

"Hurry up and let's get you changed," she says. "It's getting late."

"Changed? Into what?"

"Well, you're not wearing that to the clinic. You look like an extra on *The Brady Bunch*."

"I thought you said . . . never mind."

I follow her to her truly magnificent closet and she hands me a pistachio-green Christian Dior tracksuit. "Christian Dior makes . . . tracksuits?"

"Under a pen name, of course. All the big designers do, so we rich bitches have something to wear after plastic surgery."

"It's so soft! Is it velvet?"

"Nope. One hundred percent mink," she says proudly. "Mink that's been pulverized and reconstituted into paper-thin fiber. It's haute couture . . . that looks like Tommy Hilfiger."

"Wow." I stare at the tracksuit like I just discovered ice cream. The label says Cardinal Window.

"Get it?" Addi says. "Cardinal Window . . . just like Christian Door!"

I slip into my new best friend, the pistachio tracksuit, and it feels like bunnies are hugging me. Then we hop into Addi's sleek black Mercedes and head for the clinic.

Unlike her methodical sister, Addi drives like a drunk stuntman who's upset about something. She tears down the driveway before my door is even closed, and as we're lurching onto the street she cranks the stereo up so loud it makes the windows vibrate. She waits till we're shrieking at top speed onto a freeway entrance to reach across my lap and dig out a pair of big black sunglasses. We fly past a cop car, which I point out, and Addi shrugs. "They wouldn't dare touch me. I got a deal with the governor. I pay for the Policeman's Ball every year."

"Why?"

"Why do you think? So they can't touch me!"

We arrive at Medi-Spa, which is part clinic, part hospital, part spa . . . and all expensive, as Addi says. "Now, I signed you up for a few more things," she says as we go inside. "The trick is to get things done *before* you need them."

My jaw drops when I see the treatment price list. A facial starts at $500 here. That's more than my car payment. Plus, Addi signed me up for the Titanium Package, which will take two weeks to complete and will cost . . . "Seven thousand dollars?"

I look up at the perfect chesty blonde named Cristal behind the desk.

"It's standard pricing," she says.

"Christ, just sign the form already," Addi says.

"I don't know. I better ask Brad first."

"Why, so he can say *no*? Jennifer, the *first* rule of marriage is that forgiveness is far easier to get than permission."

"I thought it was something about honesty."

She makes a face at me. "You know, I can't figure out if you're funny or just . . . stupid."

"Little from column A," I say, "little from column B."

"Jennifer, you'll never get permission for *anything*. But you'll almost always get forgiveness *if* you look fabulous. Screw honesty! Men want to believe we're sexy naturally. Trust me, Brad doesn't want to know you're getting your anus bleached or your pussy steam-cleaned."

"*I* don't even want to know that."

"Jen, you have to start taking charge. If you don't keep your ship in shape, Brad'll row off with some little dinghy, and don't give me some bullshit about it not being fair, *life's* not fair and nobody asked you to be here, so shut up and just wax your damn pussy."

"Wow." I nod at her. "That should be a bumper sticker."

"Jen, you need to play this game if you want to stay in it. Plus, do you know how hard it was to get you this appointment? Medi-Spa isn't even taking new clients right now. The waiting list is *two years long*. Do you really want to wait that long before you look fabulous? More important, does Brad?"

"Okay." I look at her and I take a deep breath. "Okay. Let's do it."

Cristal hands me what amounts to a work order form and I sign away seven grand. It's terrifying. Brad's gonna hate this. Unless of course bleached anuses are really his thing.

Time will tell.

I get my first procedure done that day. A skin technician studies my face, a giant eye swimming overhead like a huge squid staring at me through a thick clear plate of magnified glass. Then a team of nurse-technicians and skin specialists go to work on me. They start with deep cleansing and move merrily along to Dermaplaning, which is exactly what it sounds like. They use a blade to scrape your face and peel the top layer of skin cells off.

Then I get microdermabrasion and a chemical peel, where "mild acid" is spread on your face and allowed to set, burning off unwanted layers of your epidermis. After that is fractional resurfacing. They use a powerful laser to zap unwanted freckles and age spots. I'm concerned when I see smoke rising from the zap-it gun. The doctor says smoke is normal.

What is not normal, apparently, is hair. Hair is only allowed in two places on the female body: the scalp and, to a minimal degree, the eyebrows. All other hair is unwanted, unseemly, unsightly, and embarrassing. Every crack and crevice must be as soft and bald as a baby's butt. This is accomplished by using a gruesome battalion of red-hot lasers, which feel like lit cigarettes being pressed onto your bare pudenda. I'm told the burning sensation usually remains for mere minutes . . . but sometimes it lasts for weeks.

Next stop: anal bleaching. Population: one. I have to get up in a gynecologist's chair and put my feet in stirrups so the nurse, Brunhilda Von Rough Hands, can daub cold bleaching solution on the old "chocolate starfish," which is a name she finds unamusing. Maybe that's why she warns me about the bleach solution feeling cold . . . but not about it burning. When the searing white-hot sensation hits me, I yell at her to stop. Actually I yell, "Starfish is burning! Starfish is burning!" She says not to worry. It's a normal situation.

I contend to the jury . . . it is not a normal situation. At all.

I get my vaginal steam bath next, figuring I should get all the paid violations over with. But I quite enjoy it. You squat on this ergonomic rocking-chair thing and position your hoo-hah over a big steaming bowl of boiling tea. It's pungent stuff, some blend of mugwort and wormwood, which sounds like a British crime-fighting duo to me, or a medieval venereal disease. The tea also smells like hot chimp feces, which is pretty uncool, but I fall asleep in the chair and afterward, my pussy feels like it's been to Las Vegas. Best of all, the steaming plumps the whole package up. So Brad will feel like he's trying to jam a watermelon into a pudding cup.

Finally I meet the Tin Man himself, a silent Polynesian doctor with a perfectly bald head. He uses injectable fillers to plump up the lines around my mouth and give my lips and cheeks a lift. He recommends liposuction for my belly, butt, and legs. I say no thank you. That's a major medical procedure and I'm not ready to wrap my brain around that yet. He just nods politely and says, "Your brain might not be ready for liposuction, but the rest of you is."

He gives me prescriptions for Lunesta, alprazolam, and Trimexa, so I can sleep at night, chill out during the day, and lose weight 24/7.

Better living through pharmacology!

I meet Christopher for lunch and he starts squirming when I tell him about all the procedures at my spa visit. Especially when I tell him I had my yacht club steam-cleaned.

The thought of it makes him want to retch.

"It was awesome!" I tell him. "You don't know, you don't have a yacht club."

We call vaginas yacht clubs and penises yachts, because Christopher suffers from acute icky-word syndrome. If he hears a really icky word, he seizes up in these painful cringe-flinches that take chiropractors and/or new Armani couture purchases to undo. We keep icky words chipper, like, "That sailor had a seriously small yacht. More like a dinghy. He could've moored ten of them side by side at the yacht club and still had room in there to wave a bottle of Veuve Clicquot." We name specific yachts and yacht clubs. I named my yacht club Mother Teresa and Christopher named Jeremy's yacht Farfel. He named his own yacht King Filippe Roheim III.

Christopher and I go shopping. With Addi and Ellie's encouragement and Brad's corporate credit cards, I begin to buy more clothing than I've ever owned cumulatively in my life. As the girls say, I'm worth it and Brad's good for it, so why not get it?

Suddenly my enormous walk-in closet seems terribly small.

The overstuffed racks and packed drawers are brimming with shimmer and glitter and silks and satin and faille. Oceans of cashmere, supple folds of charmeuse and chamois. Twinkling crystal, amethyst, and pearly peridot buttons. Colors I could eat with a spoon. Almond, oyster, apricot, pearl. Custard, dusty rose, violet, and hickory. Even the names of these designers sound like faraway kingdoms, exotic places you'd like stamped on your passport. "Now boarding for Versace, Prada, Cavalli, Balenciaga."

In the ongoing effort to fit into these works of art, I join an expensive gym in the warehouse district called the Sweatbox. Hillcrest has a gym, but according to Ellie nobody works out there. They work out at the Sweatbox, with "the best trainer in the world," a big muscle-bound man everybody calls Big D. I make an appointment with Mr. Big D and go to the gym wearing my awkwardly new pink and white workout togs. I feel like a prostitute named Candy Cane. The girl behind the counter at the gym is wearing an official orange and gray Sweatbox sweatsuit. "You want Big D?" she says. I nod. I'm obviously a special client. "Okay . . . well, I just saw him outside," she says. "Just go down the hall and out the door by the vending machines."

"Is there a locker room where I can freshen up?"

"Absolutely!" She hands me a shiny chrome credit card, which opens the security door to the VIP clientele locker room, which looks like a futuristic lounge or intergalactic nightclub. It has chrome walls, glass benches, and blue glass floors that look like liquid and are lit from below. Inside my space-age, bacteria-free, antimicrobial, self-ionizing metal locker is a complimentary orange and gray Sweatbox towel and mini bottles of Sweatbox-brand shampoo, conditioner, and "moisturizing salve." I have no idea where to put the salve. There are also complimentary orange flip-flops for the shower, a pair of orange plastic sunglasses for the tanning bed, and a big jumbo orange plastic water bottle that says GET SWEATY AT THE SWEATBOX. All items are labeled eco-friendly, animal friendly, and BPA-free.

After changing into my workout clothes, I follow the hall and go out the heavy metal door by the vending machines. Outside, in the brilliant winter sunlight, a large black man wearing a sweatshirt that says SWEATBOX is sitting on a folding chair eating an orange in the sun. "Hey!" I shout. "You Big D?"

He turns and squints at me. "Yes, ma'am!"

I come out and we shake hands. I thought it would be freezing out here, but it's nice and toasty; there are outdoor heat lamps running overhead. A few of the other trainers are out there having a smoke break, which charms me. I sit down on a chair next to Big D and tell him a little about myself and what I hope to get from training. I tell him about my general concerns and specific problem areas, my milk-udder arms, my pear-shaped butt, my persistent muffin top. He shakes his head when I'm done and takes out another orange, which he slowly begins to unpeel.

"You gotta get rid of that microscope, baby."

"Microscope?"

"Don't nobody look good that close up. You keep looking down, you always find trouble. Just look up at the sky, let your mind set on a cloud. Now, take a deep breath. Let your mind loose. Shake out your arms and legs. Just get up. Jog in place."

"Jog in place? You mean, now?"

"Sure, go ahead if you want to. Just keep it light and keep your head up. Stay with that cloud. It's all about how you feel inside. Like that. How you feel?"

"I feel . . . good," I say, running in place. "I feel really, really good!"

"That's it," he says. "Just remember Muhammad Ali. Float like a butterfly, sting like a *bee*! That mean to me, be heavy but feel light. You can't listen to what other people tell you about yourself. No, sir. You read in the paper that true north is moving?"

"Wh . . . what?" I'm feeling a little winded now.

"True north. Magnetic north. Where every compass in the world s'pose to point." He pulls out an old battered army-green compass and holds it in his palm. "Everybody in the whole world including Jesus and Einstein said true north can't never move. Never ever. Guess they forgot to tell *old true north*. Ha! 'Cause he movin'! Nobody can tell him nothing now! He got a style now. You know what else that means?"

"No . . . I . . . I . . . don . . . don't."

"True north moves, that mean every map they ever was in the world before now is wrong. Dead wrong. You see? Those old maps can't getcha where you wanna go no more! Need new maps, young lady, and that's where you and me come in. Why you stop runnin'?"

"Water."

"Well, all right. Don't take too long now, they gonna say we havin' a tea party."

"Sorry . . ." I quickly cap my water bottle and get back to jogging.

"Whole lotta men been telling people how to get places with the same maps. Only if those maps is wrong now, then those mens is wrong. And that means don't nobody get to tell you how to go now. You go your own way. See? Who says you got a fat ass? Who tole you that?"

"Well, nobody, but I have eyes and I can see what my ass is supposed to look like in magazines and on television and—"

"*Maps!*" he bellows "All maps. All dead-men maps. I told you . . . they done now. So you don't use them peepers to go peepin' on dead-men maps. You hear?"

"I hear."

"Get yourself lost that way. See here, I'm looking at my compass, and it is pointing me to true north. I take a map out, it tell me to go the other way. I got to hang to my own compass to get where I'm going. You see? You got to hang to your compass to get where you wanna be. You don't listen to the rest of 'em. If they is no maps that tell the truth no more . . . we is one thing."

"Wh . . . What's that?"

"We is free."

12
Faux Halcyon

Christmas slaps us like a sharp wreath of holly right in the face. It seems like it was summer yesterday and now Christmas carols are droning and ho-ho-ho-ing everywhere you go.

You can't even pump gas without hearing them and you start feeling rage flowing inside you. Then you feel *bad* that you're so damaged you hate Christmas carols, and your anger ebbs as you convince yourself these tin-eared tunes aren't a premeditated attack, they're just what the healthy people like to listen to. But then "Frosty the Snowman" comes on and your rage flows again. This shit happens every year! This is manipulative! This is brainwashing! This is America—forced joy should be illegal! It goes like this all season, your rage flowing, then ebbing . . . then flowing again . . . then ebbing . . . then *flowing, flowing, flowing* . . . and somewhat ebbing . . . *flowing!*

Keller's loves Christmas. Products we sell year-round get slapped with a red bow and 15 percent price hike for the season. The lobby is decorated from deck to halls, from Candy Cane Lane to a huge hanging wad of papier-mâché mistletoe. We have a big Rockefeller Plaza–type Christmas tree in the rotunda, right next to the special-needs shoe collection. Santa Claus, who is being played by Lenny this year, sits there on his throne for ten hours a day. Lenny wanted to make some extra money. He's endlessly patient and will let kids sit on his lap for as long as they want to. Even the moist ones.

The helper elves are supposed to promote special deals and hurry kids along; they say stuff like, "Okay! Time to go, Johnny! Santa must go shampoo his reindeer with specially formulated Ultra-Prell, now available in the pharmacy!"

Not many special deals get mentioned when Lenny's there, and nobody rushes the kids. If they do, they usually do it only once. If an unwitting elf says, "Okay, time to go, Johnny!" Lenny will calmly set the child down, stand up, and immediately drop character, even though Johnny's still right there. He'll get right in the elf's face and say, "*What* is your Goddamned problem, huh, hotshot? Trying to rush Johnny off, huh? Well, guess the fuck *what*, numb nuts! That little motherfucker will sit on my fucking lap until the Goddamned cows come home if he wants to! Understand? Because *I* am motherfucking Santa Claus! Hear me? And *no* elf steps on that! You just bought yourself a time-out in the Cookie House, elf! Go get in the Goddamned Cookie House!" Then he'll calmly return to his seat, plop the bewildered child back on his lap, and say, "Ho ho ho! What's next on that Christmas list of yours, Johnny?"

Meanwhile the banished elf will usually trudge off. Although I've seen one or two try to open the door of the Cookie House, which is just a prop gingerbread house used just for decoration. It has no working doors or windows, it's just a big box decorated with Styrofoam candy canes and lumpy mounds of snow that they set over a yellow light so the windows glow. Lenny thinks it's the elves' break room.

It's a good Christmas. The lines at Keller's grow delightfully long, and the managers all report high numbers. Sales are good. Best of all, the Christian Lambs of God have decided to invest generously in Keller's and they're shipping job lots of merchandise to our loading docks from all over the world, so everyone's in a festive mood. Plus Ellie and Addi spread delightful gossip about me with their girlfriends who shop at Keller's, and suddenly when I go to the store, I'm greeted with a new respect, even from the cosmetic girls, who say things like, "I heard your husband bought you a diamond bigger than a walnut!" and "A little bird told us Mr. Keller is taking you to Paris!"

It's all untrue, but I confirm every rumor with a sly smile.

Not everyone is smiling at me. Christopher summons me like a bishop down to his lair and points accusingly at the Olya doll boxes lined up against the wall. The Prophets of Profits at CLOG Industries are pushing a Russian peasant doll for Christmas, Olya from Olkhovka. Unfortunately she's not a big seller. Dressed in loosely stitched, tattered clothes and with gray strips of glued felt for shoes, Olya the peasant girl is supposed to incite warmth and sympathy in others, but even kids know a doll with acute depression when they see it.

"These dolls are from some toxic waste dump!" Christopher says angrily.

I shush him. "Christopher, I know you're upset but keep your voice down. The CLOG guys are in the store today."

"Where?"

"They're tied up in meetings. Don't worry about it."

He demands to speak to them and I tell him that's not going to happen.

"Then *you* ask them," he says. "You ask them why these dolls have hazardous-material warnings hidden behind the shipping labels, just like the Angel Bear boxes." He peels off a sticky-backed shipping label, revealing yet another large yellow diamond with a black skull in the center.

"Great." I sigh.

Christopher snorts. "Great? Sure. Have a very merry plutonium Christmas."

I tell him I'll see what I can do.

Meanwhile there's an avalanche of holiday parties to go to. Since Brad usually has to work, Ellie and Addi escort me to cocktail parties, dinner parties, charity auctions, club functions, museum receptions, wine tastings, fashion shows, theater premieres, and symphony balls. Addi hosts a charity auction and fashion show at her house every year for the cancer society. I go over to help her. Two hundred guests are due in an hour for cocktails and a fashion show and storm clouds are gathering over her Excelsior mansion. Downstairs, close to a hundred staff people, caterers, sound and lighting technicians, event planners, valet parking attendants, models, hair and makeup artists, and jewelers buzz about the place.

A transparent Plexiglas runway has been installed a half inch beneath the water in the indoor swimming pool for the event—and for local designer Johann Johansson. "If there's a blizzard, I will tear my Goddamned hair out," Addi says from the styling chair in her master bathroom, where a makeup artist puts on the finishing touches.

The two-hour event involved a three-day production that began by laying a wooden floor on the snowy lawn and pitching an 1,800-square-foot tent above it for cocktail hour. The big top houses a bar fully stocked with top-shelf liquor and Veuve Clicquot champagne and a kitchen area where Christafaro's catering staff whips up thousands of canapés and servings of caviar. As arrangements of white hydrangeas and roses from

Larkspur & Co. are placed on each cocktail table, guests begin to trickle in—and the snow begins to flutter down. Just before the fashion show begins, a woman in a sparkly black dress uses her strappy high heel to drag industrial floor mats over the stone steps that lead guests from the tent into the house.

Happy guests are seated in rows of white Chiavari chairs beside the runway. Bright lights and specially choreographed music accompany a team of Miami models wearing chic fashions—and several million dollars' worth of Cartier jewels.

Oohs and aaahs ensue.

Afterward the auction takes place back in the tent, where the highest bidders take home such tantalizing prizes as dinner for two with Bobby McFerrin, a vacation rental home at Sundance, and a year's fur storage at McPhee's Furs. All in all the event is a success, except that the day afterward Addi discovers two used condoms in her guest room and vomit in the Ming vase upstairs.

Ellie's son catches the measles, so I offer to host her holiday book club. I pick Virginia Woolf's essay on Coventry Patmore's poem "The Angel in the House." The poem is about the ideal Victorian wife, who was immensely charming and completely unselfish. She excelled in the domestic arts and sacrificed her own desires daily. She was eternally devoted and endlessly submissive. She lived to serve her family and thought nothing of herself. Self-sacrificing, pious, and chaste, she was also kind, loving, and powerless. She spoke softly. She never lost her temper and remained charming in even the most unsettling situations. She never needed help. She was always smiling and beautifully dressed and smelled lovely. I thought we'd talk about modern feminism and unrealistic ideals, but instead of discussing any of that, I hear a shriek from the kitchen.

Addi has discovered the Ice Empress. The ladies make me give them a full demonstration of the geisha's repertoire and

Addi starts giggling, then snorts wine up her nose. She speaks Japanese, and apparently our little ice princess has been cursing at us and calling us names.

Her daily greeting, *"Naniga hoshiino?"* means "What the fuck do you want?"

Her cute little sign-off, *"Kutabare!"* basically means "Go fuck yourself."

All of our names are nasty. "Inpo Pho" means "Pho the impotent weakling."

"Brad Baka Ka," the term she used for Brad, means "Brad the stupid asshole."

Christopher's name, "Chin-Chin," means, quite simply, "Dick."

"Shine, Star Fan!" means "Die, Star Fan!"

My favorite name of course is my own. Elegant yet simple. "Jen Aho-Onna" means "Jen the dumb bitch." Only Trevor's name is nice. "Akiko" apparently means "Bright child."

Perfect.

In the kitchen, Addi laughs so hard, I think her sides are going to split open. She says it's probably a special program that runs just for Americans.

I smack Pho. "I *told* you to tell her we were *Canadians,* didn't I?"

He shrugs.

"I told you nothing good *ever* happens to Americans! You'll see!"

He rolls his eyes and leaves. Enraged, I smack the refrigerator screen and angrily confront the Ice Empress. *"Naniga hoshiino?"* she says. *"Moshi-moshi,* Jen Aho-Onna!"

"Don't you *moshi-moshi* me, you dumb bitch. I *know* what my name means." I tell her I have a new name for her. "Dead!" I shout, and dive down to the floor, where I yank the industrial electrical cord like hell, grunting, "Ehn . . . ehn . . . ehn . . ."

while everyone's screaming at me to stop, the refrigerator will fall over, I'm going to get crushed . . . until I rip the cord out of the socket and the refrigerator powers down. The screen goes blank. I sit there panting on the floor, holding the limp cord. "Pho!" I shout. "This is your chance!"

Pho pops his head out of the study cubby. "What now?" he says.

"You're a cyber-ninja, right? Well, this thing's just a cold computer. So reprogram it."

He frowns at me. "What?"

"Reprogram it! Rip off the doors, yank out the wires, cut the mother-effing motherboard in half. Just make her *obey me*."

"I can't . . ."

"I'll pay you. A lot."

"But I don't know how to—"

"Ten thousand dollars."

"What?"

"I will pay you *ten thousand dollars* to make this Goddamned bitch *behave* . . ." I sit there on the floor, panting, still holding the limp cord. "So?" I wheeze. "Do we have a deal? Come on, Pho, this is probably exactly how Bill Gates got his start."

"Okay." He shrugs. "Deal."

I look at everyone in my kitchen and say, "Well . . . 'tis the season to be giving!"

I decide to pick a charity cause of my own, which is animals. At first I wanted to do something specifically for Ace. Since a snobby elitist dog show like Westminster would never let "damaged goods" like Ace into their precious special competition, I thought the world could use another dog show: the Handi-Capable Dog Paralympics. A special dog show for "special dogs" who want to compete in dog shows too. There could be physical competitions, like a three-legged dog race and a wheelchair obstacle course with a special textured lane for the blind. We could have a mentally challenged division for the inbreds, with a stick fetch-off for the stick obsessed, a tail-chasing competition for the neurotic twirlers, and a blue ribbon for the best incessant barker. Alas, I cannot find enough like-minded souls who share my vision, so the Handi-Capable Dog Paralympics will have to wait.

Luckily I have another idea. I set up a special fund called the Ace Award at the local emergency animal hospital. It's for pet owners who can't afford emergency care for their pets. I get the idea when Ace eats a bottle of aspirin and I have to take him to the animal emergency room. There's only one in the city. It's open twenty-four hours a day and it costs a fortune. The emergency room vet gives Ace a tablespoon of hydrogen peroxide and he throws up. The bill is three hundred dollars.

"But a tablespoon of hydrogen peroxide costs *ten cents*," I argue at the front desk.

"Well, the room it was administered in cost *ten thousand dollars* to renovate," says the stalwart bulwark of a woman at the front desk, a vet tech named Greta. She's huge. Her face looks like an angry beach ball. I pay my bill, muttering, and as I'm packing up Ace to go home, a sobbing couple comes in with their bulldog, Scout, who was run over by a Lexus SUV. He'll need extensive surgery right away. I overhear Greta tell them the procedure will cost three thousand dollars and they'll need payment up front before they can operate.

"But we don't have that much money!" the woman cries. "Can't you operate anyway?"

Greta says she's sorry, but it's policy. The woman sobs louder and the guy offers to pay in installments, says he'll call friends and family, that they'll raise the money right away, but Greta just calmly shakes her head and says she's sorry. *It's policy.* I'm shocked. I start arguing with her again. "You mean to tell me you're just going to let that bulldog die in here?"

"It's out of my hands," Greta says snippily. "It's none of your business anyway."

Anger boils up inside me and I reach for my wallet. "It's my business now," I tell her, and I slap down Brad's gold card and pay for Scout's entire surgery, thinking that'll wipe the smug look off her big face. The couple is so shocked they don't know what to say. A week later I get a handmade card in the mail from their six-year-old son.

Dear Nice Lady,

Thank you for saving Scout. He is our dog.
You saved his life. He is my friend.

I Love you,
Daniel (age 6)

That's when I decide to help as many animals as I can. Imagine bringing in your dog and not being able to save it because you don't have enough cash or room on a credit card. It's inhumane. People love their pets as much as they love their human children, sometimes more. Imagine bringing your child to the emergency room and the nurse telling you they can't sew his arm back on until the bill is paid. Disgusting.

I call Greta and set up the Ace Award, a fund for pet owners who can't afford emergency treatment for their animals. In the very first month the fund saves six dogs, fourteen cats, and a mallard, which was attacked by one of the fourteen cats. Believe it or not, the mallard was clearly the winner. The animal hospital texts me whenever there's a need, and I okay it. I've said yes to every request so far except the snake, because people who own snakes are weird, and the hamster with internal bleeding, because I suspected it was being used for nefarious purposes.

I throw my first fund-raiser at the country club and Greta gives a PowerPoint presentation featuring some of the wounded animals they've saved at the hospital. She's a superstar, choosing to show my genteel audience only cutely wounded animals: kittens with bandaged paws, bunnies with bandaged ears, a puppy with a cast on one leg, and a turtle with one tiny eye sewn shut and a small bandage on his head—he looks like a little pirate turtle saying, "Arrrrghhh!" I even got Scout, the bulldog who inspired the Ace Award in the first place, to make an appearance. The couple who owned him agreed to bring him, along with six-year-old Daniel, who slayed every heart in the audience when he climbed up on a chair in order to reach the microphone and then said, "Pweeze, everybody, pweeze help dee animals. Dey need you!"

Not a dry eye in the house.

We raise sixteen thousand dollars that night, which Addi says is the best haul for a new charity that she's ever heard of. Soon I've raised so much money I have to hire a tax accountant and Brad complains about the cost. He complains about money all the time now; I have no idea why. He's the front-runner to become the president, but he says that doesn't put any money in the bank right now.

I ask the Kellers if they'd like to help and Ed's all for it but then he says, "My cousin Ada used to work at the animal shelter. She's one special person, that Ada!" and Mother Keller looks

furious. She glances over at me sternly, twisting her ornate diamond rings around her fingers, and says if I'm so interested in
volunteering, why don't I start showing up at the church youth
group subcommittee meetings? "You're a committee head," she
says, "but I've never seen you at a meeting once."

The girls and I attend a charity event at the Minneapolis Museum
of Art, a fund-raiser for their permanent collection, which
mostly features dead artists from other centuries. The theme of
the event is a funeral wake, a festive dirge; patrons wear black
veils and sip evergreen absinthe as sad cellos play throughout the
galleries. Everyone who pledges a thousand dollars or more gets
a small headstone carved right there for them, in their honor.
The girls think it's a hoot. Addi buys us all headstones and tells
us to pick our epitaphs.

Ashes to Ashes, Dust to Dust
ADDI RATHBONE
Left everything in a children's trust.

Here lie the remains of
ELLIE RATHBONE
I might be GONE—but I'll be watching!

R.I.P.
JENNIFER KELLER
She thought life would be more . . .
something.

I can't finish.
Something makes me too sad. The cello music presses uncomfortably in my head, reminding me of the calypso music

from my honeymoon, and suddenly everything seems doomed, decaying, made of dirty water and bitterness and blue ruin. I feel like I'm a bumblebee trapped inside a cello. Maybe it's the absinthe. Maybe it's the diet pills or the prescription painkillers I always seem to be popping. I don't know. I don't care anymore.

I leave early and go home, only to discover I'm brutally, inexplicably, unforgivably *out* of any pills that could aid or assist me here in my time of melancholy need. No Vicodin, no Ativan, no freaking aspirin? *How can this be?* Even Bi'ch and company are sound asleep. There's no begging for exotic cures or medicinal herbs. I settle for unhappily soaking in a hot tub. Unhappy, I am. It's true, but I love my porcelain sanctuary, and there amidst the fragrant splendor of blooming gardenia oil and pink rose petals I sink my brittle frame into the warm eggshell-shaped embrace of my astronomically expensive bathtub, steeping myself in warm pearly-white water. Drawing a thick cowl of bubbles up around my collarbone, I think they seem so happy. Shiny green, oystery blue, pearly pink little bubbles, and so social, as though they've come from great distances to be together there at that moment.

I close my eyes.

Perhaps this bath, a mere moment in time for me, is also a grand event. An opulent, effervescent All-Bubble Ball, a magnificent occasion, demanding that each small transparent guest wear their finest, most glimmering-shimmering frippery. I sit up and study them. The bubbles dance together. I get lost watching them crowd each other in graceful interconnected and randomly clumping orbits, merrily joining one another in jolly groups or pairing off in romantic seclusion. My favorites are the wee singles, the lone bubbles that drift off on their own and seem even happier once away, as if escape allowed them to look back and see the mesmerizing beauty floating serenely behind them in peaked clouds on a silky white sea.

It must be the absinthe. I must remember to get some absinthe.

I study the lone singles, and they seem to become intoxicated by some invisible, vibrating, percolating velocity as they go along their travels, most usually near their death. They seem to know the dance is almost over. Sailing about, they become bigger and brighter every moment with a sharp iridescent green; they hurry, tacking hard across the harbor, gathering up all the most beautiful sights. Then, as though they cannot withstand their own sheer happiness, or perhaps the orchestral frequency of their brothers, they pause, quivering with incandescence and washed with pearly faces, all luminous, shiny, and bright. Then they . . .

Pop!

A tiny shout. A cry of joy and the bubbles burst apart at their iridescent seams. Not a shout of warning or weakness or worry . . . not that. They give a shout of unstoppable, incandescent glee. Then they're gone. This is the way bubbles die. I watch legion after legion of them die, until the milky bathwater is all but spent. No bubbles remain.

When the water becomes less warm, I draw myself up and wrap a large terry-cloth towel around my pale body. I step out of the tub gingerly, onto the cool porcelain floor, and climb into bed. There I write deep thoughts in my journal, using neat handwriting, until I fall asleep with all the lights on. My journal is still open, the pen rolling off the page, staining the white sheet a darkly blooming permanent blue, as my last thought hovers, abandoned on the page. It's this. There can be nothing happier or better on earth than to be a little bubble, a bubble that lives an entire life in just one day. Especially if that very short day is actually a long, magnificent dance.

Brad comes home with an apple-green Lamborghini, to celebrate his rising star at Keller's, a Lamborghini Gallardo LP570-4 Superleggera, to be exact. I shake my head. "How much did that thing cost?" I ask him.

"Isn't it insane!" he shouts at me over the roaring engine.

"Yes, Brad, it is. Especially since it's winter . . . in Minnesota."

"It's sick! She goes two hundred and sixty miles an hour!"

I cross my arms. "I see. And is there an autobahn somewhere nearby that I'm not aware of? Indoors, perhaps? Or with heated roads?"

At Brad's insistence I climb into the ridiculous green car, my head bumping the ceiling. You could slide this car under a school bus if you weren't careful. Brad puts the beast in gear and guns the engine, which roars so loudly I cover my ears. We take off, my stomach lurching, and with each turn I think I might vomit inside his new car. The whole ten-minute drive he's laughing like a maniac while I scream, *Slow down! Slow down! Slow down!* We veer around the lake so fast, we actually hit a bird *in flight*. Not one on the road, one that's actually flying through the air. A crow smacks right off the windshield and Brad curses it, the vehicle screeching to a halt. "My God!" he says. "Did it crack the windshield?"

Soon after we get back home, a car honks outside. "That's the Brock!" Brad shouts. "He's gonna shit his pants when he sees the new Lambo! Wanna go for another test ride with us?"

"No, thanks. I think I've killed enough birds in flight for one day."

For New Year's Eve Brad flies to Tokyo and Addi takes me and Ellie to some artist's party in the warehouse district, where guests pour back champagne and gnaw on lobster claws. The semifamous artist throwing the event takes plaster casts of willing participants' genitalia behind a tasteful Japanese silk screen.

Addi is first in line to sit on a bucket and have her hoo-hah planted in a tub of cold wet plaster. Then we all line up, drunk on the extraordinarily strong mojitos. After he's done, the artist's assistants set out plaster pussies and penises on a long table under flickering candles and guests guess which organ belongs to whom. One thing is certain: There are some really weird-looking vaginas walking around in the world, with orchid-like stamens and ham-steak-size labia.

"Wow, Jen," Addi says. "You have the cutest one of all." She's joking. My vagina looks like a smashed bat stuck on the grille of a car. Of course, Ellie's isn't pretty either. Her vulva looks like a meat-eating orchid. Addi's looks like Edvard Munch's *The Scream*.

13
Yokemate

In January the weather gets weird-ugly. It warms up and thaws, warms up and thaws, creating a week of weird warm sloshy slush, followed by a frigid week of brutal black ice.

Everyone on earth has the flu, including me. Two weeks of fever, headaches, body aches, and painfully coughing up butter weasels. By the tenth day I hold my arms aloft and say out loud, "Death, I welcome thee."

Even when I get better, something is off. The world around me looks the same but feels different. Like the wrong music is playing. The club feels stuffy, the cocktail parties get boring. I've heard every conversation before, eaten every appetizer already. Brad is always away on business trips these days. I go to almost every social event without him, and I notice lots of wives of wealthy men do. I spend more and more time with the girls at the club lunching and talking. Addi regales us with horror stories from the unhappy housewives field. Souring marriages, acrimonious separations, and sticky divorces fester in every corner of the club. We talk about the trouble with marriage, everyone gladly joining in.

Does your husband do that? My husband does too! Drives me crazy. We ask each other constantly, *What's wrong with men? Why can't they clean up after themselves? Why do they leave dirty socks on the floor and damp towels on the bed? What's the deal with their thermostat control issues and remote control fetishes? Why do they forget our anniversaries but remember to turn on the game when we're trying to have sex in bed?* The rhythm and predictability of these conversations is comforting in a discomforting way. You feel better while you're doing it but worse afterward. Hollow, like a tunnel.

All this complaining inspires another list for Emily.

Top Ten Mistakes New Brides Make

1. *Cooking too often.* If you cook seven fabulous dinners the first week of marriage . . . you have now set the tone. Anything less than cooking a fabulous meal every night will be regarded as your "slipping." Do everyone a favor and cook nothing until about three months in. Then make it something simple and burn it.

2. *Cleaning too much.* See above. Picking up socks on day 1 leads to picking them up on day 1,001. Set the standard early and buy four shop vacs with wide-mouth hoses, one each for the bedroom, bathroom, den, living room, etc. When you see a pair of socks on the floor, vacuum them up. Your husband will think elves took them. The vacuum is an excellent hiding space for almost anything. Your hubs will never look in the vacuum. He will not think to change a filter, no matter how many years you own it.

3. *Enjoying sex like a man.* Just like cooking, the more often you slap it down on the table, the more often your

man will expect to see it slapped there. While everyone feels romantic in the beginning, it's better to pace yourself. Keep the shenanigans down to once a week at most. Less is more. There's nowhere to go but up!

4. *Encouraging his "friendships."* Your husband's friends are now officially your foes. Even if you liked them before, they are now your adversaries. They will work actively to lead your husband astray. They will be there for every dumb idea and weak moment he has, egging him on. Don't make more work for yourself later by initially encouraging these wolves in pleated khakis. Best bet is to get them all married off. Fast.

5. *Encouraging hobbies.* Hobbies cost money and take time. The last thing you need is your husband spending all his hard-earned income on some dinky little trains or shiny golf clubs. God forbid he starts a band. Should one of these nasty hobbies take hold, consider breaking his habit for him by staging a robbery. Should he replace the items lost, stick to your guns and steal it all again. Eventually his willful spirit will become too exhausted to fill out another insurance claim.

6. *Allowing him to spend too much time alone.* Don't let that little squirrel of yours go storing up his nuts without you! Lord knows what they get into when nobody is watching. You'll never have to find out if you always know what he does. Pay off secretaries and gym valets for intel. It's worth it.

7. *Letting up on him.* Not insisting the hubster do his chores is tantamount to electing for a divorce. Consider the Stanford Prison Experiment, which proved prisoners will act exactly like you expect them to. If you expect hubs to be lazy from time to time, he will be. And more

so and more so until it's you living with a chimp who complains bitterly, does nothing, and has his own car keys.

8. *Not severely punishing him.* You must punish your husband for any infraction, no matter how small. Sled dogs are trained when they're puppies. At their first mistake, their owner violently shakes them . . . and they never make that mistake again in their noble lives. Now, your hubby's no puppy. Imagine how hard you're going to have to shake him.

9. *Conceding defeat.* Never give up. Never surrender. This will take time and no path is easy. Consider your husband the biggest and most unending renovation project of your life. It will take time and resources, and lives may be lost.

10. *Fighting over every little thing.* Everyone argues, but bickering left unchecked becomes a way of life, a native tongue you must speak when you enter the door. Put aside these childish ways and settle your differences the way tycoons do: trade them away. Offer to give up clipping your toenails in bed if he'll start taking the trash out when he's supposed to. Get everything in writing, just like lawyers. If marriage is an institution, then you're cochairs of the organization and you should communicate properly, through certified letters and not goofy little Post-it notes with hearts on them.

The main complaint we yokemates have, ironically, is absenteeism. Ellie says she sees her husband, Rick, for about a half hour a day, and that's hardly enough time to tell him everything he's screwed up and has to fix and/or needs to leave alone. I feel sorry for Ellie. Everyone thinks her life's so perfect, but I wouldn't want to live even one day of it. She and Rick never touch each other. Ever. They never kiss, never hold hands, never have sex. They apparently don't talk much outside the most necessary exchanges; intimacy on any level is nonexistent. Ellie says back when they were dating, they had a passionate sex life, but as Rick's hedge fund began to take off, he worked longer and longer hours, often coming home too tired to take off his shoes, let alone to make love to his wife. Ellie felt rejected and angry.

Whenever Rick did have time for her, she enjoyed turning the tables on him and rejecting his advances. Ellie says she learned to use sex as a weapon, withheld it whenever she was angry or upset or even mildly irked. By the time she finally cooled off, it was then Rick's turn to give her the cold shoulder. So the game went on until they both just shut down. Rick started to pull even longer hours at work. Ellie's convinced he's cheating on her. Now they live together as hostile roommates who never speak to each other. They only communicate through their precocious, robust, and ruthlessly intelligent eight-year-old son, Cody. So there they are, like silent planets of stone, orbiting each other, each unable to get closer to the other or break away.

I guess I shouldn't be so judgmental. It's not like my marriage is going to win any awards. Addi says she'll never get married again. She says any woman who decides to get married is crazy. Right now, I'd have to agree. Brad's never home anymore and when he is, we fight like crazy. Over dumb things. Stupid things. Like the toothpaste war. It started with my "inability" to replace the cap after using our toothpaste. I researched it online, and toothpaste caps are one of the top ten reasons couples fight.

Top Ten Reasons Couples Fight

1. Money. Spending it, saving it, who has it, who doesn't, and why your credit card bill is now larger than the national debt.
2. Assuming a fleet of maids will clean up all the toothpaste/beard stubble/soap gunk left on the sink.
3. Assuming a jaunty elf named T.P. replaces the toilet paper when it's empty.
4. Using an excessive amount of glassware/dishware and leaving it strewn about so the house continually looks like a party just ended.
5. Depositing damp towels on the bed and making the comforter damp, so sleeping becomes like a survival story in the rain forest.
6. Leaving the dishwasher door open and nearly killing people.
7. Leaving dirty socks and skid-marked underwear on the closet floor for your spouse to see, like a special art exhibition.
8. Leaving the toilet seat up and causing your spouse to have Startling Drop and Shockingly Cold Ass syndrome.
9. Leaving the lights on or leaving the lights off. Flicking the remote control. Opening the garage door or not opening the garage door. Basically any switch or device that can be toggled causes marital woe.
10. Heat. To turn up or not to turn up? That is the eternal question. Someone is constantly trying to freeze or bake the other one to death. That much we know.

Any of these complaints and many, many, many others are sanctioned reasons to seek out marriage counseling and/or start a blog called Things He/She Does to Make Me *Crazy*!!! Statistically it's husbands who more often commit these offenses, but in our house I am the main perpetrator. I'm always losing the toothpaste cap and it drives Brad nuts. Naturally I switched to toothpaste with an attached flip top, but that did little good. I just wrench the damn thing off, usually in the morning after a night of drinking too much wine. I can't help it. I have superhuman strength sometimes. Usually when I'm holding the toothpaste. The fact is, everybody on earth falls into one of two camps.

Those who cap the bitch . . . and those who don't.

Personally, I'm not sure why toothpaste caps are so important. Probably because I'm a non-capper, and non-cappers don't understand why anybody worries about a missing toothpaste cap. More important, we fundamentally *don't care*. Why get so bent out of shape about a dinky bit of plastic? When Brad asks, "Where's the toothpaste cap?" I usually shrug and say something like, "I have no idea, maybe it rolled away. Maybe it fell down the drain. Maybe a ladybug wanted a hat. *How should I know?* Get over it already. Move on. You can worry about dinky bits of plastic after cancer is cured and they figure out where the Mayans went, okay? Solve those mysteries first."

Brad is rarely amused by this. This is not the way cappers view the world. They see a missing toothpaste cap as a rift in the universe. Nothing can move forward until (1) the toothpaste cap is located, (2) it's screwed back onto the tube, and (3) an adequate explanation for the cap's disappearance is provided. The problem with this last requirement is that no acceptable explanation exists on earth. No matter *what* happened, no matter *how* compelling the story (e.g., a vicious crow flew through the open window and attacked you, flying off with the toothpaste cap and leaving you with bloody stumps for fingers), it doesn't matter. It's inadequate. *Why?* Because replacing a toothpaste cap takes "all of three seconds." Even in the event of an emergency, like vicious crow behavior, it would be simple to do.

At least this is what Brad tells me.

So fine. No big deal, but even the tiniest smear of toothpaste on the sink sends him into paroxysms of rage. He says my careless toothpaste droppings are ruining all his suits. He hunts for toothpaste infractions like a toothpaste forensics specialist. No matter how angry he gets, I can't take it seriously. *It's toothpaste.* Judging by Brad's complete disgust for the tingly paste, however, you'd think it wasn't toothpaste smeared around the sink but the fecal remnants of some wintergreen elves living in the medicine cabinet. So that's who I start blaming. The naughty little elves that live in the medicine cabinet and poop minty-white diarrhea paste. I even made a Christmas centerpiece based on them. A large potted poinsettia encircled at the base by pinecone candle holders set the stage for my merry little wintergreen elves, who were carefully posed in miniature scenes among the leaves enjoying various wintergreen-elf activities, like boinking.

Brad remained unamused.

Eventually I flee downstairs, defecting to the guest bathroom, and I brush my teeth there. In all honesty, I'd gladly keep the ball-sack cap on the cumwad toothpaste tube, and I'd do so religiously, if only the praise I received for capping the toothpaste was even remotely close to the punishment I received for *not* capping it. Uncapped toothpaste = utter disgust/ensuing insults/probable fight. Capped toothpaste = no reward or reaction whatsoever.

Ellie and Addi tell me to ignore Brad and his constant complaining. Ellie says her husband goes ballistic if she leaves shopping bags in the front hall. He hates anything not put away and snaps at her about clothing on the floor, newspapers on the table, and coffee cups on the counter. I tell her he sounds a little irrational and she says that's nothing. Her pet peeves include forks loaded into the dishwasher with their prongs down, food in the refrigerator that's facing "backward," and when the toilet paper is on the roll the wrong way. "Yikes," I say. "Remind me not to marry either of you guys."

"It's just that couples who live together for a long time slowly become unhinged by even the smallest things," Ellie says. "I never used to care which way the toilet paper roll was, but over the years I started to notice he put it on a different way, and I took it as a sign of disrespect."

"Does he still put it on the wrong way?"

"The maid puts all the toilet paper on the rolls these days," she says. "I just pay her extra to put it on the right way."

Addi says her ex-husband clipped his nails for hours on end in bed and ate cereal like a "jackass." I tell them I keep thinking if I could just stop annoying Brad he might look at me like he used to. Like he wants me. I'd give anything if he'd look at me that way. "Oh, please!" Addi rolls her eyes. "Men always complain about something. There's no point in trying to please them. Trust me, I know."

"You're divorced," Ellie says.

"Exactly. I know everything about being a wife. I have three ex-husbands to prove it."

The truth is none of us is exactly happy with her domestic life. We soothe ourselves by hunting down things that please us and are perfect. We search tirelessly for the perfect massage, the perfect handbag, the perfect carpaccio. It's a particular thorn in our side when we think we have the best of something, only to discover there's something better. I bought a new Prada handbag and was about to show it off to the girls when Addi walked in with an Hermès. I just shoved my handbag under the chair and didn't say anything.

People tease me about how "picky" I've become, but the truth is I'm a lot more educated about quality. I can tell cow leather from calfskin ten yards away. And I now know the difference between a skilled facial technician and an ape flinging crap at my face. Still, people frown upon pickiness around here. Christopher commented on my "increased sensitivity" last week, when we went to Hillcrest for lunch. I ordered a seafood salad with no scallops, extra lemon wedges, and dressing on the side. An order that would've seemed monastic to the club girls seemed "fussy" to him.

I don't care. I like how I am.

Not really.

Reverend Coy comes for a visit and I ask about the Olya doll. He says she originated from an impoverished village in Russia called Olkhovka. "If you could only see these families," he says. "They have nothing . . . we dressed Olya up in clothes most children from the swamp dream of seeing."

"Swamp?" I ask.

"The Olkhovka Swamp was contaminated by radioactive water leakage, from the Beloyarsk nuclear power plant nearby. They've cleaned everything up now, of course."

"Of course," I say, inching away from the Olya doll sitting on the table.

"So now we must find a way to get the village back on its feet. Let them grow strong again! Praise Jesus!"

"Yep . . ." I nod. "He's got a heckuva world going on down here."

I tell Brad about the nuclear-leak dolls and he's completely unconcerned, if not annoyed I'm bothering him with these unimportant details. "But, Brad," I say, "how do you know those dolls have no contamination in them? Do we test them?"

He says oh yes, *hardy har har,* every doll goes to Leningrad for testing and then a special spa in Minsk. "Jesus, Jen." He sighs. "I know you're not a business major but even you know commercial products are made with chemicals."

"This isn't chemicals, Brad. This is radioactivity."

He rolls his eyes. "Fine," he says. "You want to test the dolls? Test away, darling. You do keep things from getting boring." I take the matter very seriously and send a sample doll away to a lab recommended to me by the animal hospital.

I finally attend Supper Club, my first one in months. I go because finally my family's not annoyed with me. I've been missing in action for some time, but I gave Lenny and Hailey a super baby present: one of every single item sold in Keller's Peapod Department, which is what they call their infant section. Blankets, bedding, clothing, strollers, appliances, everything. Brad went ballistic but it was worth it, because everyone in my family is smiling at me again.

The other reason I show up is this week's Supper Club theme is the state fair. Everybody brings their favorite dish from the state fair; it's sort of a way to bring a little bit of summer into the dead of winter. It's also a way to get food, *any food,* on sticks. Everything is on a stick. Corn dogs on a stick, fried green tomatoes on a stick, barbecued rib fingers on a stick, fried jalapeño peppers on a stick, corncobs on a stick, pizza on a stick, walleye cheeks on a stick, cheesy pretzels on a stick, deep-fried pickles on a stick, frozen bananas on a stick, etc. . . . My favorite is martini on a stick. A frozen alcoholic Popsicle.

We also exchange belated Christmas presents, since everyone was somewhere else for the holidays. Hailey and Lenny went to Brainerd to visit Lenny's family (scary), and my mom and dad booked a Caribbean cruise like the Kellers, in the hopes that some warm weather would make my dad's health issues go away. He's been working too hard and gets worn down easily. I give Mom and Dad a new flatscreen TV. I give Hailey a gift certificate to Keller's for new clothes and I give Lenny a new box of ice-fishing lures.

They didn't get me anything. Nobody. Not even my mom and dad. They smile and say I have everything already, don't I? This makes me mad for some reason, even though it's completely and totally true. In the midst of the rest of them opening presents I find myself childishly wanting attention and I announce that I'm opening a college fund for each of the twins.

"Opening a what?" Lenny asks.

"A college fund, Lenny. It's like a coffee can, but bigger."

At home that night I find Pho has updated the Ice Empress. She appears with a big X of electrical tape over her mouth, a result of my telling Pho to "just shut her up!" Now I wince as she mumbles incoherently. I put a Post-it note on Pho's Yoo-hoo sitting on the counter:

> Pho Fang!
>
> Please degag the Ice Empress. It's creepy.
> Just give her new words or something.
>
> Love, Auntie J

I go exercise with Big D. We have a standing appointment for every Wednesday at three. We usually go jogging, and often through dicey neighborhoods. He says it makes me run faster.

On one of our jogs, I get a pebble in my shoe and stop to fix it, but Big D just keeps jogging faster, shouting, "I wouldn't slow down around here, white girl!"

"Big D, stop!"

"Why?" He turns around, jogging in place. "You under arrest by the Holy Spirit?"

"No! I have a pebble in my shoe!"

"Lord, now she got a pebble in her shoe."

"My leg is cramping too."

"Uh-huh. You some kinda flaw junkie, lady."

"I'm a what?"

"A *flaw junkie*. Always lookin' for problems. Any itty-bitty little thing. Then you go, '*Wooooo!* I found one. I found one! I found me a flaw. Looky here, big beautiful world. You can suck my dick. I found me a little pebble in my shoe. *Woooo.*'"

"'Wooo'? I don't go 'Wooooo.'"

"You go '*Wooo!*' Shit, woman, all you do is wooo."

"Sorry. My foot *hurts*. Should I keep running and get a big blister? I *hate* these shoes. I always get blisters when I run in these. Always."

"Lord, now she Godzillafying."

"*I'm what?*"

"Godzillafying. Makin' everything huge. Knockin' down buildings get in your way. Shoot, can't you just take a Goddamn pebble outta your shoe and get on with your damn day? You think *this* here's the worst day of your life? Sun shinin'. God smilin'. Woman with big titties over there."

"*Big D!*"

"Mmm-hmmm." He shakes his head. "Love big titties. Come on, you givin' me a headache, woman. Let's go!"

I'm still sore the next cold wintry morning when I have to don my heavy coat and troop down to Keller's Department Store to sign more papers in Todd Brockman's office. Why I have to sign these damn documents there, and not at home, is a mystery. Todd's on the phone with his door closed when I get there, so I visit Brad in his office. He tells me to close the door and says I'm spending too much money. "How much money did you spend at this Medi-Spa place?" he asks me angrily. I tell him to stop shouting at me. I'm supposed to spend money; he said I had to make everything perfect. "Not so *much* money, Jen! Jeez! Todd Brockman saw your monthly spa line item and freaked."

"Line item? What line item? Who the hell is looking at our monthly expenses?"

"Todd Brockman!" he says. "He checks our monthly spending report!"

"What monthly spending report?"

"The one that tracks our costs, utilities, transportation, food, clothing, and expendables? And your stupid spa treatments."

"What else is in this report?" I ask him suspiciously. "Can *Todd Brockman* see how often I buy tampons?"

"If you put it on a credit card, it goes in the report."

"No." I shake my head. "I will *not* have that slimy little toad making pie charts about my tampon drawer!"

"Ahoy there, Jen!" Todd Brockman is standing right behind me.

"Ahoy . . . *Todd*." I sigh. "Be right with you."

Todd knocks on the door twice and says, "Righty-o!"

Brad says pie chart or no pie chart, we have to cut down on our spending. His mother says the only people who spend money like I do are the wives of sheiks in Dubai. I'm incensed. "She's allowed to look at our spending reports too? Where did she pick up that little tidbit about sheiks? Does she watch *The Real Housewives of Dubai*?"

"My mother's part owner of the company," he tells me. Then

he says, "Did you in fact give Pho, the son of our maid, ten thousand dollars? Tell me you're joking."

"Pho is our maid's grandson, and I didn't give him the money; he worked for it. He fixed that big stupid refrigerator from your Japanese friends. I called the regular repairman; they didn't even know where the electrical panel was to fix it."

"Get the money back," he says.

"No!"

"Yes."

"Brad, how can you stand there and tell me to stop spending money when you buy a freaking Lamborghini?"

"Because I'm the one who *works* for a living," he says. "It's *my* money!"

"*Your* money?"

"*My* money," he repeats.

"Funny," I say. "With all that marriage-vow crap, I thought it was ours."

I turn around to leave.

"Hang on," he says. "One more thing. Is there anything else you have to tell me?"

I stare at him blankly. "Like what?"

"Like . . . about any new family members you might be having?"

"New family members?"

"Courtesy of Lenny and Hailey?"

A slow dread crawls over me. "Oh. Right. I forgot to tell you, Hailey's having twins."

He crosses his arms. "You *forgot* to tell me?"

"I thought I did tell you. Didn't I tell you?"

"No, you didn't. My mom is furious."

"She is?" My mind races. "Why?"

"Because she's not stupid, Jen! She found out from somebody

at church and figured out when they were conceived! On our honeymoon? Jesus! *You're* the one who's supposed to be having babies!"

"Well, it's not like a competition or something! Hailey and I don't share a uterus; I have my own eggs, you know. I'm perfectly capable of having a baby."

"You sure about that?"

"What's that supposed to mean?"

"It means you should've gotten pregnant by now. My parents expect us to have a family."

"I hate to break this to you, Brad, but you have to have *sex* to have a baby."

"Of course, blame everything on me."

"You are a pretty important part of the puzzle, Brad! I can't get pregnant without your piece!" His phone rings and he takes the call. What a jerk. What an insensitive creep!

I storm down to visual display in the basement, hoping Christopher will get a coffee with me, but he's in a bad mood too. Everybody freaking is. He starts in about the cheap merchandise he's handling and how at this rate he'll have to find hospice care for a fabulous gay man with umpteen forms of cancer. I tell him to lighten up and he flies off the handle at me. He says he doesn't even know who I am anymore. He thought all this trophy wife stuff was funny at first, but he doesn't want to play the game anymore. I've changed. I'm insensitive and mean now, I'm a terrible friend. He doesn't even think he can be friends with someone who's as callous and insensitive as me.

Oh, whatever. I don't have time for the drama. I can get coffee without him. I make my way to the third floor and weave through the crowded skyway. I pass the Cinnabon counter and a voice says, "Going somewhere?" The Cinnabon girl smiles at me. I should flex my Keller royalty credentials and force her evil empire of icing out of the skyway altogether, but then where would I eat my secrets? "Free sample!" she says, holding up a tray of piping-hot, freshly iced sinning.

I step back and shake my head. "Sorry," I tell her. "I'm on a diet."

"I won't tell anyone," she says coyly. I stare at her. Damn her circular thinking. I pounce quickly, grabbing a sticky cinnamony sin ball, which I stuff in my face and swallow almost immediately.

"I'll take three more," I tell her. Why the hell not? I'm on diet pills, I'm paying top dollar to be irritable and nauseous twenty-four hours a day, why not wolf down some Goddamned hot lard if I want to?

The Cinnabon girl nods at me. "Diet pills?"

"Absolutely," I say. "Trimexa."

"Everyone's taking that stuff," she says. "Our sales have doubled."

"I'm so *happy* for you."

"Toilet line has doubled too."

I look down the hall at the public restroom, the only restroom on this stretch of skyway, and I panic. There's a line snaking out of the ladies' room. "No," I gasp as my stomach rumbles.

"No worries," Cinnabon girl says. "I let my best customers use our employee bathroom. It's in the back."

"Thank you," I whisper, starting to push the swinging door open.

"Not so fast." She stops me. "I said my *best* customers." She smiles and taps the Cinners Club sign on the swinging door.

I look at her in horror. "Seriously? That's where you were going?"

She smiles at me unkindly. "I think we both know where I was going. I get a commission for every new membership I sell."

"Fine, I will, right after I . . . I just need to . . ." I try to push my way past her, but she holds the swinging door shut. Evil witch. She makes me fish out my credit card and hand it to her before she lets me in. I dash past her and into the back room, where I use the smallest, dirtiest employee bathroom I've ever seen. When I come out, the Cinnabon girl hands me a membership card and a copy of *Cinn and Bon, the Cinner's Club Monthly Newsletter*. I snatch them up and march onward . . . then stop short. "Nice try," I say.

She looks up at me. "Forget something?"

"No, not me . . . *you did*. Give it."

"Give . . ." She looks around quizzically. "Oh! Of course. Sorry." She digs under the counter and tosses me a Cinnabon scratch-n-sniff key chain. I snap it up like a shark on a hunk of plastic scratch-n-sniff steak. "Sorry!" she says again as I start to leave.

I look back at her and shrug. "Aren't we all?"

14
Queen of Hearts

Last year on Valentine's Day, both my sister and my ex-boyfriend got married. I suppose I should be grateful it wasn't to each other. This year will be different. The whole thing's scheduled. While Brad spends the day at the office, I'll spend the whole day at the spa getting primped, plumped, plucked, and prepared. Then I'll go home and put on my perfect Valentine's Day dress, a red Valentino that Addi found for me at a New York fashion show. Then Brad will come home and we'll take a limo to the annual Hillcrest Valentine's Day Sweetheart Ball.

It will be perfect *or* I will kill myself.

Everything goes according to plan; there are no mishaps at the spa, no unfortunate waxing incidents or anal bleaching burns, no getting locked inside the sauna for six hours. On the way home my mother calls to wish me a happy Valentine's Day. "So, hon," she says. "I just wanna make sure you're wearing your big boots tonight."

"Um . . . I wasn't planning on it."

"Honey, I'm serious. You have to stay warm. It's two degrees below zero."

"I know, that's why I rented a limousine. So we'd stay warm."

"But, honey, you still have to get from the car to the door."

"And I'll get frostbite during that time?"

"You could slip."

"I won't slip."

"You can't go out in this weather without boots on, hon."

"Mom, I'm wearing a five-thousand-dollar Valentino gown. I'm *not* wearing boots."

"Well, there was a story on the news last night about this poor girl whose car broke down near Brainerd and she walked for miles and miles to find help, but she went the wrong way and she wasn't wearing boots. She *froze* to death, so . . ."

I wait for her to continue. She doesn't. "So *what*, Mom?"

"So bring your cell phone and a map."

"A *map*?"

"Oh! And there was a woman who got attacked by some guy who tried to *you-know-what* her, but she got away. She threw a hot cup of coffee in his face. That's smart thinking."

"Okay, Mom." I sigh. "I'll carry around a hot cup of coffee with me tonight, and a cell phone and a map. Anything else?"

"Oh, you shouldn't drink coffee anymore. The beans are picked by children."

Later that night, I give Ace his Valentine's Day gift, a big rawhide and a postcard of a sexy poodle taped over his water bowl. Then I give Valentine presents to the Fang Gang. A fluffy pink robe for Bi'ch, a red beanbag chair for Pho and his study cubby, and a big box of chocolates for Star Fan. Pac Man gets a $500 gift card to Toys "R" Us.

I go up to the refrigerator and say, "Ice Empress?"

She appears with a big blue gangsta do-rag on her head and says, "S'up, baby?"

"Um . . . is the champagne chilled?"

She winks and says, "Shit yes, bitch! Check this out . . . I iced your shit up good!"

I go get Pho's Valentine's Day card and add to it:

Pho, please deghetto the Ice Empress. It's going to upset Mr. B. Just class her up or something.

Love, Auntie J

Upstairs, I fling rose petals all over the bedroom and strategically hang my complicated lingerie in the closet, for maximum speed putting it on. I just have to remember the fishnets go *over* the super-elastic girdle snaps. Get it wrong and there could be a wardrobe malfunction.

I slip into my silk, oxblood-red Valentino dress, with coquettish fluted skirt and fitted empire waist, and a matching pair of oxblood-red shoes, and grab my oxblood-red sequined clutch purse. The outfit is stunning. Even better, my Wonderbra hikes up my breasts so much, it provides ample room in my cleavage to tuck my cell phone.

I dawdle and dabble with finishing touches, tweaking and tweezing until I realize it's late. Brad should be home by now. I call him at the office and his secretary puts me on hold. Then Brad gets on and says he's sorry, but he has to work late tonight. He'll meet me at the club later on. "But what about your tuxedo?" I ask him, and he says he'll just come in his suit.

Drat.

How boring. I wanted to pull up at the club in a limo together. Then it occurs to me that the romantic move here would be to take the limo downtown and wait for Brad outside. Dutiful and dressed in haute couture. What a lucky devil. Fifteen minutes later I pour myself a to-go cup of pink champagne and head for the gleaming stretch limo waiting in the driveway. Only, it's not waiting in the driveway. I call the limo service. The line is busy. A prerecorded voice says due to increased Valentine's Day call volume, I should leave a message and someone will get back to me on Monday. *Monday?* I panic. I should've booked a backup limo.

I call Addi and Ellie. No answer. I start to call Christopher and remember we're not speaking. Finally I call Hailey. "It's an emergency," I tell her. "Does Lenny know anyone who drives a car? I need a limo in like . . . fifteen minutes."

"Oh really?" she says. "That's so sweet! And here I thought you'd *forgotten* it was our one-year anniversary!"

"Oh. Right. Um . . . happy anniversary."

"You forgot that we're throwing an anniversary party tonight, didn't you."

"No. No! I just . . . Yes. I did. Okay? I have a life too. Can you just ask Lenny?"

She screams for Lenny and I tell her that can't be good for the babies, they'll be born deaf. She says with an aunt like me, they'll thank her. Lenny gets on the phone and says he has a buddy. He'll call me back. Five minutes later the phone rings and Lenny says everything's set. His buddy'll pick me up in twenty-five minutes. I thank him, hang up the phone, and go pour myself a vodka tonic as big as my head.

Twenty-two minutes later, a car pulls up in the driveway. A *hearse*. A hearse converted into a stretch limo. The driver gets out wearing a bright safety-orange poncho with a fur collar and he grins at me, like this must be the greatest moment on earth. My abject horror over the vehicle is temporarily clouded by an abject confusion over his *face*. I know this guy. I squint hard at him. "*Nick?*"

"Um . . . yeah?"

"It's me, Jennifer Keller."

"Who?" He frowns.

"*Jennifer Keller?*" I step closer. "We've met a couple of times? At the vet, and at my brother-in-law's house?"

"Oh. Who's your brother-in-law?"

"Lenny? The guy who asked you to come over here?"

"*Lenny?*" He smacks his knee. "That fat bastard is your brother-in-law? Man! Was I drunk at that guy's wedding! Got a black eye that night, can't remember how. Wound up going home with one of the bridesmaids, can't remember which one. Might explain the black eye. Man, was that a good time!"

I put a hand on my hip; I'm getting seriously annoyed now. "I was *in* that wedding," I say flatly. "I was a bridesmaid."

"Oh. You were? I didn't . . . go home with *you*, did I?"

"Are you serious? Oh my God. No. You didn't."

"Whew! I didn't think so. That woulda been weird. She stole my wallet too."

Unbelievable. We stand there outside, in the cold, staring at each other, as slow snowflakes drift by. Finally he cracks a huge grin and slaps his knee. "Ah heck, Jen! Come on, I'm foolin' you! I know who you are, I knew before I got over here! I knew when Lenny gave me the address!"

I'm not amused. Not tonight. "You know, I'm actually late," I tell him. "Can we please go?" He tips his flap-eared aviator hat at me and opens the back door.

I sulk in the cavernous backseat. A freaking hearse on Valentine's Day. I never should've trusted Lenny. I can feel my blood pressure getting higher and my mind starting to whirl with disaster scenarios until I'm ready to spin out of control and we haven't even left the driveway yet. *Okay. Stop. Just relax. Breathe. I can do this.*

Don't be a flaw junkie. Don't Godzillafy.

Find the beauty in this moment. There's beauty in every weird, crappy, suck-storm moment. I ask Nick if this limo is his and he says it is. He bought it last year and fixed it up. Just a part-time thing, for when he's in town. He travels a lot. Takes photographs or something. "There isn't a bar in here, is there?" I ask hopefully, and he smiles at me in the rearview mirror.

"Your wish is my command, chief!" Then he hits a button and an old Art Deco bar appears, with mirrored panels and chrome railings. The bar has a wide array of liquor options, all mini-bottles, and many have strange names like Sex on Helium; Burn, Hobo, Burn!; Screaming Tarantula; and Dirty Little Girl Scout.

"I'm a whiskey man myself," Nick tells me, "but the kids love weird-ass drinks that taste like candy. Try one!"

I open a little bottle of something called Nipplewhipped. It's bright pink and tastes like bitter bubblegum, but it goes down fast and warms my stomach. Next I try a little bottle of Urinal Cake, which is bright blue and tastes just like a . . . urinal cake. Sweet, though. He's right, they really do taste like candy. Finally I down a bottle of Screw the Poodle, which tastes remarkably like sweet felt.

By the time we pull up in front of Keller's, I'm a bit tipsy. Nick parks by a glass window display showcasing a whole wall of those obnoxious blue and white Angel Bears. Hundreds and hundreds of them. They're holding up some glittery letters that say ALWAYS BE AN ANGEL & SAY I LOVE YOU THE KELLER'S WAY! "I'll be right back," I tell Nick. "I'm just going to tell my husband we're here."

Nick helps me out of the car and I nearly slip on the ice.

"You should wear boots," he says. "Those shoes are dumb."

"They cost more than your hearse," I say.

"Then they're Goddamned idiotic," he answers. I flip up my

collar against the biting cold and zip across the sidewalk to the cold frosted glass doors, my breath short puffs of smoke, my fingers shivering. You really can get cold in between the car and the door. I swipe my executive ID card on the brass panel beside the door, and the little green light goes on. I push the doors open. Inside, it's dark. The store is closed. It's eerie being there all alone with no other people; all the red exit signs are lit up like creatures watching me from the trees. The elevators take me up to Brad's floor, which is also dark and empty. I crack the door to his office open and freeze. I peer into the darkness. I can hear something. "Brad?" I whisper into the darkness. *"Brad?"*

Silence.

I hear something crash onto the floor. I step back, suddenly trembling. What am I doing in an empty building downtown at night? What if that's not Brad? What if it's a . . . department store killer? What if he wants to you-know-what me? *Why didn't I listen to my mother and carry around a cup of hot coffee?* My eyes suddenly focus and land on two shadowy figures on the desk. I hear . . . grunting noises. Images of the sex club in Saint John flash through my head. Two people are having *sex* on my husband's desk. They don't hear me. I'm too far away. I stop breathing. Stay frozen like a statue. Then it occurs to me like a fist to the gut . . . that one of them is my husband.

At this moment, many people might investigate further. They might fling the door open, turn on the lights, and point an accusing finger, demanding an explanation. Maybe they'd wait in the dark to see who came out of the office. Not me. I turn and run.

I never look back.

I just flee, punching the elevator button seventy-two thousand times, and when it doesn't come quickly enough, I bang down the escalators, my heart twisting into painful knots. I can't breathe. Oxygen unavailable. I sprint down the escalators, rushing past floor after floor of silent mannequins, all dressed up in ribbon and lacy lingerie. Perfect women. *No mouth, no brain, no blood*. No voice at all.

Hot tears burn my eyes as I hit the lobby. Charging toward the exit, I see the reflection of hundreds of Angel Bears in the window. I hate those stupid bears. I stare at them, rage pooling in my stomach. *I've got to get ahold of myself!* Maybe it wasn't even Brad in the office. Maybe it was the janitor or a . . . I cruise past the perfume counter and it hits me. I smelled Brad's cologne. In his office just now.

The distinct aroma of musky vanilla.

He was in there, all right.

With somebody.

Anger churns and rises, then surges forward. Always be an angel . . . my *ass*! Next thing I know, I'm standing inside a Keller's store window, knocking over the Angel Bear display that Christopher and his Gay Bee Brigade just finished putting up. I'm going crazy, knocking everything over. *What am I doing?* I don't know what I'm doing. I'm running on pure madness and adrenaline. I step back, panting. I've rearranged the teddy bears.

Before I got here they said:

ALWAYS BE AN ANGEL & SAY I LOVE YOU THE KELLER'S WAY!

Now they say:

WE'LL KILL YOU ALL!

Then I hear something tapping on the glass behind me. A group of people have gathered outside, standing by the widow pointing and laughing. A camera flash blinds me. Then I hear honking and see Nick through the window, waving and shouting.

"*Yo!* Let's go," he says. "*Time to go!*"

Squad-car cherry lights reflect off the snow and I scramble

quickly out of the window, cameras still flashing. I dash outside, sucking in the sharp air, and the hearse's passenger door is wide open. I dive into the backseat just as the squad car pulls up alongside. The cherry lights are flashing. Oh my God. *I'm going to be arrested.* My heart hammers, cold panic rising. I can see tomorrow's papers: WOULD-BE KELLER'S QUEEN ARRESTED FOR STORE-WINDOW SICKERY AND TEDDY BEAR MOLESTING . . .

Nick sits calmly at the wheel. "Quiet now," he says without looking at me. *"Stay still."*

I do. I stay perfectly still, crouched down on the floor.

"Easy now," he whispers.

Then he shouts at the officers. "Hey, fellas! Mind if I get out? I gotta pick up my fare!" Next thing I know we're rolling forward, nosing around the squad car.

We turn the corner and Nick says, "All right, chief, the coast is clear."

He doesn't ask me what happened or why I was in a store window trashing the Angel Bear display. He just asks me where I want to go next. I wipe away my tears and tell him to take me to Hillcrest. "Looks like I'll be spending Valentine's Day *alone*," I tell him.

He says, "Well, not quite alone. You got me, chief."

We pull into the snowy circular drive of Hillcrest Country Club and there's a long line of cars ahead of us, waiting for the valet. Over the club entrance is a big silver banner that says SWEETHEART BALL and is covered with big red and pink hearts. I slump back in my seat as we wait in line. Finally I sit up and tell Nick to pull around the cars. I don't want to go to the dance anymore. He nods in the rearview mirror and says, "It's a fair request."

When we pull out onto the snowy road, he asks me where I want to go. I have no idea what to tell him, so I tell him the truth.

"I don't know where to go. I don't want to go home." I wipe away a bleary tear and try to laugh. "I don't even know where home is anymore."

"I know a place," he says. "Real quiet."

He takes me to the banks of the Mississippi River. I stare skeptically at the stairs, which trail off at a steep incline into a thick swatch of black trees. Beyond them I can see the river, a winding band of swiftly moving dark water.

"We're going out there?" I ask nervously.

"Sure." He shrugs. "I live down there."

"In what? A cardboard box?"

"No, a metal box. I renovated an old barge."

"A barge?" I raise an eyebrow. "Like a *barge* barge, that brings big mountains of coal down the Mississippi?"

"Exactly. Only she's got no coal, but she does have an espresso machine."

I stare at him.

"Also it has a massage chair," he says.

"Right. This sounds so *To Catch a Predator*, it's not funny. Is there an ice cream maker and lots of toys too?"

"Actually," he says, "yes."

Certain of my impending death, I still want to see it.

"First let's get you a coat and some boots," he says. "I don't know what you're thinking, wearing those damn shoes." I look down at my frozen feet and for the first time realize they're blue. I wait in the backseat while Nick digs out a pair of big black hunting boots and another big safety-orange parka from the front seat.

"Here," he says. "Put these on."

I do as I'm told and feel much, much warmer. I follow Nick down the stairway slowly, stopping every other minute. "Wait!

Stop, I can't see anything! Where's the railing? Why wouldn't you put up a railing? Do you know how much this dress cost? Did I rip it? Why are there no lights? Or railings?" Finally Nick turns around, grabs me by the waist, and carries me over one shoulder. Just like that, as though I'm lighter than a sack of cotton balls. It makes me feel so tiny and dainty and quaint . . . I love it. I holler at him the whole way down though, despite that fact. I protest his technique and the odds we'll survive it. I say this is the worst idea anyone's ever had. I don't want him to know I'm thrilled.

One wants to *appear* to be a lady.

The trees thin out and we arrive at a moonlit riverbank. Nick takes my hand and leads me across the frozen ground. The wind picks up and the moon casts a bright blue light across the glistening snowbanks, so they look like sheets of waving diamonds. Along the riverbank is a collection of houseboats all lit up with cheerful orange windows and tied to rickety wooden docks. "People live down here?" I ask Nick.

"Only the brave ones stay year-round."

"Brave?"

He takes me to the last boat in the lineup, which is a small barge with iron sides and coal beds. The coal beds have been emptied out and remodeled into big studios. Now they have hardwood floors, built-in bookcases, and solar glass ceilings.

"You live here?" I marvel.

"Best part is she's seaworthy. I can take the SS *Nevertheless* anywhere."

"That's the barge's name? SS *Nevertheless*?"

"Yep. I got the name from that old movie with Humphrey Bogart and Katharine Hepburn . . ."

"*The African Queen!*"

"You know it?"

"Do I know it? Are you kidding? It's only like my most . . . um, yeah. I like it. It's okay."

"I wanna show you something else. Come on up here." He takes me up on deck, to the butt end of the boat, which he calls "aft." He really does not like it when I say "butt end." There, behind the old wheelhouse, is an igloo. He built it right on deck, with big chunky frozen bricks of snow. It's nearly six feet tall and gleams like an ice-blue dome of light under the moon.

"Can we go in?" I ask.

He nods and says, "Wait here. I'll grab some whiskey."

We have to kneel down and crawl through the igloo's narrow entrance, but once inside it's roomy. There's a small wood-burning stove at the center of the igloo, packed in a big block of snow so it doesn't melt the inside. Around the perimeter is a bench made of snow, and several niches cut into the wall have small oil lamps in them, which he lights.

Soon the cheerful little igloo is as toasty as a tiny baker's kitchen. Nick pours us plastic thermos cups full of whiskey. "I mostly come out here to watch the stars," he says, and points up to the ceiling, where a hole is cut. The metal stovepipe runs out through part of it, but through the other part, you can see the stars up above burning brightly.

"Bet you bring a lot of girls out here, don't you."

"In all honesty, I'm already in a relationship."

"Oh?" I say sadly, all the ugliness of the evening returning. "Committed relationship?"

"Yep. She lives here with me. A gorgeous blonde named Tandy. You might meet her."

"Nice," I say, and shift uneasily. "You know, it's getting late."

"Really?" he says. "Time to go already?"

"Probably should." I sip my whiskey. "I do have to . . . pee, though. Any chance this rig has indoor plumbing?" I tell him I prefer indoor plumbing when wearing Valentino. He tells me not to worry. "Don't get your Valentino in a bunch," he says. "Hold on a second. We got indoor plumbing . . . it's indoors." He puts out the lamps and the woodstove, then leads me back to the metal door of the cabin. Inside the warm hallway, we're greeted by a friendly golden retriever. The dog nearly knocks me over trying to kiss me. "Jennifer," Nick says, "meet Tandy."

I look at him suspiciously. "This is Tandy?"

"She's the love of my life . . . sadly. Hey, Tandy girl!"

The barge is filled with old vintage furniture and black and white photographs from Nick's travels. In his messy office, crammed with books, there's a large map on the wall covered with red thumbtacks, marking all the places he's been. It's impressive.

"You've been to Kuala Lumpur?" I ask him.

"Yep. Shot monkeys at the Batu Caves."

"You . . . *shot* them?"

"Not with a gun. With a camera. I take pictures for assignments. Got a freelance gig with the Nature Conservancy."

"Do you travel a lot?"

"Not too much. Some. Enough to keep me driving a hearse for money."

"What are all those clocks?" I point to the other side of the office, which is covered with all these different clocks. Chrome clocks, cuckoo clocks, old clocks, new clocks. None of them is ticking and they're all set to different times.

"Those?" Nick says. "Those are for all the different moments in my life that I want to remember. That one there is set to the exact time my mom died: two forty-two. Over there, that one is set for five forty-three; that's when I first reached the summit of Mount McKinley. Little hobby."

"Wow," I tell him. "Pretty . . . cool hobby."

"Didn't you say you had to pee?"

I use the bathroom, which has a solar-powered toilet and is uncharacteristically clean for a bachelor pad. I wash my hands. Tucked into the mirror is a creased photograph of an old woman smiling and blowing out a birthday cake. His mother, I think. I dry my hands and notice a small blue glass vase filled with dried seahorses on the shelf next to the sink. Perfectly preserved, all standing together, as if they were riding in a subway car and waiting for the next stop.

I come out of the bathroom and Nick's made coffee. Espresso, on his shiny little machine. "Wait a minute . . ." I say, pointing at him. "I know why you're familiar!"

"Don't tell me that you saw me in your dreams," he says. "That's what women always say."

"No! I saw you at that Mexican restaurant. Last year!"

"El Salsaria?"

"Yes! Yes! Oh my God! You were standing outside when my husband and I were . . . fighting. Arguing. Having a discussion."

Nick tilts his head and nods slightly. "Oh yeah . . . I think I remember that. You were yelling at him . . . for not killing spiders."

"That's right! That was us! I remember you. I remember your orange parka! I kept thinking, *Why is this creepy guy watching us?*"

"Frankly," Nick says, "I was a little worried about the guy. I thought you might choke him. Didn't he order some video online? I remember you yelling at him about some video he bought called *Grannies Who Chug Cock*." Nick snorts. "You *married* that guy?"

"That was not our . . . best moment."

"I remember that fight pretty clearly now. You said he was cheating on you."

"Did I?"

"Well, was he? Cheating on you?"

"No! No. Of course not. I was . . . insecure at the time. Speaking of time, it's late. We should really . . ." My cell phone suddenly rings and I dig it out of my cleavage. "Hello?"

It's Hailey.

She's out of breath, talking so fast I can't understand her.

I say, "Hailey, slow down. What happened?"

She takes a deep breath and repeats herself. She says it's Dad. He's in the emergency room, he collapsed an hour ago. I have to get to the emergency room quick. They don't know how long he'll hang in there. I get off the phone, stunned. My heart has no beat. I blink and look at Nick. "It's my dad . . ." I tell him. "He's had a heart attack."

Nick drives me there on two wheels.

I sprint through the glass emergency room doors, my breath in short sharp bursts. I nearly crash into a woman leaving the hospital with a bright bouquet of sunflowers; they seem wrong and grossly inappropriate. I have to wait in line for what seems like an hour but is probably five minutes. I regret telling Nick to go. He tried to stay but I told him I'd be fine.

Which I'm not.

How can you be expected to ask about your critically unwell family member without crying? Or shouting? I never find out. The intake nurse herds me to a private room, separate from the main lobby and its lost ocean of empty blue chairs. There, my family is waiting.

"My God," I say, staring at Hailey's belly. "You're huge."

"Thanks," she snarls. "You're dressed like an idiot."

She's right. I *am* dressed like an idiot. I'm wearing a five-thousand-dollar dress, a safety-orange parka, and huge black hunting boots. I forgot to give them back.

I sit down on the peach-colored couch. My mom tells me they arrived twenty-eight minutes ago. The doctors are still running tests and assessing his condition.

"Why'd we get a private room to wait in?" I ask.

Hailey shrugs. "The nurse just said it was more comfortable."

More comfortable? Why do they want us to be comfortable? My heart begins to hammer. We sit on the scratchy apricot couches, staring into space. I become focused on a rage-inducing pastel print hanging on the wall, a starfish lying on a beach; beneath him it says LOVE LAUGHS WITH NATURE. I don't get it and I hate it. Lenny arrives with coffee. I dial Brad for the millionth time and leave another message. He's nowhere to be found. Then the waiting room door opens and we all sit up.

Blood roars through my head like a rushing ocean and splotches of the room turn gauzy, filmy white. *Am I having a stroke?* I think I'm having a stroke. I will have my stroke quietly so I don't distract the doctors. The air is cold like stone. My fingers worry the scratchy peach fabric. The sand-colored walls press in around me. No, you must tune in to what's happening, Jennifer. *Tune in!* I catch words. *Condition . . . critical . . . ICU . . . still testing . . .*

I focus harder. I breathe.

Whatever it is, you can handle it. What can they do? Can they kill you? So they kill you. Imagine all the frustration you'll avoid. No more pantyhose. No more parking at grocery stores in subzero weather. I breathe slower.

I tune in.

Dad's condition is not good, but it's stable. Stable is good. Stable means he's not getting worse. They have him up in the ICU. We collect our things and troop to the elevators. We see him in his room for the first time, so thin and frail under white sheets. My heart clutches, and I feel silently hysterical. The nurses take us to the ICU waiting room.

The doctors are running more tests.

We sit and we wait. Somebody goes to get food. Hamburgers. Another nurse comes in. There's a problem with Dad's insurance. They can't keep him in ICU. The doctors want him to stay, but the insurance policy says he must move. Hailey starts arguing. Mom starts crying. I freeze up completely. Then the door flies open. Brad is standing there, eight feet tall and full of fury. He takes command of the situation. He takes control. He asks the nurses specific questions. He speaks with authority to doctors. *Was this test done? Are those results back?* He summons new rounds of specialists. He makes phone calls, he makes requests, he stays on top of everyone. The nurses start moving more quickly. Answers start appearing. He seems like a genius. A hero. All talk of removing my dad from the ICU disappears.

I'm so grateful to him, my legs almost buckle. Then Hailey starts bellowing and there's water all over the floor. It's like a surreal Fellini film, with more irony than explanation. The angel of death hovers over my father and my scene-stealing, attention-nabbing-to-the-last-minute-of-every-day, stupid sister . . . has gone into labor.

Typical.

15
A Walnut in the Muffin

I need to get pregnant.

Fast.

My father's health scare steeps my tender brain in inky black images of the angel of death. My demise seems imminent, should my parents ever leave the planet completely . . . and they both look weak to me suddenly. Frail. If they went and Brad kicked me out I would surely die quickly, and probably somewhere tragic, like the woods behind Bennigan's.

Conversely Hailey is quite literally bursting with life. Two lives. She gave birth to Billy and Buddy, the biggest twins on record at the hospital. They're bruisers with blocky heads who look ready to rumble or belly up to the baby bar and toss down a pint before lifting Fisher-Price dumbbells at the Playskool infant weight room. Lenny is over the moon about them. Hailey seems less enthusiastic. Every thirty seconds she's sending him for more chipped ice or a lemon Coke or more painkillers, which she needs because of the cesarean section, which Lenny watched and about which he says, "It was like watching high-definition Syfy channel!"

Between my sister and father, my entire family more or less lives at the hospital for a full week, which is ten times what the insurance companies allow—most new moms get the boot within twenty-four hours of giving birth, but Mother Keller is at the helm now and the doctors give Hailey and the twins extra-extra special-special treatment. Mother Keller pays for a full-time nanny to move in with them and builds a state-of-the-art nursery at their home.

Dad's weak but recovering. The doctors say he can go home. Mother Keller gets a state-of-the-art hospital bed and a bunch of heart-monitoring equipment and has it installed in my parents' bedroom. She hires a full-time home health care worker, a nurse named Susannah, who takes care of my father.

At home we arrive at another unexpected event.

The reporter from the annual Heck of a Home Designer Home Showcase had visited the house while I was gone, and Bi'ch let her in, graciously allowing her and the photographer she brought along with her to see the whole house. Together they chronicled all the unique details of my life, including my junk food stash and failed sex toy collection in the closet, my library of mewling how-to-save-your-marriage literature for insecure wives, the dirty laundry heaped up on the floor, Ace's poop museum behind the couch in the living room, and the foul-mouthed Ice Empress in the refrigerator.

The featured item in the catalog, which was delivered to hundreds of thousands of homes, was of course on the table in the front hall. The artist himself delivered it and set it under the warm lights: a statue of my vagina, cast in bronze. My slick, gleaming vagina outshining all other calamities and still looking like a smashed bat stuck on the grille of a car. Brad takes one look at it and doesn't say another word.

I think it's a sort of truce.

Mother Keller doesn't say anything to me about the catalog either, but two weeks later we get a supplement in the mail and both her house and mine have been crossed off the list.

Nick calls to see how my dad is and I say much better. I thank him for all his help that night. Then I hang up. No distractions. Not anymore.

I need to focus on my life with Brad. I got lucky with the Angel Bear fiasco. The security cameras did show a wild woman destroying the store window, but the angle never shows my face. The only thing recognizable is my dress and my shoes. I burn them both. Actually I just wad them up in a Walgreens bag and throw them away . . . but in my heart I burn them. I burn any doubt. I decide to completely forget Valentine's Day. All thoughts of Brad's possible deceit drain from my mind. I mean, I never saw exactly who was in his office. I wasn't even supposed to be there. He could've been anywhere, and so what if the office smelled like his cologne? Of course it did. It's his office. His office could easily smell like his cologne even if he wasn't there. Probably. There are holes in my logic, but I don't care.

I need Brad. I need his family. What would I do without them? They pay for everything; they house me; they employ my brother-in-law, who supports my sister. They gave my dad one of his biggest insurance accounts. He might not even be alive without them. How do you walk away from that? The world is filled with terrible people and terrible situations. For some reason I'm being protected. Cared for. So is my father. This is not something you walk away from.

This is something you hang on to . . . and I'm going to.

I seek counsel from the girls at the club. They're there with their families and they unanimously agree there's only one sure cure for keeping Brad. "Have a baby," Addi says. "Get a walnut in that muffin, *quick*." They say having a baby is the only guarantee I won't be tossed out and replaced by some vicious delphinium from the Lancôme counter. I agree completely. The only problem with this plan is that Brad and I don't have sex. Ever. So, how do you get a walnut in the muffin when you can't even get the tricky little squirrel in bed? Even when I do wrangle him, I don't think he enjoys it anymore. I make a mental list for Emily. Most men and women think about very different things during sexual intercourse.

Top Ten Things That Women Think Men Think During Sex

1. God, I really love her.
2. I have never felt this connected to another person before.
3. We truly are soul mates.
4. We should probably get married.
5. I wonder how I should propose. Flash mob at the Mall of America or hot-air balloon?
6. Sometimes I want to cry in front of her, but I'm afraid to reveal my weakness.
7. I wish she texted me more often.
8. I want to write a poem about her and me and our souls' journey together.
9. I hope she sleeps over.
10. I'm going to get up early and make her favorite strawberry waffles.

Top Ten Things That Men Actually Think During Sex

1. Bang! You've now officially banged all of the Sullivan sisters.

2. Crap. Which one is this? Kristen Sullivan or Kirsten Sullivan?

3. You call that a blow job? You should get some tips from your sister.

4. Could I get Kirsten and Kristen to do a three-way?

5. Easy! Don't come too soon . . . Think dead pets, dead pets, dead pets . . . whew.

6. Easy now . . . Think about baseball . . .

7. That's it . . . rock her world!

8. Man, the schwang is rockin', buddy!

9. Damn. Foot cramp.

10. Let her rip, buddy, then let's get her outta here and eat bacon!

I try to increase the chance I'll get pregnant during sex. I make appointments at a prestigious fertility clinic, and the MD there says there is absolutely nothing wrong with "my system." I'm perfectly capable of having a baby. Brad's doctor has told him the same thing. "So why can't we get pregnant?" I ask her, and she shrugs.

"Maybe your head wants to, but your heart's not in it."

"That's absurd," I tell her. "My heart's leading the way! My heart is strapped into the very front car of this stupid emotional roller coaster!"

"Our bodies are highly calibrated machines," she says. "I suggest that if your body is refusing to get pregnant . . . you listen to it." Poppycock, as Christopher would say. What I need is drugs. I consult doctors and nutritionists and talk with other women who had to use unconventional techniques to get pregnant. I take everyone's advice and use it all at the same time. I fill the house with ovulation prediction kits, fertility monitors, digital thermometers, and big chunky fertility crystals. I wear Incan fertility jewelry, I do headstands, I take Japanese herbs, eat oysters, carry fertility talismans, take prenatal vitamins, and do "fertility yoga" every day, adopting the fertility mantra "The strong sperm swims to the good egg." I even drink the fertility tea Bi'ch makes me, a potent Hmong brew I sip every morning and every night. I don't know what's in it, but it tastes like yak's ass.

Next I try to increase the likelihood that Brad will have sex with me voluntarily. I incorporate various diets, eating only whole foods, no gluten, big protein, strict portions, set times, no eating after eight P.M., etc. . . .

I work out three times a week with Big D. We don't do much weight training, mostly cardio; he believes getting the blood pumping is more important than a whole hell of a lot else. He says the last thing I need is to show up for some fancy high tea looking like Popeye. We always talk during our jogs and his pearls of wisdom can be both unexpected and insightful. He says, "Shit, girl. That dog don't hunt . . . Speed the plow, now! Speed the damn plow! Girl, nobody can ride less you bent . . . You got unlived lives in your head? Live 'em, girl, or they gonna fill your coffin with what you never done. Hear me? Just a big box of dead dreams. Nothin' else. Listen now, Big D is tellin' you. No man can ride you, girl, less you already bent."

I scour bookstores for baby-making self-empowering reading options. *Miracle Babies Happen Every Day. Baby Now! How to Give Birth to a Perfectly Perfect Baby. Nine Months to Your Life Beginning! Babies Are for Everyone. Healthy Baby-Making Made Easy. Fertile Myrtle Says YES! Alternatives to Traditional Forms of Conceiving. Not in My Uterus You're Not! If We Don't Have a Baby . . . Why Are We Even Here? A Precious Pea for Every of One of God's Pods.*

After I read about the power of positive thinking for the childless (aka, deciding something is real even if it's patently untrue), I decide to take matters into my own hands.

I build a nursery.

I convert the upstairs guest bedroom. First I hire a crew to repaint the room vibrant non-gender-specific yellow. Then I hit Keller's broadside and tell the shop girls that I want one of everything, two if it's a bestseller. They send over a truckload of stuff, much of which, it seems, has the blue CLOG logo on it, featuring a tiny dove sitting on the "G," or possibly stuck on it. Anyway, I make a pile of Christian Lambs of God products, including toys, clothes, baby bottles, blankets, crib pads, etc., that say "Made in Japan," *"Hecho en Mexico,"* "Imported: Russia," *"Afrique du Sud"* . . . Just imagine what creepy-crawlies could latch on to them.

Once I set up all the furniture, though, I'm missing one thing that is actually in the CLOG pile: a mattress for the crib. There's one from a Hong Kong district called Mongkok, which sounds like Montauk, an idyllic beach town in the Hamptons. So I rip open the plastic, open up the box, and carefully put the little mattress in the crib. Cute! Then I drive out to my parents' house and load up all my old toys and stuff from the attic. I drive them back to Lake Minnetonka and lug the boxes of my old retro kitsch up to the nursery. I begin unpacking all my old vintage toys, Japanese paper lanterns, collectible Kewpie dolls, and a plaster replica of Princess Diana's wedding cake. It's a little unconventional, but babies should be inspired and educated by their environments, not dumbed down with boring colors or insipid cartoon characters. Not *my* baby, anyway; my baby will require decorations exactly like these. Nude geisha prints and Vargas Girl calendars. Hmmm. Technically those are Asian porn stars and 1950s prostitutes. I wonder which my baby will be?

Okay, it's not perfect, but I'm ridiculously happy that my

dollhouse made it here. It's an heirloom, which I've filled over the years with quirky miniatures, tiny figurines, and pint-size antiques. It's cheap therapy. An hour playing with those goofy little pieces is completely soothing to me. I especially love the stars of this little freak show: the Tinkertoy family.

They're the worst. They have lives that are more confusing and upsetting than my own. Little Husband cheats. Little Wife is a pill-popping nympho and both the little Tinkertoy children worship Smoking Monkey, who controls all of their minds from the breakfast nook. I sigh and arrange my Tinker people, realizing how stupid it is that they're this soothing to me. The truth is, I get a perverse pleasure from lording over this mucked-up little family, whose lives are even more complicated and poorly thought out than mine.

Once again, things aren't looking too good for my little family. Little Husband is back in rehab and Little Wife's started up with G.I. Joe again. The Tinker kids are building a meth lab in the doghouse. I smile to myself and nod. I'm glad that something around here is still normal.

A week later, however, I discover something's wrong with my nursery. Furniture is moved around in the dollhouse, like a buffalo roamed through. Things that were brand-new, like blankets and stuffed animals, seem frayed and ragged. I find little piles of fluff here and there, clearly shed from items across the room. Who knows.

I shut the door and forget it.

I want to have Brad's baby . . . but the problem with having a baby is it doesn't matter one ova how fertile you are or how sexually appealing you become; if you're not in the vicinity of sperm, there is not going to be a walnut in the muffin. No walnut. No muffin.

It seems like Brad always comes home now too late and too

tired to have sex. Even if I do manage to ensnare him in my Delilah grasp, he peters out before the job is done. I can't even get him hard half the time; it's like there's no sensitivity in his dick anymore. I consider wrapping his cock in a sheet of sand-paper before giving a hand job. Maybe he'd feel that.

Two weeks later I walk into the nursery and there is a mon-ster rat in the crib staring at me. I scream. Then I hear some-thing behind me and look over at the dollhouse, where, I freak you not, there are forty-plus rats staring at me from inside the dollhouse. From *inside* the dollhouse. It's like they've moved in. I scream even louder when I see them and throw my stack of towels or whatever I'm holding and I run. I refuse to set foot in the house again until an exterminator named Hutch comes out to catch those . . . those . . . things. I'm hysterical. I sit in my car in the driveway, but I never would've stayed if I'd known what the old craggy Vietnam-vet exterminator would come out and say. I would've gotten Valium first. Hutch claims to have caught the big rat I saw in the crib . . . but it'll take him a while to catch the dollhouse ones.

"They don't move outta a dollhouse easy," he says. "Usually one of us has to burn it down first. Ma'am, tell me, you brought something in this house from Mongkok, didn't you."

"Um . . . How did you know?"

"What was it? Opium pipe? Hash log? A rolled-up Tibetan rug? Don't worry, old Hutch isn't here to turn anybody in. No, sir. I've transported my share of illegal artifacts and shoved sub-stances up my ass; I only ask because I need to know what we're dealing with. You ever hear of a Mongkok Slasher?" he asks.

"A what?"

"A Mongkok Slasher! I was stationed there back in the army. Mongkok is the most beautiful crowded cesspool on earth. Like diamonds floating in shit, you know? You fall asleep on the train standing up . . . and you don't never fall down, hear me? They got rats there the size of porcupines. Have sharp yellow teeth like needles. They can slash their way through drywall, steel plating, bone. What you got here, lady, is an advanced Hong Kong Mongkok Slasher infestation."

"Glad I don't have to say that twice."

"What was it you brung from Sin City?"

"The crib mattress!" I tell him "I put a baby's crib mattress . . . in the crib . . . it was so cute . . . with little butterflies on it . . ."

"They love cute!" he says. "Why don't you just lay out saucers a milk for 'em and knit their babies socks? Better knit fast, though . . . I'd say a pair a minute." Hutch whips off his hat and slaps his own knee. "Sonofabitch, lady! Pardon my Mandarin, but you might as well've called up a Mongkok rat nursery and had them ship you a batch of babies. These things can breed as fast as fruit flies. Faster!"

Brad and I have to move in with his parents while the house is fully fumigated.

"Now do you believe me?" I ask Brad at the Keller dinner table. "Our child could've been in that crib . . . your grandchild, Mrs. Keller. Do you know what rats do to babies? Brad, your son might've gone through life with a face like Hamburger Helper. Now, you swear to me, Brad Keller, swear you'll stop working with those horrible Christian Lambs!"

Brad looks down and promises.

Mother Keller and Ed promise too; that's the one good thing that comes from staying with them. They're witness to my emotional breakdown.

I think I finally got through.

Desperate to see my family, I happily go to this week's Supper Club. The theme is baby food, and everything must be blended or pureed, in honor of the twins. Neither Lenny nor Hailey has a single beer the whole time, and in the backyard there's a huge banner that says WELCOME TO EARTH, BILLY AND BUDDY! It's as though they aren't children but visiting extraterrestrials. "Look at these boys!" Lenny comes over with an infant tucked in each arm. "I'm gonna build them a super fort in the backyard."

Hailey smacks him. "No you're not, Lenny!"

"Like hell I'm not! My boys need a super fort!"

"They're *infants,* Lenny. Infants don't need a super fort."

"Like hell they don't!"

"No fort."

"Fort!"

I'm sitting on a wagon-wheel bench, trying to eat a "liquid taco," when Hailey drops a baby on my lap. "Here," she says to me, "hold Billy."

"That's Buddy," Lenny says. "He's got the crazy eye."

"He does *not* have a crazy eye, Lenny. Stop saying that."

"He's got a big wiener too."

"You can't tell them apart by *that,*" she whispers. "They *both* do."

"Lord, *don't I know it!*" Lenny hollers, and slaps his knee. "Chucker, you gotta check my boys out. They are *huge.* I mean it's like little racks a beef tenderloin hanging out there. *Hooowee!*"

"You know," I say politely, "I probably shouldn't hold the baby. These pants are silk."

"So?" Hailey thrusts the blue bundle at me. "This baby is a *baby.*"

"Give him to me," Mom says, and I gladly pass it over.

I stay late at the Supper Club and drink too much. Lenny drives me home. "You doin' okay there, kid?" he asks, and I tell him I'm doing great. Any day now I'll be pregnant and I'll probably have triplets, who will kick his twins' butts.

"Right on," Lenny says. "It's a date!"

I invite him and Hailey to come for Easter brunch with the rest of my family. It's good for everyone to spend time together, create a sense of community. I had no idea that brunch would be so important . . . or when such big news would hit.

We're all there, gathered around the table for brunch at the club on Easter Sunday. The dining room is packed. Everyone we know is there with their families. Waiters zip around the room delivering special-order omelets and more iced tea while expertly dodging sugar-crazed children who're tearing around the dining room hopped up on Easter candy found during the annual Easter egg hunt. Trevor got a time-out and had to go sit in the car after overdosing on sugary pink marshmallow Peeps.

Then Ed stands up. He says he was moved by something during the sermon at church that morning. When Pastor Mike spoke about the father and the son, and how we must repent to be forgiven for our sins, that's when it hit him. "Ladies and gentlemen," he says. Then he pauses and looks around the table. "Where's Lenny?" he asks, and everybody scans the room. "He's getting more pancakes!" somebody says.

We wave him over. Lenny nods. He's at the pancake trolley with the twins, loading up his plate for the third time. Lenny has a remarkable ability to hold both the twins while he's doing anything. Right now he's holding them squished together in their little pink Easter Bunny outfits with one arm, while he holds his pancake plate out with the other. Hailey meanwhile asks the waiter for more iced tea. Lenny returns and Ed resumes his speech. "My son has repented," he says. "Brad has shown me over the past several months his dedication to the Keller's company." I sneak a peek over at Sarah, whose face freezes, her pale skin porcelain white, her glossy lips pressed into a grim line.

Ed goes on to say the decision to pick a new president is always a hard one, especially when both candidates are your children. Nevertheless, in order to prosper, a company needs a leader . . . and he needs a better handicap on his golf game! The table titters at his lame retirement joke. We titter tensely and we all lean in.

"I've decided the next president of Keller's will be . . . my son . . . Bradford!"

"Dad!" Brad leaps up, knocking over his water glass, and hugs his father.

Meanwhile the water from his glass races across the table and dumps right into Sarah's lap, and she jumps up like a cat bit her, springing away from the table.

"Yep," her husband, Bill, says with a sigh. "Tonight's gonna be a long one."

Poor Bill.

Brad and I go home that night and for the first time in weeks we have sex. He even initiates it. He pushes me up against our bedroom wall and kisses me. He says I'm the best wife in the entire world. "I have no idea why you've put up with me," he says.

I tell him neither do I.

Then he opens a bottle of champagne.

"Champagne?" I say. "Are you sure you want to be . . . drinking?"

"Why not, baby!" He whips off my high heel and pours bubbly into it.

"Brad!"

"*What?*"

I stifle the urge to tell him drinking champagne is considered a real no-no for recovering alcoholics. Struggling even harder, I refrain from saying those are seven-hundred-dollar Manolo Blahniks.

"We did it!" he says, gulping down bubbly champagne from

the heel of my shoe. "It's time to celebrate!" He holds the high heel up to my mouth and tips it back, into my lips. I laugh as a cold stream of champagne surges forward, running down my neck and pooling in my cleavage. We drink three bottles.

He makes love to me passionately, wildly, all over the room, like a merchant marine on shore leave. I'm so excited I can hardly get my underwear off. I can't help mentally noting that I'm ovulating, according to my handy fertility calendar.

He finishes early. I roll and groan and tell him I want more. We bang on the sofa, the dresser, and the closet floor. It's three in the morning by the time we stumble into bed. I manage to set my alarm clock, remembering tomorrow's an important day.

I can't oversleep, no matter what.

16
On Fire for Jesus

I oversleep.

Groggy and uncomfortably hungover, I leave Brad in our tangled, sweaty bed and stumble out the door wearing my official yellow camp sweatshirt that says GRACE-TRINITY YOUTH COUNSELOR! Grace-Trinity's teen worship rally is happening up at Camp Wapi-Wapawee in Minnetrista.

An hour later I'm getting on a Grace-Trinity shuttle bus, leaving the church parking lot. My tongue tastes like wet kitty litter; my skin feels sandpaper. I wear dark glasses and sink as low as I can in my seat. The only other people here are a teenage boy wearing a Camp Wapi-Wapawee baseball hat and a silent, stoic, stern-faced Native American driver. As I board the bus, the driver hands me a paper satchel. I don't ask him what it is. He hands the teen, who boards after me, an identical paper satchel and the kid rips it open right there. "Is this the orientation package?" the kid asks, peering inside. The driver says nothing. "Does this have the meal plan sign-up sheet? They told me to get a meal plan sign-up sheet. Mom didn't give me lunch money. Is this it?" He digs in the bag. "Man, I gotta find that meal plan . . .

Hey look, cookies!" He pulls out two large chocolate chip cookies and looks at me. "Hey!" he says. "Did you get cookies?"

I lean over so I won't throw up.

The driver says nothing. We lurch forward and I stay crouched in a ball for the entire forty-minute drive, while the teenager peppers the silent driver and me with questions, none of which receive answers. Not one. "So were lotsa kids on the earlier shuttle buses?" he asks. "Did you see any girls with long brown hair and a ring in their nose and wearing a black hat? Like a ski hat? Maybe a puffy coat too. A black one. She's got this black puffy coat. I think she's coming. She should be coming. Did you guys see anyone like her? Have you seen Camp Wapi-Wapawee? Do you know what 'Wapi-Wapawee' means? Is that, like, Ojibwa? Someone said it was, like, Ojibwa."

The driver turns the radio on.

Forty minutes later, and with both my eyeballs pulsing independently of each other, we pull into Camp Wapi-Wapawee's parking lot. Two totem poles loom up outside the bus and a roiling melee of screaming, shrieking teenagers swarms between them.

Oh dear God, what have I done?

The driver parks the bus and pulls open the door. The kid scrambles up, bolts down the aisle, and sprints off the bus. Then he scrambles back onto the bus, stumbling, and jogs back to his seat, where he grabs his paper satchel. "Almost forgot the fucking cookie bag!" he says, and sprints back off. The driver's eyes flick up and study me in the rearview mirror. I sigh, achingly stand, and lumber slowly down the aisle. Nightmare, here I come.

Grace-Trinity needn't have worried about inner-city kids coming; they've poured in, and within minutes I've seen more members of minority communities than I've seen in the entire past year. The campers are much older and more sophisticated than I thought they'd be, and nobody looks that underprivileged. I wasn't expecting emaciated orphans with dirty faces and torn clothes or anything, but I also wasn't expecting so much electronic equipment, so much sparkling bling, or so many expensive sneakers. Martha Woodcock goes whipping past me with her rage counter wristwatch going *beep beep beep!*

I stop in the Counselors' Headquarters Hut and guzzle down three cups of coffee. I beg one of the interns for aspirin and get three pink baby aspirins, which are the only kind allowed on the campground. Bastards. Someone gives me a name badge that says JENNY K. on it and an orientation package with schedules and maps other various doodads stuffed inside. I'm supposed to meet the Louises for our final rundown meeting, so I walk through the maze, an impressive construction assembled by a professional event company using all donated hay bales. Inside, the tall scratchy chambers are filled with shrieking ghosts and thick fog. The ghosts are mostly wadded-up garbage bags and ripped gauze strung on wires, but one ghost is Gordon, the church janitor. He really wanted to be a ghost in the hay maze, he lobbied for it, and the committee ladies decided to let him. In Minnesota it's never a good idea to piss off anyone with access to your boiler. I find Gordon almost immediately. He's crouched in a corner and wearing a long white sheet. He holds up two hands while screaming, "*Ayiiieeeboooooo!*" He stops and peeks out from under his white hood.

"*Pssst!*" he says. "*It's me, Gordon!* I didn't scare you, did I? I don't want to scare anybody too bad! Specially not the kids! Was that okay?"

"Perfect!" I tell him, and he gives me a big smile.

I hurry on my way. I can't find my way out, though; I have to follow a group of teens, who I think are smoking marijuana cigarettes, in order to get out. At the exit a shrouded angel of death looms overhead and a prerecorded voice urges us maze walkers to accept the Lord Jesus Christ as our Savior and to pick up a free goodie bag.

In the goodie bag are miniature liquid soap samples, mouthwash, a mini deodorant stick, a travel toothbrush, a coupon for one free Chubby Cub sub sandwich, a sparkly plastic water bottle that says HEARTS ON FIRE, and a T-shirt that says I'M ADDICTED . . . TO JESUS!

It's everything an indigent teen might need.

Big Louise walks up grinning. "Jen! Isn't a miracle?"

"Which miracle, Louise?"

"*Them*. So many of *them* came." She beams.

"Who?"

"Pastor Mike said they'd come, he said they'd hear God's call and they'd come!"

"He said *who* would come, Louise? The Communists? The squirrels?"

"*Them!*" She rolls her eyes at a passing group of African-American campers who are wearing colorful ski jackets. "*Those ones!*" she whispers.

Oh sweet Jesus. I roll my eyes at her, which is painful but unavoidable whenever Big Louise is nearby.

"*Louise! Stop!* Do not refer to *anyone* as 'them' or 'those ones' . . . okay?"

"Why not? I didn't—"

"Because it sounds awful, Louise!"

"Well, I didn't call them *black*."

We're late to meet Dirty Louise in the mess hall, and we make our way slowly through the thronging crowds of semi-wild and mostly screaming teens. Of course, all these inner-city kids came because *Jesus* called them. Not because it's an all-expenses-paid vacation away from their schools and parents, complete with free transportation from and to the city, a hospitality tepee loaded with beanbag chairs, free popcorn, big goodie bags, and a "Chillaxing Zone" where a live DJ spins big beats all day. No way. *It was Jesus.*

I follow Big Louise's ample rump to the mess hall. We round the corner and I let out a yelp. Not at the mess hall, a large log cabin building overlooking icy Lake Minnetonka, but at the massive wooden structure below, on the snow-crusted beach. It's an enormous wooden cross. Taller than most of the pine trees and I'm sure easily seen from the highway or across the lake and probably outer space. That is some scary-looking cross. You could crucify a small apartment building on that thing . . . or a tall semi truck standing up on one end. *"Jesus,"* I whisper, but Big Louise is gone. She didn't even stop to look; she barreled ahead and is now just disappearing into the tall-timbered entrance of the log cabin mess hall. I hurry to catch up with her.

Inside the mess hall, there are long rows of split-log picnic tables covered by red-check tablecloths and crowned by large stainless steel condiment holders. An empty salad bar with smudgy sneeze guards banks one wall and a long buffet table filled with empty chafing dishes and stacked trays banks the other. "Halloooo there!" Dirty Louise calls over to us. She's sitting at a log table on the other side of the room, with a cup of coffee.

"Any more of that?" I ask, and she says there's a pot in the kitchen.

In the cramped, greasy kitchen, where some beleaguered kitchen crew slops out two hundred meals a day, I find the coffeemaker and pour myself a cup. As I pour some cream in my cup and stir, I read the smeary dry-erase board next to the stove, heralding tonight's dinner menu:

Chicken patties & fish fingers
Tater tot hotdish, sweet peas
Brownies & vanilla ice cream
Choice of milk

My eye catches the stainless steel shelf above the stove, which is crowded with economy-size bottles of seasonings and spices. There, tucked between the paprika and taco seasoning, I spy the unmistakable label of a Johnnie Walker whiskey bottle. Must be the cook's.

Who can blame him? I'd drink too if I worked here.

In the other room, Big Louise lets out a loud snorting cackle and that's when it hits me: the only thing that might ease my hangover is the hair of the dog. I quickly look around and then grab the whiskey from the shelf, splashing a dollop in my coffee.

At the table we get to work. The Louises both shuffle around their various activity schedules and church bulletins and camp memos; they plot out and replan their detailed tasks for the big bonfire tonight, which they're having despite the frigid weather. My stalwart Bonfire Committee did a super-fine and extra-anal job ensuring the campers' comfort at tonight's bonfire. The ladies organized forty extra cords of wood to be brought in and set up hay bales close to the fire pit so these inner-city orchids wouldn't flee just because of chilly weather.

The Louises still have doubts—and plenty of them. Big Louise is leading a Christian sing-along tonight and she's worried about wolves, errant bonfire sparks lighting her on fire, and the possibility of her sheet music being carried away in an arctic wind. Dirty Louise is telling campfire stories and she's worried about her speaking voice, her spinal posture, and if her decision to blend secular campfire stories with Christian-values tales was misguided. What if she put too much secular into the mix? What if her story causes teen fornication? Then Dirty Louise looks at me and asks if my show's all ready to go.

"*Show?*" I smile sweetly. "What show?"

Apparently I was in charge of the big bonfire talent show. I didn't even know we were *having* a talent show, much less that I was in charge of it. I show no sign of panic and tell them I'm *completely* ready. Meanwhile, cold hard panic sets in. If Mother Keller finds out I screwed up at the helm of my committee, she'll have a freaking field day with it! "Oh, and Jennifer," Dirty Louise says, "I'm so sorry about forgetting to put the sign-up sheet in your talent show info pack. I hope it wasn't too much trouble to make one. Your mother-in-law said it wouldn't be a problem."

"What?" I look at her. "My mother-in-law?"

"I gave her the info pack to give you. She gave it to you, right?"

My eye twitches slightly. I take a deep sip of coffee. "Oh, she gave it to me, all right."

The Louises start chattering about something else as my brain starts to wildly swirl.

My mother-in-law? *Of course!*

That witch *knew* I was supposed to organize the talent show and she deliberately didn't tell me to sabotage me! Unbelievable . . . and evil. What proof do I have that she never gave me the info pack? She'll just say that she did. She's probably already planted the damn thing in my house somewhere! I can't fail at this . . . I have to make my marriage work. I can't give Brad any reason to think I can fail! I jump up from the table, nearly knocking over my coffee cup.

"What time is it?" I ask, gathering my things.

"Why?"

"I have a . . . rehearsal."

"A rehearsal?" Big Louise frowns. "Right now?"

"Yep, right now! Five minutes ago, actually! Kids wanted to do a run-through before the big show."

Louise creases her forehead. "But we haven't even—"

"All right then, ladies," I say. "You're doing great! Thank you . . . see you all tonight at the show!" I take off quick-walking out the door. Then I pop my head back in. "Um . . . what time is it again?" I smile at them. "The um . . . bonfire?"

"Six o'clock," Big Louise says, arching an eyebrow.

I wave good-bye and then say, "I forgot something in the kitchen!" and I dash into the kitchen, grab the bottle of whiskey, and shove it in my bag. *Sorry, kitchen staff, bad break. You're gonna be pissed when you find your whiskey is gone . . . but you should see how bad the kitchen crew on Saint John has it.* I nearly sprint out of the mess hall. I wind up speed-walking around in circles through the campground, with no idea where I'm going.

What do I do now? Where do I go? Who can help me? I'm screwed! Totally screwed! I call everyone I can think of, everyone who won't judge me . . . which is Lenny.

"Hell, just round up some a them freaky Jesus kids and slap 'em on the stage!" he says. "They all got talent-show tricks! I remember this one kid in my Sunday school class could—"

"Thanks, Lenny!"

I hang up and tell myself, *Just breathe, relax.* I can do this. Lenny's right. All I need for a talent show is . . . talent. I just have to find some campers who do magic tricks or yodel or something and convince them to perform tonight onstage.

How hard could that be?

Very.

I quickly discover there aren't many teens willing to perform in a church youth group talent show, especially not in front of a big unruly group of inner-city kids, who will undoubtedly beat them up on the shuttle buses later. Nevertheless, I manage to convince a few campers they should publicly humiliate themselves and the acts I secure are as follows: a freshman who can belch "Yankee Doodle Dandy"; a Korean foreign-exchange student who can juggle cabbages; a girl wearing a back brace who can twirl a baton, but since her baton is at home, she'll use a canoe paddle; a chubby sixth grader who will recite a famous poem; a pale girl with dark kohl eyes who will read a short story; and some karate kids who will attempt to karate-chop a plank in half. Also the camp nurse said she could teach everyone CPR.

It's looking a little grim.

But then I catch my big lucky break in the chillaxing tent. A bunch of teens are lounging around on beanbags, including three nearly identical doe-eyed lip-glossed girls, all from the Grace-Trinity gymnastics squad, otherwise known as the Jumping Jacks. They agree to do a performance and I say, "Fabulous! You'll be the stars!" Then behind me I hear a voice. Someone says, "Hells, lady, *I'm* a star."

There's a white kid standing behind me. He's short, skinny, looks almost like an albino . . . possibly with a thyroid condition. He has spiky white-blond hair and pale, paper-white skin that offsets his startlingly blue eyes, and he has arms and legs that both seem too short for his torso. He wears big baggy oversize clothes and a baseball hat that says BIG JC! I step back and say, "You're . . . a star?" I didn't mean to sound quite so uncertain.

"Hells yes, I'm a rap star! I'm Iced-Tea. That be me. The best God rapper there is, 'cause I only sing for the big JC!"

I stare at him.

"The big JC?" he says, pointing to his hat. "Jesus?"

"Oh! You're a Christian rapper?" I feel my heart beat faster; I think I just hit pay dirt. "Do you go to Grace-Trinity?" I ask him, and he says, "Hells no! Lady, I'm from south central!"

"South central . . . L.A.?"

"South-central *Minnesota*! I cook it Burnsville style! But I raps all over; ever heard of the Funky Jesus Rappin' Road Show?"

"No. Seriously?"

"I'm the *star* of the Funky Jesus Rappin' Road Show. I got fans all over and they is *for real*! You put out the word that Iced-Tea is rappin' center stage tonight and my people will come, like sweet sure sugar, 'cause Iced-Tea peeps is *for real*. I even got my music with me." He pulls out a CD from his baggy pocket and hands it to me. I read the track titles.

Pimpin' 4 Jesus
Da Rapture
Holy Sh*t!
Holla Back, Jesus
The Notorious Big J.C.
Funky Jesus
Saved Soulja Boy
Jesus Is My N-Word
Are You There, God? It Be Me . . . Iced-Tea

"Good enough for me." I shrug. "You're on."

"For . . . reals?" he says. "For *really-reals*?"

"Yep, for really-real super-reals. Just be at the bonfire by six o'clock. All right?"

"Lady, you will not be sorry! Hells yeah. Play track two, 'Da Rapture.'"

I walk away, my heart singin' all gangsta style. *This is perfect*. Perfect! Sorry, Mother Keller, but I rule. I hurry to find a media guy who can run a power line down to the fire pit on the beach while Iced-Tea power-rehearses with the church's dance squad, who I bamboozled into performing with him. I find the bonfire is already going in the large stone-ringed fire pit next to the lake, the giant cross looming overhead. Electricity is no problem; in fact they already have a whole sound system right there, cleverly hidden in a nearby grove of plastic bushes. A big group of campers is already sitting around the fire pit, and suddenly the Louises come up beside me. "All ready then, Jen?" Big Louise asks.

"Oh, I'm ready," I tell them. "*Very* ready."

More and more campers file down the beach and take their seats on hay bales around the campfire, until there are no more seats left. It's standing room only. Then more campers come and there's not much standing room either. "Where are all these kids coming from?" Dirty Louise marvels. "There are way more here than there were during the day."

Pastor Mike uses a megaphone to welcome everybody and leads the group in a prayer, in which he blesses sinners and saints alike. Then the pre-sermon entertainment starts.

Dirty Louise is up first. She bravely goes onstage, takes a deep breath, clears her throat, and tells the teens a carefully crafted campfire story that has both a camping theme *and* a Christian theme, which is . . . odd. The story is something about a serial killer with a golden arm who murders teens having premarital sex in the woods. He finds these sinful teens camping and *zip!* He cuts their heads right off with his golden arm, which also has some sort of knife- or saw-like attachment. The police try hard to catch him, even though they understand his desire to correct sinful deviant teen behavior, but the teen-sex killer is too clever for them. He never leaves any clues, except somehow everybody knows he has a golden arm with a knife- or saw-like attachment.

Dirty Louise says it was on a night *just like this one* that the crazed teen-sex killer was about to strike again. He found some teens camping in the woods and he crept up outside their tent. He assumed they were sinning because (A) they were teenagers, (B) they were in the woods, and (C) they were making some pretty strange sounds inside the tent, which turned out to be them just trying to open a pickle jar, but he didn't know that. The fiendish killer raised his horrible golden arm up high and *slash!* He ripped the tent wide open and found the teens engaging in . . . Bible study? The killer lowered his arm. The situation was confusing for everyone.

You see, these were good, godly, nonsinning, *nonsexing* teens who had gone camping in the woods, and those godly teens showed that mean old teen-killer a Bible and he read it. He realized he'd better change his ways if he wanted to go to heaven and not to hell, where all those sexed-up teens would be. He cried and repented right there in the woods and the godly teens baptized the killer with Mountain Dew, because that's all they had, but that was good enough. Then the killer went to the police and confessed all his hideous crimes and begged the parents of all those sexed-up teens he killed for their forgiveness, which they gave him because even though they were mad at him, they also understood his desire to correct sinful deviant teen behavior. The killer went to prison, but he was happy, because he knew the Lord loved even him and also he got an operation to replace his golden arm with a simple wooden one, which the church paid for and which was the kind Jesus would've worn if he needed a prosthetic while on Earth, because he was a king but he was also a carpenter.

The end.

Dirty Louise finishes her story and stands there onstage. It's quiet. Real quiet. Nobody knows what's going to happen next, not even the crowd. I think to myself, *Oh boy, here we go. They're gonna kill her* . . . But they don't kill her, they start . . .

clapping? Slowly at first and then louder and louder, like it's the best story they've ever heard in their lives. Pastor Mike says the spirit moved them. I say Dirty Louise's plotline completely baffled them, but who knows. The Lord works in some damn crazy ways.

Big Louise is up next. She dusts off her butt, marches out onstage, tells the audience they're going to sing, and attempts to lead them in a not-quite-rousing round of "When the Saints Go Marching In." It bombs. Then she tries "Michael, Row the Boat Ashore." *Bomb.* Even good old reliable "Amazing Grace" . . . *Big fat bomb.* The campers become restless. A few start booing, some start shouting. One kid yells, "Man, who the fuck is *Michael* . . . and why is that motherfucker always *rowing*?" Sensing their disinterest, she switches gears and they all sing "S.O.S." by ABBA. "Ha!" someone heckles. *"Total lesbian! Knew it!"*

By the time Pastor Mike pulls Big Louise off the stage, it's a catcalling contest and thrown soda cans are skittering across the stage. *Great.* Thanks, Louise. Great act to follow. I pace around in the staging tent and I panic, I sweat, I consider the consequences of stealing a church shuttle bus and fleeing for somewhere God can't find me. Better yet, I pour the remaining contents of the stolen whiskey flask into my water bottle. My heart nearly stops when it's our turn. Pastor Mike introduces me, shouting through his megaphone, and I take the stage, hands trembling as I hold the microphone. The next hour is a blur. I can't remember much of it, but I remember enough that I can't say it went . . . well.

The belching freshman chokes.

The Korean foreign-exchange student can't find any cabbages and so uses raw eggs, which he drops all over the stage and a few of which he sends sailing into the crowd, clearing large sections out as girls starts screaming.

The chubby kid reads a *Star Trek* poem, which might've been fine, but he chooses to read it in Klingon. Some kid jumps on-stage next to him and starts a phony erotic translation. Then the girl with dark eyes reads her short story, which is an epic saga of depression, bulimia, and contemplating suicide. And that's the uplifting part.

The girl in the back brace twirls her canoe paddle right off the stage, nearly decapitating a counselor. The karate students couldn't find a plank and try to karate-chop a red plastic lunch tray instead. They fail miserably, despite trying for nearly twenty minutes.

I finally introduce the last act. The grand finale.

"Kids and adults!" I say. "Please welcome *Iced-Tea*! Accompanied by the Grace-Trinity Jumping Jacks!" The intro music kicks up and the Jumping Jacks bounce onto the stage doing cartwheels and flips. Iced-Tea, however, is still backstage.

"Get out there!" I hiss. "Get out there now!"

"Why they screamin' for *Ice*-Tea?" he asks angrily. "You say my name wrong?"

"No, I didn't say your name wrong! Get out there!"

The sound guy pulls his earphones off and says to the kid, "You never heard of the rap star Ice-T?"

"No!"

"Ice-T, the father of gangsta rap? The legendary icon who started on the streets of South Central and became a hip-hop superstar? Recorded Grammy-award-winning megahits like 'Home Invasion' . . . 'Straight-Up Nigga' . . . 'Cop Killer'? You never heard of him?"

"I'ma *legendary icon* your face in one minute!"

I grab Iced-Tea by the shoulders and push him onstage. "Get out there or so help me I will hunt you down and bust a cap in your white ass crack! *Go!*" Iced-Tea bounds onto the stage, hollering out to the crowd. They seem confused. People start booing.

"*That ain't Ice-T!*" somebody shouts. "*They said Ice-T was playin'!*"

Then they're throwing stuff, liquid soap samples, mini mouthwash bottles, and toothpaste kits from the goodie bags. They bounce off the big wooden cross and plunk into the fire, which smells like burning mint.

Thwap.

A chunk of hay from a nearby hay bale catches fire and rolls to the base of the cross. Iced-Tea keeps right on a-rappin' away, unfazed by the situation, which makes me wonder if he's familiar with it. The girls who are dancing most definitely are not used to being booed. Uncertain of what it means, and having never experienced miniature bottles of mouthwash being chucked at them before, they cling fiercely to their routine, speeding it up and performing with wild expressions of smiling terror frozen on their faces.

I finally tell the sound guy to cut the music, which is unnecessary. The song is just ending, with Iced-Tea belting out the last lines of his freestyle rap. In all the commotion I hadn't really heard his . . . violent, sexist, racist, homophobic, horrifying lyrics, which end with the catchy line: "*That's what Jesus told his Jerusalem bitches. Talk back again and you gonna need stitches. PEACE, MOTHAFUCKAS!*"

That's the cue for the girls to do their finale triple flip and I don't really know what goes wrong. One minute they're up and dancing and the next minute they're stumbling into the fire pit. Chaos ensues. Bouncy Blonde is pulled safely out of the fire by some quick-thinking counselor, who rips off the streamers that are on fire and trailing behind her. "Just what the hell was that?"

Big Louise thunders, marching up with her arms akimbo. I start rattling off a nonsensical list of details that might've caused all this until Dirty Louise looks up and whispers, "Dear Lord . . . No." It turns out the quick-thinking counselor who tore off the burning streamers chucked them out of harm's way . . . and onto a hay bale. Counselors rush in to stamp the flames out. Big Louise throws her can of diet soda, which bounces off the cross and rolls away. Then she grabs my water bottle and throws its contents on the fire too, assuming there's water inside, not whiskey.

Poom!

A bright fireball flash.

Within moments the giant cross catches fire and we stand there frozen, looking up, mouths agape. Roaring flames race up the cross and beat into the sky, burning so brightly you could see them from across the lake. The crowd swells as campers abandon their various hidey-holes and hay bale party rooms and come running to see. The number of black campers present has just about quadrupled.

Using drill whistles and megaphones, counselors direct kids away from the fire and herd them toward the mess hall, where they get hot chocolate and finally hear Pastor Mike's cool fireside sermon. I forgot about the sermon. The one where he was going to save all these poor underprivileged kids from the inner city who've been recently traumatized.

Right. Not betting on it.

As the crowds part, maintenance crews wheel down industrial pumps and toss long hoses to the lake. I find myself standing next to the Louises, their eyes squinting and watering from the smoke. Everything seems so surreal; I keep hoping I'll wake up. Soon people will want answers . . . and what could I say? "Everything would've been fine if Big Louise hadn't thrown my Goddamned water bottle filled with whiskey into the fire"?

Why was she getting involved anyway? Is she a certified fire-fighter? No, she is not. Probably not. Maybe. She does have CPR training.

It doesn't matter what I say. I'm dead. The Trinity Committee will hang me and Mother Keller will . . . oh God. *Mother Keller.* My stomach does a queasy flip. Everyone else is over on the other side of the fire and we stand there. Big Louise, Dirty Louise, and me. Somewhere in the crowd I hear Martha Woodcock's rage counter going *beep beep beep! Beep beep beep! Beep beep beep! Beep beep beep!* Then Gordon comes out staggering around, wearing his white sheet.

"Oh no . . ." Big Louise whispers. "He looks just like a . . . a . . ."

I turn to her and shout, "A guy from the fucking *Ku Klux Klan,* Louise!"

"What?" She blinks at me. "I was thinking of—"

"Shut up already, Louise!"

I hate Big Louise.

17
Odd Man Out

By the time I get home, it's almost midnight. I'm exhausted and shaky, and my hair smells like burning cross. Brad's car isn't in the drive. He's not home, which is a small miracle. I wonder if his mother already called him. I shudder to think of the expression on his face when she tells him. Shame, anger, remorse. An I-told-you-so eyebrow arching up on the left. I don't need to be there to see it. I already can.

I go to the Ice Empress.

"Ice Empress." I sag against the refrigerator. "Chardonnay?"

The Ice Empress appears with a small royal crown and scepter. "Right away, Your Highness! Cheerio!" She has a posh British accent now and an annoying British personality. "However, might I suggest a more refreshing beverage? Perhaps an icy-cold Yoo-hoo?"

I rest my head against the cool chrome door and groan.

The house is quiet.

Too quiet. Nobody is home, not even the Fang Gang, which is . . . unheard of. Bi'ch and Pac Man shouldn't be out this late. I start to get worried. Brad wouldn't . . . deport them, would he?

No, they're from Milwaukee. Still, maybe he deported them to Milwaukee. I call Brad's cell phone but he doesn't answer. Then I find a note from Star Fan saying they're out looking for Ace. I look around . . . where's Ace? Why isn't he here? I can't find him anywhere. I look all over the house, calling his name, and then run outside, shouting for him and clapping my hands along the lake. Panic rises inside me. I reluctantly call Mother Keller and there's no answer there either.

I start to panic.

I call my neighbors, but nobody in this neighborhood picks up the phone this late at night. I call the police and they say to call the pound. That's where they take lost dogs. The pound, however, is closed for the day. I finally call Greta at the animal hospital and ask her what to do. She makes a few calls on my behalf and fifteen minutes later she calls me back, breathing strangely, which unnerves me. This is a woman who's seen every conceivable tragedy there is and I've never heard her so much as let out a sigh.

"Jennifer?" she says. "He's at . . . the pound."

"Are you serious?"

"I called my friend who volunteers down there. She said they had two dogs delivered today and one was white with three legs."

"Who delivered him?"

"I don't know. She's going to fax me a copy of his intake form in the morning, but you don't have that long. You have to get him out of there before six in the morning."

"It's closed until nine."

"I know, but, Jennifer . . . he's scheduled for termination at six."

Within minutes I'm driving in the car, careening through city streets and clipping curbs. I blow through a red light and don't even look back. My mind is working in a peculiar gear. I'm familiar with the panic that's coursing through my veins, screaming at the top of its lungs, and seething anger is also there, but there's a strange new flower blooming in the night garden of my soul. I feel calm. Not overwhelmed calm or Zen Buddhist calm . . . it's more like a seasoned Navy SEAL has arrived in the situation room. I will allow panic when I can afford panic, which is not now. I have to think clearly now. There's no time for mistakes.

I call Nick. "Jen?" he says. "What's up?" I tell him I need him to meet me at the pound in fifteen minutes. He should wear dark clothes and bring any tools he has that can cut, pry, pull open, or break into things. He pauses, and then to his credit he says, "I'll be there." I hang up and the Navy SEAL commander approves of the decision. Nick will be a worthy crewmember.

The pound parking lot is empty. I leave the car running and start circling the building. I'm looking for any open door or sign of someone like a security guard. They probably have cameras watching me right now, which is fine. Lock me up tomorrow and throw away the key. Tonight, I will be getting inside this building. I find the gloomy entrance closed up tight. The big metal security doors are padlocked. Every window is barred and there's not a night janitor to be seen.

Nick's truck pulls into the lot and parks next to my car.

He hops out of the car and says, "What's the plan, chief?"

"Ace is inside that building, and we're getting him out."

"Okay . . ." He looks up at the ominous shadowy building. "Whatcha thinking?"

"The entrances have metal doors and double padlocks. Too hard to go through that way."

"Yep." He nods. "Never liked doors much myself."

"The first-floor windows are all barred, the second-story windows aren't."

He looks up. "Second story, then?"

I nod. "Unless you have enough steel cable or chain link in your truck."

"Well then, let me take a look."

I'm gauging the height of our vehicles and measuring them against the building, all the while vaguely aware of him rooting around in his truck. Then I hear a loud clank and a heavy metal chain dragging on the ground. "I'm thinking those little window bars over there might pop out," he says, and I agree. I move his truck and reposition it closer to the building as Nick drags the heavy chain over and clamps it with a thick U-bolt to the metal bars on a window. Then he bolts the other end of the chain underneath his idling truck.

"Ready?" he says. "Just keep the wheels straight and gun it."

"You want me to do it?"

"Hell, sweetheart, this is your rodeo."

"All right. Here we go." I get into his truck and slam the door shut. Then I take a deep breath, shift her in gear, and punch that pedal down for every ounce I'm worth.

Vroooorovrooom! The truck lurches forward, the chain goes taut, the engine starts straining. "Come on, you son of a bitch!" I grip the wheel with both hands, nearly standing on the gas pedal with my full weight. I hear a metal groaning and then *bang!* The truck leaps forward like a bronco from the gate and the iron frame bursts from the brick window well, clanking across the asphalt. I hit the brakes and stick my head out the window.

"Did we pop it?" I shout at him.

"We popped it!" he shouts back.

Nick just helped me break into a city building. Not only does Jennifer the girl think that's sexy, Jennifer the Navy SEAL commander does too. I repark his truck so the bed is right beneath the window we just violated, and we climb up, hoisting ourselves through the window. Inside the dark building we run down the empty halls, our footsteps echoing off the floors of polished cement.

We find Ace in a lonely chain-link cage with cement floors and a big padlock on the door. He's all alone, without even a blanket to comfort him in there. Ace whimpers when he sees me and limps over to the door. "Hey, buddy!" I whisper. "We're gonna get you out of here, okay? Don't worry." A sheet of yellow paper is clipped to his cage. The top line reads "ACE"— IMMEDIATE TERMINATION.

I snatch it up and rapidly scan the form for contact information or a signature. My jaw clenches when I see it. Of course. I'd recognize that spidery scrawl anywhere.

Mrs. Edwin Keller. The cocky bitch signed it at the bottom.

"Hey, Nick! We're gonna need a hacksaw or—"

"Some bolt cutters?" He whips out a pair of industrial bolt cutters from his jacket.

"Where were those?" I hiss at him.

"Don't worry about it," he says as he snaps off Ace's lock, which clatters to the floor. We hear another dog whimper in the cage across the way, a skinny greyhound who's shivering nervously. On the cage door it says "TOGGLE"—IMMEDIATE TERMINATION.

"She said there were two dogs delivered. We'll have to take this one too."

"Already on it." Nick snaps off Toggle's lock. Then we wrap the dogs up in our jackets; I carry Ace and he takes Toggle. We hear something in the other room and we both look at each other. Then we get the hell out of there.

I go through the window first and stand on the truck bed as Nick hands Ace down to me. I set him down and tell him to stay, and for the first time in his life, he obeys me. Nick carefully lowers the greyhound down and I hold her while he climbs out onto the truck bed. He takes Toggle and I take Ace and we quickly leave the scene of our crime. I call him on the cell phone as we drive away and say thank you.

"Shit, I think we should do that once a week," he says. "Travel the land and become professional dog-nappers!" I thank him again and tell him I'll call him to check on Toggle tomorrow. Then I hang up and drive for twenty minutes or more before I realize I have no idea where I'm going.

At a red light I catch sight of the little Travel Angel on my dashboard. I lean forward, crushing it with my fist. "Ace," I say, "from now on, we look out for ourselves. I've about had it with angels. No one will *ever* hurt you again, as God is my witness."

I drive to the house but I can't go inside.

Brad's car is now parked in the driveway. It makes me writhe with rage. I turn around and keep driving. By this time it's nearly three in the morning. I go the only place I can think of, the only place I know where I can turn up this late, or rather, this early.

Ted's house.

Ted, my bookmark guy. Always in place when I need him.

I drive over to his apartment and knock on the door. A pretty blond girl with a perky ski-jump nose answers. She's wearing red flannel pajamas that are covered with big white snowflakes. An enormous beagle waddles up behind her. He sniffs at Ace, who growls at him. "Sorry," I say. "I thought my friend Ted still lived here."

Then Ted appears in the doorway. He's also in red flannel pajamas covered with big white snowflakes. I look at them and say, "What the hell is going on here?"

"Jen?" Ted smiles. "Are you okay?"

"Yep!"

"This is Jen," Ted says to the blonde, and she blinks at me. Then her face lights up.

"*Jen?*" she says. "Your Jen?"

"My Jen," Ted says, grinning.

"Come in," the blonde says. "Come in!" She seizes me with freakishly strong hands and pulls me into the apartment. Before I know what's happening, I'm sitting on the couch and my coat is off. "Vine!" the blonde says. "Vee have alcohol! Ted says you are always drinking the alcohol. I will bring the biggest bottles vee have. Vait here!"

She bounces off to the kitchen.

"Where'd she'd come from?" I ask. "A Swiss Miss can?"

"Pretty much." Ted nods. "Norway. Her name's Kjersten."

He pronounces it like *Shears*-ten and smiles weird when he says it.

"What . . . is Kjersten like your girlfriend?"

"No. Not anymore."

"Well, thank Norwegian Jesus I missed that episode. She's so cute I might vomit."

"Now she's my fiancée."

"Don't be stupid."

"She is, Jennifer."

"I like that couch. Is it new?"

"Oh right, like you really care." He sighs. "I chased you for three years in that marketing department and you never gave me the time of day. Now you're acting jealous? You crack me up. You really do." Kjersten returns carrying a tray with two wineglasses and a mason jar filled with aquavit. The mason jar is for me. "I vant to meet you for so long!" She smiles and it's like her face is the sun. "I hear so much about you!" she says. "How much talent you have, how you're so funny, so pretty . . ."

I raise an eyebrow at her. "Ted said that about *me*?"

"Yah! He says you eat more than most men."

Yep. There it is.

"But he never lets me meet you!" she says. "I think he made you up to impress people!"

"She did." Ted smiles. "She said I made you up to impress her."

"I get that a lot."

"Oh look!" Kjersten smiles. "Miss Biggles remembers you!"

Mrs. Biggles? My . . . cat? I smile and look down. The room tilts. There she is, my long-lost companion, the one I gave up when I married Brad.

"She was your cat, yes?" Kjersten asks me.

"Mrs. Biggles is *still* Jen's cat," Ted says quickly. "She'll *always* be Jen's cat. Our friend Lana was watching her, but then she got a job in New York and now . . . we're watching her." He shrugs happily. "Hey, the more the merrier. We love the Biggles."

"I love Miss Biggles too." Kjersten grins. "She sleeps vith me every night."

That's it. My heart, or whatever was left of it, finally gives way and clanks on the floor. I kneel down to pet my old friend. I kiss Mrs. Biggles's sweet head and start weeping. Ted puts a hand on my shoulder. "Jen," he says. "Listen to me. You can have Mrs. Biggles back any time you want her."

"It's not that," I whisper. "I don't want to take her. I can't even provide her a . . . safe home." Then I start weeping. I tell them everything, about Brad and Mrs. Keller and the dog-napping. I tell them I want my old life back. I can't stop talking. Damned Kjersten wraps a blanket around me and makes herbal tea. She's so freaking sweet it's ridiculous. I pull myself together and splash water on my face in the bathroom. I collect Ace and his things, despite the fact that he's curled up on the floor in postcoital delight with the beagle. He's stretched out belly-up so Kjersten can rub his tum-tum. Just like my beloved Mrs. Biggles, he seems perfectly willing to live here now. I can't say I blame him. Even I don't want to go home.

In the car I call Addi. I tell her I'm fighting with Brad and worried about Ace, and she demands I come over with Ace and stay. She'll have the guest room ready. She won't bother me, I can do my own thing. I drive over there, thinking I won't sleep there but will just have a glass of wine. Right. Here's the recipe for a meltdown: Start with a hangover, add one public humiliation and a terrifying ordeal. Pour into a shaker with complete exhaustion, semi-moderate heartbreak, and a jigger or two of bittersweet memories recalling times gone by. Top off with copious amounts of white wine and garnish with no clean underpants.

Shake.

Before I know what's hit me, the tears spring forth and flow for everything. I weep for my life, I weep for my choices, I weep for Rome.

Then the sun comes up.

I'm asleep in the guest bed with a kimono on. "Ace?" I sit up and panic as I run to the kitchen, where Addi is hand-feeding my dog applewood-smoked bacon.

"Who is the most precious little dog in the world?" she coos. "You are!"

Ace and I go home. Funny to think he's safer in Ted's drafty little low-rent apartment with mismatched furniture than he is in my sprawling mansion on a lake. It turns out heated floors can't keep you warm and locks don't make you safe. I'm driving to one of the wealthiest neighborhoods in America, where all my neighbors are millionaires, but to me it's quite literally . . . a civil war zone.

I go to the gazebo and start to look through old wedding albums. Symbols of my ruined dreams, my buttercream candied-violet fantasies. I was going to be Wedding Day Barbie, all tiny-waisted and misty-eyed. Instead I wound up being Debbie Downer Divorcee, all chunky-butted and red-eyed. I hear someone whistle. I look up and there's . . . Christopher.

Hallelujah.

I had called him and asked him to come over. I tell him about everything that's happened, about burning down the cross, about my awful Valentine's Day, about Mother Keller tossing Ace in the pound and Nick helping save him.

"When I saw Ace inside that chain-link cage," I tell him, "it's like I never really cared about how anyone treated me . . . but Ace? No. I'm sorry. That's not okay. Hurt me all you want, but touch my dog and we're done."

"I once had this hairdresser," Christopher says. "Brett. Jeremy always said I only went to him because he looked like an Abercrombie and Fitch model. He gave me terrible haircuts."

I tell him I remember that. "The guy who gave you a half Mohawk."

"Exactly. I believe you said I looked like an eighties pop star who survived a car accident."

"Barely survived."

"Anyway . . ." He sighs. "It didn't matter who told me I looked terrible, I didn't believe them. I thought Jeremy was just jealous, and you? I never listened to your fashion advice. Still don't. But the point is, I only realized the truth when *Jeremy* went to Brett and got a haircut."

"I remember. He looked like Tina Turner in *Beyond Thunderdome*."

"I never saw Brett again. It was only when I saw what Brett did to someone I love that I realized what he was doing to *me*. Understand?"

"Unfortunately."

We sit there for a moment.

Finally I look up at him. "You know what?"

"What?" He squints at me.

"I have to leave. I have to leave . . . Brad."

A rusting Mazda pulls into our driveway and parks. A girl in a floppy red hat gets out carrying a big cardboard box and Christopher stares at me.

"You got the Cinnabon girl to *deliver?*"

"Satan made me join the Cinners Club," I tell him. "So she owes me. Down here, Satan!"

She makes her way to the gazebo and hands me the large cardboard box, which says CINNA-NUM!

"They're still warm," she says. "Like you wanted."

"Can you drive a stick shift?" I ask her.

She shrugs and says sure.

"Then here you are. Have a Lamborghini." I toss her the keys and she smiles at me.

"You want me to move your car or something?"

"Christopher, do you see an envelope around here with . . . oh, there it is." I hand her the manila envelope I have with me in the gazebo. "Here you go. Title and registration. You'll need those to prove you own it."

The Cinnabon girl frowns at me. "You're giving me a car?"

"No. I gave you one."

She peers up the driveway. "That green Lamborghini right there?" She holds the keys above her head and clicks the button. *Beep-beep!* The Lamborghini's headlights flash twice and its venom-yellow eyes wink open.

"Um, Jennifer?" Christopher whispers.

"Not now, dear. We're transacting. All right, Satan?"

"I can't take this."

"Well, of course you can. It's for years of service. You provided more comfort and advice and support, frankly, than any psychologist. Take the car, because, as my friend Addi once said, *life's* not fair and nobody asked you to be here, so shut up and just wax your damn pussy."

The Cinnabon girl looks back at me. Then she heads up the lawn and a moment later we hear the Lamborghini's engine roar to life and the car peels out, followed by the sound of laughter, and then . . . we see a red hat go sailing *up, up, up* into the blue sky.

Christopher looks over at me and says, "I think someone's in love."

"I think I just figured out something about love."

"Spill it."

"Well, last night when I found myself demolishing a government building with a pickup truck in order to save my three-legged dog, I realized something: that finding true love and finding true north are the same thing. You just toss the maps and use your own compass . . . because true love can turn up anywhere and it can look like anything. Even something super freaking unusual, even like a three-legged dog by the side of the road, eating out of Pampers. True love is saying, 'I love this creature . . . even if no one else wants me to.'"

"Welcome to being gay," Christopher says.

"True love is saying, 'This is a bad idea . . . and I'm doing it. This bad idea . . . *it's mine.*' You can lock it in a building or put it on the moon. You can pass a law that says it's illegal. It doesn't matter. Do what you will . . . I will never give up on it. I will always come back for it. I will find it every time, because I've got a compass that shows me the right way and all you have is maps that don't know where true north is anymore."

I look over at Christopher and he's staring at me.

"So." I sigh. "Want to help me get out of this crappy marriage?"

Christopher squeezes my hand and nods. "Honey, I've been dreaming about it ever since your wedding day."

"Good. Then we'll launch my new plan: Operation Awful Wife."

Christopher smiles at me and nods.

"Of course," he says. "You had me at 'Awful.'"

18
Operation Awful Wife

Brad's pretty irritated about his Lamborghini. I take the simplest road out and tell him I was moved by the Lord to give it away.

"You gave my Lamborghini away?"

"Well no, of course not!" I tell him. "I sold it for a dollar. God told me to."

He looks for his beloved car. He places ads and calls the police and is told if he wants to get it back, he'll have to find the new owner and negotiate a deal. Brad asks me *who the fuck I sold his car to* and I say I can't remember. When he starts to yell at me in earnest, I call Pastor Mike and schedule marriage therapy counseling. I say Brad seems inordinately attached to material things. When Mother Keller finds out we're about to go into marriage counseling and embarrass her in front of the whole church, she calls Brad in a fury and he never mentions the Lamborghini again.

Winter drains away and spring blooms. I told Christopher exactly what the divorce lawyer told me: If I walk away from this marriage without justification, I'm screwed. It's the prenup

I signed. I'll get nothing, less than nothing. Brad will get to keep everything, the stocks, the money, the property, the cars, the furniture, even my clothes. The prenup says whoever leaves without cause gets nothing. It also says anyone caught *cheating* gets nothing. Anyone caught committing adultery automatically forfeits all assets, joint and otherwise.

"The real question," Christopher says with a sigh, "is why'd you sign a prenup? Who on earth would sign a prenup?"

"I was an idiot." I sigh. "Like every girl getting married. I was in love. I thought my marriage would last forever. I would've signed anything."

Christopher groans.

I tell him Brad's mother made us sign a prenup, so neither of us would quit early or cheat and run off with all the family's money. Christopher nods and looks impressed. "Well, at least she did her homework," he says. "She knew to nail your shoes down."

"But the infidelity clause works both ways," I tell him. "If Brad gets caught cheating on *me*, then he gets nothing and I get to keep everything. See?"

"Um . . ." He looks around, confused. "No, not really."

"We need to catch Brad cheating."

"What if he isn't cheating?"

"Well then . . . we have to make him cheat."

"Make him? How do you make your husband cheat?"

Top Ten Ways to Make Your Husband Cheat

1. Tell him he can.
2. Leave him alone with your cute friends.
3. Reduce/eliminate talking to him. Walk out of the room when he walks in.

4. Cut off all sex, including masturbation. Bang into the bathroom while he's showering.
5. Make yourself look like a lesbian folksinger. Wear baggy clothes and stop shaving all your leg and armpit hair. Glue extra hair on for added effect.
6. Smell French. Refrain from using soap, perfume, or deodorant.
7. Stop feeding him. Stop shopping for him. Stop cleaning up after him.
8. Cancel all social engagements with him. Never have fun together. Look disappointed when he comes home.
9. Take long trips away from home. Suggest he do the same and bring his secretary.
10. Hang a big "Honey Do" list, aka "Nag Board," on the wall, filled with lots of smiley faces and hearts along with nasty chores and ways he can improve himself. *How 'bout going to the gym, honey? I'm worried about your blood pressure* ♥ *... Also, you're getting a gut ... I bought you a nose-hair trimmer because it looks like two miniature gorillas moved into your nose ... I canceled your golf game and made you a doctor's appointment—time to get checked for colon and prostate cancer!* ☺

First things first. I tell Brad he can have an affair if he wants to. Big mistake. I thought he might take me up on it, look surprised but delighted, and say, "Really?" But no, he looks at me with suspicion and then around the room as if I'm filming this. Right away I backtrack and say I'm kidding. I smack his arm and remind him we're cleaved together till death do us part. Of course, the way he eats and takes care of his body, that might be sooner rather than later. That triggers an argument about how I always nag him, which is exactly what I wanted to have happen.

We are soon shouting at each other and quickly diverted from the topic of cheating.

Whew.

I move on to the next plan. Christopher and I launch into gear by . . . buying gear. Spy gear. We need *hard evidence*. I learned from listening to all of Addi's divorce stories that eyewitness testimony is worthless. I could walk in on Brad balling the Dallas Cowboys cheerleaders and it wouldn't mean a thing, not even if they testified against him as well and signed legal affidavits stating they were all pregnant with his baby. It still doesn't count. We need to catch Brad on tape. Red-handed. In the meantime I have to act normal; I can't let on I'm leaving. Addi says that's mistake number one that most women make. They blurt out that they want a divorce before they've gotten ready and stashed assets away for later.

We order a boatload of creepy spy gear online, and using the dollhouse, we decide where to install all the spy cameras we bought. We have cameras disguised as a pen, an ashtray, a dictionary, a fluffy pink teddy bear, and a tabletop gumball machine. I find all of those items highly suspicious and unlikely to be in any home, but the spy gear website guarantees results.

We call the pen-cam "Mr. Inky" and stash him on Brad's desk. The ashtray-cam, or "Li'l Smokey," goes on our bedroom fireplace mantel in case there are unsanctioned shenanigans going on in our bed. The dictionary-cam, or "Brainy Boy," is shoved into the bookshelf in Brad's office. The fluffy pink teddy bear, "Gay Ted," goes in the front hall, so we can see who comes and goes. The gumball machine, "Chewy," goes in the kitchen and looks absolutely retarded.

We struggle with our roles as domesticated spies. Mr. Inky is out of the game after Brad grabs it, thinking it's a real pen, and scribbles furiously on a piece of paper. Then he chucks it in the garbage can under his desk. Mr. Inky dies. Li'l Smokey is placed too high up to record anything useful, Brainy Boy is half obscured by a hockey trophy sitting on the bookshelf, Chewy records the Ice Empress insulting people, and Gay Ted falls over on his face repeatedly, the camera lodged in his nose making him top-heavy, and he records no footage whatsoever.

We're not completely amateurs, though. I get Pho to reprogram Brad's Audi R8, which he bought to replace the Lambo, so the voice commands all do different things than they're supposed to. Normally if Brad says something like "Adjust temperature" or "Turn on radio," the car responds to those commands exactly. We make a few adjustments to the system, however, so now if Brad says any of the key words we've programmed in, the car will give us clues. If Brad says "pussy," "wet," or "girlfriend," then the left backseat seat warmer goes on. If he says "How much?" the right backseat seat warmer goes on. If he says "blow job," the passenger-side headrest rotates to the right. If he says, "Oh baby, yes!" the rearview mirror clicks two notches to the right. Now I'll know if Brad is having sex in his car. Or eating a really good sandwich.

I follow Brad to work and wear disguises so he won't recognize me. I love the feeling of becoming someone else and stalking him like a blond, brunette, or redheaded panther into the store. I watch who he talks to and how; I sit through employee seminars and watch him just like I used to do when we were dating as smarmy seminar guys extol the virtues of change. *Change!* (Cue the sound of pennies dropping.) I follow him down hallways and peer at him through makeup displays and watch him through racks of clothing. I stand behind him as he rides the escalator. To my disappointment, he never speaks to anyone unusual or out of the way. I expect him to be cavorting with the whores behind the hosiery counter or with the sluts selling Clinique lip gloss, but he doesn't. He's always talking to or meeting with someone quite appropriate, like his father or his sister or fellow members of senior management.

Infuriating.

But I don't give up. I follow Brad after work, to restaurants and bars, where he sips and sups with a variety of people. Nothing about it is scandalous, except that the amount of time he spends with Todd Brockman should legally be considered a crime. The man is heinous. It's at one of their favorite sports bars downtown that I run into my ex, David. David, my longtime love, whom I loved since second grade, when his family moved in down the street. Everyone thought we'd get married . . . including me. Instead of a wedding, however, all I got was a long, grueling, tortuous on-again, off-again "relationship" with a hipster doofus who had a drinking problem, a tendency to borrow large sums of money that he never paid back, and a horrible garage band he loved called Obscure Cold.

They were awful.

David smiles at me. He says I look great and asks if he can call me sometime. I sort of bat him off uninterestedly and say, "Sure, whatever." An action I would've thought was inconceivable until recently. Now, however, I'm someone quite different from the girl he used to know. Now I'm doing things I never thought possible. Like ordering two hundred Patty Wee Wee dolls from a remarkably inexpensive wholesaler in Taiwan, who ships them to the house express overnight. I unpack the black-eyed dolls wearing diapers and line them up like a firing squad in our bedroom.

"What're all these freaky dolls doing everywhere?" Brad shouts at me when he sees them.

I tell him I've started a new charity for incontinent children.

"These dolls are freaky as shit!" he says. "I'm sleeping downstairs."

I continue to make the house as unpleasant as I can. I have Pho reprogram the Ice Empress to be the most annoying person I can think of: Brad's mother. I have him download Tammy Faye Bakker's voice and Billy Graham sermons, so whenever you ask her for anything she spits out a Bible verse. It goes like this: "Ice Empress, can I have a bottle of water?"

"*Amen!*" she shouts. "Verily I say unto you, that through the valley of the shadow of death I was hungry and *He* gave me food. I was thirsty and *He* gave me drink. Behold!" (Panel flips open and bottle of water appears in frosty nook.) "I was near death!" she says. "And *He* gave me a generous donation! At 1-800-GO-JESUS!"

I make sure I myself am as gross as possible too, so Brad won't want to touch me. I stop shaving and cease wearing deodorant. I tell Brad that I have sleep apnea and wear a CPAP machine to bed. I wear baggy boxy clothing from my absolute favorite new clothing designer: the Mormons. They sell Fundamentalist LDS dresses on the Home Shopping Network now to raise money for their compounds or jail funds or whatever. The dresses are all handmade and totally porn-on-the-prairie. They're made of worsted felt and have high necklines, floor-length hemlines, and little peaked, tufted shoulders. They're boxy and big. I look like I'm wearing an enormous felt tea cozy. The opposite of sexy . . . in a dress.

I make sure my activities are disgusting. I take up the lost art of Victorian hair jewelry and spend hours with pale women from the nearby Mennonite community, who join my regular hair-weaving roundtables and sing hymns and braid long tresses of dead hair in the kitchen. Afterward I forget to sweep. I hire a graphic artist to paint random religious murals on the walls. The crucifixion of Christ stares at us from our bedroom ceiling. I sell all our traditional furniture and replace everything with big blocky modern furniture . . . so modern I often I don't even know what the furniture is. A couch or a collapsible bed? A rug or a wall hanging? A lamp or a flower vase? Who knows. I give up after I put what was a porcelain bidet in the living room, thinking it's a wet bar. I routinely rearrange the furniture, especially upstairs, so Brad trips over things when he goes to the bathroom at night. I sigh when he does this and call him Mr. Klutzy.

I ramp the Fang Gang show up to high volume. I tell Pho to use the house as cyber-ninja command headquarters. I tell Star Fan she can invite all her friends over anytime, day or night. I tell Bi'ch that she and her Hmong singing group can use the house as a rehearsal space. Soon my home looks like a Hmong rec center. To be honest, I've never had so much fun.

I call the animal hospital and tell Greta to send me their most unadoptable animals. That's how I wind up adopting a tattered band of abused alpacas. I start an alpaca refuge in the backyard, installing the beasts in a large pen that takes up most of the shoreline. I tell Brad the truth. They're rescue animals. That's why they spit. "If you knew what those poor creatures had been through," I shout when Brad complains. I insist they eat nutritious homemade alpaca kibble made from a complicated, smelly recipe I find online.

I find a pan-flute player to stand on the front staircase and play the pan-flute five hours every day, even on the weekends, because the music soothes the alpacas. When the pan flute player is done, I let my old boyfriend rehearse in the garage with Obscure Cold. They practice at all hours of the night and keep their drum kit in the bay where the apple-green Lamborghini once lived.

Next I launch Operation Toothpaste Smear. I hit every surface of the bathroom day after day and tell him Trevor did it.

Then I forbid him to say one word to Trevor about it . . . because if we yell at Trevor, that wouldn't look too good to his grandparents, would it?

I monkey with the neighbor's Swift-Away harmless insect replacement system. The Swift-Away system has intake pipes that peep up from the manicured hedges, like a row of miniature tubas crouched in the bushes, bells pointed up at the sky. The tubas suck up any flying insects within ten feet and shoot them headlong into the ether. If a bumblebee ambles by, *whoomph!*, the green tuba sucks the bumblebee up. If a butterfly flutters into the frame, then *whoomph!*, the green tuba swallows the butterfly whole. The intake pipes suck up the mosquitoes and moths and any other hapless insect that dares to trespass against them and shoot them cannon-style out of the hedges and into outer space.

I simply reposition the mouths of the tubas so they're aimed at our property, at about chest height. Judging by the number of dead, damaged, and wingless insects that pelt Brad as he tries to get in his car every morning for work, I don't think the engineers at Swift-Away have the "harmless" element of their technology down pat yet. Brad comes charging back into the house every morning with squashed bugs all over his shirt.

"What is happening?" he shouts. "Look at this!" He points to the pulpy yellow insect goo smeared across the lapel of his suit. "What the *fuck* is this?" he shouts.

"A dragonfly, maybe?" I guess, and he stomps off, muttering, to change his suit.

I mess with Brad's food. I grind up weight-loss pills and put them in his protein shakes so he can experience volatile gastric events at the store, just like I did. I set up a dating profile for Brad on ExplodingHearts.com. I make his profile pitch-perfect for every crazy stalker and gold digger in the nation and direct phone calls to his office. *Wealthy executive seeks loving woman to adore and pamper. Age unimportant. Kids terrific! Looking for one-night stands, meaningless hookups, and long-term relationships only.*

I hire a stripper to be our new auxiliary maid. An actual stripper that I hire from an escort agency. She's also a local porn celebrity, and after she shares the titles of some of her favorite films that she's starred in, I'm inspired to make a list.

Top Ten Worst Porn Stars

1. Great-aunts
2. Cheesemongers
3. New York cabbies
4. Ladies of the PGA
5. Hoboes
6. Mermen
7. Amish sadomasochists
8. Hirsute Taco Bell employees
9. Amateur taxidermists
10. Danny DeVito

My stripper's name is Diamond and she shows up wearing silver lamé shorts. I tell her all she has to do is cook and clean in the sexiest manner she can think of. I'll pay her five hundred bucks a day, and if she tape-records herself having sex with my husband, there's a thousand-dollar bonus. Diamond throws herself into her work, treating it as risqué burlesque. She's actually a better maid than Bi'ch and seems to have a real grip on what men like. Her second day here I find her grilling T-bone steaks outside while wearing nothing but stilettos and a purple thong.

"Did you see our new maid?" I ask Brad.

"Seems pretty creative," he says, reading the paper.

I have her do striptease acts while cleaning the stove, her head stuck up in the vent; I tell her to polish the woodwork by oiling up her lunch box and sliding down the banister repeatedly; I have her design a "cleaning supply saddle," which she wears on her back like a horse, and crawl butt-naked around the house, wearing nothing else but kneepads and cowboy boots.

Nothing. Zilch. It's like Brad is gay . . . but even a gay man would adore the production value we're putting into this show. Lenny stops by to drop something off one day and I hear him hollering in the front hall. "Lenny?" I shout. "What's wrong?"

"Oh Jesus!" he hollers. "Oh God, I saw naked titties! Big ones! Pressed up on the window outside!"

"Sorry." Diamond shrugs. "I thought he was—"

"Never mind, Diamond. It's okay. Lenny, you can open your eyes."

He shakes his head and moans. "Oh Jesus . . ." he says. "*Diamond?* The porn star?"

"Um, yeah." I nod.

"Lord, why'd you say her name? Now I know her name and Hailey's gonna *know* I know her name. She's gonna *know* I saw naked titties!"

"Don't be ridiculous. I won't say anything."

"*You don't have to,*" he whispers while looking around the room, as though Hailey might spring out at any moment pointing her accusing finger at him.

"Lenny, forget about it."

"Sorry!" Diamond grins.

Lenny's phone rings. He looks up at me, ashen, and says, "*It's her!*"

"Are you serious?"

Lenny leaps out the front door while answering the phone. "Hon?" he says. "Hang on, I got bad reception here. Hang on . . . Stop yelling at me!"

He runs out to his truck. At least he cares what his wife thinks. My husband—and I snort every time I use the word—could care less what I do or think.

I'm out of ideas.

I can't take this house or this life anymore. I tell Pho to make the Ice Empress normal again. "Okay," he says. "And what's normal this time?"

"Make her like when she first came to us. Mean and nasty. At least one of us will be who we really are."

Mom calls to wish me a happy birthday. She's one of the few who remembers. I get my annual Bacon Club rasher of bacon from Christopher. He signed me up for it like five years ago and it's sort of lost its . . . charm. I'm not complaining. At least he remembers. Well, the bacon people remember. Brad forgot my birthday last year and he got me a gift certificate for a massage two days later. He told me to go buy something sexy. Wow. Right on. Nothing says Mr. Great Big Hard Cock . . . like a gift certificate. Mom reminds me about Supper Club and she asks if everything's all right. I tell her everything's fine . . . pretty okay . . . sort of all right . . . actually, not so good. She says I can always come home for a while if I want to. "We're always here for you, sweetheart."

I smile and say, "Mom, you're awesome."

"But, honey," she adds quickly. "Don't drag over a bunch of stuff you can't use."

"*What?*"

"I just got the Salvation Army to pick up all those garbage bags of old clothes I had on the back porch all winter. The ones I cleaned out of the attic. Say, I pulled out a cute little dress you threw away. You said you didn't want it, but it's just adorable. It's a white dress with blue piping?"

"Yeah, Mom . . . I remember it. The armpit is torn. I don't want it."

"Well it has a cute little jacket and everything."

"I don't want it."

"It's perfectly good. It just needs a few stitches in the armpit."

"Mom, I don't want it. It never fit me right, the armpits always pinched. I only wore it twice in ten years. Plus I got ink on the front and the hem pulled out."

Silence.

"*Mom?* I don't want the dress."

"You can fix the hem."

"No, Mom, I can't."

"I don't see why not. It'll just take a few stitches and a little bleach to fix it."

"Then *you* fix it. *You* wear it. I don't want it. If you like it, keep it."

"Me? Well, I don't want it, honey."

"Why not?"

"Because it's all torn up and there's ink stains on it."

"Good-bye, Mom, love you."

I hang up the phone and close my eyes. How can you love someone and be so . . . so . . . thoroughly irritated by them at the same time? I'd donate any organ that my mother needed, both my eyeballs, both my kidneys, all my teeth. I'd defend her to the death if I had to, but one thing is for sure: I cannot live with her. I cannot move back in with my parents.

I'll never make it out alive.

I stop going to the country club. I've been declining all social invitations, but that's been the hardest one to pull off so far. Ellie isn't too pushy, but God help you if Addi feels scorned. That woman will go teenage batshit crazy and leave drunk messages on your phone demanding answers, which she's done now several times. She corners me in the bathroom. She asks why I've been avoiding her and I tell her I've just been busy. I'm just working on things and Brad and I are spending more time together.

"Bullshit," she says.

Didn't sound true to me either, but still, I personally don't need more than a hint when someone wants me to go away; Addi needs a frying pan to the head. We get into a huge fight right there in the bathroom, yelling and shouting. The fight bleeds out into the dining room as we stumble toward the front door, two grown women yelling at each other right there in the club in front of everybody. I feel bad for Addi, but it's not fair that she doesn't respect boundaries. "See, you push people until they get to this point," I tell her. "To where they have to hurt you in order to get you away. Now . . . who else on earth has that problem but a junkyard dog?"

She gasps at me. "Did you just call me a junkyard dog?"

I did, and even I'm flummoxed by the statement.

"Why you filthy little piece of . . ." *Sploosh*. She throws a drink from a nearby table right into my face. Louie arrives and says, "Okay, Ms. A and Mrs. J. I think you gotta go or things are gonna get real messy today." Louie hustles me out to the valet stand, while the rest of the staff keeps Addi inside. "Guess I won't be coming back around here again." I sigh remorsefully. Louie nods at me sadly as my car rolls up.

"Prolly not, Mrs. J. Okay. Bye-bye."

I refuse to go home and sink into a sticky mire of self-loathing; instead I drive straight to the gym to see Big D. It's not our normally scheduled time, so I don't know where to look for him. He's not on the loading dock, where we usually meet; he's not inside the gym on the floor. I ask the fake-tan blonde behind the counter if she's seen Big D. "Um . . . Yes. He's standing right next to you." I look over at the black man standing beside me, writing on a clipboard. He has coiled pythons tattooed on his arms. "Your name's Big D too?" I say. "That must get confusing."

"Ma'am?" He looks at me. "I'm Big D."

"You're a trainer here too?"

"Cardio, weights, Pilates . . ." He watches a brunette passing by. "Hey, Laura! I still need a ride downtown."

"Fuck off," she says.

"I don't think I have any open sessions right now," he says to me. "But you can check the schedule in the front office."

"I already have a trainer. The other Big D."

"What other Big D?" He looks at me. "There *is* no other Big D."

"An older gentleman? Gray beard?"

"Don't think we have any trainers around here with gray beards . . . We like to keep it tight, right, ladies?" He smiles at a group of women walking by. "Hey now, Mrs. Magney, Mrs. Jewson . . . how you doing, Mrs. Hoyos? Looking good, ladies! Looking good!"

"Um, Big D . . . you never worked with a woman named Ellie Rathbone, did you?"

"Sure!" he says. "How is Mrs. E? Haven't seen her in a while now . . ." The brunette appears with a stack of towels. "Need help with those, Laura?"

"Fuck you," she says.

I shake my head, confused. "I usually meet Big D on the loading dock, but—"

"Oh, you mean Dizzy Bee?" says the blonde. "He lives back there. The manager said as long as he didn't build another smokehouse he could stay."

"Stay where?"

"In the alley. He lives right out there." She points to the loading dock. I make her come outside and show me. She points at a pile of garbage on the other side of the alley.

"Hey, Dizzy Bee!" she shouts. *"Hey, Dizzy Bee!"*

The pile of garbage moves.

"Why you holler like that?" Big D shouts at her. "Do I come to your house and holler when you in bed? A black man did that at your house, the police would kill him! Just kill him right there. Tell everybody he slipped an' hit his head. Shit. What you want, girl?"

"He's *so* sweet," the blonde says. "We just love him."

It turns out Big D isn't a trainer. He's a homeless man living in the alley behind the gym. He gets his clothing from the Dumpster behind the gym, which is why he wears sweatshirts with official Sweatbox logos. "Big D," I say. "What are you doing here?"

He looks at me sideways. "I ain't here to impress you," he snaps. "I ain't here to get your vote. Why wouldn't I be here? I got the diabetes, don't I? And that dumb-ass juice bar throws away shitloads a *fruit*!"

"I don't understand why you'd pretend to be a physical trainer."

"What the hell's that?"

"A physical trainer, someone who coaches you, gets you to work out."

"Ain't that a thing! I'm a physical trainer!"

"No, you were pretending to be one."

"Pretend? Pretend, my sweet ass! I coached the hell outta you. I got you off your ass, every time you come around. That ain't no small thing. You lazy as hell!"

"You should've told me who you really were."

"Who I was? You shoulda tole me who *you* was. You rude,

you know that? You lazy and rude. I was set right there minding my own business, getting my oranges, when you come up going all firecracker in my face, talking 'bout *your big butt* and how *I'm* supposed to do something about it. Then we off running around the city like crazy people. I almost turned you in at the police station. I thought you was an escaped crazy person."

"B-but . . . Big D," I stutter. "I . . . I mean, Mr. Bee, didn't you wonder why I was telling you all that stuff, everything about myself?"

"Hell *yes* I wondered. Shit! You talk the ear off a dead man, woman. I didn't understand a damn word you said. Something 'bout what-all and who-knows. White-girl problems. One thing got clear quick, though. You was in over yo head and didn't have the sense of a betsy bug. You afraid of yo own shadow. Felt sorry for ya. I got a daughter. She don't talk as much, though."

My mind is reeling. "So you just . . ."

"I just *what*? I just ran your ass off so you could fit into them skinny jeans!"

I have no idea what to say. So I just shrug and say, "Same time next week?"

"You bet, girl. Bring me a chicken sandwich too." He clamps his headphones on and starts singing the Isley Brothers' "It's Your Thing." *"It's your thing! Do what you wanna do! I can't tell you who to sock it to . . . Ow!"*

My cell phone rings. It's Hailey.

"Can you pick up the twins?" she asks, out of breath.

"Sure. Where are they?"

"Lenny took them down for a catalog shoot. Christmas angels, I think. Then some unexpected delivery turned up at the dock, a refrigerated shipment scheduled for next week. I'm stuck at the doctor's office, and the twins are probably stuck to the hood of his forklift with duct tape. I need them home in an hour so I can feed them. Can you get them home by then? You can take the car seats out of Lenny's truck."

"You bet I can. I'm on my way."

When I get to the shoot, they're just finishing the last shot and the twins are dressed as shepherds herding small stuffed sheep. They look ridiculous. These big beefy babies wearing white robes and glue-on beards. Billy keeps chewing on the sheep they gave him. It's practically soaked. That's when I have a funny feeling in my stomach and I ask someone where the sheep came from.

Nobody knows.

I run around until I find the boxes in the loading dock. There they are, all stacked up and pretty as you please, with a CLOG Industries symbol stamped surreptitiously behind the shipping label on each box. I freak out. Brad swore he'd never use those Jesus thugs again. He lied to me. The sheep could be stuffed with anything—cancerous fiber, crushed coca leaves, pulverized plutonium. I wouldn't put anything past them. I ignored the fact we are selling bizarrely dangerous crap to the public; now it isn't me paying, it's my newborn nephew. "Lenny!" I shout at him as he rounds the corner driving his forklift full-tilt.

"Hey!" he shouts. "What's up, peanut butter cup? Got the boys okay?"

"Lenny, listen to me, I *have* to find the ship's manifest for the CLOG sheep shipment, okay? It's critical. I don't care if we have to drive to Duluth or Chicago or wherever, we need to find the ship's manifest now. It's a matter of life and possibly death, God help me. So, get on the phone, get your jacket on . . . do whatever you need to do and find out where the *fuck* it is!"

"Sure," he says, grabbing a clipboard off the wall next to him. "It's right here."

"What?"

"Yep." He hands the clipboard over. It's the ship's manifest.

"Lenny, I *asked* you how to find these months ago and you said you didn't know!"

"No, you asked me how to find *cargo ships* months ago and I'll be damned if I know where any motherfuckin' cargo ships are. We keep all the manifests on this wall. Help yourself . . . Gotta go."

I take the manifest for the CLOG sheep shipment, and I fax it over to Greta at the animal hospital. I ask her to look it over and tell me if there is anything poisonous or harmful to humans on it. There isn't, thank God.

Not this time. But there will be a next time and a time after that, if I don't do something. I find CLOG truck deliveries scheduled clear into the new year. Brad has no intention of discontinuing CLOG's products. Hell, he'd even give them to his own family. It's high time that Rome started burning. The empire needs to come down.

All I need . . . is a match.

19
The Ice Empress

O ur one-year anniversary finally arrives.

It took a Herculean effort, but when the big day finally comes, everything's ready. Our glorious moment will be celebrated at Keller's Department Store. Where else? Mother Keller arranged everything months ago, taking control of the event and citing my near-lethal investor dinner and my recent giant cross burning as proof I cannot be trusted.

I sort of had to agree.

Mother Keller decided to combine our anniversary celebration with Ed's official announcement that Brad is to become the new Keller's president. She thinks it's an ideal day to showcase family values and moral correctness, since the Minnesota senate is voting on the hideous Family Equity Act the same afternoon. Mother Keller can't resist flaunting her thoughts on the severe consequences of passing such a law, a law that flies in the face of matrimony, Christianity, and all heterosexuals' God-given right to monopolize legal unions.

Before the press conference, there'll be a celebratory champagne brunch at Hillcrest Country Club. Everyone will meet there to welcome the new president with toasts and melon. Afterward we'll all take a limousine to the store, where we'll park in the underground VIP parking lot so we can enter without crossing any nasty antigay picket lines outside.

There are always nasty antigay picket lines outside.

After Ed gives a speech introducing the world to his chosen one, he'll mention it's also his son's one-year wedding anniversary. Brad and I are scheduled to kiss as a banner unfurls behind us that says HAPPY FIRST ANNIVERSARY! Then doves will be released. Doves are the symbol of love and peace, and an ominous reminder of Noah's ark and the flood and what happens to godless nations who allow gays to run around all married and free.

Then we'll eat cupcakes.

The whole thing is captured on video, thanks to Pho, who works hard to install cameras all along our journey. He edits all the footage himself. I'll see the final video almost a hundred times, and I'll never get tired of watching it. It will become one of my favorite possessions. If there was a fire, I would run through open flames to retrieve it.

The video starts with Pho filming me in the kitchen.

"So today's the big day, huh?" he asks me.

I nod and ask the Ice Empress for some chipped ice. She flickers onto the screen and smiles at me. *"Naniga hoshiino!"* she says cheerfully. *"Moshi moshi,* Jen Aho-Onna!"

"Can I get some ice, please?"

"Hai!" she says. "Ice! *Pinpooooon!"*

A landslide of ice shoots through the dispenser and rattles into my empty glass.

Pho and I start to giggle.

We can't help ourselves. The Ice Empress just said, "What the fuck do you want? Oh, hi, Jen, you dumb bitch! Ice? Sure, have some ice! Yay!"

The Ice Empress rocks. I can't believe I ever wanted to shut her up.

Soon Brad bellows that it's time to go and Pho follows us out to the car. It's stifling hot outside and even though I'm wearing my yellow Chanel suit, which is too warm for the day, I'm still cool as a cucumber. I am the Ice Empress.

"Bye, Mr. B!" Pho waves. "Bye, Mrs. J!"

The Audi pulls away and Brad blasts the air conditioner. On the way over to the country club he lectures me. "I need you on your game today, Jen. You've been acting weird lately."

I tuck my hair behind one ear. "Have I, dear?"

"No strange behavior today, right?"

"Of course not. Why're you so nervous?"

"Oh, I don't know!" he barks at me. "Maybe because it's a pretty big day? You know?"

"Well, you've gotten through far bigger days than this, darling." I give his knee a little pat. "This is nothing! I mean, what could happen? All you have to do is give a little speech and accept the presidency. That's it. The odds of you getting a spontaneous nosebleed or having a stroke are so unlikely . . . they're almost insignificant."

"Why would I get a spontaneous nosebleed or have a stroke, for God's sake?"

"Well, you wouldn't! People do get them every day. Every minute of every day, technically speaking. I saw a TV anchor have a grand mal seizure on live TV once. It was awful. Her body went all rigid and her mouth was stuck in the letter O. She started drooling and foaming. She'd never had a seizure before; it just hit her out of the blue. I guess that's how it happens. *Wham!* They think it was the lights that did it. So just don't look into the lights. There's nothing to worry about. Don't

worry about nosebleeds or seizures or falling. But you know . . .
don't look at the lights."

When we arrive at Hillcrest, Brad gets out of the car and
nearly falls flat on his face.

"Jesus!" he shouts.

"Honey, are you okay?" I help dust off his jacket. "Honestly."
I smile. "You're so klutzy sometimes!"

The Kellers are already in the dining room and at the table.
They brought Trevor with them and he comes running up to me
shouting, "Auntie Jen!" He hugs my knees. It's a good thing he's
there. He's the only one who is happy to see me.

"Hello, *Jennifer*," Mother Keller says with a tight smile. She's
wearing an impossibly flouncy, gauzy dress, which is the exact
color of putty, or a Band-Aid.

"Hello." I smile pleasantly. "You look . . . lovely today. Very
frilly."

"It's chiffon," she sniffs.

"Quite flammable," I say. "Stay away from the candles."

"Yes, well." Her eyes narrow slightly. "You'd know."

"Auntie Jen!" Trevor tugs on my yellow jacket. "Can I sit
next to you?"

"Of course you can, buddy!"

"Mommy's home crying," he says, and Mother Keller pats his
head to shush him. She says Sarah wasn't feeling that well this
morning and decided to stay home. Bill decided to stay home
too. "Must be something going around," she says, inspecting a
nail.

"My, yes." I nod. "There is definitely something going around."

We take our seats at the head table. Waiters whisk in glasses
of orange juice and plates of dry scrambled eggs as the even
drier speeches begin. It's as boring as waiting for water to boil,

but halfway through the sliced-melon course, things perk up a bit when Trevor gets a gushing nosebleed.

"I'm bleeding!" he shouts. "Auntie Jen, I'm bleeding!"

The whole room looks over at us.

Mother Keller rolls her eyes and I push my chair back, hurrying Trevor off to the bathroom. There I try to rinse out the bright red stains on his white oxford shirt. Fifteen minutes later Mother Keller bangs in through the swinging door, exasperated.

"Wonderful!" she says, shaking her head. "Just wonderful."

"Gramma, I got Pop Rocks!"

She shushes him. "What on earth are we going to do?" she asks me. "There'll be press at the store and there's the big family photograph later. I guess we can rush him up to the boys' department and grab him a new shirt."

"It's not a problem," I say, and turn off the water. "I'll just run him home and grab another one." Mother Keller looks unsure. I tell her I'll just take Brad's car and he can ride with them to the store. "We'll just meet there." I shrug. "No problem."

She shakes her head and sighs. "I suppose that'll have to do. Look at that shirt. Ruined."

"Gramma, want some Pop Rocks?"

I catch him before he falls off the sink. "Grandma doesn't want any Pop Rocks, Trevor. Come on, let me wash your hands."

"All right, you two." Mother Keller looks at her watch. "I'll see you down at the store . . . but, Jennifer, do put him in something decent. Not any of those garish colors he likes."

"Pink!" Trevor claps.

"No pink, young man. Do you hear me?"

"Yes, Gramma."

"Honestly. See if you can find his blue pinstripe, Jennifer." She sighs and smooths down her diaphanous putty-colored skirt. "Oh, and best not to disturb Sarah. She's in a bit of a mood today." *A bit of a mood?* I bet she is. I bet she's in more than that. I bet she's in a bit of a *planning to sue you all* mood. Trevor and I leave the club as Ed takes the stage. I check my watch. If everything goes according to plan, I have exactly an hour.

"Come on," I say. "Pick it up, Trev. We gotta keep moving."

He changes shirts and I buckle him into the backseat.

"Okay, buddy, you remember our plan?"

"Yep!"

"Good. Hey, you were a regular stuntman back there. You know? Everybody thought it was real blood."

"Want some Pop Rocks?" he asks, offering to pour some bright red powder into my palm.

"No thanks, buddy. Let's do this."

"Yeah." He nods and puts on his pink Barbie sunglasses. "Let's *do* this."

We drive on and emerge from Hillcrest's wrought iron gates, turning the corner. I pull up to the hearse parked on the street in the shade and roll down my window.

"Ready?" I ask.

The hearse's window rolls down. Nick grins at me from the front seat. "Ready, chief."

"So whatever you do, keep them occupied until noon."

"Got it. Hey, Trev, how'd you do back there?"

"I'm a regular stuntman!" Trevor shouts.

"Excellent."

"All right then." I take a deep breath. "See you soon. Better wish me luck."

"You don't need any luck, chief. You're making your own."

Trevor and I drive downtown and park in the store's public lot. We hurry up to the fourth floor by the girls' department and Kjersten is waiting for us right where I said her perky little nose should be. "Kjersten here is going to watch you for an hour or so," I tell Trevor. "Okay?" He nods.

"I told her about our deal. You get to buy *anything* you want today."

"Anything? Even pink Barbie doll roller skates?"

"*Especially* pink Barbie doll roller skates, buddy. Today we let the freak flag fly."

"Yay!" he shouts. "Freak flag!"

I thank Kjersten again and hurry off to find Christopher. I phone Pho on the way. "How's the elevator going?" I ask him, and he says good. "And . . . how was the drive over?"

"Awesome," he says. "That car is fierce! She even let me drive it."

"Wow. That's pretty . . . um, can you put her on, please?"

She takes the phone and I say, "Hey, Satan."

"Hey," she says.

"Car running good?"

"You know. Like liquid sex on quicksilver dreams."

"Right. You were just supposed to drive him *here*. Not let him *drive* it."

"Well, he was awesome. We just did some loops around the parking lot."

"Well. Don't let him do it again. Okay?"

"Okay."

"The last thing I need is Brad seeing his green Lamborghini out there whipping around the parking lot being driven by a fourteen-year-old, you know?"

"Totally get it."

"You're going to let him drive it again, aren't you."

"Definitely."

"Okay, but you better get over to the country club."

"No worries. On my way. That car is fast. It can outrun

trains, planes, and cop cars . . . and I'm speaking from personal experience."

"You worry me. I'll see you guys . . . soon."

"Yep. Bye."

I go find Christopher, who's in the VIP lounge surrounded by the Gay Bee Brigade, who buzz about with extra energy today. Christopher's so nervous, his hands are trembling. "Just hang in there," I tell him, "and wait for my cue." He hugs me with tears in his eyes and says he's sorry for anything bad he ever said to my face or behind my back. He says I'm the best friend a gay bee could ever have. I kiss him on the hands and go downstairs. The lobby is filling up with reporters and cameras.

Watching the video, back at the country club we see the Kellers just leaving. "Where did Jen run off to now?" Brad says as Mother Keller straightens his tie.

"I told you, she went to get Trevor another shirt. She'll meet us at the store."

Brad uses a finger to loosen his collar. "Whatever," he says. "Might be better if she doesn't show up at all."

"Now, darling." Mother Keller smiles at him. "It's your wedding anniversary."

"Right," Brad snorts while fixing his tie. "Don't remind me."

"Where's the damned limo?" Ed says. "It's getting late."

Todd gets out his cell phone. "I'll call the service."

"Wait." Mother Keller peers down the drive. "Here it comes."

The hearse pulls into view and Ed pulls a face. "What the hell is this?" he barks. "They sent a hearse? Why the hell did they send a hearse?"

Mother Keller sighs and pats her husband's arm. "Now, dear," she says. "Let's not overreact." Nick rolls up and gets out of the limo in his brown suit.

"I'm here for the Keller party?" he says, smiling. Ed starts to grumble and Mother Keller hushes him. "Just get in, darling," she says. "Let's just get there. We don't want to be late, do we?" Nick holds the door open for her and Mother Keller slips into the backseat. Ed follows unhappily behind her and the board members all get in after him.

"Almost there, buddy!" Todd thumps Brad on the shoulder and Brad shakes his head.

"Not soon enough for me," he says, and they both chuckle as they get into the hearse and slam the door shut. Inside the hearse Pho hid the ashtray spy cam in the backseat on top of the bar. It provides a fine view of the group as they get settled. Nick pulls out and ambles down the leafy drive. Then we switch to an exterior camera that shows the hearse leaving Hillcrest Country Club. We see the long black hearse exiting through the wrought iron gates. Nick carefully turns the corner and then . . .

Ka-thunk!

Mother Keller looks up, startled. "What was that?"

"We hit something." Ed squints through the window.

"Oh dear Lord!" We see Mother Keller's expression as she looks out the windshield at the confused scene outside. Nick pulls over and everyone piles out. The exterior camera shows everyone gathering around a disguised Bi'ch, who lies sprawled on the ground. Beside her kneel Dizzy Bee and Star Fan. "Grandmother!" Star Fan shouts with emotion. "What have they done?"

"You done hit this old lady!" Dizzy Bee shouts. "I seen it!"

"What's happened here?" Ed barks.

"You hit this poor old lady and her chicken!"

"A chicken?" Mother Keller clutches at her gauzy neckline, which blows in the wind. "What on earth is he talking about?" Someone points to the old woman's wicker basket, which is now lying upside down beside her, its captive chicken now running free down the boulevard. "We must get the chicken!" Star Fan pleads as Bi'ch groans pitifully.

"Well, help her, for God's sake!" Mother Keller orders.

"Should we call the police?" a white-haired board member asks her.

"Don't be stupid," she says. "Just help her off the street. We have a press conference in twenty minutes."

Star Fan begins crying. Her acting skills are superb. "Please help us," she says. "We must get Grandma's chicken! He's been blessed by the high priest and we must catch him. Otherwise, it is Hmong custom to sue."

"To what?" Mother Keller clutches her throat.

"Please, ma'am," Star Fan says pathetically. "We are a peaceful people. Our Hmong chickens are highly revered in the community. They're an endangered species."

"Oh dear Lord." Ed sighs. "Perfect!" He turns to Nick. "Had to hit an endangered chicken! Today of all Goddamned days!"

Nick apologizes and offers to call the police.

"Hold on now," Mother Keller says. "Let's not be hasty."

The department store, meanwhile, is now filled with eagerly waiting employees and reporters. I'm standing off to the side. I check the clock and take a deep breath.

It's time.

I step up to the microphone. My hands feel cold and my head feels oddly disconnected from my body. It's so strange to be up here alone. I wish there was even like a potted plant or something beside me . . . but there isn't, there's just me. Just here, right now. *Just breathe. Relax. You can do this. Remember the twins.*

I lean into the microphone and say, "Ladies and gentlemen, there's been a slight change of plans today. The Kellers have been detained, unfortunately, by circumstances beyond their control . . ." The microphone squeals with feedback. I hold a manila envelope in one hand. Inside it are the Olya doll test results. I sent one of the dolls to the animal hospital and Greta forwarded it on to their toxicology lab. The report contained good news and bad. The good news is the dolls are not radioactive. The bad news is . . . they're made out of untreated post-consumer garbage, which is largely comprised of chemical sewage. A sludgy mix that was superheated in a conductor oven until it melted and gelled into resin. Then it was spun into waxy strands of hair. I told Brad, "Darling, you're selling dolls made of shit and garbage."

He didn't care. He was mad . . . at *me*. Not at the shit-and-garbage-doll people, but at me! He couldn't believe I'd actually sent a doll to the lab. He called me a pain in the ass and a "muck-raker." Well, I guess he's right. Here I am about to rake some serious muck. I also have the report from Addi's private eye, the one I hired to investigate CLOG Industries. He dug up enough dirt on the Prophets of Profits to cover a landfill.

The lobby is more crowded than I ever remember it being. I clear my throat.

"Hello, good afternoon, thank you for coming. I'm Jennifer . . . Keller, and I'm here today because there's been a delay in the official naming of the new president."

The crowd buzzes slightly and I clear my throat again.

"I'm here today to deliver some sad news. The Keller's name has always stood as a symbol of quality and family integrity. But regretfully that good name has been tarnished in recent months by inadequate product safety policies." I expect some reaction to this, but there's just a sea of faces staring at me. I clear my throat and say, "Keller's has recently discovered that the popular Angel Bears, which Keller's sold for Valentine's Day, were in fact imported illegally. They were filled with fibrous DDT, a cancer-causing material that's currently banned in the U.S. entirely." The crowd starts to murmur.

A few reporters raise their hands.

I tell them that the Angel Bears were sold to Keller's by a religious import/export conglomerate named Christian Lambs of God, or CLOG, Industries, which is controlled by some of the largest churches in America. The men of the cloth travel around the world to some of the poorest places on Earth and routinely exploit those very people they've been tasked with helping. They employ foreign factories with substandard safety protocols and often use underage employees. They buy in bulk from illegal sweatshops, sometimes even opening their own, in order to ship low-cost product back to the United States. Now the room starts getting excited. Reporters begin pushing closer, jostling each other to get their microphones near me.

"What does Ed Keller have to say about all this?" somebody asks.

"When can we get a statement from the family?"

I tell them that the Kellers will be issuing a formal statement shortly, but for now . . . they'd like to invite everyone to very special event.

"A wedding," I tell them. "To celebrate the Family Equity Act."

The room gets very quiet. All the Keller's employees look at each other. No one's heard about any special event. Little do they know that the Gay Bee Brigade's been working feverishly night and day for this moment. Christopher's design lab was the rehearsal space.

They have no idea what we've prepared for them.

I smile and say, "Keller's Department Store is *proud* to host the very *first* gay wedding in Minnesota!" The room freezes. Everyone looks up at me, confused. For a second I wonder if I'm dreaming. There's no sound, no motion, nobody says a word. I thought there'd be a big uproar. I start to panic. Maybe this was a big, *big* mistake.

Then a short, myopic reporter in the front row raises his hand. He says, "Um . . . could you please repeat that?"

I clear my throat and tell them that the Keller family wishes to host the first gay wedding in Minnesota—for one of their most beloved employees—in an effort to extend their support of the Family Equity Act, which they hope is passed speedily with a unanimous vote.

The myopic reporter raises his hand again. "Do they know the Family Equity Act hasn't actually passed yet?"

Then some big guy in the crowd wearing a blue jacket shouts at me. "You're lying!" he says. "No *way* did the Kellers okay some faggy gay wedding!"

I swallow hard. I wasn't ready for that reaction. I regain my composure quickly, however; I've survived much worse than this in my lifetime. I survived five years of online dating, which made me *many* unattractive things, including a quick liar. I know from blunt experience that there are only two ways out of a lie. You can either say you have to use the bathroom and flee the scene, or hold your ground and go down deeper.

Seeing as this is not the time for a bathroom break, I firmly repeat myself. "I can assure you, the Kellers have sanctioned the wedding."

"Then where are they?" Blue Jacket shouts. I hate that guy.

"The Kellers will be along shortly. They've been held up at the senate. They went there to personally express their support for the Family Equity Act to lawmakers. As you know, Keller's is a family-owned company. And it's not just any family. The Kellers are a family with strong values. It's no secret that they're also quite religious and they've prayed about the issue of same-sex marriage. They've looked into their hearts and they respectfully disagree with the church's stance on the matter. The Kellers believe that *love* is what makes a family. They believe that true love—real love—is under the jurisdiction of *God*, not the courts."

Flashbulbs start popping, which somehow relaxes me.

"It's true the Family Equity Act hasn't passed yet," I say. "But the Kellers hope to send a *clear message* to the community that we must all stand *together* to support the great institution of family. They hope lawmakers realize that times aren't changing . . . they've already changed."

I pause and the space is filled with whistling and clapping. I smile at the room. Suddenly this seems easy. I stand on the podium, and still shaking slightly, I raise both my arms.

"Welcome!" I shout. "To Minnesota's first gay wedding!"

Then the banner behind me unfurls and instead of saying HAPPY FIRST ANNIVERSARY! it says HAPPY FIRST GAY WEDDING!

The room explodes in an uproar. Thunderous applause, shouting, cameras flashing, reporters jockeying with one another to ask me questions. The guy in the blue jacket manages to muscle his way to the front. "Bullshit!" he says. "The Kellers didn't sanction this, did they!"

Bolstered by the room's reaction, I smile widely at him. "Oh no?" I say. "Then why is *this* happening?" I snap my fingers and suddenly the large curtain draped across the marble staircase opens, revealing a sixteen-piece string ensemble. The conductor taps his little wand twice and they begin playing the wedding march.

The crowd gasps.

Everyone looks around the room until someone whistles and points up.

The room turns to see Christopher and Jeremy at the top of

the escalator. They're both wearing black tuxedos and they're both beaming. I've never seen either one of them smile like that before. As they step onto the escalator and begin their smooth descent to the lobby, everyone starts cheering.

The hearse-cam catches the chaotic scene unfolding in the back of Nick's hearse. Everyone piles into the backseat, only now they're joined by four new passengers. Dizzy Bee takes up almost a whole bench. Several board members are crammed in too; they look like white Styrofoam packing peanuts stuffed in around him. Mother Keller is wedged in between Bi'ch and Star Fan. Star Fan holds the flapping, squawking chicken on her lap.

"Wouldn't the chicken be happier back in his basket?" Mother Keller asks tightly.

Star Fan says *no,* Hmong chickens need space.

Mother Keller rolls her eyes. She asks again if she couldn't *call them a cab*—which would take them anywhere they want to go—but Star Fan declines adamantly. They're headed downtown too; catching a ride in the hearse will be much quicker. When Mother Keller tries to insist they take a cab, the fearsome Star Fan sits up and points a finger at her. "Are you insulting my people?" she asks out of the blue and quite indignantly.

Mother Keller looks startled. She says *no, no, of course not. . .*

Then Brad sits up and stares out the window with a weird look on his face. "No . . ." he says under his breath. "It . . . it can't be!"

Mother Keller looks over at him. "What?"

"Look over there. Is that . . . Is that my car? Fuck! That's my Lamborghini!"

"Where?"

"Right there!" He rolls down his window and starts shouting at the driver of the apple-green Lamborghini, which is idling on the other side of the street. "That's my fucking car!" he shouts. "Hey, asshole! Jackass! I know you can hear me! *That is my car!*"

Mother Keller starts fanning herself. "Bradford, I cannot condone this swearing."

"Hey, jackass!" Brad tries to flag the driver down, but the girl in the driver's seat just waves at him and guns the engine, peeling out in the opposite direction. "No! Fuck! Follow that car! Dude . . . driver guy . . . follow that fucking green Lambo!"

"Bradford! Stop it this instant! We are *not* chasing down some car!"

"Dude!" Brad lunges toward the driver's seat and pleads with Nick. "Dude! I'll fucking give you *five thousand dollars* to catch that fucking car!"

"Righty-o!" Nick says cheerfully.

"*No!*" Mother Keller shouts.

"*Go, go, go!*" Brad shouts. He lunges right over the privacy divider, scrambling into the passenger seat next to Nick for a better view. The chicken breaks free, squawking and flapping wildly around the hearse, bouncing off the seats, the ceiling, and many of the board members. Bi'ch seems to be feeling much better and begins singing a shrill duet with Dizzy Bee, who bellows "Old Man River" in his deep baritone voice.

Mother Keller's face is a portrait of fury. She demands they stop the car and Brad tells Nick to ignore her. He keeps upping the price he's willing to pay until they hit fifteen thousand dollars. Mother Keller keeps on shouting at Brad and Brad tells her to shut up.

It's his car, for Christ's sake!

Ed shouts at Brad to stop speaking to his mother like that and all three of them manage to keep up the heated argument. Nick chases the Lamborghini onto 394 East, headed away from the city. Mother Keller starts frantically calling people on her cell phone.

It only takes the Cinnabon girl a half mile to lose the hearse . . . but it takes Mother Keller three more miles to convince Brad to let Nick turn the damn car around. After she checks her messages, she turns quite pale. "Hurry!" she says. "Something's wrong down at the store."

"What now?" Ed sighs. "What a Goddamned shitstorm of a day."

Mother Keller makes a face. "I can't hear very well . . . but I have a message that says Jennifer's holding a press conference . . . by herself?"

"Well, I'd like to see that!" Ed chortles. "She can't very well introduce a new president when he isn't even there!"

Mother Keller tries to hear better and finally she roars, *"Silence!"* so loudly that the whole limo goes quiet. Brad stops shouting, Dizzy and Bi'ch stop singing, even the chicken stops squawking as Mother Keller's face transmogrifies into a contorted knot of fear and confusion.

"What is it, Mom?"

"Jennifer's not introducing the new president . . . She's . . . throwing a gay wedding."

"How? Where?"

"Drive!" Mother Keller suddenly shouts at Nick. "Drive, Goddamn it! Drive faster! Drive fucking faster!"

Meanwhile, Christopher and Jeremy make their way down the aisle slowly. They've waited a long time for this and they take their time, smiling at friends and waving as hundreds of cameras pop and flash at them. Christopher and Jeremy step on a gold aisle runner and loud club music starts pumping as another curtain swings open, revealing a DJ with a huge mixing board. They dance the rest of the way. They boogie down the aisle together, and they have clearly practiced their routine. The delighted crowd cheers even louder for them as cameras start popping and flashing even faster. When Christopher and Jeremy reach the altar, I step up, holding a bouquet of all-white roses.

I'm Christopher's best man.

There's a clap of thunder from above. We look up and a large glittering disco ball descends from a billowing cloud of smoke near the ceiling. Inside the disco ball is none other than Black Janet Reno the drag queen, Christopher's all-time favorite. Black Janet Reno is lowered onto the altar and hops out wearing six-inch glittering stilettos. Picking up a microphone, she says, "Honey-children, can I get a *hallelujah!*"

The whole room shouts, *"Hallelujah!"*

"Is today the day our Lord has made?" she shouts. "If it is, say *hallelujah!*"

"Hallelujah!" we shout. Tears well up in my eyes. Maybe because I'm emotional or terrified, or because everyone is shouting so . . . *loudly.*

Black Janet Reno presides over the ceremony. She's the entertainment and the wedding officiant. We rehearsed this and she knows to move quickly, but when will I learn, you can't put a drag queen in front of camera crews and expect her to leave willingly. I'm not too nervous until Nick text-messages me: ALMOST THERE!

I try to keep calm and message him back: PHO READY!

Pho is definitely ready, but that doesn't keep me from sweating bullets. How long is this freaking ceremony anyway? *Can't they hurry up?* Black Janet Reno sings "You Are So Beautiful" and the boys read a poem they wrote together for the occasion. An ode about two yachts that pass in the night . . . the USS

Farfel and the *King Filippe Roheim III*. I start tapping my foot while nervously watching the elevator doors right behind me. I stood here on purpose, so I'd know when the Kellers got here and could body-block if things got ugly.

Now it seems like a really stupid idea. I imagine gruesome scenarios in which the Kellers burst through the doors with the police in tow, right before Christopher and Jeremy say, "I do." I can't let that happen. Among all the other things that are happening, my best friend is getting married, and that's more important than all the rest of it.

Back on the highway, the hearse careens and exits at the downtown ramp. Everyone inside the vehicle is hanging on to each other for dear life and the chicken has started pooping on people. Ten minutes later Keller's security camera catches a hearse squealing into the underground parking lot and lurching to a stop in front of the open elevator doors. Brad bursts out of the limo and runs for them, his parents close behind him. Mother Keller shouts at her husband to hurry while Nick holds the doors for everyone and they all pack into the elevator together. Todd, Brad, Mr. and Mrs. Keller, and the whole board of directors jam in there, eager to find out what's happening upstairs.

The chrome doors of the elevator close and Nick looks over at his partners in crime, Dizzy Bee, Bi'ch, Star Fan, and a chicken. They all refrained from getting on the elevator.

They just nod silently at each other and take the stairs.

Meanwhile, my little cyber-ninja, Pho, was able to hack into the elevator's mainframe and access its operating system as well as the fish-eye security camera inside. In the video we see the beleaguered Keller crew, so close to their destination, all scrunched inside the elevator as Brad repeatedly punches the button marked LOBBY. Nothing happens. Then the elevator rockets one floor and a screeching sound is heard as the elevator jerks to a stop.

"What happened?" Ed shouts. "Why aren't we moving?"

"We're stuck between floors," Brad says, trying to pry open the chrome doors with his manicured fingertips.

His mother looks at her cell phone, furious. "We can't let this happen on company property," she says. "We can't let her marry a couple of fucking . . . queers!"

Back in the lobby, my phone vibrates. It's an emergency text message from Pho, who's monitoring the elevator from a computer terminal upstairs. HURRY! BRAD FIGURED OUT HATCH!

Crap! The elevator was supposed to hold them hostage for another fifteen minutes!

I give Black Janet Reno the emergency signal. Why did we pick thumbs-up for an emergency signal? It looks like I'm saying everything's okay! I have to flash thumbs-up at her two more times before she sees me. Her eyes go wide and she nods, and she quickly brings the ceremony to its legal conclusion. "Hopping quickly along like little bunnies!" She smiles, her glittery lipstick sparkling. "Do you, Jeremy, do you take this little snack cake of a cutie, Christopher, to be your lawfully wedded husband?"

"*I do,*" says Jeremy.

Suddenly a loud clanking noise comes from the elevator. Everyone looks. Mostly because besides the clanking, there is the very audible sound of Brad swearing his head off. *Shit!* It sounds like he's prying open the doors with a freaking crowbar . . . "Hurry!" I hiss, but Black Janet Reno is unfazed. "And do you, Christopher, take this luscious hunk of man meat, Jeremy, to be your lawfully wedded husband, forever and ever and ever-ever?"

I gasp as Brad stumbles out of the elevator smeared with grease.

"What the fuck is going on?" Brad shouts.

"*I do!*" Christopher grins.

"All right, honey-children, then by the power vested in me—"

"Stop right there!" Brad shouts.

Black Janet Reno puts a fist on her glittered hip and says, "Who's gonna stop me? *You, white boy?* We didn't come this far to get knocked down by some greasy cracker. No, honey . . . by the power vested in me by God and these very fine Manolo Blahniks I am rocking, I now pronounce you honey-babies *groom* and *groom*!"

The newlyweds kiss and the crowd goes wild.

I look over as Mr. and Mrs. Keller crawl out of the partially open elevator doors. They too are smudgy and dirty. One arm of Mrs. Keller's chiffon dress is ripped.

"What've you done?" she says. "What's going on?"

Ed looks confused as reporters rush for him. They ask him if it's true that the store sold cancer-causing teddy bears and that he now supports gay marriage. Ed just looks around, bewildered, and Todd steps in, snake-oil salesman that he is, and gives the cameras some bullshit statement about Keller's continuing to be committed to the community.

"Look, Gramma! I'm a ballerina!" Mother Keller gasps as her grandson sails past wearing pink roller skates and a blond Barbie wig. He whirls around grinning and does a pirouette for her. Mother Keller spins and viciously grabs my arm, her claw digging into my skin.

"What have you done?" she hisses.

I look at her and blink innocently. "Nothing that you wouldn't do, Mother Keller. I just went after what I wanted tooth and nail, without any concern for what I destroyed in the process. It's a page from your playbook. I did exactly what I thought needed to be done."

"I see. And you think you're going to *get away* with this?"

"Oh, I hope not," I tell her. "In fact, what I'm *really* hoping you'll do is go right over there to those reporters and tell them that this whole thing was *my* idea, that the wedding wasn't sanctioned by Keller's, because then as *a bonus* the entire world will *know* that . . . by all definitions . . . I beat you."

Her eyes narrow like she's a snake ready to strike. "You're a filthy little—"

"Of course you *could* take responsibility for the wedding yourself and tell everyone you were in charge. Say it was an experiment, an olive branch, a PR stunt. Whatever. That way no one would ever have to know that the great queen was undone . . . by a mere pawn."

"Oh, you're in a world of hurt now, honey," she whispers.

"Actually that's where I've *been*. In a world of hurt. Totally my own fault, for marrying your son and letting you and your family control my life, interfere with my happiness. Now I'm going to do a little interfering of my own." I signal Ted, who's standing over by the elevators with my guest of honor. He picked her up from the airport himself. He also brought Ace.

Love that Ted.

"Ace!" I whistle for him. "Here, boy!" Ted lets him off the leash and Ace bounds across the lobby toward me, wagging his tail all the way. Mother Keller scowls.

"So? You rescued your crippled fleabag. I can get him back again."

"True, but I think you might be tied up trying to get something else back again." I call over to Ed, who's surrounded by reporters. They follow him as he makes his way over to me.

"Did you do all this?" he asks, face red.

I look over at Mother Keller and smile. "Speaking of true love, Ed, there's someone here to see you." I nod at the small woman advancing toward us. She's petite, wearing a dark purple suit, and has dark short-cropped hair.

Mother Keller gasps. "No!" she whispers.

"Oh *yes*." I nod. "Ada is here."

Mrs. Keller hurries over to her husband's side. Ed looks pale. They both watch the small woman walking toward them.

"Ed, you remember your cousin Ada?"

Ed just keeps staring.

I sigh. "I just thought somebody should tell you."

"Tell me what?" he whispers at me hoarsely.

I smile. "Ada . . . she's not your cousin."

He looks over at me. "What?"

"Ada's not your biological cousin. She was adopted."

"She was *not*," Mrs. Keller says.

"She was, actually! Got the paperwork. Ada's not your blood relative, Ed. Right, Ada?"

Ada nods and smiles sweetly. Ed blinks at her and steps forward. Mrs. Keller just clutches her neckline and cries out, "Ed! What're you doing!"

Ed's blue eyes begin welling. "Ada? Is it you?"

She nods at me. "It's me, Eddie Bear."

The ever-vigilant news cameras catch Ed Keller rushing forward, ignoring his wife's protests completely, and grabbing Ada, dipping her down, and kissing her deeply. "True love wins!" I shout, and every gay bee in the house starts cheering. Brad, however, is not cheering. He's scowling in the corner and waits to pounce on me when the reporters aren't looking. He's so mad he's almost speechless . . . but not entirely. He pulls me aside and demands to know *why* I've done this horrible thing. I ask him, "Which horrible thing, Brad? Warning the public about unsafe products or helping my best friend achieve one of his lifelong dreams?"

"You're fucking insane!" he says. "I'll make sure that you don't ever—"

"Oh, whatever, Brad. You know, I'm sorry, I just can't. You're so . . . *boring.*"

"Boring?"

"Boring! I never realized till now! I just wanted to be in love with you so I filled in all your blank parts with fairy tales. But man, are you boring. If you were a plant, Brad, you'd be mold. If you were an animal . . . you'd still be mold. If you were a beverage, you'd be like leftover hot dog water or something. Maybe something was floating around in there once, but it ain't there now, and—*hey!* That's my song!"

"What?"

"Sorry! Gotta dance!" I bound off for the dance floor. Dizzy Bee is singing my theme song by the Isley Brothers. *"It's your thing! Do what you wanna do! I can't tell ya who to sock it to . . . Ow!"* The music kicks up louder. My entire family has shown up and they're all dancing. Mom is smiling, Dad looks terrific, Lenny has ahold of Hailey with one arm and grips both the twins with the other, Christopher twirls Jeremy, and the whole Fang Gang has dropped into some sort of Hmong boogie, along with a hundred of their Hmong friends. Best of all, Nick taps me on the shoulder and we dance all night.

The reporters stay late too, eating caviar and swilling pink champagne before they go racing off to their newsrooms to deliver the incredible story of the first gay wedding in Minnesota, which was paid for by the Kellers and had nude bartenders, ball-gagged slave waiters, a nude trapeze artist swinging from the ceiling, and white horses pulling the newlywed grooms away in a pink carriage. Meanwhile the DJ—a hip newcomer named Iced-Tea—spins dance music till we nearly drop. I told him before he got there that he wasn't allowed to do any singing.

20
Wayward and Wanton

There are repercussions for my actions.

Many.

The next morning more big news hits. The Minnesota senate passed the Family Equity Act just in time to make Christopher's marriage legal.

"But wait!" Christopher says, panicking. "Do I really *want* to be married?"

"Ha-ha," I say. "Welcome to being straight. It sucks."

Experts speculate that the bill passed in large part because of Keller's endorsement. The majorities in both houses at the legislature make clear they could not ignore such a large conservative organization backing the clearly controversial bill. The senators were in session as Jeremy and Christopher sashayed down the escalator. An anonymous source says hundreds of cell phones suddenly lit up across the senate floor and that the session "perked up" right after news of Keller's "big gay wedding" got out.

The second indication of divine intervention is that Keller's stock begins to soar. Suddenly the stodgy old humdrum department store, which catered only to Republicans and AARP members, becomes the go-to shopping destination for all sorts of new demographics. Gay bees make it a point to shop there, which means everybody else follows. Even the drag queens began to buy their wigs at Keller's and have personal shoppers running around like mad in search of size 14 stilettos and industrial-strength undergarments that could conceal the Foshay Tower.

It's a miracle.

I'm actually happy for the Kellers. As I keep insisting to my friends and family, I never wanted to *destroy* them, I just wanted them to start being honest with the public and stop selling teddy bears stuffed with cancer. I got my wish, too. Mr. Cartwright at the Public Health Department announces that Keller's Department Store has discontinued all foreign imports from unregistered factories. I keep track of his findings online. A month later he says no further health infractions have been found at Keller's Department Store and no citations have been issued. Keller's has been given a clean bill of health. Six months later Mr. Cartwright is happy to report that Keller's status has not changed, but he continues to refuse all Keller dinner invitations.

Another unexpected turn of events occurs.

I'm thrown in jail.

Christopher's with me when it happens. As the squad car pulls away he shouts he'll come and get me . . . but he has no idea where they're taking me. Detective Wojek, the dick cop who picks me up, is clearly being paid by the Kellers to harass me, and he takes his sweet time booking me on purpose. Nobody can find you if you're not in the system. He leaves me in a locked interrogation room for what seems like eight hours but is probably more like forty-five minutes. I'm trying to keep calm but I feel a panic attack coming on. It's like a geyser of cold water that keeps trying to bubble up. Then all of a sudden I hear a familiar voice in the hallway. "Well, you damn well better hope she is! Do you hear me?"

I sit up, my heart lurching wildly. Could it be her?

"See this?" she shouts. "This is the mayor's home phone number. Do you have it on your cell phone? Want me to call it? I will wake R. T. Rybak up *right now* and tell him that you're the motherfucker who told me to! Now open this fucking door before I get the governor to come down here and fire you himself!" The interrogation room's metal door bursts open and the dick cop comes in, his head hung low. Behind him a coiffed blonde sails in, draped in silks and satins, cuffed with sparkle-chunk diamonds. It's Addi. I feel such a rush of relief when I see her that I burst into big blubbery tears. "How did you find me?"

"Christopher called. He said you were arrested because you threw a . . . gay wedding at Keller's?"

"No, the wedding was actually legal. They dragged me in on some trumped-up loitering charge."

"I'm going to pretend that you invited me to your epic event–slash–scandal of the season and blame my absence on the fact I was in Paris."

"Were you?"

"Of course. How else was I going to get over our fight? I bought shit! Anyway, Christopher called every precinct in town trying to find you, and when nobody had you in the system he panicked and called me. I found you in like . . . four minutes? Three?"

"Thank God." I smile, wiping back a tear.

The dick cop pokes his head in and Addi glares at him. "What?" she says.

"Um . . . want coffee?" he asks hopefully.

"Seriously? I don't drink the brown anus water that you call coffee! Why don't you do something useful and tell me when we can leave."

"Um . . . that. Right. It's a little tricky, I have to actually book her before she can go."

"No!" Addi smacks her hand on the table.

"I'll do it as fast as I can."

"You can't be serious. You're going to book her? All right." She narrows her eyes. I've seen that look. You do not want to be on the delivery end of that look. "You know what? Now I'm actually pissed. I was going to let this whole thing blow over, call it a misunderstanding, but if you think I'm going to let you book my friend on some bogus charge just so you're not in hot water with the chief for unjustified harassment of a beautiful high-tax-bracket citizen . . . well then, prepare to meet the Fist!"

"Um . . . okay," he says, and shuts the door.

Addi whips out her cell phone and punches #3 on the speed dial. She starts barking to someone in German. "Henckles, Luststerben and Grump?" I ask her.

"You know it, sister. Henckles, Luststerben and Grump!"

Twenty minutes later, three large women in matching charcoal-gray suits and black orthopedic shoes show up. They smell vaguely of cabbage and have severe faces like knuckles or gargoyles with dead shark eyes. They wear no makeup, and their short oily hair is bobby-pinned viciously into place. Their suits look as stiff, their arms like stuffed German sausages. They're aggressively ugly. Without their saying a word, it's clear they enjoy making people uncomfortable. Detective Wojek openly perspires when he sees them.

The smallest woman is the only one who speaks. "Detective Wojek, I'm Ursula Henckles. These are my associates, Elke Luststerben and Astrid Grump." Ursula speaks in a strange hoarse whisper, which sends chills down your spine and invisible spiders running into your ear. "We are attorneys from the law offices of Henckles, Luststerben and Grump. The woman you are currently illegally detaining is our client. You have two options at this point. You may release her and we will be done here . . . or you may pursue whatever avenue you're quite mistakenly on and we will become entangled in a most pointed way. Since you've held our client illegally, we will be pressing charges against you, Detective Wojek. *You*—not the department—and if you think the chief will be eager to spend his precious legal defense funds on a rookie who's actually lost his squad car while on duty and who has two strikes against him already, not to mention a history of Vicodin abuse . . . think again. Think hard, Detective Wojek. This decision will determine how you spend the next year of your life. With us . . . or without us. Any questions?" Detective Wojek blinks. "Very good. You have seven minutes to make your decision. At that time we will proceed with our prescribed course of action. Good day."

She spins on her heel and marches out. The other women follow.

I'm not sure . . . but I think I peed my pants.

Four minutes and thirty-two seconds later, I'm free. Outside in the delicious fresh air. We all pile into the oily black Henckles, Luststerben & Grump minivan and I start crying again, thanking them for saving me. Addi says if I don't shut up she'll slap me. Ursula urges me to leave town as soon as possible. "The Kellers hired a dumb cop that time," she tells me. "Next time might be different. Your best strategy is to make sure there *is* no next time. Understand? I don't enjoy police stations. I'd rather not fetch you from one again."

"Do what the Fist says." Addi nods. "Let's hop on a plane somewhere."

Ursula snorts. "Have I taught you *nothing*? They'll be looking for you too, Addi. They'll track your credit cards, your plane tickets, your passport stamps. The Kellers have nothing to gain by leaving Jennifer alone—and everything to lose."

They won't stop harassing me. They'll continue to try to arrest me, dirty up my record, besmirch my character, toss me in jail for anything, not caring if the charges stick. They'll just want to build up a case that I'm an unsavory character whom they tried to help and who turned around and betrayed them.

Ursula says I should leave town and not use credit cards. They'll have someone watching my bank accounts. "Do you have someone you can stay with?" she asks. "Not your family or friends. A place they can't find you, a person they don't know about."

Hmmm. I just might.

I call Nick from a pay phone. I tell him I'm looking for a temporary hideout, a sanctuary for wayward girls, and he says, "Look no further!" He invites me and Ace to come stay with him on the SS *Nevertheless*. On one condition: I have to promise to sleep in *my own* cabin and to keep my hands *to myself* and to *not* sexually harass him unless he *asks* me too. I tell him I don't think that will be a problem. "Maybe not for you," he says. "But I'm down here on my own . . . *a devastatingly handsome man*, who's allowing a *wanton female* to come into his home."

"*Wayward*," I say, correcting him.

"Wanton, wayward, whatever," he says. "You're a woman who's gone wild."

"True. Which is why I can't promise you anything. I'm not responsible for my actions."

"Good enough for me!" he says. "Come on down."

That night, I move into my cabin. There's a sign on my door that says WANTON FEMALES ONLY. A greyhound sleeps on my bed. "Hey, Toggle girl!" I say, kissing her forehead. "She looks so much better!" When Nick first took her to the vet, we found out she had severe meningitis, and they didn't know if she'd pull through. The disease is often fatal and it's expensive to treat, which is why her previous owners had "opted out" and given poor Toggle to the pound for "immediate extermination." Luckily, of course, we found her and Nick took excellent care of her. Toggle pulled through.

Nick makes us dinner—baked potatoes and grilled pork chops on greasy paper plates—which we carry outside into the cricketing, croaking soft summer night. We sit on deck and eat our dinner, watching the sky darken overhead and the slowly twisting ribbon of chocolate-colored Mississippi slip past our feet. Ace, Tandy, and Toggle are on hand, all snoring away with full rounded bellies. They ate pork chops too.

Another sign that God might not be drunk at the wheel after all is that the good old boys from the Christian Lambs of God go down pretty hard and take large chunks of their churches with them. Cool Coy Jones gets a ten-year sentence and the IRS fleeces the coffers of Atlanta First Baptist. The megachurch is sold to developers and turned into a VA hospital. Pastor Joe gets five years at Joliet, where he plans to start his own prison ministry, and Deacon Davis flees the country. I imagine he's mining for diamonds in Bembezi, Zimbabwe.

Nick suggests we pull up anchor and throw off the lines. Take the SS *Nevertheless* on a trip downriver. That's when I get the idea. If we're going to travel . . . why not work on a travel assignment at the same time? I call Susan at Frontier Travel. The stories she offers us to cover are small and I'll make shit for money, but like Susan says . . . Today's column about pie festivals is tomorrow's exposé on sex trafficking. Admittedly with a few stories in between. I tell her it's all right, give me the little stories.

I'm in.

Nick is in too; he takes the photographs for my articles. We travel all over together working on them. Our itinerary is plotted by where the paying assignments send us and where we want to go. I'll be honest, we're not quite *National Geographic* material yet. Technically, we've only left the United States once. We drove up to Canada to write an article in Thunder Bay called "Do's and Don'ts for White People Attending a Powwow."

Do negotiate prices on native art and craftwork.

Don't ask if anything costs "big wampum."

Next we sail the SS *Nevertheless* down the Mississippi to Saint Louis for the big Saint Louis Pirate Festival. Which is . . . weird. I've never seen so many yoga moms with peg legs or a gas station with a sign that says THANK YOU FOR NOT TALKING LIKE A PIRATE. Next we go to New Orleans for an article about the oddest events at Mardi Gras, which are the "sexiest steak" contest, a voodoo curse-a-thon, and the ever-controversial fat baby parade.

We mostly stick to the Mississippi and to destinations we can reach by water, because we love living on the SS *Nevertheless*. It comfortably houses us, plus all the dogs and Nick's hearse, which we drive around upon reaching our destinations. It went over very big at Mardi Gras. Not so much at the powwow.

Our latest destination is the most exotic so far, though it's still part of the United States: Saint John in the Caribbean. I'm back. This time I'm not staying at any awful all-inclusive Christian resort where the staff kills dogs. This time I'm there with my dogs and living in my lovely houseboat-barge with a person I love. Nick and I sail the barge out across the ocean and we're not even docked at port for a whole day when I sit up in bed, having just finished an afternoon romp with Nick and some DNA-rearranging sex. I gather the sheets around my naked body while the far less modest Nick gets up buck-naked and heads for the galley to make us an espresso—his standard after-sex drink, so he can gear up for more sex.

The man is a titan.

The first time we made love he went into his office and set one of the clocks to the exact time we started making love. "Seriously?" I arch an eyebrow at him.

"Hey, I mark all the momentous occasions in my life this way. Sorry, chief." He chuckles. "But you count as momentous."

My satellite phone rings one morning and I wrestle it out of the sheets. It's Ursula Henckles, from the esteemed law firm of Henckles, Luststerben & Grump. She took my divorce case on right before I left town. I haven't heard from her in months; the judge and lawyers have all been locked in tedious stalemates. It's all been quite boring, but her voice is a pleasant surprise.

"Miss Johnson," she says. "There's been significant action on your case lately. I'll tell you now that we have to get through an oddity, an unpleasantness, and an indecency before we get to the fat sugar cube."

"Pardon me?"

"It'll be a shitstorm for a while," she says, "but you'll come out smiling. Okay?"

I say okay, mostly because I have no idea what she's talking about.

THE ODDITY

Ursula says when I filed for divorce, all my accounts, both personal and joint, were immediately frozen. So were Brad's.

Whatever assets we had were frozen wherever they happened to be. All our money waits in big blocks of ice until some judge makes a verdict. That's the bad news. The good news is that all this endless waiting around with nobody being able to move any money allowed her financial forensics team to really dig in and hunt for things.

"And when we hunt for things, Miss Johnson, we find them."

She says she found something very unusual in my account. Then she asks if I knew that Brad had been transferring stock into my name. I have no idea what she's talking about.

"Are you sure?" she says. "I can defend you if you tell me."

"What stock?" I say. "Seriously? How?"

Apparently, her crackerjack financial forensics team uncovered Brad's illegal activity. He'd been hiding shares in my name almost the entire time we were married. He hid them under my duplicate social security number. The one I never use . . . the one I gave Emily. He wasn't alone; he had quite a few people helping him, including Todd and Mother Keller.

When I ask her why Brad or his mother would hide their own stock, she reminds me of the bylaws, which say no single family member is allowed to have controlling interest in the company. Nobody can hoard stocks in order to gain power. Brad was probably stashing away stocks to be used at a later date, like after he was president and had nominated enough new board members to change the bylaws. Once he did that, he could march out all his little hidden shares and take control of the company completely.

"Well, that explains Brad," I say. "But why would Mother Keller hide stocks?"

"Good question. We believe there were plans for an impending hostile takeover."

"Brad's?"

"I don't think so, and that brings us to . . . the unpleasantness."

"Terrific."

THE UNPLEASANTNESS

"So," she says. "Did you know your refrigerator was spying on you?"

"No . . . but I always thought the coffeemaker was stealing money."

She's serious.

Ursula says our Ice Empress 3000 routinely videotaped us and recorded thousands of our conversations. It was being activated by remote satellite and transmitted everything it recorded to an unknown location.

I ask her, "Who would do such a thing?"

"The people who gave it to you, of course."

The Japanese investment group. The ones who'd come to dinner. They'd been planning a hostile takeover and had been using the Ice Empress to spy on us for the past *year.* That's why they sent us a ten-thousand-dollar refrigerator. To spy on us. It was like a Trojan horse with a cheese-aging drawer. Ursula tells me that according to her sources, the Japanese investors were never planning on doing actual business with Brad, except by way of a hostile takeover. They undoubtedly came to dinner for reconnaissance purposes only—to make sure their spy fridge was working, to plant more listening devices, and to snoop around for sensitive documents.

"So *that's* why Ace was acting so weird! He kept barking, he wouldn't leave the top of the stairs. Someone must've been trying to snoop around up there and he stopped them! Well, bless your little three-legged butt, Ace!" Ace starts barking and I tousle his ears. "Man, what a dog! And people say I rescued him."

"I wonder who else rescued you that night."

"I don't know, but I nearly killed those men. I almost poisoned them with bad fish and then our chandelier came within inches of crushing them. I ran them out of the house in under half an hour. Plus there was no furniture on the first floor."

"No? Why not?"

"Because my mother-in-law was hell-bent on ruining the dinner. She deliberately screwed up the catering and then had a steam-cleaning service pick up all my furniture hours before the party. I had no couches, no chairs, no dining room table . . ."

"Brilliant. Nowhere to put a listening device."

"Pardon?"

"No furniture, no listening devices—and where was all the paperwork?"

"Paperwork? What paperwork?"

"Your office, filing cabinets. Financial papers. Where were they?"

"Well, that was all in Brad's office, but—"

"It was stripped clean too."

"Um . . . yes."

"You see, I think your mother-in-law somehow knew about the Japanese takeover. That's why she was hiding stocks and that's why she destroyed your dinner."

"No, I'm pretty sure she just wanted to make me look stupid. It's her hobby."

"If she just wanted to ruin dinner, why clear out Brad's office?

Why remove paperwork? You see, I think her goal was to ruin not your plans . . . but theirs."

"Um . . . No. You'd need to know her. She was definitely trying to ruin my dinner."

"Didn't you say she always wanted to keep Keller's Department Store in the family?"

"Well, yes. Keeping Keller's in the family was like her prime objective in life, besides torturing me and having a not-gay grandchild."

"So, wouldn't she naturally detest the idea of 'foreigners' coming into her empire?"

"Detest? Um . . . That would be accurate."

"You said she's always meddling in everyone's business. Isn't it possible she knew these Japanese businessmen were up to something? And if she did . . . look how brilliantly she foiled them. They could take nothing, because nothing was there to take. They could leave nothing for the same reason. They were uncomfortable, left early, and never came back. There was even a government official there to assist in their departure. Most amazing is that she orchestrated all this without anyone knowing she did. That takes skill. I wonder if she's CIA."

I'm not fast to accept the idea . . . Is it possible she's right? I mean, what happened right after the Japanese were gone? We wound up with Christian investors that she met at church. That sounds like a Ma Keller plot if there ever was one. I'm suddenly flooded with conflicting emotions. What if this monster I hated had actually been trying to protect us, without our knowing about it? I hadn't even thought of the possibility. I was too blind with rage at her. One thing is certain: She is as brilliant as she is evil. I suddenly regret not getting to know her better. The real her. Whoever that is . . . underneath all those layers of shellac and chiffon. I wish she would have let me in on some of her evil plots. I'd make a very good sidekick for a villain, I think.

I certainly could have helped with her wardrobe.

Ursula tells me she must make one confession. It wasn't her computer forensics team that found the clues that led to this information. "It was not my men," she says. "It was yours. I received an unscheduled visit from your maid last week. She did not have an appointment."

"Bi'ch? She's my ex-maid."

"She brought her grandchildren with her."

"Star Fan and Pho? Was baby Pac Man there?"

"That is no baby, Mrs. Keller. I can assure you. Babies cannot run down the hall with a fire extinguisher. Anyway, they brought me the information about the Ice Empress."

"It was Pho, wasn't it?"

"Yes. The Pho boy is most intelligent, and I do not like children."

"No surprise there."

She says Pho uncovered the code that revealed just how long the Ice Empress filmed us, which was apparently from the moment we plugged her in to the moment I unplugged her during book group. When I told Pho to reprogram her, the original espionage software was corrupted and she stopped filming us. Then when I asked Pho to reactivate her original voice, he rebooted her system, restarting her original programming, and the camera was reactivated. She says Pho was able to extract some very interesting video footage.

"Oh God," I groan. "This is the indecency, isn't it?"

"Big-time," she says.

THE INDECENCY

"So . . . a video of what?" I ask, feeling queasy. "What was on it?"

"Miss Johnson?" she says. "We *caught* the sonofabitch!"

"Pardon?"

"Your husband! The video Pho brought me . . . it contains *concrete proof* that your husband was engaged in an affair. It is absolute, concrete proof!"

"Oh!" I sit down on the bed, suddenly winded. A dull aching hurt rises like a gray balloon in my stomach. Brad was cheating? I had somehow convinced myself that he hadn't been. Stupid, I know.

"We hit the jackpot!" Ursula says again gleefully. "We got him damn good!"

I ask her what's actually on the tape and she says the Ice Empress caught Brad and a brunette in stilettos having sex on the center island. "And, Miss Johnson," she says, "not only is the footage time-stamped, the Ice Empress camera was perfectly aimed for *irrefutable* evidence that penetration did occur! This is a rare treat for me . . ."

"Oh, and for me too."

"It means an airtight case, Miss Johnson. I've already contacted Brad's lawyers. God, how I love to hear grown men cry . . ."

I tell her I don't want to hear any more. I only have one more question.

"Do you know who the brunette was?"

She sighs and mutters something under her breath in German. "I do," she says, and I'm just about to tell her I don't want to know when she says, "Miss Emily Goodhue."

I pause. I chuckle. "Emily? *Cute Emily?* No, that's not possible, there must be some mistake. She would never . . . She's Todd's secretary. They worked together, that's all. She's the sweetest girl, so friendly!"

Ursula just sighs. "Can you can hear yourself yet?"

"Yes. I can . . . but Emily . . . she was getting married!"

"Here we go. The nine-hour 'This can't be true' marathon. I can do this with you if you don't mind being billed five hundred dollars an hour for it."

"Isn't Emily getting married?"

"Well . . . yes. We have confirmation that Brad proposed to her."

"She's marrying Brad?"

"I thought we would just rip that Band-Aid off fast. Now, I have very good news for you that we should move on to. Ready?"

"What are you talking about . . . Brad is marrying Emily?" I feel funny. Like I'm having a stroke. My heart races. I can't seem to puzzle out the words she just said, but the reptilian part of my brain has registered that something very bad just happened.

"Okay," Ursula says. "Good riddance to bad rubbish . . . Right?"

"I—"

"Onward, Mrs. Keller!"

I'm actually grateful for her gruff tone. It reminds me to straighten my shoulders. Now is not the time to fall apart. Now is the time to keep calm and carry on. I'll fall apart later. In private. Probably after drinking a bathtub filled with cheap red wine. For now, in this moment, I must be brave. Get all the facts and assemble them. Not show my weakness. The truth is, my heart is breaking just a little . . . Possibly more for Emily than for myself. *"That poor girl . . ."* I whisper quietly.

"Exactly," Ursula says. "Now, you want a fat sugar cube or not?"

"Yes." I nod. "Please."

"It's a fat one!" she says.

"I have . . . no idea how to take that."

"It's actually one of the fattest sugar cubes I've ever seen."

"Starting to get terrified."

THE FAT SUGAR CUBE

Ursula thinks I'll figure out what the fat sugar cube is before she even says it out loud. She generously offers to give me a Henckles, Luststerben & Grump beer koozie if I do.

She reviews everything we've already talked about. The fact that all Brad's and my assets were frozen wherever they happened to be when the judge froze them. The fact that this caught Brad off guard. The fact that he'd been putting large amounts of stock into my name without my knowing it . . . and logically therefore hoping I would not find out about it. He of course was hoping to get all the assets himself . . . but he has been unsuccessful.

Now there is new evidence against him . . .

Concrete evidence of a most damning nature.

"The video the Pho boy found changes everything," she says. "It's a categorical violation of your prenup and because of this, negotiations are over."

"Over?"

"Over," she says. "Naughty boys get nothing and winner takes all. Get it?"

"Look, Ursula, I know you're waiting for me to put something together, but I have news for you: My nerves are a little shattered over here . . . I'm not completely over the unpleasantness and I'm *really* not over the indecency . . . and I'm about to pass out, because for all I know a 'fat sugar cube' means something so awful it defies description."

"No, my dear. In this case your fat sugar cube is the fact that Brad cheated. Because of your prenup you get everything in the estate . . . including all the stocks he hid under your name. They're all yours now. Legally."

"Okay. How many shares are we talking about?"

"Well, Miss Johnson, a great deal. When your divorce is final, you will have a controlling interest in Keller's Department Store."

"What does that mean exactly?"

"You own it."

"It? What do you mean . . . *it?*"

"I mean all of it, darling! You will *own* Keller's Department Store! The entire thing. Lock, stock, and barrel. For the first time in its history, Keller's will not be owned by a Keller. Maybe you should change it to Johnson's! Strange, isn't it? So sudden. But I told you it was a fat sugar cube. Those naughty little bunnies hid all their eggs in your Easter basket, thinking you'd never find them . . . and even if you did, you'd obey them. They never imagined you'd be so clever. They never saw this coming, did they, Jennifer? . . . Jennifer?"

21
Elegantly Invincible

Flash forward a year.

A fairly boring year actually, filled with court cases, legal battles, and unsuccessful lawsuits as the Keller family frantically tried to "sue my ass off" and get their company back. At the final trial, when the judge delivered her final verdict and declared me the rightful owner of Keller's, the Honorable Ann Nelson brought her shiny black gavel down with a sharp *crack!* And then she looked at me and winked.

She did. She winked.

What a world! Suddenly I owned Keller's, but I confess, it didn't take me long to figure out I was a really crappy CEO. My first action was to close the store for a week and give all Keller's employees a proper vacation, which ended up costing us . . . I don't like to recall the exact number. I never was any good with money or sales projections and profit forecasts, which turned out to be a big part of the job. My dad is much better at it. Plus he likes having a big fancy office downtown. I have an executive office too, but I don't use it much. Usually the only occupants are an ever-growing tribe of dust bunnies under the couch and a bronze sculpture that sits on my desk and looks very much like a bat smashed against a grille.

I don't even have a secretary.

Emily's desk sits empty. I was sad, in a way, when I heard she'd left, and I packaged up all those lists I made her. I sent them to her along with a note.

> Emily,
>
> I'm not sure if you're still planning on marrying Brad, but if you are, you're going to need these a lot more than I am. Look out for yourself, Emily . . . you might be the only one who does.
>
> —Jennifer Johnson

I'm not mad at her anymore. I'm too happy traveling around the world with Nick and the dogs on the SS *Nevertheless,* and even though we hardly ever come home now, I never worry about the store. I left it in quite capable hands. Not only is my dad the head bean counter, Lenny is the head of infrastructure management, and I hired a new president.

The new president was a big deal.

I knew I wanted him, but it took months of courting him and weeks of salary negotiation, not to mention having the entire executive suite remodeled exactly to his specifications, before he agreed to take the position. Everyone loves him. He's quirky and creative. Every day he sits at a vast Lucite desk, and he spins around in a huge pink vinyl wingback chair. "Okay, ladies!" he says. "Grab your fairy dust, we have work to do!"

Yes.

Christopher is the new president of Keller's Department Store.

Best decision I've ever made.

No contest.

Seemingly overnight he transformed our dowdy, frumpy department store into a chic upscale shopping destination. He put in endless hours, obsessed with removing all traces of the old regime. He purchased all new product lines and banished anything cheap or poorly made. Whenever "previous Keller" merchandise surfaced—an old box of skorts or a crate of nude pantyhose—he ordered a ritual fire. He wants nothing from the past. His team worked relentlessly, painting and redesigning every floor as Christopher oversaw every imaginable detail. He even took down all the big oil paintings of the Kellers and the long-gone board members that had hung in the conference room since the store opened. He purged the place until not a single image of any Keller remained.

"I want *fresh* ideas, people! *Chop-chop!* Dear God, *no*, honey. Take it away, before my poor eyes start to blister. How many times must I say it? We don't *do* downtrodden anymore. Everyone listening? We don't do downtrodden anymore. Or oppressive. Or soul-killing. Got it? Listen to me . . . and please somebody tell me there's a triple-foam latte in this office for me . . . because I'm not trying to sound dramatic, people, but if I don't get a coffee, I may— Oh, thank you! Wonderful! Thank you, darling. *Delicious!*"

He works his staff hard, but he works himself harder and with more clarity of vision than anyone else could. They call him Queen Bitchy Bee. He routinely asks his assistants if they know that he had the first legal gay wedding in Minnesota, thanks to Keller's CEO.

Yes, his assistants moan. *We know.*

"Did I tell you she paid for everything?"

You did.

"She said to me, 'Christopher darling, I'm throwing your dream wedding. I'm paying for the whole thing and I don't care what happens afterward, so make it gay, honey.' I said, 'Are you sure?' Because she had that whole horrible Christian Keller militia breathing down her neck all the time. And she said she was sure. When I asked her, 'How gay should I make it?' she just looked at me and said . . . *As gay . . . as gay gets.*' Isn't that wonderful?" (Here I'm told there's usually the welling of tears.) "Gentlemen"—he sighs—"there's only *one* Jennifer Johnson in this world. No one else even holds a candle."

Very sweet but totally untrue. I know a few people who are quite a bit more amazing than me. Greta now spearheads my international animal-rescue organization, ACE (Animal Care in Emergencies). I gave my Lake Minnetonka house to the Fang Gang, partially because they deserved it and partially because Mrs. Keller deserved it. Pho runs his thriving cyber-ninja business from the house and Bi'ch teaches survival training there with Dizzy Bee, who moved into the guesthouse. Star Fan married a very nice marine and is now pregnant. I knew we didn't have long with her. Pac Man is my angel. He's fearless.

Lots of changes happened in the Keller family too. Sarah opened her own clothing boutique, and Brad moved to Los Angeles to pursue a career as a songwriter . . . so he'll be coming home soon. Sadly, Mr. Keller left his wife for Ada, a fact that made me feel a little bad, until Mother Keller herself remarried and was happier than anyone had ever seen her. She married Pastor Mike at Grace-Trinity, a real coup by any standards, and it catapulted her into the highest echelons of church-lady power. So basically she's in heaven. Her own Lutheran Jerusalem. Martha Woodcock defected across the street, to Mount Holyoke Lutheran.

All I know is life is designed to be a disaster.

In every way you can possibly think of. We get lost, we fall down, we marry the wrong people . . . life is a mess. It's also oddly, eerily perfect. Rough seas and stormy passages build something quite ferocious inside us. Something uncontainable and even ugly to others but something wildly free.

Strange miracles come in odd packages. The people who wound up helping me the most weren't rich and famous. They were surly Hmong teenagers, limo-hearse drivers, homeless old men with diabetes. They taught me that if you want to come in from the rain, stop searching for shelter. Look for something else that needs help and protect it, because when we shelter something else, no matter how small, we become shelter ourselves. We never need to look for it again.

Magnetic north is shifting, which means the old maps are wrong and getting wronger. Old routes won't take us where we want to go. So we must find the new ways ourselves, slowly, carefully, often in the dark, and sometimes falling down. We are the new mapmakers. Strange miracles are hurtling toward us right this very moment, so hang on. Miracles are coming as fast as they possibly can.

Acknowledgments

The author would like to acknowledge the fact that many people helped her with this book, including the unstoppable Jeanette Perez, the saintly Amanda Bergeron, the irreplaceable Carrie Kania, the indomitable Cal Morgan, the full-of-savoir-faire Alberto Rojas, the unkillable Jen Hart, the adorable Mary Sasso, and the mysterious Julia O'Halloran. Special thanks to Laura Cherkas, my production editor, and to Natsuki Schwartz for Japanese translations. You're all as much a part of this book as I am . . . which may call for certain apologies.

Deep thanks to all my agents, my lawyers, and all those who would sue . . . the fiercesome John Stout, the dapper John Larson, the lovable Tom Weiss, and the indefatigable Stephanie Unterberger. Also to the lovely Elizabeth Sheinkman at Curtis Brown London, and the sharpshooter duo of Debbie Deuble and Steve Fisher at APA. God love your wily, sharky hearts, every one.

Many friends helped me with this book, probably because I had their phone numbers. Rick Bursky sent poems, Billy Collins wanted to, Joyce Carol Oates provided ongoing sparks, Neil Gaiman told me I could . . . so I did. Special thanks to Harry Drabik, who provided sanctuary. Marcy Russ took notes, My

Lee Xiong double-checked my Hmongs, Ari Hoptman killed all the joy, Jeffrey Hagen took pity on me, Jodi Ohlsen counseled, Chris Strouth knows his bad porn, and Christian Barnard sent treats in the mail. Andrew Bendel could have been helpful but wasn't. Tim Peterson was available for caffeine infusions, Bart Regehr always astounds, and Andrew Peterson is a living idea machine. David Sunderland makes everything pretty. Love to the Breadloaf Kittens 2000—I always am grateful to you—and Matty Dillon, Jim Zervanos, Leslie Blanco, Speed Weed, Miss Meghan Cleary, Thom Didato, and the other hardworking Borts out there all writing away in the dark.

Thanks and apologies to the Ludington-Klings for the completely inappropriate use of their beloved dog's name, Farfel, and to high school friend Billy Davis for becoming a deacon against his will, and to the Swenson gang for wacky authenticity, and also to the Morganthalers, a lovely family in every way. Hurrah to the hale souls of Key West, specifically Judy Blume, who inspires me; Grand Vin, who let me write on their porch; Tom Favelli and friends; Meredith and Michael, who conjure 3-D poetry; Michael Baier, my cajoled mentor; my adopted German family the Seigerts; and Pepper, Tennessee Slim, Cookie-Man, Deb, and all the rest of the Key West gang . . . my world is better and much weirder because I know you. My deep love and sympathy to the Commodore and Jane McKean, along with the whole schooner *Appledore* crew, who lost their first mate, J. C. Smith, while I was writing this book.

The author's family endures a lot. Love, thanks, apologies, rain checks, and IOUs to Judeman, Colly, H.K., J.T., Katie, Oscar, and a myriad of cats, who stood by helping every which way they could. So did Cindy, Becky, Paul, and all the Nelsons from afar. You're one heckuva family. Who else expects you to show up with vodka and pie?

Big love to Sir Lawrence Swenson, who truly is wonderful in every way and who makes me smile constantly. Lastly, thanks to Walter, my egg-roll-shaped pug, whose ongoing wants and immediate needs make me a better, stronger, and vastly more patient person.

I love all of you.

BOOKS BY HEATHER MCELHATTON

PRETTY LITTLE MISTAKES
A Do-Over Novel

ISBN 978-0-06-113322-0 (paperback)

"A chick lit-meets-noir [novel] where the choices are tougher, the stakes higher, and the characters sexier and far more disturbed."
—*Curve* magazine

MILLION LITTLE MISTAKES

ISBN 978-0-06-113326-8 (paperback)

You've just won $22 million in the BIG MONEY SUCKA! lottery. Will you keep your job or quit? If you're a tidy, goody-two-shoes rule-follower in real life, you can break the mold and make decisions you'd normally never make in this follow-up to McElhatton's first do-over novel.

JENNIFER JOHNSON IS SICK OF BEING SINGLE
A Novel

ISBN 978-0-06-146136-1 (paperback)

"You might think this is just chick lit, but keep reading. This brash and funny novel plays with the form, with a dark, intelligent and wholly unexpected conclusion."
—*Minneapolis Star Tribune*

JENNIFER JOHNSON IS SICK OF BEING MARRIED
A Novel

ISBN 978-0-06-206439-4 (paperback)

"Jennifer's a wonderful narrator—honest, witty, self-deprecating and sharply observant—which more than redeems the story's familiar aspects (gay best friend, high maintenance sibling's pending nuptials, lame Internet dates). McElhatton blends just enough cynicism into the whimsical narrative, creating a fun romp through a woman's manifold insecurities."
—*Publishers Weekly* on *Jennifer Johnson is Sick of Being Single*

Visit www.AuthorTracker.com
for exclusive information on your favorite HarperCollins authors.

Available wherever books are sold, or call 1-800-331-3761 to order.

12 V 7/13